It might be the excitement of performing that turned him on; maybe he was actually more of an exhibitionist than he wanted to admit.

It really didn't matter, anyway. The women didn't know the difference. They shrieked and waved more money in his direction, hands reaching for his dick or his ass or any part of him they could reach. Sometimes panties would fly at him from the audience, and quite often he'd find business cards stuffed into his g-string along with the cash. Once, a woman had scribbled her phone number on his calf with a fucking Sharpie. 555-2283. He remembered it distinctly, because it hadn't washed off his leg for almost a week.

Tonight there were no panties, no rabid fans with Sharpies—just fistfuls of crisp fives, tens, and twenties, with the odd single thrown in once in a while.

Finally, his dance was over. He scooped up the scattered pieces of his costume and blew a final kiss to the audience as he walked backstage, his g-string stuffed with money. He counted out nearly two hundred bucks, a good take for one dance. He had two more sets before he would be finished for the night, and if he did as well during those, he might just buy the plasma screen television he'd had his eye on.

"Hey, Aiden! Wait up!"

This is a work of fiction. Names, characters, places, and incidents either are the product of the author's imagination or are used fictitiously. Any resemblance to actual events, locales, organizations, or persons, living or dead, is entirely coincidental and beyond the intent of either the author or the publisher.

Kegs and Dorms
TOP SHELF
An imprint of Torquere Press Publishers
PO Box 2545
Round Rock, TX 78680
Another Believer Copyright © 2008 by Stephanie Vaughan
Reading Between the Lines Copyright © 2008 by Jane Davitt
Secui Domus Copyright © 2008 by Kiernan Kelly
What It's All About Copyright © 2008 by Tory Temple
Cover illustration by Alessia Brio
Published with permission
ISBN: 978-1-60370-527-1, 1-60370-527-9

www.torquerepress.com

First Torquere Press Printing: November 2008
Printed in the USA

**If you enjoyed Kegs and Dorms,
you might enjoy these Torquere Press titles:**

Fireline by Tory Temple

Family Matters by Kara Larson, Chris Owen, Sean Michael and Alexa Snow

OC Pride: Jumping the Fence by Stephanie Vaughan

Riding Heartbreak Road by Kiernan Kelly

Wild Raspberries by Jane Davitt

To Adrianna...
Stay in school ☺
Tory T.

To Adrianna,
It was great meeting you!.
Kiernan Kelly

Kegs and Dorms by Jane Davitt, Kiernan Kelly,
Tory Temple, and Stephanie Vaughan

Torquere
Press
Inc.
romance for the rest of us
www.torquerepress.com

Kegs and Dorms

Table of Contents

Secui Domus by Kiernan Kelly   9
Another Believer by Stephanie Vaughan   83
Reading Between the Lines by Jane Davitt   165
What It's All About by Tory Temple   231

Kegs and Dorms

Secui Domus
by Kiernan Kelly

Chapter One

The houselights dimmed, multicolored spotlights swirling across the curtains, the murmur of the crowd swiftly growing into hoots and catcalls. Aiden Barrows stood alone in the wings, dressed in his favorite costume—the nerd—waiting for his introduction. He wore plaid, floodwater pants that stopped several inches short of his ankles, black socks, sneakers, green suspenders, a striped, button down shirt complete with pocket protector, and a pair of horn-rimmed glasses taped at the bridge of the nose. His hair was a carefully arranged mess of black, spiky hanks.

The audience liked the costume because it was comical, but what they paid to see was the body beneath it. Honed to perfection, thanks to a combination of good genes and a regular work-out schedule, there wasn't an ounce of fat to spare on Aiden's six-foot frame.

Aiden loved the nerd costume for a different reason. The audience didn't know it, but it reflected the *real* him.

He wasn't really the self-assured exhibitionist everyone thought, although he wasn't shy by any stretch of the imagination. He stripped only because it was the one job he found that would more than pay for tuition, his dorm room, books, lab fees, and food, and still leave him the study time necessary to maintain his 4.0.

The work was easy, the money was great, and he couldn't beat the hours. The club was a drive, nearly twenty miles away in West Caulfield, but the money made the commute worth it. He worked two days a week, Fridays and Saturdays, four hours each night, and never cleared less than six hundred for the weekend. It left the rest of his week wide open for school. It was perfect.

The first thunderous beats of *The Stroke* by Billy Squier echoed in the room, his cue. The screams of the women in the audience increased exponentially when he walked onstage, his nose stuck in a book. The extra large printing on the cover read, "*Algorithms for Love*" in black letters. He reached center stage and paused, ostensibly too engrossed in his reading material to notice the couple of hundred women screaming and vying for his attention.

Suddenly, Aiden picked his head up, cocking it as if he heard something. He pretended to notice the audience and did a double take, his mouth dropping open. First he looked at the audience, then the book, then the audience, then the book again. A slow smile creased his cheeks as he tossed the book over his shoulder and faced the screaming women. By the time Billy Squier began singing "Stroke me, stroke me," Aiden had discarded his glasses, pocket protector, suspenders, shoes and socks, and was unbuttoning his shirt.

His hips thrust in time to the beat of the music as he peeled it off, revealing broad shoulders, a finely sculpted chest, and an abdomen rippling with muscle. Naked from the waist up, he walked down the narrow runway, playing to the women who lined it. He licked his lips, wiggled his ass, and played with his nipples, working the crowd into a barely controlled frenzy.

Finally, he walked to center stage, turned his back, reached between his legs and pulled hard on the material of his pants. Fastened together with Velcro, they came off easily, revealing the red satin g-string he wore underneath. Faced with his firm, naked butt, the women went wild, drowning out the music.

Aiden went into his routine, an easy bump-and-grind, flashing his impressive pecker now and then. Money appeared in the hands of the crowd, waving at him. He selected the highest denominations, dropping to his knees so the lucky women who proffered a ten or twenty dollar bill could stuff it into his g-string and cop a feel at the same time.

Quite often he'd get an erection, courtesy of the grasping fingers. Eight and a half inches of hard cock was always good for tips, but it never failed to surprise him when his body reacted to their touch—Aiden didn't swing that way. He liked women well enough, especially when they were generous with their tips, but they didn't do anything for him sexually. Onstage he might get hard, but offstage, no matter how beautiful the woman, his cock remained as soft and pliant as a wet dishrag.

It might be the excitement of performing that turned him on; maybe he was actually more of an exhibitionist than he wanted to admit.

It really didn't matter, anyway. The women didn't know the difference. They shrieked and waved more money in his direction, hands reaching for his dick or his ass or any part of him they could reach. Sometimes panties would fly at him from the audience, and quite often he'd find business cards stuffed into his g-string along with the cash. Once, a woman had scribbled her phone number on his calf with a fucking Sharpie. *555-2283.* He remembered it distinctly, because it hadn't washed off his leg for almost a week.

Tonight there were no panties, no rabid fans with Sharpies—just fistfuls of crisp fives, tens, and twenties, with the odd single thrown in once in a while.

Finally, his dance was over. He scooped up the scattered pieces of his costume and blew a final kiss to the audience as he walked backstage, his g-string stuffed with money. He counted out nearly two hundred bucks, a good take for one dance. He had two more sets before he would be finished for the night, and if he did as well during those, he might just buy the plasma screen television he'd had his eye on.

"Hey, Aiden! Wait up!"

Aiden turned at the sound of his name and saw Bobby Hatcher heading toward him, all well-muscled six-feet two inches of him, dressed in a pair of short, denim cut-offs, flannel shirt, suede vest, cowboy hat, and boots. Bobby liked to stick with the tried and true routines, like the cowboy or the cop. A little boring, but Aiden had to admit Bobby's coffee-and-cream complexion made a striking contrast to the white vest and hat. *Then again,* Aiden thought, *anything short of a gorilla suit would look great on him.* "Hey, Bobby."

"Did you hear about the dorms?"

"What about them?"

"They found fucking asbestos in the buildings! Some schmuck called the EPA, and now they're making a big fucking deal about it. It was on the news and everything. Got the whole damn place cordoned off. We can't even get in to get our stuff!"

"What? Aw, please tell me you're shitting me." That was the last thing Aiden expected or wanted to hear. "Everything I own is in my room! My books, computer, notes... my whole fucking *life* is in there!"

"I know, mine too. It's a mess, Aiden. The EPA is saying it's gonna take months to clean it out!"

"What does the college have to say about it?"

"Who the fuck knows? Nobody in Administration is talking, except to try to pass the blame to the contractors who built the dorms."

"Shit! I guess I'm going to have to try to find a room off campus."

"Good luck. I've been calling all over town. There's not a room to be had for fifty miles in any direction," Bobby said morosely. "I'm thinking about dropping my classes, putting everything on hold and going home until they re-open the dorms."

"Jesus. That's going to screw with your GPA and your scholarship, Bobby." Not to mention their friendship—he and Bobby met as freshmen and had been friends ever since. Bobby was the one who'd turned Aiden on to the strip gig.

"No shit, but I have to sleep *somewhere*, man. The Red Cross came in and set up cots in the gym, but there was only enough room for fifty people, and they went fast."

"There has to be something we can do!"

"Well, if you can think of anything, I'm all ears. My brain is fried from trying to figure a way out of this mess. Look, I gotta go—I'm on next. Let's go down to FUBAR after work and grab a beer. Maybe we can think of something. If not, we can at least get tanked. God knows I need a drink right about now. If we're lucky, maybe Hank will let us catch a few winks in the back room."

FUBAR was the local gay bar, run by a beefy ex-Marine named Hank. He'd christened the bar after the military acronym, *Fucked Up Beyond All Recognition*, because, as he liked to say, that was usually the way his patrons left his establishment. They also usually left it with the intention of screwing each other at the earliest possible moment, often getting no further than the parking lot before whipping their dicks out, which led to the abbreviated nickname favored by some of the patrons—FUB, the Fuck U Bar.

"Yeah, okay," Aiden agreed. He felt like he'd been sucker-punched. Five minutes ago, he'd known exactly where his life was headed and how he was going to get there. He had less than a year left of school before he graduated with his Bachelors in Fine Arts. He was going to take the next year off, get an apartment, work full-time dancing for the first half of the year, save his money, and spend the next six months touring Europe, studying art, and seeing all the great masterpieces up close and personal.

He had his itinerary all planned and marked with red pushpins on a wall map in his dorm room. The National Museum in London, the Louvre in Paris, the Van Gogh Museum in Amsterdam, and the Museo del Prado in Madrid. Afterwards, he'd return home a seasoned traveler, go back to school and get his Masters.

Within the space of five minutes, all his plans were shot to shit. He was homeless and nothing was certain anymore.

The only thing he was sure of was that going to FUBAR and getting plastered sounded like the best idea he'd heard all afternoon.

As it turned out, he and Bobby weren't the only ones looking to drown their sorrows. When they arrived at FUBAR the place was packed, although the atmosphere was much more subdued than it usually was when it was crowded. Aiden recognized most of the patrons as residents from the dorms. No music played, no one was throwing darts or shooting pool, no one was making out in any of the darker corners, no laughter rang out. It was as if everyone was in mourning—and they were, for their academic careers, Aiden realized.

He and Bobby took seats at the bar, the only ones still unoccupied, and ordered a pitcher from Hank.

"You boys need a place to spend the night, too?" Hank asked, sliding a pair of tall glasses and a full pitcher in front of Aiden and Bobby. "Most of 'em in here are singing the same sorry tune. I told everybody the bar closes at two, but everyone's welcome to spend the night at Hank's Hotel." He smiled, gesturing toward the bar room floor.

"Thanks, Hank," Aiden said. His skin crawled thinking about sleeping on the dusty, scarred and scuffed floor, but it was at least marginally better than sleeping outside under a tree in the park, or cramped up in the front seat of his VW Bug, which seemed to be his only other options.

"It's a shame you boys got kicked out of the dorms," Hank said, pouring them each a beer. "A lot of 'em are talking about quitting school and going home."

"Doesn't seem like there's much else we can do," Bobby said. "There aren't any apartments available in town, and most of these guys couldn't afford them even if there were. They live on shoestring budgets and ramen noodles as it is."

"Yeah." Hank grew quiet, chewing his lip, looking distinctly uncomfortable for a moment. Then he sighed, as if in surrender. "Hey, y'all wouldn't be interested in renting my house, would you?"

"What house?" Aiden asked, ears perking up. "I thought you lived in an apartment upstairs?"

15

"I do, but I own that big, gray house over on Challenger Drive."

"That's *yours*? How much do you want for it?" Aiden asked, feeling a faint stirring of hope, already mentally adding a couple of days at the club to cover his new costs. Myrna, the manager at the club, had been after him to do more shows, anyway. Mondays maybe, and Wednesdays... no, not Wednesdays—he had a lab on Wednesday nights. Thursdays then, and Fridays and Saturdays, of course. He couldn't hope to match what he made on the weekends on a week night, but it should be enough. Then something struck him, making him curb his burgeoning enthusiasm. "Wait... if you own it, why don't you live in it?"

"I bought that house just before I left for 'Nam. I had a boyfriend back then, thought it was going to be a forever thing, you know? We were going to move in when I got back and open the bar together, but things between us didn't work out. I couldn't bring myself to live in the house alone, but I couldn't part with it, either. I never rented it to anyone connected with the college before, and before you ask, the reason ain't nobody's business but mine. Renters I got now are moving come the end of the month."

"We'll take it!" Aiden cried, high-fiving Bobby.

"Whoa, hold on," Hank said, holding up a hand. "Just so you understand, the place is livable, but it needs a lot of work. I've been letting it go—money's been tight these last few years. That's the reason the current renters are leaving. It has four oversized bedrooms which you can probably split into eight smaller ones, and three bathrooms, but it needs a new roof, new plumbing..."

"So, we fix it," Aiden said again, decisively.

"With what money?" Bobby asked, quirking an eyebrow. "Somebody die and leave you a Swiss bank account?"

Aiden's mind raced, but then his cheek hitched in a devilish smile as an idea occurred to him. "How many people does Myrna's club hold? Two hundred, two-fifty maybe?"

"Yeah, I guess. So? What's that got to do with anything?"

Aiden ignored his question. "FUBAR can hold almost as many, right? Myrna's club charges... what? Five bucks a head to get in the door? Two drink minimum?"

"The cover is ten dollars. Why? What's going on in that pointy little head of yours, Aiden?"

"That's two thousand dollars a night to see the same three men strip down to a g-string two or three times. I wonder what they'd pay to see ten men strip? Or fifteen?" Aiden said, watching the light try to wink on over Bobby's head as he fought to understand. "Because we'd hold the show here at FUBAR, we'd get the queer crowd, too. We'll have a packed house every night." He turned toward Hank. "Hank, if we put on the show here, your bar receipts will only go up. The people coming to see the show will drink like fucking fish! You just said you could use more money, right?"

Hank was a little quicker on the uptake than Bobby. "I did at that. I suppose I could let you boys have this place a couple, three nights a week," he said with a grin. "Two drink minimum, huh? Shit, you can have the damn weekends—you keep the door, and I'll keep the take from the bar."

Aiden grabbed Hank's grizzled face and planted a big wet kiss on his lips. "You're a life-saver, Hank!" He jumped up from his stool, surveying the crowd of newly homeless students. "I see a few possibilities already. Come on, Bobby. We've got work to do," he said, ignoring the stunned and confused look on Bobby's face.

It would work. Aiden would make sure of it.

Chapter Two

Overnight, FUBAR became Ground Zero for the displaced students from the men's dorm. While some of the students affected by the closing of the dorm gave up, packed it in and went home, and a good number of them found temporary quarters, bunking in with friends or relatives—although most had to travel a long way back and forth to school to do so—some elected, by choice or necessity, to continue sleeping on the floor of the bar. Most were gay, some were straight, and all were desperate. They ate at the cafeteria at the school, or used Hank's microwave to warm up frozen dinners or cups of ramen noodles, and used the Athletic Department's showers, but spent their nights sprawled across the floor at FUBAR, wrapped up in blankets scored from the Red Cross.

The town fathers—who usually sniffed out infractions of business licenses with the unerring accuracy of bloodhounds—looked the other way at FUBAR doubling as a boarding house. They didn't want the streets of town crawling with homeless college students sleeping in their cars or in the park, and possibly end up featured on the evening news as the worst college town in America. At least if the kids were staying at FUBAR, they were out of sight, and out of mind.

The students returned to FUBAR after their classes, sitting around, commiserating with each other while trying to do homework or write term papers. For the first time in FUBAR history, men could be found sitting at the battered wooden tables drinking nothing stronger than orange juice and debating politics or philosophy, or typing term papers on laptops while dressed in their jockeys. In a way, Aiden realized, the name of the bar had never seemed more appropriate. Their lives certainly were fucked up beyond recognition.

At least they put their pants on during Hank's business hours. After all, he was nice enough to let them stay there—he couldn't afford to shut down FUBAR completely. At seven o'clock every night, the blankets and pillows were rolled up and tucked away into the back room until two a.m., when the bar closed and Hank's Hotel officially reopened. It sucked for the guys who had early morning classes, but it was the best Hank could do, and they were all grateful.

Aiden and Bobby comprehended one thing immediately—if they were going to succeed in their plan to rent out Hank's house, they were going to need a *lot* of help. The first task they tackled was making a list of possibilities. Half of the list was composed of seniors who formerly lived in the dorms and either had majors or family businesses that might be useful. Seniors were too close to graduation—they had more to lose by putting off their education, and were apt to try harder to make Aiden and Bobby's plan succeed.

There was Frank Willows, an engineering major, who might be able to help with the renovating the house. John Greenhouse was a business major, Peter Dumont was a film and video student who might help with staging, lights, and music for the show. Desmond Lincoln was a marketing major who could do promotion and advertising for it. Grant Silverstein's father owned a construction company. Arthur Fenkle's dad was a plumber. There were several others, all having special skills to bring to the table.

The second half of the list had nothing to do with academics or connections, and everything to do with physical fitness. They were the men who would help fund the pseudo-fraternity—the dancers. Every man who made the short list had a singular quality that made him stand out among his peers—his looks. Tall, short, black, white, Latino, Asian, conservative, radical, GPA, nothing mattered except one thing—that he look fabulous in nothing but a g-string.

At the moment, they were having a conversation with a tall, athletically built guy with swarthy skin and dark blue eyes, named Keshoe. He was a drama student, someone at home in front of an audience, and perfect for their needs. Aiden knew Kesh personally—*intimately*, in fact—and didn't hesitate to throw down the "former lover" card to coerce him to agree.

"Kesh, it's the opportunity of a lifetime! I know you, Kesh. You *live* to perform, and you're good at it! Plus, you've got the body of a god! Where else can you get a captive audience to watch you perform?" Aiden noticed a slight frown crease Bobby's brow as he talked about his and Kesh's past history, but chalked it up to stress. Bobby hadn't cared while Aiden was actually *fucking* Keshoe— why should he care whether or not Aiden talked about it now, especially if it would help sway Keshoe to help them?

Keshoe gave them a dry look. "I doubt seriously they'll be interested in hearing a monologue from Hamlet. Not unless I can teach my cock to act it out in pantomime."

That seemed to snap Bobby out of his funk. "Can you *do* that?" he asked, raising an eyebrow and looking directly at Keshoe's substantial package.

Aiden elbowed Bobby—hard. "We can work it out, Kesh. Every dancer has to have a specialty, something that makes his strip stand out from the others. Acting can be yours." He went on before Keshoe could say no and mean it. "Besides, where else are you going to live with the dorm closed? Do you really want to continue sleeping on the floor of the bar? Or are you considering chucking your education and going home to sell cars at your dad's dealership? Come on, man... we need you. Please?"

Keshoe looked around at the bodies lying scattered across the floor of FUBAR like a child's discarded set of pick-up sticks. "Okay, I'm in."

Aiden allowed himself to savor a short-lived jolt of victory before he and Bobby moved to the next man on their list. Granger Halifax was a computer science major who possessed all the personality of a brick, had a vocabulary that rivaled Merriam-Webster, and usually smelled vaguely like tuna fish. However, Aiden could tell from a glance that he had six-foot-something of hard-bodied geek packed into his collared t-shirt and Dockers. True, he'd need a make-over of nuclear proportions before he could be deemed fit for public consumption, but Aiden knew—not from personal experience, sadly, but from having seen Granger in the showers at school once or twice—that he had enough below the waist to fill out *three* g-strings.

Bobby caught Aiden's elbow, pulling him to a stop. His eyes slid toward where Granger sat, nose buried in a book. "*Granger*? I thought we were talking to potential dancers?"

"We are," Aiden answered. "Trust me on this one."

"Aiden, have you lost your mind? Look at him!"

"I am. *You're* seeing what's there, but *I'm* seeing the possibilities. With a little work, he can be outstanding, Bobby!" Aiden said, pulling Bobby along to Granger's table.

Granger looked up, his eyes widening as Aiden and Bobby sat down at his table. His listened to Aiden's spiel, but didn't look impressed.

"It won't work." Granger said, as soon as Aiden finished his carefully rehearsed speech. He whipped out his pocket calculator and began tapping the keys. "What you're proposing stretches the laws of probability like

Silly Putty. I doubt seriously that there will be enough women to support a regular schedule for a show like the one you're proposing. There are roughly eight thousand women in town, including the twenty-four hundred who attend school here. Of that, the age range breaks down to forty percent under the age of twenty-five, thirty-five percent between twenty-five and forty, twenty-five percent over forty. Roughly two-thirds of the women over thirty will have children. Seventy percent of all the women are either married or a have a significant other, and taking away the small percentage which might have an illness which keeps them housebound, that leaves—"

Aiden interrupted him, losing patience within the first few minutes of Granger's argument. He slapped a hand down on Granger's calculator, pulling it away from under Granger's fingers. "You've thought a lot about this, haven't you? What do you do, Granger? Sleep with the census under your pillow? I didn't think you were that interested in women, since I see you hanging around in FUBAR all the time." Alone, Aiden remembered, always alone, but there nonetheless.

Granger blushed fuchsia. "I'm bi. I think. Maybe. Maybe not. I'm not really sure. I don't have enough experience to make a sound judgment. Statistically speaking, I mean."

"Uh, how much experience is 'not enough,' Granger?" Aiden asked, too curious not to ask.

"Um… none."

"Wait, I'm confused. Do you mean none with men or none with women?" Aiden asked, unable to stop himself. It was impossible that this guy, who—if one took the time to look beyond the horn-rimmed glasses and outdated wardrobe—was as hot as a greased griddle in the middle of the desert, regardless of his questionable grooming habits, could be a virgin. Given half a chance,

Aiden would jump his bones right there in the middle of FUBAR.

"Neither." Granger's cheeks glowed red, and he averted his eyes.

Whoa.

Granger wouldn't make eye contact with Aiden. When he did look up, he focused on Aiden's mouth or hairline. Aiden realized Granger suffered from a crippling shyness. Not a good thing, especially when Aiden was asking him to prance around in front of a pack of screaming men and women while wearing nothing but a strip of dental floss.

Granger would take a lot of work.

Aiden took a closer look at him. Granger's skin was clear and smooth; a natural, light golden brown that Aiden knew just by looking would tan richly. His eyes were green and gold behind the thick lenses of his black-rimmed glasses, and framed by long lashes; his nose and chin were strong, and his lips, full and sensual. His hair was thick and had a slight, natural curl. Aiden already knew the body under the clothes was outstanding. With help, Granger could be a knock-out.

All he needed was a little self-confidence and a firm, guiding hand. Aiden decided the hand in question would be his, and Bobby's, too, if he was up to it. *First things first,* he thought. *Step one is to gain Granger's confidence. We can go from there.*

"Bobby, do me a favor?" Aiden said, turning toward him. "Go grab Dee before he leaves. I want to talk to him later."

"Huh? Dee? Oh, *Dee*! Sure," Bobby said, although his face was a mask of confusion. "Dee" was a secret code word they'd shared since their freshman year. It wasn't a name but the letter of the alphabet, and stood for "*depart.*" They used it when one of them was trying to hook up with someone and wanted a little privacy. He shot Aiden an unreadable look, said goodbye to Granger, and drifted off toward the bar.

"So, what are your plans, Granger?" Aiden asked once they were alone.

"After graduation? I've been accepted to MIT. I'm supposed to start my Masters program there next fall."

Well, it wasn't exactly what Aiden wanted to know, but it did explain why Granger hadn't pulled up stakes and gone home, choosing to stick it out instead, sleeping on the floor of the bar. He needed to graduate or risk losing his place at one of the most prestigious technological universities in the country.

"I sort of meant *tonight*, Granger," Aiden said with a smile. "I was wondering if you might want to catch a movie. Maybe get some dinner."

Granger's eyes widened and he looked more than a little shocked. He must have been startled, because his eyes actually met Aiden's for a moment. "Like... on a date?" he whispered.

"Well, yeah."

"With *you*?"

"That's the plan." Aiden chuckled.

Granger fell silent, lowering his eyes, fingers fidgeting with the calculator he'd taken back from Aiden. Finally, his eyes flicked up. "*Why?*"

"I like you."

"You don't even know me."

"Okay, fair enough, but I like what I *do* know. You're smart, nice, and I think you're cute. That's enough for wanting a date, right?"

"You don't need to do this just to get me to help you, Aiden. I'll help. I need to stay here, and don't want to have to spend the time sleeping in a bar. I'm still not convinced what you're planning is feasible, but I'm willing to give it a go."

Yeah, but you don't know what it is I want you to do, yet, Aiden thought. "I'm glad you'll help us, but that's not the reason I asked you out. If it was, I wouldn't still be asking you, and I am. How about it? I have to talk to a few more people, but then we can split. Go grab a bite at the café down the street and catch a show later on."

Granger stared at his hands, fingers turning the calculator around and around.

"Granger? Please?"

"Okay." The word was uttered so softly that Aiden nearly missed it.

"Great! I'll be back in a few." Aiden smiled, patting Granger on the hand. He tossed Granger a reassuring wink, then went off to catch up with Bobby.

"*Dee?*" Bobby asked the moment Aiden was within earshot.

"Yeah. I needed a few minutes alone. I have a date," he added with a grin.

"With *Granger?*"

"Yes, with Granger," Aiden said, feeling a little annoyed. What was wrong with Granger that everyone, including Granger himself, thought he was un-datable?

"Don't do it, Aiden. Don't mess with the poor guy just because you want him to strip."

"Do you think I'm that much of a jerk? He already said he'd help us. I asked him out because I wanted to," Aiden insisted. He knew it wasn't the whole truth, but he felt the need to defend himself. Besides, Aiden really did think Granger was all the things he'd said—smart, nice, and cute. "He's a sweet guy, and he's going to clean up real pretty. We're only going to eat and grab a movie, not fucking elope. Besides, he can use a boost to his self-confidence."

"Did you tell him exactly what it is you expect him to do? No, I didn't think so. You're playing with the guy."

"No, I'm not."

"Yes, you are. You're pretending to be Henry Higgins using Eliza to win a bet. Pygmalion for the new millennium."

"Leave it be, Bobby," Aiden snapped. "Who's next on our list?"

Bobby didn't look pleased. As a matter of fact, he looked downright pissed off, but that was just too damn bad. Who Aiden dated and for what reason was Aiden's business, and no one else's. *What the hell is wrong with him, anyway?* Aiden wondered. *Bobby never cared who I was seeing before. As I recall, he used to tell me I needed to get laid more often. Said I got cranky when I went too long without.*

He shrugged it off and chalked it up to the stress they were all feeling. He reached over, grabbed the list, and zeroed in on their next candidate.

Chapter Three

Out of the twenty-five names they'd written down on what they referred to as their Entertainment Crew, Aiden and Bobby succeeded in scoring fifteen commitments that afternoon, and had hopes of convincing a few more, in time. All of them were hot, buff men willing to grease up and strip down for the benefit of what became known to the insiders as *Project Secui Domus*. Well, fourteen, if you didn't count Granger, who really had no idea what he was signing up for... yet.

Bobby was the one who came up with the name for their proposed new house. He dubbed it *Secui Domus*—Party House in Latin. Mostly, it was because of the way they hoped to earn money for its renovation and upkeep, but also because they planned to throw one of the wildest keggers in the history of the college just as soon as they were safely situated within its walls.

Aiden and Bobby's hunt for candidates with technical and practical skills went equally well. They now had a future lawyer, engineer, computer specialist, and several others signed up and ready to roll, as well as a few with connections to a contractor and a plumber.

The first big meeting for Secui Domus would take place the following night, at FUBAR, at four p.m. sharp. During the meeting they hoped to rough out a budget needed for repairs to the house. Frank Willows, their engineering student, and Salvatore Grecco, whose father was a home inspector for an insurance company, had already left to visit the house and make a list of what needed to be done. Sal's father had agreed to meet them at the house and do a quick walk-through.

At a second meeting the following night at the same time, the Entertainment Crew would gather to discuss the first benefit show. They needed to move on the show relatively quickly—the house would no doubt require major work before they could even *begin* to move in, and for that they needed cash—and lots of it. For starters, the bedrooms had to be split into smaller rooms to accommodate the number of men living there. Furniture had to be purchased—bunk beds and writing desks, a kitchen table, and a living room set. After that, they could move in. The roof and the plumbing could be worked on while they were living in the house.

Aiden sighed, sitting back in his chair and surveying the room. Everyone was keyed up, excited over the possibility of having somewhere else to sleep besides the floor at FUBAR. It was the first spark of life he'd seen in the bar since before word got out that the dorms were closed down.

Personally, he was bone-tired. Not physically—he hadn't done more than move from table to table—but mentally, he was exhausted. He'd done some quick thinking and even faster talking, dancing around the finer details of the plan—easily done, since there really *weren't* any details as of yet—and throwing enough bullshit to bury the bar knee-deep. He was more than ready for a little well-deserved R&R and, dragging himself to his feet, he headed toward the table where Granger still sat.

Poor guy hadn't moved an inch in over four hours. He was sitting hunched over, fingers nervously drumming on the table, worry lines creasing his forehead. He looked as if he thought Aiden asking him on a date was a joke, and he was waiting for the punch line.

It was time to put him out of his misery, Aiden thought, approaching Granger's table. "Hey Granger! Ready to go?"

Granger looked up at him. "Huh?"

"Go. Us. A date. Remember? Jeez, Granger... should I

have programmed it into your Palm Pilot?" Aiden asked with a lopsided grin.

"Oh. Uh, yeah, I'm ready," Granger mumbled, standing up. He stood up, and Aiden was surprised that he'd never noticed just how tall Granger was, topping—the six foot three mark easily. His golf shirt had a ketchup stain smack dab in the middle of it, and his Dockers were wrinkled and shredded at the cuffs, but other than those two little things, he didn't look half bad at all, Aiden decided. His grin stretched into a full, wide smile as he grabbed Granger's elbow. "Come on, then! I'm starved."

They passed Bobby on the way out the door, and Aiden didn't miss the black look Bobby shot him. He made a mental note to find out what bug had crawled up Bobby's ass when he returned to FUBAR after his date.

Aiden hauled Granger out of FUBAR, leading him down the street. Two blocks over was a little café, the Blue Moon Pie, where the sandwiches were thick, the soup was hot, and most importantly, the price tag was more than reasonable. It was frequented by locals, visitors to the college, and students who were sick to the gills of ramen noodles and who'd managed to scrape a couple of bucks together for a real meal.

They got a booth near the back of the restaurant and slid their tall frames on either side of the Formica table. Aiden plucked two laminated menus from behind the napkin dispenser and handed one to Granger. "Here you go. Order whatever you want, Granger. It's on me."

"No, you don't have to do that, Aiden. I can pay for my—"

"Date, remember? I asked you. I pay. That's the way dates work, Granger. You can pay next time, if you want," Aiden said, waving a dismissive hand in the air. "I'm thinking about getting a Monte Cristo or maybe the roast beef with horseradish dressing. Nah, on second thought

29

I think I'll have the beef, on sourdough, with a bowl of chicken noodle soup. What do you want, Granger?"

"Uh, the same?"

Aiden cocked an eyebrow at him. "You asking or telling?"

Granger laughed softly, the first time Aiden ever heard him laugh. He had a good one, the kind that was naturally contagious. "Telling, I guess. Roast beef, but no chicken soup, thanks. I'll have the beef barley."

Aiden signaled for the waitress, a perky young woman with cheerleader legs and a pink stripe in her hair that matched the color of her shirt and socks. He ordered for both of them, adding a couple of Cokes and two orders of fries. Aiden noticed the interest in her eyes when she looked at him, and wondered absently if she'd be one of the women who they hoped would become a regular at their shows. He gave her a warm smile, just in case.

Aiden and Granger made idle chitchat until their food arrived, talking mostly about school, their class loads, and the closing of the dorms. As Granger relaxed and warmed up, Aiden found him to be thoroughly likeable—a little on the serious side, but ingenuous and intelligent, as long as the conversation remained in what Aiden came to regard as "safe zones," such as school, academics, and politics.

Quite often during their conversation, between bites of rare roast beef on thickly sliced sourdough bread, Granger's guard would slip, his eyes sparkling and his gestures growing unselfconscious and animated, particularly when the subject delved into familiar territory for him—computers, or more specifically of interest to Granger, computer *games*.

"I use a high end 3D graphics and modeling program called *Maya*, and the C++ programming language to create and animate the characters. I just finished skinning a character for the game I've been programming for my final project in one of my classes. Man, he's a thing of beauty, if I do say so myself. He's a Dwarf in full-out battle armor. You can count the freaking hair on his head! I'm really proud of him. I had a problem with the forward and inverse kinematics, but I think I've got it covered now—"

"Wait—you created a character? I thought you only dealt with zeros and ones and crap?" Aiden interrupted.

Granger laughed. "You're talking about binary code. Nobody writes programs in binary—it's too complex. It's fine for computers, but virtually impossible for anyone who actually uses optic organs to read. I usually use C++, although I've done some Java and other languages, too. I've actually got a double major. Programming *and* Graphic Design, because I wanted to be able to do it all—program the game, design the characters, the whole enchilada."

Aiden took a bite of his sandwich, chewing thoughtfully. "So, if I wanted you to create a game, like Grand Theft Auto or something, you could draw the characters and their world, and then make them move through that world?"

"Yup. That's the idea."

Aiden's mind was racing. A *game*. A game specifically designed for adults. How cool would it be to have a game based on the dancers of Secui Domus, where the person with the controller could make the characters dance and strip? Maybe even do *more* than just strip... an X-rated version! Players could have their own character and they could hook-up with the dancers! It would be like directing a porn movie from the comfort of your own home. Sort of like the SIMS with those user-built "adult" patches, taken to the next level. Gay, straight and bisexual. Smooth, realistic, and hotter than hell.

Suddenly, Aiden wasn't sure he wanted Granger to

31

strip after all. He had better uses for the sharp mind behind those horn-rimmed glasses. He'd talk to Bobby about it as soon as he got back to the bar.

"Aiden? How can you do it?"

Aiden blinked, suddenly aware that he'd been staring into space, lost in his thoughts. "Huh?"

"I was asking how you do it. How do you take your clothes off in front of strangers? I mean, I know you've got a killer body and all," Granger said, his cheeks flushing, "but how do you get the nerve to strip to the skin in front of people?" His face turned a deeper red, and he avoided Aiden's eyes, his voice lowering to a whisper. "I went to the club a couple of times to see you."

"You did? What did you think?" Aiden smiled. Granger was adorable when he blushed.

"You're... very talented."

"You mean I've got a big dick," Aiden said, and laughed when Granger's face turned a darker red. "Thank you. To answer your question, it's easy after the first few times, especially when they start throwing money at you. You could do it, too. I'll bet you have a really good body."

Granger tried to sip his Coke and choked. "Me? No way! I'm not grotesque or anything, I guess, but I'm not like you or Bobby or Keshoe. Nobody gives me a second glance."

Aiden frowned. "I did! I asked you out, remember?"

Granger chuckled sardonically. "I may be short on experience, but I'm not stupid, Aiden. I know why you asked me out. You want me to help with the frat house, maybe by doing something I ordinarily would balk at doing. You're trying to butter me up." He raised a hand before Aiden could object. "It's okay. I don't mind, but it doesn't change the fact that I'm still a geek."

Aiden shook his head. The guy had the self-confidence of a gnat. It was time to come clean, especially since he now might have other uses for Granger's talent. "Listen to me, Granger. You're right, in a way. I *did* want you to do something you probably wouldn't want to do. I wanted you to be one of the dancers."

Granger's jaw dropped, but then he snorted. "Oh, man. Good one, Aiden."

"I'm serious." He pulled out the list he and Bobby had made of possible Entertainment Crew candidates and slid it across the table toward Granger. He pointed to Granger's name, about halfway down the list. "See? Your name is right there, after Keshoe's."

Granger peered at the paper, then rolled his eyes and pushed it back to Aiden. "Come on, Aiden! Look at me! Who would want to see me take my clothes off?"

"I could think of lots of people — anyone with eyes, for example."

He received another ingenuous snort from Granger. "Yeah, right. Pull my other leg for a while—this one's getting sore."

"It's true. I even said so to Bobby. You're a good looking guy, Granger. All you need is a little make-over."

Granger looked away, although the expression on his face told Aiden he was pleased and more than a little embarrassed. "I take it you've changed your mind about me, though, huh?"

"Not really. I'd still like you to dance, at least once in a while, but you gave me another idea just now. Do you think you could create a game for us? A Secui Domus game, where the players can make the characters strip? Maybe even have sex?"

Granger's head snapped back, his eyes wide. "Are you serious? You want me to design an X-rated game? Do you have any idea of what would be involved in that? What you're proposing would normally take years of work and a huge crew of programmers! I can't begin to tell you how complicated it is to take a game from design to completion—"

"But it can be done?" Aiden refused to give up the idea so easily. It was a goldmine, and the residuals on the game could potentially keep Secui Domus going for years after Aiden and the rest of the original founders graduated.

"Well… sure it can, given enough time and money and resources and—"

"So you can do it?"

"I *can*… I mean, I have the know-how, but, Aiden—"

"Awesome!" Aiden grinned, as if Granger had enthusiastically agreed to his plan. Aiden impulsively grabbed Granger's face and pulled him closer, meeting him halfway across the table, and planted a big, wet kiss on him. "We've got several guys who have computer and design experience. I'll assign them to you, and you can get started ASAP."

Granger sat back, jaw slack, looking stunned. Aiden couldn't decide if the look on his face reflected the fact that he'd just been blindsided with an enormous, unbelievably complex project, or kissed. Either way, he looked positively shell-shocked.

"Well, we should get going if we're going to catch the nine o'clock show," Aiden said, signaling for the waitress to bring them the check.

"Show?" Granger repeated, looking as if he didn't understand the concept of the word. Poor guy. He looked like he'd just been hit upside the head with a two-by-four. Aiden could practically see little stars and chirping birdies circling his noggin.

"The movie, Granger. We were going to go see a movie after we ate, remember?" Aiden prompted.

"Oh, yeah. I forgot. Listen, Aiden… would you mind if we skipped the movie? My head is suddenly killing me," Granger said. He took off his glasses and rubbed the bridge of his nose between his index finger and thumb.

Aiden was solicitous, and tried to hide the smile that kept curving his lips. He had Granger hooked—he knew it and Granger knew it. Complex or not, headache or not, Granger was intrigued, and he was the type of man who couldn't—or wouldn't—turn his back on a challenge.

"Hey, Aiden?"

"Yeah?"

"I guess I'm Secui Domus' new Graphics and Gaming Director, but can I still get that make-over?" Granger asked, with a sheepish grin.

Aiden smiled back. "Keshoe?" He asked, watching Granger's cheeks pink up. "You mentioned him a couple of times."

"No, no, he'd never give me the time of day," Granger replied, shaking his head.

"Don't be so certain. Kesh is a great guy. Don't sell him short, Granger. Besides, after I get finished with you, you'll have to beat them off with a stick. Better yet, maybe *you'll* be the one *they're* beating off," Aiden laughed, watching Granger's face deepen to crimson at the double-entendre. "Come on, let's get back—I can't wait to tell Bobby about the game!"

Chapter Four

No, no, no! You step off on the *right* foot! The right... no, the *other* right! For God's sake, Bill, you only have two fucking feet! How hard is it for you to remember your right from your left?"

Aiden looked up from the laptop, his fingers poised over the keys. His responsibility was to keep track of the finances for Secui Domus, while Bobby was in charge of putting the first show together. Everyone was feeling a little edgy and a lot nervous, but Bobby was in rare form, as irritable and high-strung as any Broadway director had ever been. He continually snapped at everyone and everything, irritating the crew's already frayed nerves. At the moment, he was standing by the newly erected catwalk that stuck out from the small stage at the rear of the bar like a long, thin dick. Onstage, Bill's face was as red as his g-string. Aiden felt compelled to say something. "Come on, Bobby, give him a break! He's new at this."

Bobby spun around, glaring at Aiden with anger sparking in his eyes. "Would *you* like to teach him the routine? We have less than two weeks before our first show. If it bombs, we won't have to worry about having a second or third, and *this* idiot can't even remember which foot is his right one!"

Aiden sighed and gently closed the cover of the laptop. "Come on, Bobby. You need a time-out before the performers start burning you in effigy. You've been working non-stop on the show and are in serious need of a break." He turned toward Bill, who was half-naked and covered in sweat. "Take ten, Bill. Bobby will be back in a few."

Aiden grabbed Bobby's arm, ignoring his protests, and dragged him out of the bar into the backroom.

Bobby barely waited for the door to close before exploding. "I've had it, Aiden! I'm tired of working my ass off, of being the only one committed to this! The guys are *always* late to rehearsal, and most of them can't dance for shit! They have absolutely no rhythm—"

"Bobby, everyone has as much at stake in this as we do. Plus, the audience is paying to see good-looking, buff guys take off their clothes. They're not going to care whether or not they're off-step."

"Yeah, well I have news for you. They can't strip worth a shit, either," Bobby grumbled. The air seemed to go out of him, and he sank down onto the old mohair sofa Hank kept in the back room for the nights when one of his regulars needed a place to sleep off a bender. Bobby's head hung low, as if he was exhausted.

Aiden smiled and patted him on the shoulder. "Wait here, and don't move. I know just what you need." He raced out into the main room, ducked behind the bar and pulled two, icy-cold long necks from the fridge, slipping a couple of dollars into the register on his way out.

"Here," he said, handing one to Bobby. "It'll cool your throat and your temper at the same time." He twisted off the top of his bottle and took a deep swallow, watching Bobby do the same. The beer slid down his throat, cooling it all the way down. "I know you're working hard, Bobby, and I understand that you want it to be perfect, but most of these guys have never done anything like this before."

"Neither had we when we first started."

Aiden laughed, remembering his first time on stage. "I know, and do you remember what we looked like on our first few times out? I do. My knees were knocking together so hard they sounded like castanets. I stumbled twice over my own damn feet and nearly fell off the catwalk. You weren't much better, but we learned. So will they."

Bobby shook his head doubtfully. "I don't know, Aiden. Keshoe tried to take off his t-shirt and nearly strangled himself, and Kenny fell over on his ass trying to step out of his pants."

"That's easily fixable. Give Keshoe a button-down shirt, and Kenny can wear the Velcro pants from my nerd number. He's shorter than me, so they won't look too geeky," Aiden said, polishing off his beer. He set the bottle aside, sitting down on the couch next to Bobby. "Come on, give. There's something else bugging you. I know you, Bobby. You usually have the patience of a saint, but you've been snapping at everybody, even Hank, and *he's* not even in the show! You've been on edge ever since the first afternoon we started planning this thing. What's eating you?"

"Nothing." Bobby wouldn't look at Aiden. He stared at the bottle he held in his hands, twisting it around and around between his fingers.

"For Christ's sake, Bobby, are you going to tell me, or make me beat it out of you?"

"Like you could."

"Bobby…"

"You sleep with him yet?"

Aiden gawked at Bobby in surprise. That was the last thing he'd expected Bobby to ask him. Since when did Bobby care who Aiden slept with? Suddenly, Aiden wished he had another beer—or better yet, vodka. "Did I sleep with whom?"

"Granger. Have you?"

"Why do you care?"

"Just answer the question."

Aiden stared hard at Bobby for a minute, but Bobby refused to meet his eyes. "No. I haven't even been out with him again—just that once for dinner. Why do you care?" he asked again. "You never did before. Bobby?

You started this, let's finish it. Answer me."

"I care. Maybe I care a lot," Bobby said softly. He turned his chocolate brown eyes, dark and deep, toward Aiden.

"Why didn't you ever say anything, Bobby? We've been dancing at the same club for two years! We hung out in FUBAR's, went to Daytona every year on Spring Break together... shit, we even dated the same fucking guy once!"

Neither had known it in the beginning, but when they found out they were both seeing the same man, they would compare notes after their dates. He was playing them both, telling each of them that they were exclusive, that he was faithful. It became a contest between them to see who would be the first one to get the guy to break and tell the truth. Bobby won, reducing the guy to tears, as Aiden recalled. They both dumped the sorry bastard on the same night.

Bobby shrugged. "That was different. It was just sex, then, Aiden. I knew it didn't mean anything. This is different. Granger is different. He's sweet, an innocent. He's a keeper, not a player."

"Not for me. Granger and I are just friends. Don't get me wrong—he's a nice guy. He has a hot body, I just know it, but he's not my type, Bobby. I like a man who knows what he's doing," Aiden said with a slow, sensuous smile. He let his gaze travel from Bobby's handsome face all the way down the six-plus feet to his toes and back again, seeing Bobby as if for the first time.

Bobby was long, lean, and hard. His face was model-quality; his cheekbones high and his eyes dark, deep pools. Oddly enough, Aiden had never considered Bobby as a possible boyfriend, and now he wondered why. Maybe because he knew instinctively that Bobby—like Granger—was a keeper. Before, Aiden had just been too busy fucking everything in pants to want to settle down, but now he found the idea of having a steady boyfriend to be an appealing proposition. With all the stress he was under, having someone who understood him, who was there to listen as well as wrinkle the sheets, sounded ideal, and Bobby certainly fit the bill.

Bobby's cheek quirked in a half-smile. "Yeah?"

"Yeah. You wouldn't happen to know a guy like that, would you?"

Aiden was rewarded with a flash of white teeth and a dimple, a smile that reached all the way to Bobby's eyes. "Actually, I happen to know just the guy. Good looking, responsible. Knows where he's going and how he's going to get there."

Aiden laughed. "Ah, now, he sounds like a fine, upstanding young man. But I need more than that, Bobby. I need a guy whose hands can play my body like a virtuoso; who can kiss me blind and halfway to Tuesday, and then fuck me through the rest of the week without taking a breath."

"I know a guy like that, too, and guess what? He's the same guy."

"Wow. He sounds perfect." Aiden grinned, enjoying their little game. "When do I get to meet him?"

Aiden's smile faded as Bobby's eyes grew serious and he leaned in closer, closing the gap between them until only inches separated them.

"He's always been waiting right here. You just weren't ready to see him before."

Aiden's breath caught as their lips met in a soft kiss. Bobby's lips were supple and warm, and sent a tingle shooting through him that he felt in every fiber of his being. The man could kiss, that was for sure. He'd always thought Bobby was a knock-out. Tall and strong, sleek and ripped, Bobby's body was the stuff of wet dreams.

Aiden knew all there was to know about Bobby, all his idiosyncrasies, like the way he got hiccups when he drank cola, and the way he always put his left shoe on before his right. He never tore an envelope open, always working his thumb under the flap carefully so it wouldn't tear, and saved wrapping paper from Christmas and birthday presents to recycle. He liked liver and onions, but hated the way the meat felt to touch so never cooked it himself.

Aiden was the first to admit he didn't have a great record when it came to relationships. He could hold a job, keep his grades at a steady 4.0, hold his breath underwater for nearly two minutes, organize and follow through on any number of complex projects, but he couldn't keep a boyfriend past the three week mark. He always found himself pushing the guy away. Little things he might find endearing at the beginning of an affair annoyed the hell out of him after a couple of weeks. He knew his relationships wouldn't last, and was always on the lookout for the next hot young thing he'd be taking to his bed.

He didn't want that to happen with Bobby, didn't want to lose their friendship, so he never allowed it to progress to the next level.

Until now, that was, and as their kiss deepened, Aiden found himself unable to hold back any more. He threw caution to the wind and himself into the kiss. Aiden cupped Bobby's cheeks, pulling him in deeper. Fresh-shaven, Bobby's skin was soft and smooth against his palms.

Bobby's hand slipped under his shirt, long, elegant fingers tracing burning trails across Aiden's chest and stomach. Aiden's cock filled, and he moaned, "Oh, God. You *do* know what you're doing, don't you?" He dropped his head, his tongue sampling the delicate skin below

Bobby's ear, tasting soap and salt.

"Always did. You were just too stupid to see it."

"Not stupid. Oh, yeah, Bobby... right there," he moaned as Bobby's fingers found a nipple, teasing it with light pinches. "Maybe I was blind, but never stupid."

"Liking that, huh? Didn't know you liked tit-play."

"You never asked."

"Shut up and touch me."

For once in his life, Aiden was more than happy to comply with a direct order. He pulled Bobby's t-shirt up, exposing sleek, brown skin tightly stretched over rippling stomach muscles. His finger traced the cleft between Bobby's six-pack, circling the navel, and dipped under the waistband of Bobby's jeans. Bobby's cock pressed against his fly, a thick, hard bulge distending the material. Aiden popped the button and unzipped him, exposing plain, white briefs. The thin material, already wet with precome, clung to the shape of Bobby's dick

Bending over Bobby's lap, Aiden put his mouth over the outlined head of Bobby's cock, sucking the damp material into his mouth, tasting cotton and male. Above him, Bobby moaned, hips lifting toward Aiden's mouth.

"Come on, man. Stop teasing," Bobby whispered. "Suck me, Aiden." Bobby's warm hand slid up under the back of Aiden's shirt, then down to cup Aiden's ass through his jeans.

Aiden aimed to do exactly that, but he was hard, too, his erection trapped painfully by the zipper of his jeans. He lifted his hips, fumbling with his zipper, and released it before peeling Bobby's underwear open at the fly.

Bobby's cock was fully engorged, the blood turning it a shade or two darker than the rest of him. Aiden's head swam with his scent, musky and potent. Aiden's mouth filled with saliva, anxious to see if Bobby tasted half as good as he smelled. He wrapped his hand around Bobby's thick shaft and closed his lips over the head. Bobby's gasp was no louder than his own moan as Bobby's taste filled his mouth.

Bobby's hand found his cock, squeezing the head, stroking him. His thumb teased at the tiny slit, coaxing dribbles of precome from it. Aiden's head swam, his body overwhelmed; he felt his orgasm building already. It wasn't going to take long, and as much as he wanted to drag it out, to make it last, he couldn't hold back the pressure that was quickly building inside him.

Neither could Bobby, it seemed. He came without warning, feeding Aiden a mouthful of sweet juice. Tasting the salty, thick liquid, he licked Bobby clean, savoring every drop. Groaning, he sat up and watched Bobby's hand on his cock, heard the slick sounds, and responded with a gusher of his own, coming in hot spurts over Bobby's fist.

Bobby lifted his hand to his mouth, licking his fingers. "Mmm, mmm, good," he said, smiling. "Remind me why we never did this before."

"Because now we have a problem," Aiden said, reaching for Bobby's hand. He suckled Bobby's fingers, tasting himself on them.

"What's the problem? You and me? We fit together, Aiden. Always have. I've been waiting two fucking years for you to make a move on me. Finally, I had to take matters into my own hands." Bobby chuckled, pulling his fingers out of Aiden's mouth.

"You sure? You know how I am with guys. I don't want to lose you as a friend, Bobby."

"If you haven't by now, you're not likely to. For Christ's sake, Aiden, I've already seen you at your worst. Remember our New Year's Eve party last year? When you got plastered and organized a circle jerk? You made everybody shoot into my 'Number One Son' mug. My *mother* gave me that mug. If I'm still speaking to you after *that*, nothing you can do will drive me away."

Aiden chuckled. "Guess so." He leaned in and kissed Bobby softly, quickly losing himself again in feel of Bobby's hot mouth and soft tongue.

Bobby pulled away first, to Aiden's disappointment, fingers firmly cupping Aiden's chin. Aiden looked into Bobby's dark eyes and saw his sober expression. "There's one thing you need to understand, Aiden. If you and I are going to be together then we're an exclusive couple, got it? No more fucking around."

Aiden nodded, turning his head to kiss Bobby's palm. "Got it."

"If you feel the need to sleep with somebody else, I expect you to have the decency to tell me first."

"Ain't gonna happen, baby. Been there, done that, got the souvenir ashtray."

"I'm serious, Aiden. Don't you dare fucking cheat on me. I deserve better than that."

"Have I ever lied to you?"

"No, and don't think you can start now."

"Nope. Got me a ball and chain now," Aiden teased.

"You're lucky I don't tattoo "Property of Bobby. Hands Off" on your forehead."

Aiden laughed and ducked closer for another long kiss. "Come on. We have to get back out there before Bill busts a nut trying to figure out his left foot from his right."

"Hey... we're good now, right?"

"Hell, yeah. We're officially a couple. Joined at the hip," Aiden replied. His eyes twinkled with humor. "Maybe joined somewhere else later on, huh?"

"I'm counting on it," Bobby said, returning Aiden's look with one of his own, heat making his dark eyes sparkle.

"You gonna go easier on Bill and the other dancers,

now?"

"Guess so. I'm relaxed, recharged, and reanimated. Let's go fix this thing."

"I'm right behind you."

"For now. Later on, I plan on being behind *you*. Behind you, on top of you, under you, and in every other position I can think of," Bobby quipped.

Aiden's ass clenched involuntarily just thinking about being filled by the long, thick length of Bobby's meat. "Oh, *hell* yeah, as long as I get a shot at that bubble butt of yours."

"I don't have a bubble butt!"

"Yes, you do. Got yourself a big ol' puffball back there," Aiden said, laughing. He swatted Bobby's ass to drive home his point. "Jiggles nicely, too."

"My ass doesn't jiggle!"

"Just like a bowlful of Jell-O."

"We've been a couple for five minutes and you're pissing me off already, Aiden."

"What? That's a compliment! You know what they say—there's always room for Jell-O," he quipped, and laughed when Bobby sniffed haughtily.

Aiden thought nothing could spoil his good mood. He felt warm and sated, ready to take on the world, and it showed in his walk and his smile. First, there was Hank's last minute save with the house, and now a new relationship with Bobby. Things were definitely looking up.

Chapter Five

Granger, stand up straight! Jeez, if you slouch any more your butt will be dragging on the sidewalk."

Every time Aiden thought he'd brought Granger's confidence level up, Granger would do or say something that told Aiden he was mistaken. One minute Granger would be smiling, and the next, looking as though he was ready to crawl under a rock.

"I feel ridiculous. People are going to laugh, Aiden."

"No, they're not. You look great. Come on, straighten up, and for God's sake, smile! We're walking into a bar, not a funeral home," Aiden chided, pausing with his hand on the door to FUBAR.

He'd spent the entire day with Granger, including nearly five hours in the mall shopping for new clothes while he lectured Granger on fashion. Pant legs should brush the tops of your shoes. Color is your friend. T-shirts should be snug, not oversized like circus tents. Layering is sexy, but not so many layers that you look like you're ready to hit the tundra. Granger had dutifully repeated everything Aiden said and took copious notes. They'd bought him several new outfits, one of which Aiden insisted he put on immediately—a pair of nice, soft cargo pants and a turquoise t-shirt that hugged Granger's chest like a second skin. Just as Aiden had suspected, Granger had been hiding a dynamite body under his frumpy, ill-fitting clothing.

From the mall they drove to Aiden's favorite hair stylist, where Granger got the works—hair cut, highlights, eyebrow waxing, manicure, and pedicure. By the time the stylist finished working the last bit of product into Granger's hair, everyone in the shop had gathered around his chair, oohing and ahhing. Granger left the shop with a whole new look, and the phone numbers of two of the stylists in his pocket.

"I don't look like me. I look like a stranger," Granger said softly, staring at his reflection in the window of FUBAR. His glasses were gone, replaced by contact lenses, and his eyes were wide under his newly shaped, sleek eyebrows, his expression filled with wonder. "Are you sure I look okay?"

"Hell, yeah! Relax, Granger. Everyone's going to love the new you. Everything you see was already there, just waiting to come out. Now, come on. We've still got work to do." Aiden patted Granger on the shoulder and opened the door, ushering him inside. "You need to get back to work on the programming for the game, and I need to check in with Bobby before he decides we've run off to some exotic island together."

Granger snorted as if what he'd said was absurd, but Aiden had been semi-serious. Bobby was still jealous about the attention Aiden was paying Granger, even though Aiden kept assuring him there was nothing to be worried about. After seeing Granger's new look, Aiden figured he'd have to take Bobby into the back room and fuck him blind to reassure Bobby again that there was nothing going on between Granger and himself.

Oh, how I suffer for our relationship, Aiden thought happily, pulling open the door.

As they walked into the bar, Aiden was pleased to note the appreciative glances that followed Granger. *He's going to be a busy man,* Aiden thought cheerfully. Granger was going to have a full calendar of dates, judging from the way some of the men were staring at him. *Hell, I would've scored a second date with Granger myself, if I wasn't sure Bobby would geld me for it.*

Aiden noticed one particular pair of blue eyes never left Granger from the moment he walked into the bar.

Keshoe was watching him with a hungry look, like a hawk tracking a rabbit. Aiden wasn't surprised at all when Keshoe jumped up and made a beeline for them.

Granger and Keshoe locked eyes, and suddenly Aiden became invisible. *Well, that's that,* Aiden thought, giving Granger an encouraging pat on the shoulder. *He's just said goodbye to his virginity, even if he doesn't know it yet.* If the looks they were giving one another were any indication, Aiden would be surprised if they made it to the back room before Keshoe had Granger's clothes off.

He made a mental note to tell Granger to program a make-over into the game he was designing. It would be interesting to have a geeky character for players to transform and then fuck.

"Just you wait, 'Enry 'Iggins, just you wait." Aiden smiled as Bobby's arms wrapped around his waist from behind and sang softly into his ear. "I see you've managed to turn Eliza Doolittle into the belle of the ball. Looks like Keshoe thinks Granger's hot. The question is, do you think so, too?"

"He *is* hot. I told you he would be," Aiden said, folding his hands over Bobby's. "Not as hot as a certain Psych major I know, though."

"Good answer. I may let you live another day."

Aiden laughed and turned in Bobby's arms, meeting his lips in a deep, slow kiss. "Jealous much?"

"Only where you're concerned."

"How's the show going?"

"Believe it or not, I think we'll be ready. I finally had to paint an "R" and an "L" on the toes of Bill's shoes so he'd remember his right from his left, and told him to keep them on during his routine. Other than that, if everyone remembers to breathe and manages not to piss their g-strings, we're good to go."

Aiden laughed, hugging Bobby. "Great. Maybe we

should advertise that the performance may include golden showers."

"Nah, let's save that for the Christmas Spectacular," Bobby said, chuckling.

Still laughing, Aiden led Bobby to the bar, where Hank was polishing glasses. "Hank, did you get the lease drawn up yet? The show is on Saturday, and we're already nearly sold out. We can start the renovations on Monday. They'll only take a week or so to do, if the contractor's estimate is correct. We can start moving in by the end of the month."

"Called the lawyer yesterday. The new lease will be ready by Friday," Hank said. He looked over Aiden's shoulder and froze. "Oh, shit. Tell me I'm seeing things." His bushy brows knit in a frown, and his craggy face turning to granite.

Aiden turned, looking toward the door. A man stood just inside it, and he recognized him instantly—Wesley Ackerman, the college Dean. He was a handsome older man dressed in an expensive suit. Distinguished gray dusted his temples, but Aiden knew he had the disposition of a hedgehog—prickly at best, painful at worst. In four years at the college, Aiden couldn't remember ever seeing him smile, and today was no exception. Ackerman looked as though he'd just swallowed something slimy and foul as his eyes flicked around the bar.

What the hell is the Dean doing at FUBAR? Aiden wondered. *I doubt he's here to buy tickets for the show.*

He turned back toward Hank and was stunned by the animosity that colored those rocky features.

"What are you doing here?" Hank barked. Aiden noticed his hands had tightened around the glass he'd been polishing, his knuckles gone white.

"Believe me when I tell you it wasn't by choice," Ackerman said. Behind his wire-framed glasses, his eyes were blue chips of ice, his mouth drawn in a tight, grim line. "I've been informed that students from my college have been sleeping here."

"No shit, Sherlock. What was I supposed to do... let them sleep on the street?"

"That's not my concern. They can't stay here. This is a bar, not a hotel. If the papers hear that my students are sleeping on the floor of a gay bar, the college will suffer. Our alumni will not be pleased. Everyone is to pack up their belongings immediately and return to the college. We've arranged for tents to be set up on the Green—"

"*Tents*? Are you kidding? You want these kids to camp out on the fucking lawn?" Hank roared, slamming the glass down on the bar. It shattered, spraying the bar with glittering shards. Aiden and Bobby both jumped, along with everyone else in the bar. "No electricity, no bathroom? No heat or air conditioning? For how long? Word has it that it's going to be months before the dorms can reopen!"

"Again, that's not my concern."

"Get the fuck out of my bar, Wes!" Hank bellowed, looking as if he was ready to jump over the bar, tackle Ackerman to the ground and pound on the man until there was nothing left but a tattered pile of wool.

Ackerman stalked across the floor and shoved a paper under Hank's nose. "Would you care to explain this? You've turned my students into cheap strippers! The college will not stand for such behavior from its students! I will not have the good name of the college dragged through the mud!"

"Excuse me, Dean, but what we do on our own time is our own business," Aiden said. "Stripping was our idea, not Hank's. Besides, it's good money and there's nothing wrong with it."

"Stay out of this!" Hank and Ackerman shouted

together. Their eyes never left one another's faces, glaring at each other like a pair of snarling wolverines.

"This show will not go on. The boys will pack up their belongings and move to the tents, and that's final!" Ackerman barked. He crumpled the flyer into a ball, flinging it onto the bar.

"The boys will stay right the fuck where they are, and this is *my* bar, damnit! What kind of entertainment I put in it is none of your goddamn business!" Hank thundered. "As a matter of fact, they'll only be here for another couple of weeks, anyway. I'm renting the house out to them."

Ackerman's eyes flew open. "You can't do that!"

"It's already done."

"This is exactly what I knew was going to happen when you opened a gay bar within walking distance of the college! I knew it was going to be trouble! I warned you!"

Hank's voice lowered into a menacing rumble. "Get out of my bar, Wes, before I really lose my temper." Every muscle flexed under Hank's t-shirt, and he suddenly looked every inch the formidable, dangerous ex-Marine he was, and very close to losing control.

Aiden's eyes flew open. He'd never seen Hank so angry, so near to losing it. Even on the worst nights at the bar, when men got drunk and belligerent with him, Hank had always managed to keep a tight rein on his temper. Aiden figured it was Hank's Marine Corps training that kept his anger in check, and wondered what it was about Ackerman that drove him so close to the edge.

To his credit, Ackerman didn't turn tail and flee in the face of Hank's fury. Instead, he leaned in over the bar until his nose almost touched Hank's. His voice lowered, too, sounding as deadly and venomous as the hiss of a cobra. "This show will *not* go on. I'll go to the town council. I'll go to the mayor. I'll go to the fucking *governor* if I have to, but I will put a stop to this, Hank. You've gone too far this time. I'll shut this place down for good!" He turned on his heel and stalked out of the bar, slamming the door shut behind him.

Stunned silence filled the air, every eye in the place fixed on Hank, who didn't say another word. He stared at the door for a minute, then turned and stomped toward the back room. He disappeared inside, and the moment the door slammed shut, the silence broke. Everyone shouted questions at the same time, all of which were directed at Aiden and Bobby.

"What the hell just happened?"

"Can he really stop the show?"

"Do you think we should move?"

"Into tents? What are they, crazy?"

"What if they expel us?"

"Can they do that?"

Aiden was just as confused as everyone else. He exchanged a look with Bobby, then took a deep breath. "Okay, okay! Everyone calm down. We don't know any more than you do. Phil?" he asked, spotting a good-looking blond sitting at a nearby table, "Your dad is a lawyer, isn't he? Can you give him a shout? See if he can tell us what rights we have."

Phil nodded and pulled out his cell phone, and Aiden turned his attention back to Bobby. "I'm going to go talk to Hank. Something's going on between him and Ackerman that has nothing to do with our show or us staying here, and I need to find out what it is. I'll be right back."

"Are you sure you want to go in there? He was pretty upset, Aiden," Bobby said, glancing toward the door to the back room.

"I need to get to the bottom of this, Bobby. We only

have a couple of weeks before the first show and we've already nearly sold out of tickets. Need I remind you that I cut a check to the contractor this morning? If we're forced to refund those tickets, we're screwed!"

Bobby nodded, and Aiden trotted to the back room. He put his hand on the knob and said a silent prayer that he wouldn't meet the business end of Hank's fist on the other side.

Chapter Six

Hank was sitting on the sofa in the back room, holding his head in his hands. "Get out," he said, without even lifting his head up to see who'd come in.

"No can do, Hank. I've got a bar full of guys out there who are suddenly scared shitless they're going to be expelled. Unless I go back with an explanation, we're going to have a mass exodus on our hands and we'll be good and truly fucked," Aiden said, closing the door softly and taking a seat on the couch next to Hank. "Come on, give. I know there's something going on here besides the Dean being a hardass."

"It's nobody's fucking business but my own, Aiden."

"Sorry, Hank. That's not true. We have a lot invested here, and you know it. We've sold a shitload of tickets, written a check to the contractor that's not going to be worth the paper it's printed on if we have to refund the money for the tickets. It's not just us... it's you, too. What are people going to say if the bar doesn't produce the show we've been promising? FUBAR's reputation will be shot."

Hank sighed heavily and turned tired eyes up toward Aiden. "Do you remember when I told you I had a man waiting for me when I was overseas in 'Nam? That it didn't work out when I got home?"

"Yeah... oh, no! Not Ackerman!" Aiden was shocked. He hadn't even known the Dean was gay.

"Yeah. I thought I knew him, but it turns out I didn't. He changed in the four years I was gone. Wes wasn't like the way he is now, not back then. His hair was long and he always had a few joints stuffed into the pocket of his denim jacket. We used to spend hours smoking weed and dreaming of opening a bar together, but while I was gone somebody managed to shove a stick up his ass. I don't know what happened to him, but I suspect his old man got into his head. When I got back I found he'd gone back into the closet and bolted and locked the door, even against me.

"I came back and found him in a fucking suit, his pony tail sheared off, and his pot plants turned into mulch. He was teaching at the college at the time and only got worse as he worked his way up to the Dean's office."

"You still wanted to open the bar and he didn't?"

"Not only did he not want to own it with me, he tried to forbid me from opening it at all! Worse, he denied we'd ever had a relationship. Said he wasn't gay—that I'd confused him, tricked him somehow. He said the bar was trashy and bad for the college's image, being so close to campus. Said I needed to grow up and get a respectable job. Mind you, I'd just come home from 'Nam, and seen shit over there that would give me nightmares for the rest of my life. Meanwhile, *his* rich daddy pulled a few really long strings so Wes could dodge the draft, and he had the fucking balls to tell me *I* was immature!"

"Shit, Hank…"

"Yeah. Bastard broke my heart, but he pissed me off at the same time. I opened FUBAR that same year and kept it open just to spite him. Believe me, there were plenty of times over the years when I've wanted to pack it in, but I'll be damned if I'll give Wes the satisfaction. That's the same reason I never sold the house. I couldn't bear to live in it without him, but I wasn't about to sell it either. I wanted him to see that motherfucker every single day, so it would remind him of what could have been, of what he'd thrown away."

Aiden could see misery coloring Hank's features. It was obvious to Aiden that the decades that had passed hadn't eased the pain Ackerman caused. He realized that, no matter what Hank said to the contrary, Hank still loved Ackerman.

"And now we've finally given him ammunition to try to close you down. Aw, shit, Hank! Why didn't you tell us before?" Aiden felt horrible. It would be bad enough if they lost the money on the show and had to drop out of school, or were expelled, but they were fucking with Hank's whole life!

"It's not your fault, kid. Wes doesn't really care about you sleeping here, or putting on the show. He's been gunning for me since we broke up. He's been in the fucking closet for thirty-five years, and he's always been worried that I might out him. This is his chance to get rid of the threat once and for all."

"I've got one of the guys checking with his dad about our legal recourses, Hank. We'll work it out, and if not, we'll cancel the show. It's not worth you losing everything over."

Hank's head snapped up, his eyes sparking. "The *hell* you will! That show is going on as planned if I have to get up on that stage and strip myself! Wes ruined my life once—I'll be damned if I let him do it again, or to you boys, either."

Aiden could only nod. "Okay... if you're sure..."

"Fuck yes, I'm sure."

Aiden left Hank and returned to the bar. Bobby met him halfway across the room. "Phil's dad said that technically they couldn't stop us from doing what we want off campus, providing we don't use the college's name in any of the advertising, or any of its facilities. We're all of age. But if the *town* wanted to—and it sounded as if Ackerman would push them to do whatever they could—they could raid the bar. If they find anyone in here underage they could close Hank down permanently and file criminal charges. He also said we'd need to be careful not to show any flesh that would ordinarily be covered by a swimsuit. The local beach allows thongs, so we're good there, but the dancers need to keep their dicks covered at all times, and no lap dances. The boys can't let anybody grab them, either. No stuffing money into g-strings—the tips will have to pass hand to hand."

"Shit, the audience isn't going to be happy about that, but okay, we can deal with it. Everybody gets carded at the door. I don't care if they're ninety years old. We'll put up signs—*you must be twenty-one to enter*. Do we have any strippers who are under twenty-one?"

"No. There are a few guys who've been sleeping here who are, though."

"They'll need to make themselves scarce from here on out. They can move into the house—Hank won't mind. They can sleep on the floor in the living room while the bedrooms are being renovated—it won't be any worse than sleeping on the barroom floor. Hell, it'll probably be better—at least there's a rug. We won't have to worry about the flashing with the new guys, but anyone who's had experience onstage will have to be warned. We can post "Absolutely No Touching the Dancers" signs, too."

Bobby finally grabbed Aiden's arm and pulled him away into a quiet corner of the bar, out of earshot of anyone else. "What's going on, Aiden?"

Aiden told him Hank's story, trying to keep his voice low. "The one bullet in our gun is that Ackerman is gay and in the closet."

Bobby's face grew stony. "No. Absolutely not, Aiden. We're *not* outing him. That's the worst thing you can do to somebody! I won't be a part of it."

"Of course we're not! What kind of a man do you think I am? But it wouldn't hurt if he *thought* we might."

Bobby swatted Aiden playfully upside the head. "You

are too devious for words. Honestly, I can't decide if you're truly evil or just a close facsimile."

Aiden laughed. "You flatter me, m' boy. Come here," he said, pulling Bobby into his arms. His hip ground his dick against Bobby's hip, forcing Bobby's frown to melt into a smile.

"Nope, definitely evil," Bobby smirked. He leaned in for a kiss, then pulled away. "What do we do now?"

Aiden sighed and adjusted the boner that pressed against the unforgiving denim of his jeans. "Now I get to go and have a long talk with Ackerman."

Bobby nodded, looking less than pleased. "What are you going to tell him? No, wait... I don't really want to know. Just do me one favor, okay? Try not to get expelled."

Aiden snorted. "Yeah, I'll do my best. Will you do me a favor, too? If I'm not back by morning, send in the Marines," he said, nodding toward the back room where Hank remained.

Although he laughed and patted Bobby on the shoulder reassuringly, he was only half-joking. He knew that walking into the Dean's office armed only with a glib tongue was no less dangerous than marching into a lion's den wearing a suit made of sirloin steaks.

He was extremely glad Bobby hadn't pressed for what Aiden planned on telling Ackerman because, quite frankly, Aiden had no fucking idea.

Chapter Seven

Aiden didn't go directly to the Dean's office. He needed to formulate a plan, have all the details hammered out in his mind before he went in. Instead, he found a bench in the courtyard of the Administration Building and sat down.

The campus was quiet, much more so than he ever recalled it being. It was a small college, the sort where everyone knew almost everyone else. Usually there were students trudging back and forth between the dorms and the academic buildings, people playing Frisbee on the green, music floating in the air from radios. Since the dorms had closed, all that had changed. Students who lived in the frat and sorority houses kept to their own lawns, and everyone else... well, everyone else was in too much of a hurry to get back to wherever they were staying. The campus had lost the familial feeling it once had, and Aiden felt the loss sharply.

He'd never thought about it before, but it was true. Over the past nearly four years, the college had become Aiden's home, and the students, his family. It made him angry to think that no one had done anything more than toss a few cots into the gym when the dorms were closed down. Then to top it off, Ackerman pulled his holier-than-thou act, trying to keep the students from working out a viable solution, and threatened Hank's livelihood to boot.

His eyes wandered to the window on the ground floor that he knew to be Ackerman's office. The light was on, a clear indication that the Dean was in there, no doubt toasting his latest triumph over Hank with a glass of something expensive like Grey Goose, while poor Hank was trying to drown his misery in bottles of Bud.

The longer he sat and thought about it, the angrier he became. He shoved his hands through his hair, frustrated, but knowing that facing the Dean was his only option. He still had no definite plan mapped out, except for a short speech long on expletives, doused with a healthy dollop of death threats if the Dean didn't back off.

It probably wouldn't do much more than get him expelled, but at least he'd get it off his chest.

To hell with it! Aiden thought, grinding his teeth. *I'm going to march in there and tell Ackerman exactly what I think of him, consequences be damned. The bastard has it coming.*

He stalked up the sidewalk toward the building and pulled open the door. His footsteps echoed in the empty corridor as he marched past the deserted receptionist's desk and down the hallway that led to Ackerman's posh office. His fingers closed on the doorknob, ready to twist it open, when a heavy hand landed on his shoulder, startling him.

Turning, he found Hank frowning at him.

"Hank? I—"

"Get back to FUBAR. This ain't your fight, Aiden. Never was. I should've taken care of this years ago," Hank grumbled, giving Aiden's shoulder a squeeze.

"No, you have too much at stake, Hank. If we hadn't come up with the brilliant idea of moving into your house and putting on a show in the bar, Ackerman wouldn't have—"

"Go. Home." There was no mistaking the steel in Hank's voice—he was no longer an aging bar owner. He was an ex-Marine, and if Aiden didn't hop to obey his order fast enough, he was fully capable of ripping Aiden's head clean off if he was so inclined.

Aiden's eyebrows shot up to his hairline. He'd never seen Hank like this before, but he suddenly understood why Ackerman had found the man attractive once upon a time. There was something mesmerizing about Hank's bearing, in the way his eyes chilled into chips of ice. Hank exuded raw power, and Aiden felt a shiver trip down his spine by way of his prick. It jumped up, pushing against his fly, making Aiden want to ask Hank if he could drop and give Hank as many of whatever Hank wanted as he could.

Hank could be a scary, sexy bastard when he went into Marine-mode.

Aiden nodded, backing away from the door. He pretended to walk back down the hallway, but slowly, casually, and he stopped the moment he heard Ackerman's door slam shut and Hank begin to bellow from inside Ackerman's office. Then he ran back up the hallway and stood outside the door, intent on eavesdropping. He wasn't about to leave until he knew what was going to happen, and knew instinctively that Hank wouldn't tell him later at the bar. He didn't go as far as to cup his ear to the door—but then again, he didn't have to. Both Hank's and Ackerman's shouts came through loud and clear.

Curiosity killed the cat, his mother's voice sang in his ear.

Yeah, well, I never much liked cats anyway. I'm more of a dog kinda guy, he thought, stifling a smile. Besides, he was Hank's friend. If Ackerman threatened Hank in any way, he'd be glad to have a witness after the fact.

At least, that's how he justified it to himself.

"When are you going to back the fuck off, Wes?" Hank's deep bellow made the wooden door resonate.

"When my students are out of your bar and back where they belong!" Ackerman yelled. Aiden grudgingly gave him a little credit—Aiden didn't think the bastard would've had the balls to face-off with Hank.

"This ain't about them and you damn well know it!

This is about you and me, Wes. It's *always* been about you and me!"

"Keep your fucking voice down! Do you want the whole campus to hear you? There is no 'you and me.' There never was!"

"Then that must've been your fucking clone I used to fuck into the mattress!"

"Shut up! Shut up! I swear to God, Hank, if anyone hears you, I'll—"

"You'll what?" Hanks voice dropped several decibels, but Aiden could still hear the threat in it loud and clear. Ackerman was walking a very thin line, and Hank was more than ready to shoot if he strayed over it by even a hair.

Aiden heard the creaking of leather and the squeak of a chair and a deep sigh. Ackerman had either stood up or sat down—he doubted if Hank had taken a seat. "Why do you stay here, Hank? I know the bar doesn't make you a fortune, not enough to keep you here, anyway. Why haven't you moved on, found someone else? Is it just to burn my ass?"

"That's exactly why!"

"What good has it done you? Why can't you let go? Why waste your life here?"

"Because I never stopped loving you, you bastard!"

Aiden gasped, covering his mouth with his hand. There was a long silence, making Aiden worry. What was going on? Why wasn't Hank screaming at Ackerman anymore? Why wasn't Ackerman yelling at him? What had Ackerman done to him?

Nothing it seemed. After a full five minutes, just when Aiden was ready to burst into the office, sure that Hank had either suffered a heart attack or that Ackerman had hit Hank over the head with the brass sculpture of Rodin's *"The Thinker"* he kept on his desk, Hank spoke again.

Gone was his Marine frog voice. He sounded old, and tired, and incredibly sad.

"I can't help it, Wes. It fucking hurt when I came back from 'Nam and you... *why*, Wes? Why go back into the closet? Why pretend to be something you're not? Even if what you said was true and you never really loved me, I still know you're not straight. You never married... hell, as far as I know, you never even dated. You've got to be lonely, as much as I am, maybe even more. At least I have the bar. I have friends. All you have is this goddamn office and a school full of kids who hate your guts right now."

"Why? Because working at the college was the only fucking job I could get back then, that's why. You were gone, tramping through rice paddies half a world away, and I was stuck here, starving! In order to get the job, I *had* to go back in. You know what it was like in this town back then, Hank, and you sure as shit remember what my father was like. If he or the Board had known I was gay, I would've been thrown out on my ass. I'd never have gotten tenure, and I sure as hell wouldn't have been made Dean."

"So? That was then, Wes. What about now? Your dad is gone. Nobody would fucking care who you slept with anymore."

"Bullshit. Come on, Hank. You must know how people look at you, what they say when your back is turned. I can't have that. I can't live with it."

"What exactly are people saying?" The venom was back in Hank's voice, along with the warning.

There was another stretch of silence, and again Hank broke it. "Okay, presuming I believe you, then why go after the kids? Your problem has always been with me. They didn't do anything to you, Wes. They're only trying to make the best of a shitty situation. Nobody will connect you with them or the bar. I'll see to it. Just let them be, at least until the dorms are open again."

"I was worried, okay? God knows you have enough reason to out me. If the papers get wind of the kids stripping at your bar, living in your house, it'll be like shining a big, fat spotlight on the college... on me. Somebody's bound to dig up the skeletons I've kept buried all these years."

"Skeletons like me? Look, you know I've done a lot of shit in my life, but the one thing I've always been is a man of my word. I swear to you that you'll be safe. Nobody will even mention your name, Wes, and once the dorms are open, I'll sell the house, close the bar, and leave for good."

"You'd leave town?"

"I'll leave the fucking *state*, if that's what it takes."

Another few moments of silence passed, each second stretching an eternity in Aiden's mind. *No, Hank! Don't do it! Don't give in to the bastard*, he screamed, albeit in his head.

"Okay. I won't interfere with either the show or the students moving into the house, as long as we're agreed that they move back into the dorms as soon as they're open. That should be in another three months, in time for the start of the new school year. Then you're gone, Hank. Agreed?"

"Yeah. Agreed."

Aiden took off at a run, racing down the hallway before Hank saw him. His blood was boiling at the injustice of it all—Hank was going to close down the bar? Sell the house out from under them? Why? So Ackerman could keep his sexuality hidden like a dirty little secret?

He ran out of the building and kept running until the stitch in his side grew too painful. Skidding to a stop, he bent in half, gasping for air, holding his side. Collapsing on the grass in the middle of the Green, he stared back at the Administration Building, feeling more impotent than he ever had in his entire life. There was nothing he could do, he realized.

He couldn't let Hank know he'd overheard Hank's argument with Ackerman, or the agreement they'd reached. Hank would be furious if he knew, and there was nothing Aiden could do about it anyway. Hank was a grown man and sole owner of the bar and house. If he wanted to sell, there wasn't a damn thing Aiden or anyone else could do to change his mind.

Dragging himself to his feet, he made his way back to his car. Aiden needed Bobby, needed to tell him what had happened. He made a promise to himself not to tell anyone else, though—there was no need for the others to know. Someone might slip, might talk about Ackerman, and then everyone would be good and truly fucked— Hank, Ackerman, the students—everyone.

No, the show would go on, the students would move into the house as planned, but Aiden no longer felt the enthusiasm he once had about the project. Instead, all he felt was guilt settling on his shoulders, pressing down, a heavy, crushing weight that he could barely tolerate.

He'd been wrong. It wasn't the school's fault; it wasn't even Ackerman's fault. He was the only one to blame by coming up with the fucking idea in the first place. He should have minded his own business, let the students find somewhere else to live or go home. Instead, he'd stuck his nose squarely where it didn't belong and had wrecked Hank's life in the process.

Worse than all of it was the fact that he knew there was nothing he could do to make it right again.

Chapter Eight

Bobby hadn't moved, standing by the bar in exactly the same spot he'd been when Aiden had left him. He was deep in conversation with Granger, his brows knit in a frown that Aiden knew meant he was concentrating, trying to understand. No doubt Granger was regaling Bobby with some tediously technical aspect of the Secui Domus game he'd begun programming. Keshoe stood next to Granger, leaning back against the bar, dark eyes watching Granger's face with a hungry look.

The two had become very close over the past few days, and there was a bounce in Granger's step that hadn't been there before, a twinkle in his eye that Aiden knew could only come from one thing—Granger's days as the campus' oldest virgin were over.

He walked up and slipped his arms around Bobby's waist, resting his cheek on a shoulder and breathing in the familiar scent.

"Hey," Bobby said, turning in Aiden's arms, his eyes troubled. "How'd it go? Are you still a student here, or am I going to have to trash my plans to become a shrink and follow you into a new and exciting career in air-conditioning and refrigeration repair?"

"I didn't talk to Ackerman," Aiden said. "Are you done here?"

"Granger was telling me about his plans for the game, but I think we're through. Right, Granger?" Bobby asked.

Granger was no longer even looking at Bobby, having already turned his attention to Keshoe. From the way the two were eyeing each other, Aiden figured they wouldn't notice if he and Bobby self-combusted.

Aiden tugged on Bobby's arm. "Come on into the back room, Bobby. I want to talk to you." He didn't, not really. What he wanted to do was get Bobby naked, as quickly as possible. He needed the sort of comfort a man could only get when he was hip deep inside his lover.

"Okay, give," Bobby said as soon as the door shut behind them and they were alone. "What happened? You went racing out of here with murder in your eyes and then come back with your tail tucked between your legs, whining like a lost puppy."

"I'm not whining."

"Trust me. I know whining when I hear it. What happened?"

Haltingly, Aiden told Bobby what had happened and what he overheard. "Look, we can't let Hank know I was eavesdropping, and we can't risk anyone outing Ackerman. We have to pretend everything's okay and just let it go."

"But what about Hank?"

"I don't know. Maybe we can figure something out before the dorms open. Bobby, I feel really shitty about all of this—like everything's my fault. If I'd only minded my own fucking business, none of this would be happening."

"Don't, Aiden. It isn't your fault—you were only trying to help. This all dates back to unresolved issues between Hank and Ackerman. Don't make their problem yours."

"They were doing fine until I butted in."

"No, they weren't. Ackerman is still in denial, and Hank refused to move on."

"Yeah, well, I still feel like a first-class shit." Aiden sank onto the cot, falling backward, staring dejectedly at the ceiling.

Bobby sat next to him. "As I see it, I can do one of two things. I can try to talk you out of your funk, or I can give you something else to think about. Personally, I'm just about all talked out tonight—do you have any idea what it's like to try to keep from nodding off when Granger starts talking about albedo textures, refactoring code, and parallax occlusion mapping? For a while, I actually thought I was starting to slip into a coma."

Aiden laughed, despite his heavy heart. "Yeah, I understand completely. He's a good guy, but man, he is short in the conversational skills department. So... can I assume you're up for option number two?" He smiled as Bobby slipped a hand under his t-shirt, nimble fingers smoothing over Aiden's chest.

Bobby didn't answer. Instead, he leaned forward and kissed Aiden, long and deep. His tongue swept Aiden's mouth, over the palate, the teeth, fighting Aiden's tongue for the right to dominate. Aiden gave over, needing to be cared for, to be taken, to be *had*. He opened for Bobby fully, giving over completely to those teasing hands and sweet mouth.

Bobby didn't seem to mind. In fact, the man was quite enthusiastic, zealously plundering Aiden's mouth thoroughly before moving on to the delicate skin under Aiden's jaw, and lower still, to his chest and belly.

They stripped each other slowly, both taking care to kiss and lick every inch of skin they exposed, until both lay on the narrow cot, naked and hard, the outside world and their problems forgotten, aware only of the fevered pitch of their arousal and need for each other.

Closing his eyes, Aiden surrendered himself to his sense of touch as Bobby's lips and tongue did magical things to his body. A nipple was flicked, suckled, and pinched; his bellybutton explored by a warm, wet tongue. His inner thighs massaged by strong fingers, then teased with lips and teeth until Aiden's cock angrily began to demand equal time.

Moaning, Aiden's hands refused to stay still any longer, finding Bobby's ass, squeezing and kneading the firm flesh. A finger slipped between Bobby's cheeks, searching for his entrance. Finding it, Aiden teased it, slipping inside, until Bobby's moans made Aiden's cock protest with drops of precome and an angry twitch against his belly.

"Man, Bobby, I really want in you," Aiden breathed. His eyes widened as Bobby produced a condom and lube seemingly out of thin air. Maybe he only thought it was instantaneous—he was so wildly aroused that he was barely aware of where he was, never mind the correct passage of time. He closed his eyes as Bobby's hands stroked his cock, rolling the latex over it.

Still, Aiden needed to do little except lay back and enjoy every twinge, every shock, every bolt of pleasure as Bobby continued to do all the work. He crouched over Aiden's engorged cock and then slowly lowered himself over it, impaling himself on Aiden's slicked length.

Aiden gasped Bobby's name as his cock was enveloped in the heated silk of Bobby's body. When Bobby began to rock, to ride Aiden's cock and send shivers of sheer ecstasy rocketing through him, he decided to stop being so selfish and give back a little of what Bobby was giving him. He wrapped his fingers around Bobby's cock, the fat head slick with precome, and began to stroke.

"Faster, Aiden," Bobby ordered breathlessly. Aiden was only too happy to comply. He squeezed Bobby's cock, sliding his hand up and down the hard shaft in a faster rhythm. "Gonna come!"

"Give it to me, Bobby. Give it up!" Aiden cried. He squeezed his eyes shut as spurts of white heat covered his face. The smell of come, of man and musky sex filled his nostrils, and together with Bobby's anal muscles contracting around his cock, brought his own orgasm roaring to the surface.

He pushed Bobby away, tearing off the condom and fisting himself, striving to get past the point of no return, hand working his turgid flesh frantically.

Bobby pushed Aiden's hands out of the way and wrapped his lips around Aiden's cock, just as he began to come. "Oh, God, yeah! Drain every last bit of it, Bobby!" Aiden cried, the last syllable of Bobby's name stretching out, undulating into a hoarse moan as he bolted over the precipice and soared. His body seized, every muscle in it growing rigid as his orgasm exploded outward from his very core, sizzling through his veins at light speed. His neck and back arched off the bed; his feet dug into the mattress as if to keep him from flying off it, propelled by the power of his climax.

It seemed to last forever, much longer than usual, going on and on until he finally crested and fell, sated and relaxed, onto his back, pulling Bobby down with him. "Oh, man. Bobby, that was fucking great! You were great! I was great! Shit... we should do this for a living. We'd be multi-fucking-millionaires."

Bobby snorted, throwing an arm and leg over Aiden's sweat-soaked body. "Funny, but I don't really see a market for that, Aiden. I'm not sure anyone would want to pay us to fuck each other."

"Porn movies. We could make 'em. Star in 'em."

"Forget it. First, I am not an actor. That's Keshoe's department. Secondly, I don't even want to begin to get into what's wrong and demented with that idea. Thirdly, we have enough to do anyway, with the show coming up in another week or so."

"Yeah, I suppose. Maybe we could just video ourselves. Then we could watch us. We'd love us, you know. Make us hot enough to fuck again. Which we could video, and then watch, which would make us hot. Do you see the pattern I'm trying to establish here?" Aiden chuckled.

"You, sir, are a hopeless romantic."

"Nope. Just a horndog who's finally found a guy who can keep him satisfied."

Bobby looked pleased at that and smiled, even though he remained sarcastic. "Wow. I'm honored."

"Yeah, you should be. Now come on, get up. We've got work to do," Aiden said, slapping Bobby playfully on the thigh.

Bobby looked sober for a minute and put a hand on Aiden's arm. "Not that I want to dispel the warm fuzzies we both seem to be wallowing in at the moment, but what are we going to do about Hank?"

Aiden shook his head sadly. "Nothing, I guess. It's going to have work itself out. Either Hank will keep his word to Ackerman and sell out, or he won't. We'll put on the show. If it's successful, then we'll move into the house, at least until the dorms reopen. After that, it's all going to be up to Hank. Secui Domus may be nothing more than a really sweet memory."

"Well, look at the bright side—we should have time to throw a hell of a kegger before we get evicted." Bobby added, although he wasn't smiling. Aiden knew Bobby felt as badly as he did. Not even the thought of a Party-to-End-All-Parties could perk their spirits. They knew that if Hank was leaving and they were going to be forced back into the dorms, it would be more of a wake than a celebration.

Chapter Nine

Aiden felt like a handful of raw, screaming nerves wrapped up in a thin layer of sweat-soaked skin. He couldn't stop moving; walking from one end of the bar to the other and back again, checking and re-checking the lights and sound system, the curtain cues, and the glass racks. He haunted the bartenders, the servers, the dancers, the stage hands, and the bouncers until one threatened to stuff him inside the bar's air-conditioning ducts if he didn't knock it off.

He couldn't help himself; everything depended on tonight, on the first show, and since nothing had gone right during the dress rehearsal, he figured he had good cause to panic.

First, the light cues had been completely wrong. The audio wouldn't work right. The music would play, then spiral into a high-pitched squeal that set everyone's teeth on edge. Three of the dancers were battling intense cases of cold-feet. Bobby was running on a short fuse, which only exacerbated Aiden's case of nerves.

It was going to be a disaster, he just knew it.

Then there was Hank. He hadn't been himself since his meeting with Ackerman, although only Aiden and Bobby knew why. Morose and depressed, he spent as little time in the bar as possible, and when he was there, he only spoke when absolutely necessary. His mood cast a pall over everyone, since no one (aside from Aiden and Bobby) could understand the reason he was so unhappy.

Hank had told everyone only that Ackerman had relented on his position, but refrained from mentioning anything else of what had gone on in Ackerman's office that night. As far as the students were concerned, it was a done deal. Ackerman had backed off, and life was good, therefore they were flummoxed over Hank's depression.

Aiden didn't know what frightened him more—the fact that they'd sold out of tickets for the first show, or the worry he had that no one would show up, even after forking over ten bucks for a ticket. Worse, if everyone did come, would they like the show or hate it? Would Secui Domus become a reality?

He was about to find out. It was seven-thirty and time to open the doors. Aiden found Bobby, gave him a quick kiss for luck, then marched through the empty bar to the front doors. Nodding toward the bouncers who would be checking IDs, he gave the signal.

The doors opened to show a line of people that snaked down the block and around the corner. Aiden stood to the side, watching as the bouncers checked ID after ID, carefully scrutinizing each one, refusing to be hurried by the people impatient to get in to see the show. He nodded to himself. Good. They weren't taking any chances that someone with a fake ID would slip in and give the town fathers reason to go gunning after Hank.

Slipping through the already thickening crowd jostling to find seats, he headed backstage.

Backstage, of course, was the small room at the back of the bar, the door now hidden behind a slightly moth-eaten, red velvet curtain strung across the length of the rear wall just behind the small stage and catwalk.

Bobby stood ready to work. He was first on; they'd wanted to start off the show with a seasoned professional, someone who could get the crowd so worked up that they might overlook some of the mistakes the less-than-stellar newbies might make.

He was wearing his firefighter's costume, one of Aiden's favorites. Bobby looked hot—in every sense of the word, dressed in a helmet, turnout coat, bunker pants and boots decorated with wide strips of bright yellow duct tape.

He'd bought the costume secondhand on EBay and it was the real McCoy—heavy canvas and rubber.

Everyone else was in the process of getting dressed, knocking knees and elbows in the small room. Keshoe, dressed as a gladiator, ready to give *Spartacus' Speech to the Gladiators* as part of his routine, was trying to calm down Bill, who looked ready to upchuck all over him.

Bobby spotted Aiden and squeezed between an astronaut and a construction worker to get to him.

"How is it out there?" he asked Aiden, wincing as the construction worker nearly kneed the astronaut while trying to pull on a work boot.

"Packed house, hon. I just wanted to tell you to break a leg."

"Are we sure we're ready for this?" Bobby asked, eyeing the roomful of would-be dancers.

"No, but we're going to do it anyway," Aiden said, leaning in for a quick kiss. "It's nearly eight now. I'm going to go settle them down, get the ball rolling, okay?"

"Yup."

"Knock 'em dead, kid," Aiden said. He turned back toward the door, took a deep breath, and stepped outside. The curtain hung directly in front of his face. Feeling for the split, he pulled the heavy fabric to the side and stepped through.

Immediately the chatter of the crowd swelled to hoots and whistles, and he held up his hands, patiently waiting for it to die down. As the crowd gradually realized that he wasn't going to take anything off, they quieted.

"Hello everybody and welcome to the very first Secui Domus Strip Spectacular!"

The audience responded to his welcome—or more likely to the word "strip"—by applauding wildly and screaming at him to "take something off!"

Aiden grinned, shaking his head, holding his hands

up. "I'm Aiden Barrows, your Master of Ceremonies for the evening. Sit back, remember you have a two drink minimum, tip your waiters and bartenders well, and enjoy as Secui Domus Productions present their all-male revue!"

That was the sound mixer's cue to start up the music for Bobby's dance. The opening strains of the Talking Heads' *Burning Down the House* blared, and Aiden quickly stepped off the stage to make room for Bobby's dance. He headed over to the bar to help Hank and the two students working as bartenders hustle drinks for the waiters, keeping one eye on the stage. Aiden wasn't worried about Bobby's dance—he was a pro, knew what he was doing, and would have the crowd eating out of his hand before he was done.

It was everyone who *followed* Bobby that had Aiden worried.

Bobby's routine went off without a hitch. He danced, muscles moving fluidly under his skin, discarding pieces of his costume with grace. Down at last to his flame-printed g-string, he did a slow bump and grind that gave Aiden a hard-on and brought the audience to its feet. He slipped behind the curtain to cries of "More!" and Aiden felt inordinately proud of him. Bobby had done well, and he had every intention of rewarding his boy as soon as they were alone.

Keshoe was up next. At the sight of the tall, handsome gladiator, the crowd went wild. Keshoe paused only for a moment, eyes widening at the size of the rowdy crowd. Then he recovered, much to Aiden's relief, and launched into his routine.

Aiden exhaled, suddenly aware that he'd been holding his breath. He sidled up to Hank, who was pouring a pitcher. "How are you holding up, Hank?"

"So far, so good. Big crowd, huh?" There was barely

any inflection in Hank's voice. He sounded as if he was a robot, detached and about a million miles away.

"Hank, you don't have to be here, you know. We can handle this," Aiden said, putting a hand on Hank's beefy arm.

Hank shook him off. "Nah, I'm good. Somebody's gotta keep an eye on you kids."

Aiden nodded, unconvinced, but he had too many worries to argue with Hank. He watched as Keshoe finished his routine and the next dancer stepped out from behind the curtain.

Bill didn't dance as much as he *stomped*, but it didn't matter. The crowd loved him anyway, forgiving him his missteps and his obvious lack of rhythm. When he pulled off Aiden's Velcro pants, they banged on the tables and applauded.

Aiden didn't know what made him look toward the front door at that moment, but he did, and what he saw made his heart pound so hard that the thumping of blood in his ears drowned out the noise of the crowd.

Ackerman stood just inside the door, his face hard and grim, hands curled into fists at his sides. He looked distinctly uncomfortable and incredibly high-strung, as if he would take a swing at the very first person who invaded his personal space.

Oh, sweet fuck! What now? Why was Ackerman here? Hadn't he promised Hank not to interfere? Aiden cut a glance toward Hank, and from the stony expression on Hank's face, realized Hank was asking himself those same questions.

Ackerman made his way through the crowd to the bar. When Hank reached over and grabbed the front of his jacket, Aiden figured it was all over. Hank was going to plow his fist into Ackerman's face, the cops would be called, and the show would be over. Hank would go to jail, the bar would be closed, and the students would be homeless.

They were fucked, pure and simple.

Instead, even though Hank's fist was curled into a hard ball and his muscles bulged with tension, he didn't hit Ackerman. "Why are you here, Wes?" he hissed in a tight, angry voice.

"Relax, Hank. I… I couldn't stay away, but not for the reason you think. Fuck! I haven't slept since you came to see me! Look at me—I'm a train wreck, Hank. I couldn't stop thinking about the past, about what might have happened if I hadn't…" Ackerman suddenly deflated, going limp. His head hung down, his arms braced against the bar and Hank's fingers twisted in his lapels the only things that seemed to be keeping him upright.

"Wes? Wes, what are you talking about?" The frost melted from Hank's voice. Hank let go of Ackerman's jacket and touched the side of his face. The gentleness of the action brought a lump to Aiden's throat.

"I'm sorry, Hank. For everything. For all of it. I'm such an asshole! I threw my whole life away because I was too afraid of who I am and what I wanted. Scared of you, of us, of what we had together. Of what everyone else would say, of losing my fucking job…"

Aiden was just as stunned by Ackerman's confession as Hank appeared. Onstage, dancers continued to shake and shimmy, working their muscular bodies for the crowd, the music blaring, the audience screaming, but he didn't hear or see any of it. All he could concentrate on was the drama unfolding between Ackerman and Hank.

Aiden wondered what Hank was going to do. If it had been him, and he was faced with the man who'd broken his heart and made his life a living hell for thirty-five years, he would have dragged Ackerman over the bar and beat the living shit out of the man. He would have paid

Ackerman back for each day, every minute of pain. Aiden was sure that if Hank felt the same and went that route, he'd kill Ackerman.

His balls tried to crawl up inside his body as he held his breath, waiting for Hank to throw the first punch, to see Ackerman's blood spray the bar.

It never happened.

Instead, with a look of incredible tenderness and longing softening Hank's granite features, he pulled Ackerman closer. Hank didn't hit him, but kissed him, slowly and with such heat that it brought Aiden's recently softened erection roaring back.

No one except the two bartenders and the people crowded nearest the bar noticed. Everyone else was too busy watching the construction worker dance in his tool belt and little else to pay any attention. Still, Aiden hoped Ackerman and Hank were ready, because the few who *had* seen them kiss would have the news spread all over campus by morning.

"Later," Aiden heard Hank growl in a raspy voice. "I have to work. Don't fucking try to leave, Wes. I'll hunt your ass down. Watch the show."

"I'm not going anywhere. Not this time," Ackerman said. His cheeks were red, but his eyes sparkled, and he looked twenty years younger to Aiden.

That was the moment when Aiden finally relaxed. He felt his tension drain away and turned his head so Hank and Ackerman wouldn't notice he'd been watching them, or see the big, goofy grin that spread across his face.

On the stage, the performances went on, unaffected by the show that continued to play out silently between Hank and Ackerman, and when Aiden clapped and whistled, he wasn't sure who he was applauding for—the dancers, or Hank and Wes.

Chapter Ten

A naked guy, his body smeared with what appeared to be melting streaks of whipped cream—at least Aiden *thought* it was whipped cream—ran through the crowded living room of Secui Domus, laughing and eagerly pursued by three others.

Music pounded the floorboards and walls; the smell of beer permeated the entire house. Out on the back porch, Keshoe and Granger were working as bartenders, pumping glass after glass from the huge, silver kegs of Sam Adams and Rolling Rock.

Someone had set up a Slip and Slide in the yard, a sheet of slick plastic that stretched for several yards. Two men were spraying it with beer; a third was sliding through the foam on his belly, naked except for a pair of Speedos.

Couples and threesomes were in the shadowed corners of the house and yard, and if Aiden listened closely enough, he could make out the wet sounds of kissing and sucking over the music and laughter that filled the air.

They'd officially been living in the house for two months. The semester was over, and the party was not only celebrating the birth of Secui Domus, but the impending graduation of several of its founding members, Aiden and Bobby included.

He smiled as Hank and Wes slipped by him, heading into the yard. The two men had been inseparable ever since the night of the first show at FUBAR. Wes had not only come out, he'd come out with a *vengeance*, moving from his posh apartment into Hank's smaller, far less cushy accommodations over the bar.

There'd been a huge brouhaha when the Board had found out about Wes' sexual preference and his newly reestablished romance with Hank. It was still unsure whether Wes would keep his job as Dean.

According to Wes, he couldn't care less. He was happy for the first time in over a quarter century and wasn't going back into the closet for anyone or any reason. Hank took a slightly different view—he said he'd be making soup with the Board members' entrails if they booted Wes out of office. Aiden was just glad Wes had finally seen the light after thirty-five years. Aiden had never seen Hank as happy as he'd been these past few months.

As for himself, he and Bobby were closer than ever. In their shared room at Secui Domus, Aiden's map of Europe was pinned on the wall over the bed, except that now every location on Aiden's proposed trip was marked by two pins—a red one for him and a blue one for Bobby.

Granger and Keshoe were officially a couple, although they maintained an "open" relationship, sleeping with whoever caught their eye. Aiden didn't really understand it—he loved Bobby too much now to even consider sleeping with anyone else, but who was he to judge? It seemed to be working well enough for Granger and Keshoe, at least for the time being.

"Hey, Aiden! Wait up!"

Speak of the devil and he shall appear, Aiden thought, as he waited for Granger to catch up. Aiden often thought lately that he'd created a monster in Granger. Ever since his make-over and hook-up with Kesh, Granger had become something of a Don Juan, flirting outrageously with anyone with a dick, and sleeping with them more often than not. Aiden sincerely hoped he was being careful, and that he'd get it out of his system soon. Keshoe was enjoying their relationship at the moment, but he wouldn't wait forever for Granger to commit to him.

"I've got something for you," Granger said, handing Aiden a small, flat package.

"What's this?" Aiden asked, looking at the wrapping

paper spotted with caps and diplomas. "You didn't have to get me anything for graduation, Granger."

Aiden smiled as Bobby joined them, slipping an arm around Aiden's waist. "Whoa, you got a present? What about me? I'm graduating, too," he said with an impish grin.

"It's really for both of you," Granger said, laughing. "Go on, open it!"

Aiden obligingly ripped the paper off, revealing a thin CD case. The disc inside was unmarked, the sort that could be burned on a home computer. "What is it?" he asked, cocking a confused brow at Granger.

Granger's face split open into a wide grin. "The very first copy of the beta version of *Secui Domus, the Game.*"

"Holy shit!" Granger cried, holding the disc up to catch the light. "You're kidding me! I thought it was going to take years to program the game!"

"It will. This is just one character, and there aren't very many options programmed in yet. Still, I thought you'd appreciate it. I named the character *Aiden*. He even looks like you."

"Oh, man, Granger! This is so fucking cool! Thank you!" Aiden cried, hugging Granger tightly. He felt a lump rise under Granger's fly, pressing against his hipbone. *Yup*, Aiden thought wryly, *I've created a monster.*

"Awesome, Granger!" Bobby added. Aiden felt a tug backwards, putting some space between Aiden's body and Granger's, and it brought a softer smile to his lips. Bobby didn't like to share, particularly where Aiden was concerned, not that Aiden minded the possessiveness a bit. He felt the same way, after all.

Granger flashed them both an interested look, then shrugged and wandered back to where Keshoe waited, still pumping out glasses of beer. He knew enough not to make a move on Aiden—or Bobby, for that matter—and they watched as he happily went back to pouring beer and flirting with everyone else.

Aiden dragged Bobby off the back porch into the yard, where the party had overflowed from the house, spilling out across the lawn. He scouted the area, finally spotting a relatively unpopulated dark corner near the right hand side of the fence, and headed in that direction.

Hidden from everyone else by the shadow of the house, Aiden pulled Bobby into his arms. "Did you ever think it would all work out?" he asked, nuzzling Bobby's neck.

"Nope. Not for one minute. Sometimes I wake up thinking it was all a dream and that we're still sleeping on the floor of the bar." Warm hands slipped under Aiden's t-shirt, smoothing over his skin. Their hips ground together, sweet friction making Aiden's cock thicken under his fly.

"Damn!" Aiden hissed, arching his neck for Bobby's lips. "I can't be within spitting distance of you without getting a hard-on!"

"Hey, you two!" A deep, gravelly voice cut in, bringing both Aiden and Bobby up short. "Go find your own damn corner!"

Turning, Aiden saw that Hank had Wes facing the side of the house, hands braced on the aluminum siding. Both had their pants dropped to their knees, asses glowing white in the darkness.

Laughing, and with Hank's threats of beating them both into steaming piles of smartass mulch following them, they ran. Stripping off their shirts, they stopped in the kitchen and grabbed a couple of cans of whipped cream, exchanging identical, wicked grins.

Graduation was looming, but at the moment, Secui Domus' first ever kegger was in full swing, and its Founding Fathers were ready and able to keep the party going.

Another Believer
by Stephanie Vaughan

Is this seat taken?"

David looked up and had to make a conscious effort to close his mouth.

"Uh, no. Go ahead."

Shifting his feet, David shoved his backpack further beneath his seat and pulled his elbows in to make room.

"Thanks." Little ripples of pleasure fluttered down David's back upon hearing the smooth baritone, and maybe the cutest guy he'd ever seen sat down, tucking a well-worn duffel between his feet.

"No problem." Trying not to be obvious, David cast a quick glance beneath his lashes at the long legs and muscular thighs settling in next to him. Late August in Southern California meant that daytime temperatures were in the eighties and nineties, and shorts were still the order of the day for most people.

The legs now stretched out beside him were lean and tanned, with a light dusting of reddish-blond hair. David tried not to gawk. He'd admired the view from behind earlier in the train station, casting admiring glances and doing his best to be discreet, even going so far as to offer up a brief plea to the universe that the tall man with the seriously hot bod would be on his train. He wouldn't have had the hubris to ask that said cute guy would sit next to him. That would use up a year's worth of good luck, and there was still the dorm and roommate lottery to get through.

The train was already moving, pulling out of Union Station and into the hazy sunshine that was L.A. in the fall. Forcing himself to look away, David tried to focus on the scenery, such as it was, and away from maybe the hottest guy he'd ever seen, let alone rubbed forearms with. The empty vista formed by the cement channel of the Los Angeles River, even with its colorful graffiti and eye-catching collection of debris, was no match for the nicely muscled arm that now rested near David's. Not even close.

David's overactive imagination had no trouble supplying him with scenarios for what he'd like that very attractive forearm to do, beginning with slipping down over David's thigh and stroking firmly up and down his inseam a few times before cupping his crotch.

Aw, man.

The heat and electricity from being so close was already getting to him, and then the train jerked and the guy's arm brushed against David's.

"Sorry."

David's gaze flew to meet the other man's and he was momentarily lost in the depths of perfect, brilliant green. "It's okay. I'm David, by the way." He stuck out his hand, reaching over the armrest to shake.

"Jonah. Simpson." Jonah's hand dwarfed David's, long fingers wrapping easily around the back of David's hand. Two fingers were wrapped with adhesive tape, and David tried to hide his shiver as slightly roughened fingertips scraped across his skin.

"Cool." David retrieved his hand, rubbing it across his thigh, embarrassed at the tingle he continued to feel. He'd really have to get a grip before he humiliated himself, but he'd never been this close to anyone so perfectly beautiful.

Chestnut hair, streaked with everything from dark mahogany to strawberry blond, fell in shaggy disarray over Jonah's forehead, and a light sprinkling of freckles scattered themselves charmingly along two high cheekbones and a perfectly-sized, perfectly-shaped, perfectly-placed nose. A spare upper lip rode gracefully above a much plumper lower one, and already David had gotten intermittent flashes of a smile that was an orthodontist's dream.

David sighed.

Jonah was absolutely gorgeous.

He was even tall.

Every one of David's favorite fantasies started with a tall man, but he'd figured out early that perfect specimens like the one seated next to him didn't look twice at short, nerdy science geeks like him. It wasn't just that, though. Every bit of David's research indicated that not getting a second glance severely limited his chances of being fucked senseless by any of those perfect specimens.

Beside him, Jonah leaned over to pull out the duffel beneath his feet and began rummaging through it. When he sat up again, he had a dog-eared manila envelope in his hands, from which he pulled out a collection of documents and brochures. Kicking the duffel back beneath the seat again, Jonah straightened the pile before sorting through it.

Craning his neck a bit, David tried to get a glimpse of the subject matter, but just then Jonah looked up. David immediately averted his gaze and switched back to studying the landscape. He knew from experience that the scenery around Union Station consisted primarily of what the newspapers usually called ordinary urban clutter, but occasionally the extraordinary could be spotted. Not just garden variety graffiti and abandoned washing machines. David knew that street people made their homes in some of the channels that fed runoff water into the river during the rainy months. Since rain in August in L.A. was practically unheard of, this time of year the cavernous concrete tunnels were often inhabited. He sometimes got inadvertent glimpses of their lives and it was nothing short of heartbreaking, so, as much as possible, David did his best not to look.

"Whoa!"

Yanking his gaze around and up to Jonah's, David immediately took in the wide, startled green eyes and the attractive flush in those high, round cheeks.

"Did you see that?" Jonah's gaze fixed on David and it was breath-stopping to be the recipient of that much focused energy.

Shaking his head, David could only shrug weakly. "No. What?"

"There was a... a man." Near dumbstruck, Jonah struggled to put words together. "In the..."

When Jonah's glance strayed reluctantly back to the windows on the opposite side of the train, David's followed it. He didn't have to know specifically what Jonah'd seen; he could just flash to his own memories of some of the more comment-worthy sights he'd witnessed over the months.

Jonah's gaze strayed back to David and David reminded himself not to gawk. Those eyes really were amazing. Instead, David nodded sympathetically. "Yeah, it can kind of catch you off guard sometimes."

Mouth falling open a little, it was Jonah's turn to gape.

"You've seen—?" "

"Junkies shooting up? Pros turning tricks? Naked old dudes doing things I don't even want to think about?" Randomly tossing out some of the more frequent occurrences, David watched in delight as Jonah's eyebrows climbed higher and higher, eventually disappearing beneath the sweet fringe of hair that hung into his amazing eyes.

"It was…" A full-body shudder passed over Jonah and David took the opportunity to let his gaze briefly roam over the impressive pair of shoulders evident beneath the t-shirt that clung to Jonah's body. "He was…"

"Yeah?" Smiling encouragingly, David did his best to keep the conversation going. If the talk had to do with anything electrical or, more specifically, his special love—robotics—David could go all night. But make the conversation anything social and he was at a loss. He never really knew what to say.

"He was big. And," Jonah paused to look over his shoulder, back in the direction the steady speed of the train had swept them past. Peering into David's eyes with an intensity that made his insides quiver, Jonah somehow seemed to be willing David to believe the unbelievable. "This big black dude… was wearing nothing but a diaper. That's it. That's all he had on. His legs were… Back in the… "

David winced at the mental picture Jonah's words had conjured. Just sad. What must that guy's story be?

Jonah's distress was obvious and David instantly wanted to comfort him. He had a soft heart and he knew it. The fact that the person in need of help was so perfectly gorgeous that he made David's teeth ache was beside the point.

His need to offer emotional support was completely impartial. Altruistic, even.

It was his nature to try to help, so David reached out his hand, rubbing Jonah's arm softly. "Yeah, it's hard sometimes. I know."

Slowly, by small degrees, Jonah relaxed. The eyes got less intent; that beautiful mouth that David wanted desperately to lick softened; the muscles beneath David's hand loosened. And then, ever so slowly, Jonah's gaze dropped to watch the circling motions David only gradually realized he was making—making on Jonah's very attractive, very probably heterosexual arm.

Oh, shit.

Now he'd done it.

David closed his eyes before Jonah's horrified gaze could find his. Now Jonah was going to call him whatever Jonah's straight jock brain's nom du jour for not-straight was. Then he'd probably threaten to beat the crap out of David's skinny, obviously not-straight ass for daring to touch him.

It wasn't the thumping, or even just the threat of it David dreaded, so much as it was the look he'd no doubt see in Jonah's eyes. Coming so closely on the heels of the intense look and the sympathetic look, David knew it was going to sting just that much more.

"David?" Low, gritty, slow, Jonah's voice hung heavily in the air between them. The train swayed and rattled as it took a turn, the steel wheels clanking rhythmically over the tracks.

Random bits of conversation from other passengers floated by and David grasped at them, desperate to avoid what was about to come crashing down on his clumsy but well-intentioned head. A man asked the score of the day's ball game. A girl's flirtatious giggle was followed by a low, masculine chuckle. The automated voice of the train system announced the next stop.

"Oh. Whoa. Sorry. I'll just... Never mind." Carefully

withdrawing his hand, David turned away. Gazing blindly out the window, he was still hyper-aware of the man behind him; could feel the gaze boring into the back of his neck.

"You got a last name, David?"

Okay, this wasn't exactly what he'd been expecting. Chancing a look, David glanced over his shoulder and found something undecipherable on Jonah's chiseled face. "Yeah, Sato. Why?"

"Japanese?"

"Half. *Why?*" David knew he sucked at reading faces. But even knowing that social skills weren't his thing, this went way beyond the usual 'was that a joke and should I laugh now?'

Eyes narrowing suspiciously, Jonah slanted him a look out of those eyes that even now made David's heart beat faster, damn him. "Gay?"

Disappointment made David reckless and he opened his never-appropriate mouth and sunk whatever hopes he might still have clung to. "Gay as in likes cock and butt sex, or gay as in happy?"

Nearly choking, Jonah glanced around quickly, probably looking to see who might have overheard. David didn't care. He was going to have to get up and go find another seat now and, after standing in line for nearly an hour to be sure he got a window on the coast side of the train, David was extra pissed at himself for the wasted effort.

"Keep your voice down. Jeez." Jonah looked around again before lowering his head, bringing it close to David's. "The, uh, the first one."

"What do you think?" Folding his arms across his chest, David leaned back in his seat. Just because Jonah was hot and he knew it didn't mean David would let him get away with whatever he wanted.

"Just answer the question. Are you?" To David's surprise, Jonah followed, pursuing David into his personal space. He leaned in until David could see the exact hue and intensity of those fabulous green eyes.

Maybe it was frustration, but something boiled over inside David and he searched for the most outrageous thing he could think of to set this cruel tease of a straight boy back on his heels.

"Absolutely *love* the cock, and there's nothing I like more than riding a big hard one. All night long." He drew out the last bit, taking an evil delight in watching Jonah's eyes go wide.

"Oh. Wow." Nostrils flaring with the quick, shallow breaths he was taking, Jonah stared back. "*Nice.*"

Oh. Wow. Nice.

In the time it took to get from L.A. to Simi Valley, Jonah's day had gone from tedious and boring to very, *very* interesting.

He'd been resigned to a long, dull trip up the coast on the train and he'd picked the seat next to the Asian guy because he'd always had a thing for the whole black hair, dark almond-shaped eyes combo. Jonah figured at least the indoor scenery would be nice.

Still, he hadn't expected much. That the guy would also have that vaguely brainiac look about him was just gravy. Jonah'd taken crap for years about his preference in that area, but there was no one around now to give him grief if he did a little low-key perving.

He couldn't help it.

He liked smart guys; guys who could talk about something besides stats and standings and who got snubbed in the NBA draft. To Jonah there was nothing sexier than a guy who was really smart—who actually knew his stuff and wasn't ashamed to show it. There was just something that turned him on about the self-confidence that came from the combination of intelligence and expertise.

"Tickets, gentlemen."

Jonah nearly came out of his skin at the voice suddenly speaking behind him. The attendant's matter-of-fact delivery didn't mitigate the fact that Jonah had been so wrapped up in his conversation with David and all its wonderful possibilities, that he hadn't had a clue that anyone had approached from behind.

Turning away from David reluctantly, Jonah reached into his duffel and rummaged for his ticket. Finding it, he handed it to the attendant and smiled. "Here you go." The man verifying the information on Jonah's ticket didn't need to know that the smile had nothing to do with him and everything to do with the happy little fantasies now bubbling up from Jonah's imagination.

When the attendant handed Jonah's ticket back and turned to David with an expectant look, Jonah had the excuse he needed to turn and watch David right along with the man.

David's very proper, "It's right here, sir," had Jonah biting his lip, and he didn't think he imagined the amused flicker on the attendant's lips, either.

"You gentlemen have yourselves a good trip now, hear?" After flipping the VACANT signs above their seats to OCCUPIED, the attendant moved on.

Jonah watched the man move up to the next row before turning back to David, who still sat back in his seat, arms folded across his chest. "So, cool. He's gone. Where were we?"

"What?"

Even David's glare was darling. Jonah wanted to kiss

the scowl off his face, then remove his shirt and keep going from there. "I'm just looking." Jonah's gaze ran across David's face, loving the clean lines and high cheekbones, the fall of dark hair that slid easily across his forehead.

"At what?"

"You." Jonah smiled. "Hey, you want to go find the dining car with me?"

"Don't you have paperwork to do?"

"Huh?" Jonah had forgotten all about the pile of school registration papers he'd taken out to sort through until David nodded at his lap. "Oh, right. Well, I was going to, but you distracted me. Besides, that can wait; right now I'm hungry. I want to find something to eat and I want you to come with me."

"Why would you want me to go with you? We don't even know each other."

"So... we'll get to know each other." The lure of David's smooth, almost flawless skin called and Jonah couldn't resist any longer. He put a hand back on David's knee and let it slide down the inside a few inches, savoring the texture of soft hair he found there.

David gasped, the abrupt intake of breath expanding his chest, and Jonah was almost certain those were David's nipples now slightly visible beneath his t-shirt.

David stared open-mouthed and Jonah wondered if he'd taken too much for granted. Just because *he* was attracted didn't mean that David was equally attracted. Boldness wasn't always rewarded and, okay, just maybe a little moderation was called for. It wasn't his first instinct, but Jonah could adapt when the situation called for it.

Removing his hand, Jonah tried for a friendly, non-threatening smile. "Come on. We can grab a cup of coffee and you can tell me where you're headed."

"I don't drink coffee."

Was it his imagination, or was David's expression

growing less mulish? So maybe David hadn't shut him down completely. In fact, that last response might even indicate a glimmer of interest. "So get a hot chocolate. Juice. Whatever."

"Why are you asking me? Are you seriously that bored?"

So. David wasn't exactly the trusting type, apparently. Shrugging, Jonah opted for a portion of the truth. "Maybe I just feel like some company. I don't know a single person on this train and I'm headed for a school where I likewise don't know anybody. Maybe making a new friend seems like a good way to start."

David tilted his head consideringly. "Yeah? What school?" David shifted in his seat, still looking far from relaxed, but maybe a fraction more comfortable. Man, the guys on the team would give him no end of shit if they saw how badly Jonah had nearly blown that one. He must seriously be losing his touch.

"Mt. Scott."

"Really." David's gaze narrowed, indicating just how improbably Jonah's answer struck him, and his arms went back to their former position of folded across his chest.

Damn.

Maybe it was for the best—less distracting and all—but Jonah still had a moment of regret. "What, you don't believe me?"

"Let's just say you don't look like the typical Scottie."

It took Jonah an extra half-second to get the reference. "Oh. Right. Scottie."

"Beats the alternative."

Wha…? Oh… *Mountie?*

Together with the raised eyebrow, the arrogant little smirk that had come over David's face as he watched Jonah do the math was devastating.

That settled it.

Jonah definitely wanted this guy, and not for just a quickie, either. David was starting to show definite boyfriend possibilities. "Okay, Sato, just so you know— I'm on to you. You are *so* not what you pretend to be."

"Yeah? And what's that?" The effects of wiseass mode hadn't completely evaporated, and David still showed a hint of that condescending little intellectual superiority complex he obviously harbored.

"Mild-mannered... science geek, maybe. Good student. No threat to anyone." Jonah's gaze took in the black t-shirt, the baggy jeans shorts, the nondescript boots, ending with a measured assessment of those deep brown eyes. "I'll bet you fool a lot of people."

David's look back was equally measuring. "But not you, huh?"

"Definitely not. I'm smarter than I look, as it turns out."

"Oh, really?" There was the eyebrow again, raised and skeptical as all hell. God, that was hot. Jonah wanted to kiss him—bad.

"Matter of fact, yeah." Standing, Jonah stuck his hands in his pockets and gestured with his head toward the front of the train. "Come on. Let's go find the dining car."

David made his decision only after what seemed like ages, but was probably more like thirty seconds, grabbing the seat in front of him and hoisting himself to his feet. Jonah turned to lead the way, hiding his sigh of relief.

He had no idea how this was going to work.

As they wove their way through the various train sections to the dining car, Jonah was acutely aware of David following along at a safe distance. The logistics were going to be interesting. At six foot three, he was used to being the little guy on the team—most basketball players falling closer toward the high sixes and low seven-foot marks to make it on even a college team.

David couldn't be more than... five-seven or eight, if that. Jonah had never been with anyone that short, but the one thing he knew for sure was that he was going to find out what it was like, and soon.

Was it wrong of him to have a physical type that he knew he responded to? Those eyes. That sleek, black hair. The golden brown skin that made his fingers itch to touch. Stroke.

Cut it out, Simpson. You're going to make yourself crazy. You've got a whole day and then some to make this happen.

Reaching the dining car, Jonah cast another glance back to make sure David was still there and fought his first impulse, which was to hold the door for David. Too date-like. Something told him David wouldn't appreciate it yet.

It was only late morning, so the breakfast menu was still posted. Jonah ordered the "Big Breakfast," with eggs, toast, hash browns, and bacon—coffee and juice to wash it down with—then watched with mild alarm as David ordered only an organic soy protein drink.

"That's it? That's all you're ordering? You're not hungry?"

After finding a table for two, David peeled the lid off and took a sip. "It's really filling. Ever tried one?"

"Huh-uh. Can't say as I have." Jonah found all of that soy-based health stuff vaguely disturbing.

"They're really good. Soy, oats, banana, almonds, vanilla. Totally dairy free." Taking another long drink, David's throat worked rhythmically and Jonah's imagination began to take over. He thought of all the other things that made throats work that way until his dick began twitching, making Jonah tug discreetly on his shorts for more room.

Stop it! You're not an animal. You can keep yourself under control and at least have a civilized meal first. Then you can take the man somewhere private and tear all his clothes off.

Licking away a small mustache of the drink left on his upper lip, David cast a disparaging eye on the plate of food the bellman was placing before Jonah. "That stuff'll kill you, you know."

Jonah took a test bite of the bacon, letting the salty taste burst across his tongue like it always did. Closing his eyes, all the better to savor the flavor, a happy smile spread across his face. When he opened them again to search for his fork, it was hard to miss the vaguely disapproving look on David's face. "It's a damn shame pigs are so tasty. They're really very cool animals."

"I won't even try to follow the alleged logic in that statement." Rolling his eyes, David looked pointedly away from Jonah's plate and out the window at the passing scenery.

"You don't eat meat?" Jonah forked a pile of scrambled eggs into his mouth and hoped he wasn't coming off like a jerk.

"Not much. A little chicken; some fish once in a while. It's hard to go home and not eat my mom's Spam musubi."

Swallowing the bite of toast he'd chased his eggs with, Jonah glanced down at his plate, then back up at David. "So, does it bother you to watch me eat it?"

David took in Jonah's food, then up at Jonah's face and shrugged. "Not really. I mean, I'm not your mother, but... dude. That's a lot of grease and fat."

"Yeah?"

"Oh, come on. Unless you spent the last twenty...?" The eyebrow was back again, this time accompanied by a little snort of disbelief. It should probably bother Jonah that every little thing David did seemed too adorable for words.

"Four," Jonah helpfully supplied. "I'm twenty-four."

"Unless you've spent the last twenty-four years in a cave, you might have read. Studies have been done. Results were published." Waiting pointedly for an answer Jonah deliberately withheld, David quickly ran out of patience and picked up where he'd left off with his rant. "Saturated fat? Trans-fats? Cholesterol? Any of this ringing a bell, big guy?"

Taking a prolonged sip from his juice, afterward Jonah let his tongue flick over his lips and was thrilled at the subsequent stutter in David's speech. Just to double-check, Jonah gave his lips another quick lick, followed by catching his upper lip between his teeth.

Oh, yeah.

Silence fell.

A brown-eyed gaze fastened on his mouth and stayed there, watching.

Sweet.

Slowly nodding his head, Jonah set down his cup. "Yeah, rings a bell. I guess I just want what I want, and usually I find a way to get it. I can be very determined."

Holy cow.

Things were getting confusing and David was getting some seriously messed up signals.

This guy couldn't possibly want him—but those were the signals he was picking up.

Smokin' hot jocks like Jonah Simpson did not go for nothing-special guys like David. Much as his fantasy life might like to imagine otherwise, tall, tanned, fantastic-looking athletes with beautifully sculpted bodies didn't hit on average-looking science nerds like him.

Just as David's mind produced the 'beautifully sculpted body' thought, Jonah hitched up his t-shirt with one hand and scratched his belly. Ridges of golden brown skin and the merest hint of a happy trail showed themselves, and David's thought process ground to a halt.

Waiting breathlessly, it was only after the hand let the shirt drop again, obscuring that breath-stealing view, that David's thought processes could resume. He realized belatedly that he'd taken in every microscopic move of that hand; had in fact been rooting for it to shove down into the waistband of the shorts and possibly even hold them out of the way. Would Jonah's dick be hard? Would it be standing at attention, erect with a gorgeously flushed head, weeping a little with—

"I think I'm done here. What about you?"

"What?" Stupid and punch-drunk, that's how he sounded. David's tongue barely worked and his voice was thick with stifled desire.

"I guess I'm not as hungry as I thought." Indicating his half-eaten plate of food with a nod of his head, Jonah reached for his foam coffee cup. "I can take this with me, though. We're done here, aren't we? Are we done here?"

Even his wrinkled nose and head-tilt were attractive. Jeez, how was David supposed to withstand that caliber of charm and attractiveness? How could any normal human being?

"Sure. I guess." Like a stupid puppy, David got up and followed as Jonah made his way out of the dining car. Trailing along behind had its good points, though, because it meant he got to study the rear view of Jonah Simpson, and that wasn't bad at all.

He didn't need the taped fingers and conditioned build to know that Jonah was an athlete. A man didn't get legs like that from riding a sofa or a desk chair eight hours a day. The toned muscles helped account for the smooth, easy flow of Jonah's walk, and it only took a moment's closed eyes to imagine what that would look like naked.

Jonah must have a roommate, right? Or have had, at some point. Too old to be a freshman, he must be transferring—although it was just barely possible that Jonah had lived at home up until now. David spun a split-second fantasy of what Jonah's imaginary roommate got to gawk at on a regular basis—probably saw all the time and took for granted, damn his unappreciative soul.

"Hey, check it out." Jonah nodded at something out the window, paused and waited for David to come stand next to him.

"What?" All David could see was miles of coastline and the Pacific Ocean, its usual green-blue color.

"Look. Dolphins." Grinning like a kid, Jonah pointed with his free hand. "See?"

David squinted in the direction Jonah indicated. "No."

"Dude. Right there. There's like, four or five of 'em. Right *there*."

"I don't—"

Jonah grasped David's chin and guided it to the left and down a little. "Right there. Now do you see?"

Fighting hard not to turn and look up into Jonah's eyes, David tried to focus on what Jonah was indicating and ignore the calloused fingers touching his face. Warm and just a little rough, they were distracting as hell, though. The long arm attached to the hand and fingers was inches from David's face, dozens of fine, gold-tipped hairs lying close along its surface, beckoning.

The scent of Jonah's skin floated up and David could almost taste it. It would be clean; a little salty. David wanted to turn and just lick Jonah's forearm.

That's pathetic. He doesn't want you. David's pride

and self-respect made a late-inning appearance.

His libido argued back. *Then why is he touching you?*

"Excuse us. Excuse us! Bathroom emergency! I'm *so* sorry." A beleaguered young mother, moving quickly down the corridor of the train car, the panic-stricken face of her toddler just visible beneath her arm, approached at the speed of light. "Excuse us. I'm so sorry."

David and Jonah already took up more than half the available aisle space and there was nowhere for them to go. One arm already clutching David's face, Jonah's other arm held the foam coffee cup aloft, juggling to keep the hot liquid from spilling on either of the two of them or the mother and child.

David's gaze flew from the wide-eyed panic he read on the little boy's face to the staunchly determined one on the young mother's as they closed in on him and Jonah. The next thing David knew, he was smashed flat against the metal and glass of the train wall, while the hard length of Jonah's body was pressed firmly against his backside.

For a moment—just one moment, David promised himself—he closed his eyes and savored the feeling. Six-plus feet of solid flesh was weighing down on him and it was incredible.

The only thing that would make it better was if they were horizontal.

The errant thought had barely flashed through David's head when Jonah eased off him. It was over in moments and David was prying himself off the glass, away from the coolness that made such a nice contrast to the heat suffusing his face, as even now the memory of Jonah's body pressed to his replayed itself in his mind.

"Sorry. There was nowhere to go and she didn't look like she was going to stop." Jonah's voice was still mere inches away, and the illusion of intimacy it created made David yearn to lean back into it. That's all it was, though—an illusion.

Instead, he shook himself and glanced up quickly at Jonah's face, forcing himself to look away almost immediately. Not before he'd noticed, though, that Jonah's lashes were the same gold-fringed auburn as the hairs on Jonah's forearms.

"No, that's okay. I…" David's voice trailed off. How could he possibly attempt to hold a thought together when his body couldn't stop remembering? The heat of Jonah's body was imprinted on his mind, on his memory, until that was all he could think of.

The door to the railroad car slid open again and the attendant who'd checked their tickets made his way past, nodding genially as he passed. "Gentlemen."

"Hey." Jonah flashed another of his seemingly endless supply of friendly smiles, and David wondered how he could manage it. David was having trouble remembering how to breathe. Looking down at David, Jonah's gaze fastened on David's mouth. "There really were dolphins."

"I believe you." David gazed back; realized his mouth had gone dry and blood was filling his cock. What would a kiss from that mouth feel like? And those long arms. Wrapped around David's shoulders, or reaching down to grab his ass—how would they feel?

"Yeah, so." Jonah stepped back, and relief and disappointment washed over David in equal amounts. "Did I spill coffee on you? Let me check." Not waiting for permission, Jonah gave David's shoulder a little push and turned him around.

"I'm fine. You didn't spill on me." Surprising himself with the vehemence in his voice, David guessed from the look on Jonah's face he'd surprised Jonah, too.

This wasn't good. David needed to get out of there

before his circuits were permanently fried by too much alternating current. He knew when he was outclassed and Jonah Simpson wasn't just out of his league, Jonah might even qualify as out of David's species. "Listen, um, thanks for breakfast, but I think I'm gonna go for a walk. See ya around."

Without waiting for a reaction, David slipped under Jonah's arm and walked quickly down the corridor, back in the direction of the dining car and away from their seats. He had to get away from all of that perfectly packaged charm and charisma before he did something stupid.

Wandering for a while, David took himself on a tour of the train and all the compartments he could reach as a passenger, walking slowly to draw things out. Although he knew it was out of the question, David would have loved to get a look at the engine compartment. He'd seen pictures, and the control panels and equipment to run the train looked fascinating. It would be a total blast to get in there and see everything, but in a post-nine-eleven world he knew better than to even ask.

The train had passed the Oxnard station a while back and was now running close to the shoreline. Surfers could be seen bobbing out in the water, splashes of black in their wetsuits as they straddled their boards and waited for the next set of waves.

As close as he'd lived to the ocean, surfing was one thing David had never learned to do. He'd done some body surfing as a kid. Had loved the feeling of treading water, waiting for the ocean to swell beneath him, signaling it was time to get horizontal and start stroking and kicking like hell.

Most of the time he'd missed the waves. Too often he hadn't been a strong enough swimmer to keep up with it and the huge swell of water would pass him by, leaving him to swim back out and wait for the next one.

Once in a while, though, he'd catch it. Catch it just right and know the feeling of being part of something bigger than himself. The ocean would rise up under and around him as he swam as hard as he could—in a partnership, almost. As the junior partner, he'd be carried to shore by the wave and be dumped out, gasping for air and laughing at the sheer exhilarating joy of it.

David shoved his hands in his pockets and leaned against the window, keeping an eye on the surfers as they disappeared from sight. The train rounded a bend, rolling ever northward, taking him closer by the minute back to school; back for his last year at Mt. Scott.

He hadn't thought about body surfing or summers at the beach in a long time.

They'd had some pretty idyllic times, him and his brother and sister. Mom was a nurse and had worked full-time to help afford a decent house and educations for three kids. Dad was an electronics inspector for McDonnell-Douglas first, and then Boeing, after the merger. David had learned the principles of electronics from the time he was a kid; he couldn't remember a time when he hadn't understood at least the basics.

It was his *obaasan*—his Grandmother Sato—who'd taken them to the beach, sitting under a big umbrella reading romance novels while he and his brother and sister had played. Sometimes his cousins had come along, too, and they'd had a great time digging for tiny sand crabs and making forts, spending hours building elaborate structures of sand with moats and towers, only to have them wiped out by the incoming tide.

So if things had been so perfect, why was he on a train to a college in the Pacific Northwest, then? Why hadn't he gone to UC San Diego like most of his friends, or even Cal State Long Beach, where he could get his degree and still be close to his family? Why did he have to pick a crunchy granola geek college in a state that led the country in inches of rainfall per year?

David pressed his forehead to the glass, letting his gaze rest on nothing in particular— thinking.

He didn't make friends easily.

Too much of a geek and, at the same time, too sure of his facts to suffer fools gladly.

Why couldn't humans be as straightforward and easy to understand as his robots? David could build a robot to do just about anything and a robot either worked or didn't work, depending on whether or not the wiring and programming were done correctly. No, "Yeah, I wanna fuck. Let's do it!" one day and, "Fuck off, geek boy," the next.

At that moment, the memory of strong fingers grasping his chin and guiding his head a particular direction made an encore appearance. David wrapped his arms around himself and leaned against the side of the railway car, giving himself permission to pretend for just a few moments that it was someone else holding him.

Leaning back in his seat, Jonah crossed his arms and tucked his hands under his armpits. Eyes closed, he could trouble-shoot what had gone wrong with his plan, while inserting the occasional fantasy to keep his spirits up. He tried to step back and give his actions an objective assessment.

Breakfast.

Okay, things had seemed to be going well at that point. They'd been talking, getting to know each other a little bit and figuring out their differences. There was that whole unhealthy obsession with natural foods thing to be worked out, but it was nothing major in Jonah's mind. Admittedly, he didn't have a ton of data to go on yet, but everything he'd found out about David so far had been pretty great.

Smart. Cute. Gay. Part Asian. Jeez, did it get any better than that?

Good oral technique never hurt. Jonah's evil, horny guy side asserted itself, but he quashed it. Sure, that was important, but he wouldn't let himself think negatively. This was going to happen and he wasn't about to sabotage his efforts with a lot of unproductive thinking.

Jonah stifled his inner critique and aimed squarely for the positive side with a fantasy of him and David.

In his fantasy, the two of them were alone in a room together, facing one another, standing less than an arm's length apart.

Jonah reached across and lifted David's shirt. Raising his arms cooperatively, David shimmied out of the shirt when Jonah moved to tug it over his head. David's arms alighted on Jonah's forearms, his thumbs rubbing appreciatively over Jonah's skin.

A shiver slithered up the real Jonah's spine.

He was turning himself on, but it felt so good to think about, he couldn't find it in himself to stop.

So next, he'd unsnap the front of David's shorts, giving himself a little room to work. Then, he'd slip his hands inside and run them along David's flanks. He'd squeeze a little bit, then reach around to grasp David's butt firmly in both hands. Letting the shorts fall magically away, he'd drop to his knees and take David's pretty, flushed cock in his mouth, rolling his tongue appreciatively over its contours, slurping down all of that juicy, salty goodness and... *God!*

Jonah forced himself back to reality. He'd have to stop torturing himself before he came in his shorts. Seriously.

Maybe you could get David to help you out with that, if you ask nicely.

About to chide himself for the crassness of his thoughts, Jonah came to the sudden realization that his two sides were in perfect agreement: they both wanted David.

"Um, 'scuse me."

Jonah's eyes sprang open at his first awareness that David was back. Looking all business, nothing in David's face suggested that he would ever have said anything remotely like the explicit remarks he'd made to Jonah earlier. Unable to pinpoint what it was exactly about David that drew him so inexorably, Jonah contented himself with admiring the perfectly proportioned face and compact body, even as he moved his feet to allow David to get back to his seat.

"How was the walk?"

"Good." David sat and immediately busied himself by digging through his bag, eventually retrieving a magazine on … *robots?*

So. Okay. Cool. He could hang with that. "Good magazine?'

David looked up and Jonah got the impression that interruptions weren't something that David normally had much patience for. A cutting remark seemed perched on David's lips, ready to fall, but the response when it came was relatively mild. "Yeah."

"Which article did you buy it for?"

David's look was skeptical. "Brushless motors."

If David wanted to play reluctant interview, Jonah could go all day, asking question after inane follow-up question. Right now he was interested in establishing boundaries. Testing limits. He'd push a little and see how long it took David to push back. "Yeah? And how was it?"

"I haven't read it yet, but I'm interested in the increased

efficiency aspect. I've got an application in mind for my senior project."

"Cool. What's the project—or can you say? It's not a secret, is it?"

Openly suspicious now, David narrowed his gaze. "You can't possibly be interested in this stuff, so why all the pretend fascination?"

"Why can't I be interested?"

"Because you can't. Brushless motors?" David's eyebrow went up again. Jonah just smiled and waited, wondering if David had any idea how cute it was. "Got a jones for static armature?"

"Not usually," Jonah admitted. "But under the right circumstances, I could be persuaded."

"Really." David folded his arms across his chest again, a dubious purse of his lips adding just the right amount of 'you are so full of shit' skepticism to his expression.

"Oh, absolutely. As it happens." Jonah nodded. "Everybody knows that mechanical commutators are old school. BLDCs are the wave of the future. It's all over but the shouting."

If he hadn't been watching for it, the infinitesimal jaw-drop would have blown right by him, but Jonah had been waiting for it; been expecting it, in fact. The hard part turned out to be keeping a straight face.

"You—" Gradually, by degrees, David's face relaxed into a grin that turned into an outright laugh. "You totally set me up. You *dick*."

"Nah, I can't take credit. You set yourself up."

David was openly laughing now and that only cemented things for Jonah. David flipped every one of his switches, in fact he couldn't remember wanting anyone this much in a long time. But he couldn't be with a guy who couldn't laugh at himself.

"*You…* Now who's not what he seems to be?"

It was all Jonah could do not to bat his lashes and flirt like crazy, but he had the feeling that David needed slow courting. There wasn't time for that, though. This train ride wasn't going to last forever and, even if they ended up in the same city, that wasn't necessarily the same thing as the same destination. Jonah needed to get something going now.

"Nah, I'm pretty simple, really. What you see is what you get."

David's gaze flickered and Jonah could swear that was a spark of interest he'd just seen flash through David's eyes, but he only shook his head. "Nothing's that simple."

"Sometimes it really is." As carefully as he could calibrate it, Jonah let the smallest little bit of desire into his tone as he made deliberate eye-contact with David. Taking a deep breath and letting it out, he allowed his fingers to stray over the armrest and brush the inside of David's wrist. "Want to take a walk?"

"A walk?"

"Yeah. Wanna go see what kind of trouble we can get into?"

Just that quickly the cautious David was back—the skeptical guy who didn't seem to have the word trust in his vocabulary. "What kind of trouble?"

"Come on, it'll be fun." Refusing to even consider defeat, Jonah stood and backed out of his seat, out into the aisle. "Show me what you found when you took your tour."

"It's a train. It's really not all that exciting. Shocking, I know, but true." David's reluctance apparently didn't extend to his body, because his legs were already moving, pushing him to his feet.

"Let's go anyway." Excitement bubbled up in Jonah's veins as David placed his magazine face down on his seat and stood.

"Where do you want to start?"

Anywhere would do. Just to be doing anything with David was a start, but somewhere they could be alone would be even better. "I suppose Baggage is out of the question?" Jonah suggested. "Or what about an observation deck? It'd be cool to hang out on the back of the train, like in old movies. You know?"

"Old movies? Are you high? The liability would be huge. I'm surprised they even have windows. I mean, we could get sunburned. Sorry to stomp all over your romantic daydreams, darling, but the sleeper cars are probably more doable."

Darling? Jonah bit his cheek to keep from grinning. "Man, you're not gonna give me even a shred of hope to hold onto, are you?"

"Reality bites." David smirked and Jonah allowed himself a smile. So cute, that little hint of intellectual arrogance that was never far from the surface with David.

"Okay, what about the sleeper cars, then? What's down there?"

David's gaze strayed toward the rear of the train, his body swaying as the train rounded a turn and lurched mildly. "I guess we can see if anyone tries to stop us. We won't have the right ticket if they ask, but what's the worst they can do? Tell us to go back?"

"Exactly. Don't you want to know what they look like?"

"They're pretty small. They don't even have in-room toilets and the shower is down the hall." David led the way and Jonah followed happily.

"So you've seen them?"

David waited for him at the door to the next car, sliding it aside for them to pass through, confident in his movements. "Sure. You can go a lot of places just by acting like you belong there."

"I'm shocked. You enter unauthorized areas frequently? You must. You sound pretty comfortable about it."

"What? It's not exactly Area 51, you know." David's slightly exasperated tone was endearing and Jonah decided it was just one more sign of his growing infatuation. "If they were all that worried they'd have it locked. Or maybe that's just me."

"Good point." They were winding their way toward the back, with only a few cars left before the end of the train, by Jonah's estimation. Instead of comfortable seats, two to a side, the aisle bisected the car with compartments to either side. "Hey, David, hold up."

"What?"

"Here's the shower."

"Yeah, I know." Obviously uninterested, David was already half way down the length of the railcar.

"Hang on, I want to look." Opening the door, Jonah stepped inside, surprised at how roomy it was. A bench across the corner, even. Poking his head back out into the hall, Jonah beckoned. "Hey, check it out."

"Sheltered life, much? It's a shower, Simpson. Try to wrap your head around the concept."

"Get over here, smartass. I want to show you something."

All but rolling his eyes at Jonah's stupidity, David stepped into the little room. "Okay, dazzle me."

"Lucky for you I work well under pressure."

"Should I even try to guess at what that means?" David just shot him a doubtful look.

Stepping close, Jonah trailed a hand down David's arm. "Lot of pressure for a first kiss."

David's eyes widened, but didn't back away when Jonah lowered his head. After that first initial shock, though, they closed sweetly and David let Jonah brush his mouth over David's.

Oh, yeah.

So soft, David's lips parted slightly when Jonah turned it into a real kiss, helping himself to his first taste of David. The train swayed as they rounded another slow turn, pressing David's body against his, and Jonah reached out for support, searching for one of the stall's metal safety bars.

Groaning at the feel of David's mouth under his and the tantalizing little brushes of David's body against his, Jonah wanted to grab David and hold on—crush their bodies together harder, so he could get some real friction going. Afraid of freaking David out, though, he held onto the bar with one hand and let the other hold onto David's waist.

Since David hadn't pushed him away, Jonah couldn't resist going in for another kiss. When David finally began to kiss him back, Jonah groaned a little and pulled back. "I like the way you taste."

Slowly opening his eyes, there was still a hint of suspicion in David's eyes when he looked up. "Are you for real?"

"Want to touch me and make sure?" Jonah smiled at the picture David made—half suspicious, half dreamy-eyed wonder—and touched David's deliciously kissable mouth. "I really do like you. What about you? What do you think?"

"That you're way too good-looking to be hitting on me. That this doesn't make sense."

David's hands had settled at Jonah's waist, though, fingers curled into Jonah's sides, and Jonah could already imagine what they would feel like gripping him as they fucked.

"Makes perfect sense to me."

This wasn't real.

Things like this didn't happen to him.

Guys who looked like Jonah didn't give him the time of day. They were usually straight, and if they did talk to him, it was because they wanted help with their trig homework. Sometimes they just came right out and asked for the answers to the test.

If they were gay *and* cute, then they wanted someone every bit as beautiful as they were; it was a truism that had stood the test of time, been proven and re-proven. Guys as hot as Jonah Simpson could have anyone they wanted, and just like his car keys wouldn't suddenly fall *up* if he dropped them, tall-and-drop-dead gorgeous didn't single him out for an urgent make-out session.

It just didn't happen.

"I really like you." Jonah was touching David's mouth now, running a finger along David's bottom lip and even letting it slip inside for a moment. David was too stupefied to do much except react, so when Jonah's finger got near his teeth he wasn't thinking, he just opened his mouth and sucked it inside. Jonah groaned a little, his gaze dropping to watch his finger disappear into David's mouth, only to pull it out again. "God, you're sexy. Smart. Funny. Oh, shit, I—"

Taking David's head in his hands, Jonah was kissing him now. Really kissing him, not the lip-brushing thing they'd been doing a minute ago. Jonah's mouth pressed urgently on his and David's cheek was damp from his own saliva because Jonah's finger had been in his mouth. And now Jonah was kissing him like it really mattered and all David could do was kiss back.

How could he not?

Jonah was gorgeous and he felt incredible beneath David's hands. David knew he was being stupid, that this couldn't last beyond this one train ride, but he couldn't help himself. Jonah was hot and amazing-looking and felt better in his hands than anyone David had ever been this close to. He was even making sexy little noises in the back of his throat now, kind of moaning and catching his breath, and David was lost.

Standing on his toes, he looped his arms around Jonah's neck and hung on. Pressed his body up against Jonah's and kissed the man back. Jonah's tongue was in his mouth and—*Jonah's tongue was in his mouth!*—and Jonah's erection was pressing into David's stomach.

Why couldn't he be tall, damnit?! He hated being short. Hated always being the last one picked for sports and the one always shoved to the front when it came time for group pictures.

If he was tall, and maybe less of a dweeb, he might know what to do with someone like Jonah. When Jonah grabbed David's ass and hauled him up to rub their dicks together, David had no idea what he was supposed to do; could only wrap his legs around Jonah's waist and squeeze. Tilting his head to get a better angle, David opened his mouth to Jonah's tongue, like his body wanted to open to Jonah's dick.

Pressed together, chest to chest, there was no room for David to rock against Jonah, but he wanted to desperately. Jonah's mouth was hot and sleek, his tongue slipping in and out to rub alongside David's. Jonah's chest was hard and, in fact, there didn't seem to be an ounce of fat anywhere on Jonah.

"So gorgeous. So perfect. So *hot*." Jonah had pulled back, despite David's best effort to keep their mouths connected. Eyes slipping closed again, Jonah began dropping teasing little kisses along David's nose and brow and cheek.

If Jonah was not quite right in the head, David wasn't

going to say anything, as long as Jonah kept those hands on him and kept kissing him. He was determined that nothing along the lines of, "How long since you took your meds?" would slip out of his mouth. He just kept running his fingers through the soft tangle of hair at Jonah's nape, stroking his fingers down Jonah's neck and along the top of Jonah's spine.

Until Jonah set him down, anyway, then a little whimper of disappointment slipped out. There was something expectant in Jonah's movements as he reached a hand behind David and pushed the door closed. When a little metallic click told David that Jonah had locked the door, it was a measure of David's distraction that it took him a second to put two and two together.

David had never had anything remotely like this happen to him and he had no idea how to respond. Jonah couldn't possibly be serious. Could he? "So I guess you really like this place, huh?"

Jonah's laugh came easily, like nothing ever threw him. "You're funny. I like that in a guy."

"You're easy to please." Now that Jonah wasn't touching him, David wasn't sure what to do with his hands. He knew what he'd like to do with them, but Jonah was just watching him with that look that David couldn't quite name, and the doubts continued to build.

"Not really." Jonah reached for David's shirt. "May I?"

"Help yourself, but it'll never fit."

"That's all right—I have my reasons." Tugging David's shirt over his head, Jonah reached behind David and tossed it, on the bench, probably. But no way was David turning away to look.

"Like what?" Hideously embarrassed, David gritted his teeth and wondered helplessly what he had that Jonah could possibly want to look at. He was no athlete. He didn't even work out.

"Oh, sweet." Gaze fixed on David's chest as though David's remark hadn't registered, Jonah sucked in his breath. Smiling, Jonah brushed David's nipples with his thumbs.

Like they were wired straight to his dick, David gasped and got harder. There was no disguising his hard-on, and David knew to the second when Jonah shifted that gaze from David's nipples to his aching dick.

"Like this." Another quick glance up to David's face and then Jonah was lowering his head, licking at David's nipples, so hard now they actually hurt.

David's hand was about to make contact with Jonah's hair, having taken on not only a life of its own but free will, too, apparently. Crap! He couldn't just spear his fingers through Jonah's hair and grab hold to keep that amazing tongue close.

Could he?

Well, maybe just rest his hand there. He could touch the soft strands of Jonah's sun-streaked hair just a little— just enough to verify how incredibly silky they were so that he could call it to mind later. Like nothing he'd ever felt before, Jonah's hair slipped easily through David's fingers to fall against his palm.

Jonah moaned appreciatively, drawing the hardened nubs of David's flesh into his mouth, taking them between his teeth and tugging.

David was so hard he could feel his pulse in the throbbing of his dick. He wanted to use his hand, or—better yet—Jonah's, and cup it roughly against his erection. It wouldn't take much, just a few quick strokes and he'd be coming. A sticky, embarrassed mess.

"Can I do it? Can I get you off?"

Shit! Please, God, tell him he hadn't spoken the thought aloud. "I... I guess... You want to?" This so couldn't be happening. He must have slipped into some weird alternate reality where average guys really did score blowjobs from incredibly hot near-total strangers.

"Oh, yeah." Jonah's gaze had dropped to where his hand was now petting the bulge behind David's fly. Backing up, Jonah took a quick look around, first sitting on the triangular-shaped bench that took up most of the corner before sliding down onto the floor. Reaching out for David's legs, Jonah looked up, catching David's gaze. "This is good."

David couldn't believe it, but Jonah was so tall that, sitting on the ground, he could easily reach and go to work on David's pants. David wanted to say something, but what? What could he possibly say that would make this any less weird or even a micron more believable?

Nothing he could come up with in the few seconds it took Jonah to get his belt undone and his pants unzipped seemed remotely appropriate. "Are you absolutely sure?" didn't seem any better than, "Are you completely out of your mind?"

The point was moot anyway, because Jonah was slipping a condom over David's woefully average hard-on and was smoothing the wrinkles out of it. Stroking David's heated, rigid flesh and then he was closing his eyes and feeding David's dick into his mouth; caressing it with fervent, impassioned movements that made it seem to David like maybe the most sincere, heartfelt blowjob he'd ever witnessed.

Jonah was taking long, slow pulls at David's cock, and the way he let it slip to the side, making his cheek bulge was, oh, God, the heat was incredible. The moist suction of Jonah's velvety hot mouth scattered David's last thoughts and all he could do was clutch the shower's metal safety bars and hang on.

David's knees were already shaky and the jerky,

irregular movements of the train as it wound its way along kept him from developing any kind of rhythm. His shorts were undone, but his open-legged position kept them from going anywhere, while the cut of the material constrained his movements and kept him from widening his stance or getting any kind of solid footing under him.

Jonah's big hands slid up the back of David's thighs, gripping his ass, holding him in place while Jonah took what he wanted. It spun David's head to think that anything he had to offer could possibly be what Jonah needed, but the evidence seemed to indicate otherwise. Pulling away momentarily, Jonah fisted David's cock, sliding and measuring for several strokes, gazing at it all the while in rapt concentration.

Flicking a glance upward, Jonah smiled. "So pretty." Just a brief, throwaway comment, before he slid back onto David's dick and began working it in earnest.

The visual of Jonah's mouth fastened on David's dick, the incredible face, that magical mouth working him while strong hands held him in place and feasted on him was too much sensory overload. Jonah's hum of pleasure, combined with the downward sweep of those lush, auburn lashes, pulled David's response out of him.

David knew he'd probably never have another moment as perfect as this, where the hottest guy he'd ever had his hands on was caressing him, demanding his orgasm, and he wasn't ready for it to end. He'd never had a moment of such perfect pleasure and he wanted to draw it out, but his body wasn't cooperating.

He couldn't fight it, couldn't hold back, and he was giving it up, surrendering to the sweet hot perfection of Jonah Simpson's mouth.

Floating, breath coming in short, choppy gulps, David delayed opening his eyes as long as he could. As long as he kept his eyes closed, he could stay in the magical world he inhabited for the moment.

The one where who you were on the inside was as important as the shape on the outside.

The one where he had a chance with a guy like Jonah.

"Are you okay?"

"Yeah." David forced his eyes open to find a satisfied-looking Jonah sprawled backwards against the corner of the shower room, the rhythmic movements of the train doing amazing things for his toned athlete's body.

"You're sure about that?" Jeez, how could Jonah be that relaxed, that calm, when David was so... so *not*? This was where the hammer came down and the running away on Jonah's part commenced.

"Uh-huh. Um, thanks." It came out almost surly sounding, but David couldn't help it. Really, what was he supposed to say now? *Was it good for you, too?*

"I didn't do it for the thanks, but you're welcome."

"Then why did you do it?"

In his relaxed position, Jonah's big hands lay draped across his mile-long legs. The thumb of one hand rubbed absently back and forth, the movement drawing David's gaze, scant inches away from where Jonah's hard-on still formed an impressive bulge behind the soft denim of his shorts.

"You're kidding. Right?" Jonah's grin was back, and David was appalled at how much he wanted to believe that Jonah was laughing with him and not at him.

"Not really, no."

"Huh. Wow. Okay." The smile faded and Jonah just watched him, a series of expressions chasing each other across that open face.

Moments passed and the realization slowly dawned on David that he was standing, still half-undressed. Maybe somebody, somewhere could put himself back together with a wink and a joke, but that guy wasn't him. So he concentrated on looking anywhere but at Jonah's face and stuffed himself back into his shorts as quickly and unobtrusively as possible.

He was shifting his weight, trying to edge toward the door without being totally obvious, when Jonah coughed into his hand and leaned forward. "Where are you going?"

"Um, I don't know. Out. Finish the tour?" God, he was lame. Rolling his eyes at his own awkward behavior, David wanted more than anything to just get out of this with his pride intact. He didn't want to find out how much more time he'd have to spend with Jonah before he broke down and begged Jonah to fuck him, but he had a feeling it wasn't a lot.

The pitying rejection he could live without, thank you very much.

"So, listen, I was thinking we should maybe look into getting a room." Jonah stood and David was instantly reminded of the differences between them. "What do you say? Interested?"

"A room, are you crazy? Oh my God, do you know how much those cost?" David looked horrified. And shocked. And much more interested than he wanted to let on. "Why would you want to do that?"

Jonah realized exactly how hard he was pushing things, but he only had a little over twenty-four hours to make something happen. Like his childhood idol Michael Jordan always said, "You miss 100% of the shots you don't take."

He might be throwing up an air ball, but he was taking this shot. "I must be doing it wrong if I'm that hard to figure out."

"What—?" David pressed a hand to his eyes, turning his head for a moment. When he let his hand fall away and looked up at Jonah, the naked honesty in his dark eyes was devastating. "What is this all about, really? I don't get you."

Clenching his hands against the urge to put them on David, Jonah took a deep breath, choosing his next words carefully. "I'm very attracted to you. And I think we have a limited time opportunity here. This trip won't last forever, and I'd like to spend what's left of it with you."

Looking around, Jonah smiled, suddenly self-conscious. Had he ever had a conversation as critical as this one in less promising surroundings? What the hell. He'd already committed—he might as well follow through. "What about you? Are you at all interested?"

"I would have thought we just established that pretty conclusively." David's color was already high, just beginning to fade from his post-orgasm flush, so it was hard to tell if the pink currently staining his cheeks was new. What it was, though, was adorable as hell.

"Maybe we should use the scientific method and put it to the test." Although he'd been smiling when he'd said it, Jonah could tell instantly he'd made a mistake when David immediately reverted back to the ultra formal, talking-to-a-stranger body language that Jonah had spent all morning coaxing him out of.

"Look, I can tell this isn't going to work. It's... You're too... Thanks for, um, everything. I'm just going to go back to my seat now."

David turned with more of the quick, economical movements Jonah had admired since they met and opened the door. Jonah's legs were longer, though, and he was after David in a heartbeat.

"Don't go. Please. David. Look, that was stupid." David wouldn't look up and Jonah found himself talking to the top of David's head. All of that inky black softness was inches from Jonah's nose and he wanted to run his hands through it, see if it could possibly feel as soft as it looked. He'd like to brush his fingers along the close-cut sides before taking David's head between his hands and kissing the man again.

"David?" With the door open, though, anyone could see in, and already David's gaze was straying nervously in that direction.

Glancing up briefly, the soft, deep brown of David's eyes immediately sucked Jonah in. He couldn't wait for the chance to sit and gaze into them for hours on end— beginning immediately after they'd had sex, ideally.

"What?"

The wary, defensive look was back in David's eyes, though, and Jonah wondered what it would take to actually earn David's trust. "I know I'm not handling this very well. It's just that I really want something to happen here. What can I say to get you to believe me?"

"I don't know. I—"

"Can I help you gentlemen find something?"

The steward who'd checked their tickets earlier stood in the hallway outside. In his hands he carried a pile of clean towels, and he looked eager to carry on with his mission, but not before he'd shooed the pair of misguided explorers back the way they'd come.

"Umm..."

"As a matter of fact," Jonah hurried to get his story in before David could contradict him again, "what we were doing was checking out the accommodations."

David's eyes widened and the eyebrow went up, but he stayed mercifully silent while the attendant eyed them skeptically and tried to look past them into the shower stall.

"Really?"

"Absolutely," Jonah dropped an arm around David's shoulders to keep him from sidling away and smiled his most winning smile. "We realized that if we pooled our money, we could probably get one of the smaller compartments—what are they called?"

"Compartments? You mean a roomette?"

"That's the one. We were looking for you, actually. Can you tell us about availability?"

His expression reflecting exactly what he thought about the likelihood of Jonah's story, the attendant shifted the stack of towels under one arm and reached into an inner coat pocket. Pulling out a folded, laminated card, he consulted it briefly before tucking it back into the same pocket he'd taken it from. "There might be something open. I'd need to double-check with the steward before I could let you have it, though."

"Could you do that? That would be great. Wouldn't that be great, David?"

"Jonah..."

David's voice had a hint of what-the-fuck in it that Jonah hurried to cover. "I know, I know. It's my fault—I didn't get my ticket in time and messed everything up. Totally my fault. But they might still have something. It doesn't hurt to ask. So, do you have any idea if you do?" He turned back to the attendant.

"I'll have to check and get back to you." The look he shot them was full of meaning, and Jonah got the message as the man stepped back to give them room. "I know where you gentlemen are sitting. I have to finish my rounds first, but I'll find out and come let you know."

"Thanks. That'd be great. C'mon, David, let's get out of here."

Taking David's hand, Jonah led them back the way

they'd come, the two of them barely rounding the corner before David began whispering furiously at him. "Are you trying to get us thrown off the train? Maybe *you* have the money to get to Portland some other way, but I don't."

"Oh, listen to you. What happened to Mr. Go-anywhere-you-want-as-long-as-you-look-like-you-know-what-you're-doing, huh? Would you stop worrying? Everything's going to be fine."

Having cleared the stairs back up to the second level, Jonah could drop an arm around David's shoulders, smiling to himself at just how great it felt. David's body was amazing. Perfect. Jonah's hard-on had faded while talking to the porter, but just the thought of getting a little privacy and running his hands over David's naked body was reviving it.

"I can't afford to screw up." Flashing an annoyed look up at Jonah, David accepted the arm over his shoulders without comment.

"No one's going to screw up, so relax, okay?"

"Easy for you to say."

Jonah rubbed David's arm and pulled him a little closer. Leaning over, Jonah buried his nose in David's hair, inhaling the lingering scent of David's shampoo as well as the warm fragrance of David's skin that lay beneath. "I love the way you smell."

"Stop distracting me. I'm pissed."

David's words would have carried a little more sting if he hadn't been leaning into Jonah, rubbing his head on Jonah's shoulder like an affectionate cat.

"Yeah, I figured. I say we go find our seats and hang out until Porter Dude finds out if we've got the room or not. We can always go to Plan B if the room thing doesn't work out."

"Plan B? I can't wait to hear." The aisle narrowed

up ahead, so side-by-side wasn't possible. David slipped out from under Jonah's arm, tossing a smirk in Jonah's direction as he moved to take the lead.

Jonah squeezed one denim-covered butt cheek as David passed, grinning when David tried and failed to evade it. Waiting until they dropped into their seats to lean over and whisper in David's ear, Jonah couldn't resist adding a little lick. "Plan B would be finding a blanket and waiting until they dim the lights tonight."

The look of horror that came over David's face wasn't a shock. For all of David's breeziness on the subject of rule-breaking, Jonah had him pegged as a basically law-abiding citizen. The little accompanying shiver he'd detected was gratifying, though.

"You're nuts! Do you know how much trouble we could get in?"

Seated next to David, Jonah ran his fingers down the inside of David's arm, stroking the soft skin there as he gazed into David's dark eyes. "Nah, the worst it could be is indecent exposure or lewd in public. Don't worry, though—we won't get caught."

"Do I even want to know how you know that? You're right we won't get caught, because we won't be doing any of that."

Jonah slipped his hand down to David's knee, stroking there with the same rhythm he had used on David's arm. This time, though, his fingers strayed up under the first couple of inches of David's shorts, creeping under the material to toy with the warm skin he found there. "It's all up to you, I promise."

Despite doing his best to look indignant, David's eyes gave him away, straying again and again back down to where Jonah was touching him. The little flare of his nostrils as he breathed in Jonah's scent and the way his tongue flicked out periodically, as though wanting to taste, only confirmed that David was much more interested than he wanted to let on.

"Besides," Jonah continued, "I feel pretty good that the steward's going to come through for us and get us a room. Meanwhile, I'm going to use the time to go over my stuff from the school—I know I'm forgetting something. What about you? You finally going to read your magazine?"

David's neck was right there, though, calling to Jonah. So he leaned in and placed an open mouthed kiss on it, licking lightly at the slightly salty taste of it, letting it roll around on his tongue. Biting, tasting, Jonah hummed with pleasure. David held himself rigid at first, only gradually relaxing into Jonah, eventually even sighing softly.

"I'm going to... I'm going to, um, yeah, read that article now. Cut it out, though. I need to focus." David tilted his head, giving Jonah more room.

Kissing down to the skin where David's neck met his shoulder, in between bites Jonah murmured in agreement. "Yeah, that looked interesting. God, you taste good. I can't wait to see you naked. I want your dick in my mouth again. You feel amazing."

"*Gah!* You can't just say things like that." There was a disconnect between David's words and his actions, though, because his hand came up to Jonah's head, gripping Jonah's hair and holding him in place.

"It's going to happen. Can't you feel it?"

"Stop distracting me." David pulled away, still hanging on to Jonah's hair, but angling Jonah's head as well as his own to make eye contact. "You're driving me crazy and we're totally in public. Don't you get it? A few more seconds and I'll be jumping you—and that could cause problems."

"It wouldn't be that big a deal. Honestly, nobody cares." Personally, Jonah thought it sounded like an excellent idea, but he cut David some slack. It wouldn't do either of them any good if David had a nervous breakdown. When David opened his mouth to protest, Jonah preempted him. "But I see your point. If you get your magazine and read, I promise I'll leave you alone. At least until the steward comes back with news about the room."

Sitting up straighter, David adjusted his clothing, and Jonah pretended not to notice when he tugged on his shorts to give himself more room. He reached for his magazine and began thumbing through it, paying loving attention to diagrams and illustrations like most guys would a porn mag.

After going for his own reading material stashed in the duffel below his seat, Jonah paused a moment to admire: the thick, black silk of David's hair that he longed to get his hands in again; the smooth curve of David's ear that tempted his teeth; the slight arch of David's neck that suggested a head and mouth bent to other activities.

David must have sensed Jonah's attention, because he looked up from his magazine. "What?"

Jonah had promised, though.

Sort of.

"Nothing. Just thinking."

Maybe it was the post-orgasm lassitude finally catching up with him, but David found himself having a hard time keeping his eyes open. Over the summer vacation he'd gotten used to staying up late, tinkering with his robots and playing *World of Warcraft* online with his buddies, but today he'd had to be up early to catch the train. So it could have been that, too.

Regardless, neither the article on brushless motors nor a write-up on the hosts of his favorite geek-TV show testing a new robot system could hold his attention. Instead, David's thoughts kept wandering to endless replays of Jonah's mouth on his dick, thoughts of how very much he'd like to have that happen again—repeatedly and at great length— and wondering what universal laws of nature would have to be turned on their heads to make that happen in any known reality.

Surrendering to the inevitable, David braced his elbows on the seat's armrests, folded his hands together and used them to prop up his chin as he closed his eyes and daydreamed. He'd be naked, of course. On a table, or countertop, maybe. Near a window, because the sun would be shining through onto Jonah's hair, picking out the hundred different shades of reddish-brown. David wanted to kiss him so bad.

He couldn't, though, 'cause Jonah's mouth was full of David's cock. Since it was a dream, Jonah's lips were stretched wide, because in real life David just wasn't that big. It was a pretty awesome great dream, though. Jonah's hands were on David's ass, holding him in place, moving him just so.

Vaguely aware somewhere in the back of his mind that he was turning himself on, David knew he was getting hard again, probably. Next to him Jonah shifted. Their shoulders rubbed and David soaked up the heat from Jonah's arm; dragged a slow, prolonged breath into his lungs, inhaling the erotic scents of Jonah's skin and hair and letting them roll around inside him.

"—really?" Jonah's hushed voice beside him startled David, jerking him back to wakefulness. "That sounds great. Let me just double-check here. David?"

Jonah touched David's hand. Opening his eyes, David rubbed his neck and tried to haul himself back from dreamland and somehow project alertness. "Hmm?"

"They had a last-minute cancellation on one of the

compartments. I say we go for it. You could stretch out and get some real sleep. What do you say? Want to do it?"

"Um… how much?"

Jonah named a number and David tried not to react. Something must have showed on his face because Jonah immediately leaped in to rescue the plan. "Don't worry about it. I'll put it on a card and you can pay me back later. It's no big deal."

Running the numbers in his head, David did some rough calculations of how long it would take him to pay Jonah back. To squeeze just fifty bucks a month out of his budget would mean even more ramen noodles and tuna fish than he normally ate. And he'd been trying to cut back, because the trans-fats were off the charts in that stuff. The sodium content alone—

"David, forget it, let me take care of it. I'll just—"

"No, you won't. If I'm going to do it, we're going halves or I'm not doing it at all."

"Okay, okay. We'll figure out the details later, then. Cool." Turning back to the attendant, Jonah thanked the man and got directions to the room. The attendant took the credit card Jonah pulled from his wallet and left with it, while David caught himself checking out the quality of the leather goods. Jonah must be doing okay on money to be able to charge the cost of the room without taking even a minute to figure out where the money to eventually pay for it was going to come from. "So… I guess just grab our stuff and head down there, huh?"

"I guess." David shoved his magazine inside his backpack and zipped it closed while, next to him, Jonah was tucking his papers back inside the envelope he'd pulled them from. The duffel Jonah eventually put everything in had obviously seen a lot of use, but on closer inspection, David spotted the workmanship of the leather straps and the dull gleam of real brass buckles.

Crap.

Not only was Jonah tall and good-looking, he obviously had money, too.

Life was so not fair.

Standing back, Jonah let David lead the way, but dropped an arm around David's shoulders as soon as the corridor widened and they could walk two abreast. Jonah's skin was warm, that arm heavy against David's neck, and when David glanced up, he was struck again by the utter perfection of Jonah's features. The straight, almost aristocratic nose; the artlessly tousled mop of hair; the full lips, with just a hint of chapping—the kind that probably came from sailing the family yacht.

How much more out of his league could he be? Exactly none. Jonah looked like he could have stepped off the pages of a Ralph Lauren ad.

Just then Jonah looked down and caught David's gaze. He smiled and David wanted to smile back, but couldn't. If he let himself believe for even a minute that this was real, he was sunk. This was an anomaly. Some statistically improbable occurrence that shouldn't ever have happened—like conjoined twins or math savants. Jonah was going to come to his senses any minute now, and the less David invested, the easier that was going to be to take when Jonah walked away.

Jonah let go of him long enough for the two of them to take the circular stairway down to the lower level, but as soon as they were heading down the hall again, Jonah rested a hand on David's shoulder. The train rattled over a bumpy section of rail and David widened his stance for better stability, but Jonah didn't seem too need to make any adjustments at all—probably the yacht thing again. Every time their gazes met, Jonah just flashed him that carefree smile, as though hooking up on board a train as it made its way up the coast was an everyday thing.

The room turned out to be even smaller than David had imagined. Just a twin-sized bed, a little table and a chair, all upholstered in the same nearly indestructible synthetic material favored by most forms of public conveyance. David tried not to think about the causes of the various stains he couldn't help but notice, only to have the whole pot-and-kettle analogy hit him right between the eyes.

"Not exactly The Fairmont, but it beats the alternative, huh?" Jonah tossed his bag on the little bed before lacing his fingers together and stretching his arms overhead. Not only was he so tall his arms almost touched the ceiling, but his shirt rode up, revealing a choice few inches of tanned, flat belly.

David wanted to lick him.

Too soon, though, Jonah lowered his arms and began rotating his shoulders in alternating directions and reality set in. They were alone in this little room on a moving train for one reason, and that reason wasn't fascinating conversation. Whatever Jonah had in mind must be pretty athletic, though, if he had to loosen up for it like it was the NCAA playoffs.

"Yeah. I guess."

"You guess?" Jonah's gaze sharpened. Caught in mid-stretch, he froze for an instant. Then, with slow and deliberate motions, Jonah sat down on the single bed, locking his elbows and bracing himself as he leaned back on his hands. "So what's the deal, then? You don't really want to be here? I pushed too hard and now you're having second thoughts?"

"No, I…" Fingering the strap of his backpack as it hung from his shoulder, David had no idea what to do. Open his mouth and let Jonah see what a social incompetent he was? Or stand here, silent, and let Jonah think the worst? Letting his gaze flick over Jonah, David wondered desperately what the best thing to do was.

"What?" Jonah looked up at him with the most beautiful green eyes David had ever had the privilege of gazing into. When would he ever have a chance like this again? Did he want to be an old man, like Uncle Hiro? A quiet, careful man, who'd spent his life doing research in a lab—too cautious to ever get out and have an actual life? The silence spun out, broken only by the rhythmic clanking of the metal on metal beneath them.

No.

He didn't want that.

What he wanted was right in front of him.

So what if he couldn't have it forever? So what if he was only borrowing perfection? At least he could say he'd experienced it. He'd be able to look back later and have something to measure the rest of his life by. "No, I want to be here. I want this."

Letting his pack slide off his shoulder, David let it fall the rest of the way. He moved the two steps it took to reach Jonah and touched a finger to the chapped but still soft lips that were now curving up into a smile.

Jonah sat up and put his hands on David's waist, grinning. "Cool. Because I really like you and it would suck if you didn't like me back."

"Oh, yeah. As if." Dismissing the possibility, David slipped a hand into Jonah's hair, letting it slide between his fingers—cool and silky on top, but warm underneath. "Has anyone turned you down, ever?"

David put a knee on the bed first, then another hand on Jonah's shoulder and brought the other knee up, until he was nearly sitting on Jonah's lap.

"Believe it or not, they—*whoa!*" Just then the train that had been clacking rhythmically along beneath them lurched sharply, toppling Jonah backward and David on top of him. Jonah's head hit the corner of the window with a sickening thud and he slumped sideways at an awkward angle.

Looking on in horror, David froze. Jonah's face twisted in pain as he moved his hand from David's body and rubbed the back of his head. "Oh, shit." Unbelievably, he began to laugh. "That really hurts."

"Ow, jeez, are you all right? Here, let me feel." David helped Jonah to untwist his body and lay flat on the bed. Slipping his hand beneath Jonah's head, he immediately ran up against Jonah's. Pushing it out of the way, he gently explored Jonah's scalp. "Huh. Not much. Oh, wait. Here's a little bump."

"Ouch! Easy there, all right?"

"Sorry." David eased his hand out from underneath Jonah's head. "I'm sorry, that was all my fault."

Large, green eyes with thick, auburn lashes looked up at him quizzically. "How was that your fault?"

"Because... because it was." He stroked Jonah's forehead, brushing the hair back with his fingers, marveling at its soft waves. "I'm so sorry."

"You know, if you wanted to make me feel better. Sort of take my mind off the pain, as it were..." Jonah drew his legs up and David slid forward, his ass coming to rest atop Jonah's crotch. As Jonah's voice trailed off, one eyebrow rose suggestively. Something else was rising, too.

"I'd do that. For you."

"Yeah?" His hands on David's hips, Jonah's long fingers dug into David's ass, even as he undulated his body so that David could feel the dick hardening there.

"Oh, yeah." David's voice came out as a husky whisper, sounding totally foreign to his own ears. And why shouldn't it? Everything about this day was alien to him. The hot, built guy... wanting *him*? Unreal.

David got so lost in the heat in Jonah's eyes that forgot

he was supposed to be doing anything. And not just anything, but something kind of specific.

"I'm ready to feel better now." Jonah flexed his hips, and a wonderfully hard thickness beneath his shorts ground up into the crack of David's ass, and David lost it. The last semblance of coherent thought went up like so much vapor—just floated up on the air, getting thinner and thinner until there was nothing left of it.

Gorgeous, green eyes got a heavy-lidded look to them and that seductive mouth opened a fraction, as if in expectation. Desire. For him. For David. *Ohmygod.* David leaned forward, onto his forearms, and practically attacked Jonah's mouth. They were kissing, drawing on each other, David's tongue trying awkwardly to get inside Jonah's mouth.

He hadn't had much practice, didn't really know what he was doing, but Jonah made it easy. Made him feel like a natural. Like all he'd ever really needed was the right guy and suddenly he was competent. Attractive. Sexy, even.

David rubbed his chest against Jonah's, nipples tiny and hard, easily distinguished beneath the thin fabric of Jonah's t-shirt. Groaning at the feel of that hot, hard chest beneath him, David rubbed his thumb over one nipple, thrilled that he'd apparently done this to Jonah. Jonah groaned back and angled his head, trying for more of David's mouth.

The conductor's disembodied voice came over the P.A., announcing… David couldn't tell what. *Jonah's mouth. God!* "—arriving at—" A few words sunk in, but not much. "—in ten minutes. In ten minutes, arriving at—"

"What did he say?" Lifting his head, David met Jonah's gaze. "Could you hear that?"

"Not a word. Ask me if I care."

"Hurry. Come on! We're going to miss it. I cann*ot* miss this train." David's brown eyes were wide with anxiety, his eyebrows likewise raised in alarm. Already Jonah had developed a weird obsession, memorizing the nuances of David's eyebrows.

Like now.

So high they nearly disappeared under the shock of shiny black hair that he kept shoving out of his way, in stark contrast to when he was relaxed. When Jonah had had David's dick in his mouth, they'd been practically horizontal. Jonah couldn't wait to see where they'd be when he was balls-deep in David's ass.

Jonah shrugged. "Dude, you're the one who insisted on getting off the train here for snacks. Besides, we're fine. We've got five more minutes until departure and we're practically there. What's so special about these things, anyway?" Indicating the foam box he held in the crook of his arm, Jonah raised it up a bit and took an appreciative whiff. "They smell good, sure. But I'm guessing they're something special if you're willing to risk being left at the station. Hey, wait up."

Catching at David's arm, Jonah caught David's hand and held on. David's gaze flitted down to where his hand now lay, captured by Jonah's, then back up to Jonah's face. David looked slightly uncomfortable, but he'd just have to get used to it. If they were going to be a couple—and Jonah was surer of that with every minute that passed—David would just have to get used to it.

"They're not for me, they're for my lab partner. *Salteñas* are Bolivian and so is Guillermo—I guess they remind him of home. Anyway, these are his favorite, and I promised I'd stop and pick some up for him, but I... I got kind of distracted."

A little glow lit up inside Jonah at David's confession and he was momentarily silent. It startled him, in fact, just how moved he was. "No, that's okay. I mean, I like trying new things and it beats train food."

"Thanks for understanding."

"Not a problem."

They covered the last few yards of sidewalk and made their way through the station and back to the train. The next several minutes were taken up with threading their way through the scattered groups of people and getting back to their room. 'Roomette.' Goofy name. But Jonah didn't care if it gave him time alone with David.

He couldn't figure out what it was, but he was completely gone over this guy. He'd been hot for a guy on first sight before. Plenty of times, in fact. But he couldn't remember ever being so totally into someone this fast. Ever.

David was smart and cute and funny. Even David's prickly façade was adorable, and if that wasn't a measure of how infatuated he was, Jonah didn't know what was.

"Do you want to try one?" David set a box, identical to the one Jonah carried, on the little table that stood next to the room's only chair.

"They smell great. What's in them, again?" Jonah shrugged and sat on the bed as David removed the box from its plastic carry bag and opened the lid. The pungent aroma of meat and something baked quickly filled the little room.

"Uh, meat? I dunno. Chicken, I think. And some beef. A few vegetables. I think there's even some hard-boiled egg in there. They're pretty good. Here." David handed one to Jonah and took another for himself. "It might still be hot inside, so be careful."

Jonah grasped the warm meat pie carefully and took an experimental bite. Juice squirted out as soon as his teeth punctured the crust, dripping through his fingers and onto the floor.

"I should have warned you. They're kind of messy. Supposedly a real Bolivian can eat one without spilling a drop. The rest of us just look like buffoons." Laughing, David finished his off in a few economical bites, cramming the last of his into his mouth and smiling happily at Jonah as he chewed and swallowed.

"So explain to me again how this fits into your whole macrobiotic, healthy eater, trans-fat-Nazi persona again?" Smiling a little to take the sting out of it, Jonah took a couple more bites, and pretty soon he was finishing off his first *salteña*.

"I'm not that bad." David was laughing, but it had a self-conscious ring to it and Jonah could swear his ears were tinged with red

"Yeah, you kind of are. Don't make me play back the tape from my hidden recorder."

"Okay, there's probably lard in the crust—I'll give you that one—but the rest of it's not too bad. And I only get them once in a while; whenever I'm going back and forth from home to school. I get home more often than G. does."

"Yeah? Where's home?"

"Huh?"

The juice from the meat pie had run all down Jonah's hand and, instead of using one of the napkins so thoughtfully provided in the box, he was licking his fingers, sucking them clean one by one. David would probably be appalled if he realized how avidly he was watching, but Jonah wasn't going to mention it. "Home? Where is it?"

"Um, Huntington Beach. Harbor and Adams."

"Nice area."

"The best. I love it there. How about you?"

Jonah took a couple of last swipes before cutting David some slack and reverting to napkins. Now that he had some food in his belly and the train was moving again, it was time to get back to some serious seduction. He swung his feet up onto the bed and leaned back, propping his head up with one fist. "Hancock Park... L.A."

David shrugged. "I don't get up to L.A. very often. What's it like living there?"

"It's nice. Not as trendy as the west side, but close enough to downtown that I don't feel like I miss anything. All the best music comes to town, so that's good." Jonah scratched his stomach, letting his shirt ride up a little bit. Slipping his hand up a little higher, he thumbed first one nipple, then the other and David's eyes went wide for an instant. "You like O.C.?"

"Yeah. My family's all there... cousins, grandparents. Brother and sister, and parents, obviously. It's the best."

"That's right, you already said that. Duh. Now I'm the one who's distracted." He let his gaze travel over David's body, liking the lean, compact body. The dark brown eyes with their exotic almond shape; the glossy, nearly blue-black hair.

David stood silent, looking vaguely uncomfortable, and Jonah wondered if he was coming on too strong again. The man was just so... changeable. Elusive. One minute arrogant and superior, the next as shy as a—

Oh, no. It couldn't be. Like, seriously, the man had to have *some* experience... Didn't he?

No need to panic. He'd just have to keep a tight rein on himself and not get too carried away. But, damnit, David was nearly irresistible, with that cocky attitude and sweet body.

Jonah closed his eyes and drew in a long, controlled breath. He was just exhaling when David's voice intruded, but closer this time. "Are you all right? Is it your head? Are you dizzy?"

"No, I'm— Well, maybe a little. I should probably

lie flat. On my back, you know?" A little white lie. A gentle exaggeration of the truth, wouldn't land him in the seventh circle of Hell. Exactly.

"Here, let me help." Standing next to the bed, David's face was a picture of worry.

Jonah let David take him by the shoulders and ease him gently backward. Glancing up into David's eyes, Jonah winced and closed his own eyes again. "That hurts. Maybe you should lie down next to me."

"Why?"

"Um... because I might open them again when I talk to you, and just looking up could make me dizzy. I hate throwing up." Not his best effort ever, but he'd never been much good at improvising.

"Uh, okay."

Unbelievable.

David climbed onto the single bed, pausing probably to work out logistics, while Jonah rolled onto his side and tried to make room by squeezing up against the outside wall of the train. It took a fair amount of jostling and adjusting to get them both wedged into the same space, but it was all worth it when David rested one hand tentatively on Jonah's hip.

Jonah opened his eyes and smiled at David's closeness. "I like your eyes." It was true. Dark, dark brown, with the perfect touch of exotic Asian ancestry to push all of Jonah's buttons in exactly the ways he liked them pushed.

"Thanks." David flinched and looked away, and Jonah wondered what that simple thank you cost him in response to a compliment. "They're nothing special, though. Just brown."

Bingo. Jonah's smile broadened at the qualifier. If he'd worn one, he could have set his watch by it.

"I like brown eyes. I *love* your brown eyes." Jonah

couldn't hold back any more. He had to kiss David, so he leaned in, closing his eyes a little but waiting to see what David would do. When David's gaze dropped to Jonah's lips, after the briefest pause, David's lips parted a bit and his tongue flicked out to lick at his upper lip briefly.

Oh, yeah.

Closing the distance, Jonah pressed his lips to David's, pressing lightly at first, until David made a happy little noise in the back of his throat and Jonah took it deeper. David responded by sucking on Jonah's tongue and pressing closer, hooking a finger in the pocket of Jonah's shorts and tugging. Jonah's happiness bubbled up in the form of a moan when David lifted his leg and rested it atop Jonah's, letting their cocks find each other and bump enthusiastically.

Room.

They needed more room.

Jonah slid an arm under David's and slowly eased down onto his back. David didn't waste any time in shifting over, climbing on top of Jonah and kissing back enthusiastically.

The shirt had to go, though. Jonah slipped his hands under David's shirt, moaning a little at the slide of smooth, warm skin under his fingertips. He circled his hands a bit, delighting in the feel of David's body, eventually catching the shirt and sliding it up.

Jonah was happy when David fought breaking the kiss even long enough to get his shirt off. "Shirt. Can you…?

"Yeah." David nodded breathlessly and helped the maneuver along. "You, too."

"Absolutely." Grinning as David sat back to give him room to work, Jonah shimmied out of his shirt with David's enthusiastic help.

"Oh. Oh, wow."

Jonah tended to take his looks for granted, especially

since his body was in the shape it was more due to genetics and playing sports than to any attempt at body-building on his part. He had to admit, though, that it might be worth a little more of an effort if the results made David's reaction so spectacular. The look in David's eyes and the slight quiver in his hands as he held them hesitantly a couple of inches away from Jonah's chest were worth a few extra hours spent in the weight room, definitely.

Cupping his hands, David caressed Jonah's chest, molding Jonah's flesh and pushing at the muscles beneath the skin. It was amazing, the way something so simple could send electrical impulses licking down Jonah's spine, hardening his dick even more, if that was possible. Jonah put his hands on David's thighs, running them up under the edges of David's shorts. "How about taking these off?"

"Uh…" David's eyes went wide for a moment, his hands going motionless where they'd been massaging Jonah's pecs, seconds away from doing wonderful things to Jonah's nipples.

Jonah willed himself to keep breathing, waiting for David's next move. This had to work. He wouldn't let the possibility of failure so much as enter his mind, so instead he imagined David's hands working the snap and, like mental telepathy or remote control, David reached for the opening of his shorts.

*Take your hands off the jock and move slowly away from the bed. You're about to make a **huge** fool of yourself, and there'll be no pretending this rejection away.*

Maybe not. But there's no one else here to see or laugh, is there? The hot guy wants you, so shut up and get naked before he changes his mind.

While David's two sides argued internally, his body just kept going, his hands moving from the warm smoothness of Jonah's chest to his own shorts—unsnapping with his left hand while his right reached for the zipper. Jonah was smiling at him, and he'd do anything to keep that hot gaze fixed on him.

"All right."

Jonah closed his eyes momentarily, his nostrils flaring with each intake of breath. When Jonah opened them again, they were smokier than ever. "Show me your dick."

Responding automatically, David pulled his briefs down and to one side, his erect cock springing eagerly toward Jonah.

"Nice."

The weird part was, David actually believed him. In that moment, with Jonah gazing at him so intently, he was happy to show off his body because everything he saw on Jonah's face told him that Jonah meant what he said.

So he wrapped the fingers of one hand around his erection and pumped it a little bit, enjoying the sharp intake of breath from Jonah that resulted.

"Oh, sweet." Jonah's tongue darted out, swept quickly across his lips, wetting them, then retreated. "Come closer."

Oh, yeah.

The heated gaze directed steadily at his dick had David rising to his knees, angling closer until he had to hang onto the bed's backrest to balance himself. Just the thought of that hot mouth swallowing him down again was—

"Closer. Just—yeah, like that."

Close enough now that Jonah put his hand over David's, where it still clutched at his dick, and directed it to Jonah's mouth. That magic combination of lips and tongue caressed him again, rubbing around the head, now slippery with pre-come and Jonah's saliva.

Heat and warmth enveloped him for the second time that day and, holy crap, that was amazing. Big hands gripped his ass, first pulling him closer, then pushing him away. Working him down, moving him back and forth like a... like a...

He couldn't think while Jonah was doing that to him, sucking him hard, then backing off and using that tongue to play with David's cock. Flicking around the head, teasing at his hole, all the time squeezing David's ass and controlling his every move.

Sweet and oh, so hot, it spun David's head to see his dick disappearing into that mouth, the visual more perfect than any fantasy he'd ever jerked off to. He gave up trying to hold a thought, much less analyze or commit to memory. Jonah was working him and David let go, gave himself up to the intense pleasure of being taken.

Losing himself in how good it all felt, David's head fell back and that tingle, that unmistakable urgency, began to take over as David chased his orgasm. He pushed at Jonah's mouth, but Jonah had a firm grip on him and pulled him back.

"Wait. David, wait." Holding David firmly by the hips, Jonah licked his lips and panted, catching his breath.

"But—" *Don't whine, idiot. He might stop completely.*

"I know, I could do that all day. But I really want to be inside you when you come. Can I fuck you?"

"Of course you may." It came out stilted and stupidly formal to David's ears, but it was undeniably sincere. He'd unquestionably be Jonah Simpson's fuck toy if that was what was being offered.

"Oh, sweet." Jonah let go of David's hips and unsnapped his own shorts, urging David upward for a moment so that he could wriggle out of them.

Shorts.

Of course!

Excellent idea!

David scrambled quickly off the bed and shed his own, climbing back up before either one of them could change his mind. As he was doing it, Jonah was fishing in the pocket of his shorts and came up with a condom and a little packet of what David hoped was lube of some sort.

Jonah smiled crookedly and handed the condom to David. "Put it on me?"

Not trusting himself to speak and not say something stupid, David only nodded and took the proffered packet. He was tearing it open with his teeth when he caught an appraising look from Jonah, skimming up and down his body as Jonah fingered the clear gel he'd squirted onto the palm of one hand.

David was too far gone to do much analyzing, especially when Jonah leaned over and took his mouth in an urgent kiss, all tongue and teeth and hot suction. He got lost in the kiss—at how natural and right it seemed. How could he have lived this long without Jonah to kiss him, hold him, fuck him?

"Sorry. I can't help it. You're just so hot." Jonah's voice was slow and a little raspy, and it rolled over David's nerves like fingernails down his spine.

Entranced, it took David a second to open his eyes. When he did, Jonah reached for the hand that held the condom and guided it to his cock. David thought for a second that Jonah might have instructions for him, but Jonah just smiled and took a deep breath, shivering as David fit the whisper-thin latex over the flushed head.

"Me, hot? Not even. But—"

"Don't want to hear it." Jonah cut him off abruptly. "You're hot if I say you are, and you definitely are."

"Hmm. Okay." After glancing up quickly, David ducked his head and finished rolling the condom down Jonah's dick. So pretty. He wanted to... Oh, why not? David lowered his head took the tip of Jonah's cock in his mouth. The latex taste was bitter and nasty, but the scent of Jonah's skin was more concentrated here—musky and rich—and David sucked it down into his lungs, even as he licked at the most beautiful dick he'd ever had the privilege of sucking.

That's what it was. A privilege, and one he'd totally lucked into. But just because it was an accident didn't mean he wasn't going to grab his chance and run with it. Suck it. Whatever he could get away with.

"Wait." Fingers under his chin pushed him back before tilting David's head up. "Don't go so fast. You're making me crazy and, as much as I love what you're doing, I... *God.*" A flash of molten green was the only warning David got before Jonah kissed him again, rougher this time. Intense. A demanding tongue filled his mouth while a hand slid abruptly into his hair, twining strands between the fingers, holding him still.

Another hand swept down his side, coming to rest on David's hip, pausing for a moment before homing in on his dick.

David moaned.

Fuck.

It was so good. *So* good.

Most of his fantasies involved making slow, languid love. Taking his time and luxuriating in unhurried, deliberate touching. Kissing. Stroking. Caressing. But this...

This was exciting.

Amazing.

Being the object of urgent desire that absolutely couldn't wait.

Being manhandled by a hard-bodied, undeniably stunning, jock was his new standard of excellence.

"David. David, Jesus…" Jonah's hand was jacking him. With a efficient, twisting motion that was bringing him right up to the edge. Hips jerking, he tried to maximize the motions of Jonah's hand. "Come on. Let's do it. Ride me, would you?"

Nodding, David shifted, praying he wouldn't screw this up. He'd never done it that way—just another reminder that Jonah was a lot more experienced than he was. What if he messed it up so badly that Jonah got disgusted with him? What if he—

"Hold still a second. Did you—? No, hang on." Jonah put more lube on his fingers and smeared it around David's hole, slipping a finger inside and stroking David expertly. More lube, more stroking, then suddenly nothing. "I'll go slow. I promise."

"You don't have to. I don't care." Two big hands— one slippery, one not—bracketed his hips, guiding his movements.

"Don't say that." Jonah's gaze was fixed on a point beneath David's body—aligning their bodies, probably.

"I mean it. Just do it. Just fuck me." The fat, flushed head of Jonah's dick was pressing eagerly against David's hole and David closed his eyes in concentration. He was *so* not a pro at this. He needed to focus. Relax his body. Let Jonah in. Oh. Oh, geez, that was amazing. Thick. Delicious. A slow, sweet burn that pushed steadily upward.

One hand on the wall, David lowered himself, aiming for smooth and faux-relaxed, but really just grateful that one of them knew what he was doing. Jonah pulled his legs up a little for better leverage and then he was all the way in, holding firm, not moving.

David tried to stay still, breathing deep through his

nose, biting his lip and balancing with one hand holding the metal window frame. Eyes closed, afraid of what he'd see when he opened them, he couldn't *not* look. Jonah was too beautiful just sitting and talking. David needed to know what he looked like naked. Naked having sex.

Jonah's eyes were open, as it turned out. Intent, unsmiling, he gazed steadily up at David. "Perfect."

"Not."

"Shut up. It is." Jonah undulated his hips slowly and David was in heaven. "You are."

Jonah did it again and David sucked a breath in hard. "Oh. Oh, wow."

"Told you you'd like it." Jonah's gaze was locked on David's face now and David wanted to fall into those gorgeous green eyes.

"Did not." David answered back reflexively—honestly, because Jonah hadn't—and then wanted to slap a hand over his own mouth. *Idiot. Why are you arguing with the man?*

Jonah laughed and it did phenomenal things for his abs and pecs. God, but the man was incredibly built. Tanned chest and freckled shoulders, reddish, blondish streaked hair—*he* looked like the perfect Huntington Beach surfer boy, not David. So unbelievably good-looking.

"I didn't? My bad." As if for emphasis, Jonah withdrew, then flexed his hips and reentered and David's head reeled at the sensations.

"M-maybe you did." Jonah could shave his head and call himself the King of Siam, as long as he kept doing that. "Again. Please, do that again."

"Just for you." As he withdrew, Jonah smiled, as if he knew exactly what it was doing to David.

"Oh, God." Maybe it was a good thing that Jonah knew, because David couldn't come close to quantifying. There were no measurable results about the best thing that had ever happened to him.

On Jonah's instroke, David tried some moves of his own; tried to mimic Jonah's smooth, controlled upward thrust with the downward motion of his body, but his thighs gave out and he dropped awkwardly down onto Jonah. It didn't matter, though, because—never missing a beat—Jonah adjusted. Taking a firm grip on David's hips, Jonah held him in place just where he wanted him, and began fucking David in earnest.

It was the most beautiful, most perfect moment of David's life. Jonah was gorgeous, with a beautiful body and flawless features, and for some absurd, inexplicable reason he wanted David. Knowing that gave David just enough confidence to let it all happen.

Jonah held David's ass in his big hands and drove himself into David, over and over. A powerful thrust would send shockwaves into David's body, thrilling him with the feeling of being possessed—as if somehow in that moment he was the only one who could provide what Jonah wanted. Then with each delicious outstroke, David would moan and sigh at the sensation of Jonah moving through him.

Knowing he was giving himself away as a selfish asshole, David's hand crept down to his own dick.

To jack himself while Jonah was getting off on fucking him? Incredible. He couldn't resist.

It was too good.

Too much stimulation.

The hotness of Jonah—beneath him, inside him. How good it felt, even if it was his own fist he was fucking— it was all too much. Three or four good strokes was all David got and then he was coming, spurting all over Jonah's tanned stomach.

Which only seemed to get Jonah hotter.

Or maybe it was coincidence. Maybe Jonah was about

to come anyway, but the pace of his thrusts suddenly got faster, more urgent. He was slamming into David at light speed six, eight, ten more times and then he stilled for an instant as he came, too. Jonah's thrusting stuttered and slowed, until it eventually stopped entirely.

Now that his mind was gradually coming back to him, David had time to think. Had he done all right? Not embarrassed himself? What had he said? David couldn't remember. Had he been too needy? Begged too much?

God, why didn't Jonah say something? Cracking under the pressure, David blurted out the first thing that came into his head. "I came all over you."

Jonah's eyes opened at that, inspected his own chest, gaze gradually climbing to scan David's face. "And I got lube in your hair."

"You did?"

"Pretty sure. I say that makes us even." Reaching for a handful of paper napkins left over from their lunch, Jonah disposed of the condom and began wiping David's come from his chest. "Anyway, I'm not complaining."

"Let me do that." David wasn't sure what the etiquette of these situations was supposed to be, but it seemed to fit vaguely under the category of 'clean up your own mess,' so he grabbed some and dabbed at Jonah's chest, too.

"Don't worry about it." Jonah tossed the used napkins in the trash, then leaned back on his elbows. "If you're really concerned, we could always go take a shower."

The only thing cuter than a wide awake, aroused-and-trying-in-vain-not-to-show-it David turned out to be a sexually-replete-and-dozing one. In sleep, David's face showed all the innocence and trusting nature that he tried so hard to hide while awake.

Wearing his shorts and t-shirt again—naturally modest David had insisted—he'd fallen asleep, head resting on his robot magazine, open to the very article they'd sparred over earlier.

Jonah, on the other hand, was wide awake, too busy plotting his next move to nap.

So, the sex had been great.

Better than great, it had been outstanding.

Not that he'd been all that worried.

Still, it was helpful to have it verified in such a satisfying way that they were good together. Good was an understatement, really. David was fantastic in bed. Willing. Enthusiastic. Open to direction.

It wasn't a huge deal, but Jonah enjoyed things more when the other guy wasn't always jockeying to be top man, so it worked out nicely that David followed directions well.

And so cute. He'd looked perfect on his knees, working Jonah's dick. *Shit.* Jonah reached down to adjust himself as his cock stirred in response to the picture his mind had conjured up. That sweet little body, so eager and receptive…

Maybe it was because Jonah was around thyroid cases and the other genetic freaks like him that made up ninety percent of all basketball players, but he appreciated all the same equipment in more compact form. David was so hot, though, and there was just something appealing about the notion that he was so obviously the kind of guy who didn't give it up very often.

Maybe all athletes weren't horndogs, but the ones that Jonah worked and played next to year in and year out certainly did their best to true-up the average. More concerned with quantity than quality, a huge percentage of them didn't give a rat's ass about compatibility. Hell, when it came right down to it, gender wasn't even a sticking point, necessarily.

Give 'em a hole and they'd fuck it—a set of available genitals and they'd suck it.

Not that there was anything wrong with that, but Jonah preferred someone like David when it came to hooking up. There was probably some deep psychological meaning behind it, but Jonah liked to feel like he was more than merely a convenient collection of parts.

Just then David stirred in his sleep. Scrunched up his face for a moment, before it all melted away and his face was once again as clear and unlined as a baby's. Eyes closed, head tilted slightly up, something about David's face put Jonah in mind of an angel. An angel who gave really good head.

Reaching out to touch, Jonah ran a hand down David's shoulder as he slept, down his back and up the slope of his perfect little ass. Jonah relaxed his hand and let it shape itself to the curve of David's butt, just letting it rest there while he fought the desire to squeeze and mold it. Play. Explore.

Still asleep, David rolled over onto his side, shifting everything closer to Jonah so that it only took a couple of minor adjustments until Jonah was spooning up against David's ass. Propping his head on one bent arm, Jonah wrapped the other around David's middle and splayed his hand across David's stomach. Jonah smiled and gave up a silent thanks to the universe when David gave a little grunt and snuggled closer.

When Jonah opened his eyes again, the angle of sunlight through the window told him he must have napped, too. David was still sleeping, face down, and the magazine had fallen to the floor. He couldn't tell for sure from where he lay, but Jonah suspected that David's hand was inside his shorts—another trait Jonah found incredibly endearing.

Which raised the obvious question: how could

someone as obviously sensual and affectionate as David possibly be so inexperienced? Maybe O.C. guys didn't have the perceptiveness to be able to see past David's prickly exterior. Well, too bad. Their loss was Jonah's gain, because he sure as hell could see it.

Jonah watched the scenery out the window for a bit, breaking up the sightseeing with frequent looks back at David's sleeping form. It probably ought to disturb him, how quickly he was becoming convinced that he and David were meant to be together. Maybe not forever, because who the hell knew? He liked the way they fit together, in a lot of different ways—in every way he'd tested so far.

What if they tried rooming together? Would it be too much togetherness? He could get used to the idea of seeing David every day; didn't have any trouble picturing them sharing a dorm room, working on their separate projects.

Or maybe an apartment would be better.

Would his grades slip because he skipped class too often, sleeping late, in bed with David?

"I fell asleep." David lifted his head, rubbing a hand over his face, pushing his hair out of his eyes, barely meeting Jonah's gaze. "How embarrassing."

"Why? I did, too."

"You did not. You're just trying to make me feel better about it, aren't you? You have those impeccable country club manners, I can tell." Suspicious David, the one who'd watched Jonah so warily just a few hours ago, was back. Jonah had hoped he'd banished that guy, but as David sat up, he began edging away from Jonah, trying to make moving over to the chair look easy and unaffected.

"I'm going to take that as a compliment, even though I'm not sure that's how you meant it." Jonah's gaze flowed naturally over David's body, skimming up his lightly furred legs, his slim, muscled arms, to the serious look lurking in those dark brown eyes. "But, yeah. I did, too, fall asleep."

David's gaze fell, eventually fixing on his magazine, lying open on the floor of the little roomette. The pages did a subtle dance as they vibrated ever so slightly to the motion of the train.

"So, how was the article? Was it as good as you'd hoped?"

Glancing up, David hesitated. "Yeah, it was..." The words dammed up behind his lips as he struggled to get something out. Finally, he just shrugged. "I have no idea. I couldn't focus. At all. I kept..."

Jonah smiled encouragingly. "Uh-huh?"

"I kept thinking about—"

"About my dick?" Jonah offered.

David's eyes went wide and he stared at Jonah, but only for a moment. Dropping his gaze, David's ears grew suspiciously pink, until he eventually nodded. "Yeah."

"Cool." Jonah pushed himself up and crossed to where David sat. Kneeling in front of David, Jonah placed his hands on David's knees. "Don't be embarrassed. I fell asleep thinking about you, too."

The doubtful look on David's face got to Jonah. The guy couldn't have gotten enough positive feedback in his life if he was still this uncertain. Jonah opened his mouth to say something reassuring, but changed his mind midstream. Instead he simply closed the distance and pressed his mouth to David's.

Their lips met and meshed as David, after the tiniest hesitation, leaned into the kiss. He even hooked a hand behind Jonah's neck and tugged as, at the same time, he explored the seam of Jonah's lips with his tongue.

When David pulled back, Jonah wanted to follow, but decided instead to let David control the pace. David's responses would tell him a lot.

"Did you, really?"

"Yeah, I did." Jonah loved the hopeful look that was beginning to creep in around the edges of David's guardedness. Maybe he was finally getting through. "Can you tell what I'm thinking right now?"

"About *my* dick?" The eyebrow made a belated appearance, and a bit of the cockiness that had been so evident earlier began to bleed through again.

"Give the man a prize." Jonah murmured as he closed in on David's lips again, only this time David met him half-way. Cupping his hand over the hard-on beginning to tent David's shorts, Jonah gave it an appreciative squeeze.

David's answering moan vibrated through their kiss. "Another one?"

"Sure. Why not?" Jonah edged closer, letting their chests bump briefly. "You deserve it."

At that, David reared back, eyeing Jonah thoughtfully. *What was going through his brain at that moment? Please let it be nothing bad.* "You know what? I have to agree with you. I think I'm about due."

"Well, in that case…" Where to start? Jonah reached for the edge of David's shirt, skinning it up and over the head of a very cooperative David. "Oh… So pretty."

David's nipples tightened, peaking up into taut little spirals that all but begged to be sucked. A quick glance up at David's face confirmed he was holding his breath—in anticipation, Jonah hoped. He leaned in and licked delicately at the first, nuzzled his nose into David's sternum briefly before moving over to the other. Fastening his lips around the tiny bud, Jonah sucked; took just the tip between his teeth to tease it.

"Oh, yeah. Jonah." David's breathy sigh was all the encouragement Jonah needed. Eyes half-shut against the rush of sensation, David's hands were wonderful indicators of his overall level of distraction. First tugging on Jonah's shoulders, as Jonah applied more suction David switched to pushing Jonah away—only to pull him close again when Jonah relented.

Switching tactics, Jonah hooked the fingers that had been anchoring David firmly to the chair in the waistband of David's shorts. After a quick side trip to release the snap, Jonah didn't bother with the zipper, just slid them over David's high, rounded ass and down over his thighs and off.

He was familiar with David's scent now, loved the warm, musky smell as he took a proprietary grip on David's cock. Pumped it a couple of times; pressed his thumb into the slit and smiled at the way David nearly came clean up out of the chair.

"Are you really up for another one? Can we do it again?" Jonah chose that moment to add a firm squeeze to David's balls, even as he jacked his eager dick.

David's nod of assent was accompanied by an inarticulate, choked little noise that sounded like agreement.

"Yeah? That's 'yeah'?" Jonah wasn't above a little sensual blackmail, and gave David's cock a particularly long and loving stroke as he asked.

Fingers digging into the arms of the chair, David nodded again, more vigorously this time. "Yeah. Definitely."

"Nice. Oh, sweet. Let's, um…" Releasing his grip on David, Jonah sat back on his heels, enjoying the dazed, out of control look on David's face. When David pushed up out of the chair and moved back over to the little bed, Jonah was already working himself out of his shorts and fishing for what he fervently hoped wasn't his last condom.

When he looked up, David was face down on the

bed, arms cradling his head, ass up—motionless except for the shallow breaths making his ribs rise and fall in an irregular rhythm. *Oh, yeah. He could so get used to seeing that every day.*

"Jesus." *In the mornings would be cool, too.* "David, you're killing me."

"Huh?"

Mindlessly stroking himself, long beyond the point where the lube was adequately distributed, Jonah was so utterly taken by the sight of David offering himself. So incredibly hot. "Just…"

David rolled his head to one side, squinting up at Jonah with one eye. "And you're waiting for…?"

Oh, yeah. That's what he'd been waiting for—without even realizing it. That's who he wanted to fuck. The cute body was great, but it was the smart-mouth attitude that really tripped his trigger. "Just making sure you really want it."

"Don't waste my time, Simpson. You want some of this? Come take care of it before I change my mind."

"Don't waste your time, huh?" Jonah leaned over and applied one well-lubed finger to David's hole, sliding it in with authority. "Am I wasting your time here, Sato? Huh?"

He stroked a couple of times, looking for and finding David's prostate. David moaned appreciatively and pushed back against Jonah's finger.

"Because, goodness knows, if you've got better things to do—" He quickly slipped his finger out and replaced it with his dick, pushing inside David, grabbing David's hips for leverage. Jonah thrust hard, shoving all the way in, letting David really feel it. "You got better things to do, David? Really?"

"M—" Pulling out abruptly, Jonah thrust in again just as suddenly. "Maybe." Jonah started to pull out again, but David used his arms and pushed himself back hard onto Jonah's dick. "Not sure. Do it again."

Jonah gave up all pretense of trying to carry on a conversation and gave himself up to the pleasure; to how incredibly good it all felt and how glad he was he'd found David. Grunting and sweating, trying to balance his rhythm against the random tics and swaying of the train, Jonah had to work a little harder for the orgasm this time.

Beneath him, David was groaning with each outstroke, fisting his dick, making incoherent cries of pleasure. Then David began to jerk, thighs and ass quivering, clamping down hard on Jonah's cock and dragging him over the edge into ecstasy.

"I can't get past how many trees there are."

Settled back against Jonah, those long arms wrapped around his middle, David was having a hard time working up the energy it took to form an opinion. "Yeah. They definitely have a lot of them."

"It takes some getting used to, all of that green in one place. You know?"

Jonah's voice rumbled against his back. David thumbed over the athletic tape that wound around Jonah's left index finger; rolled his head to one side and pressed his lips to Jonah's bare arm. Jonah's tanned, bare, incredibly sexy arm. "I remember thinking pretty much those exact words my first year up here, too. Different from southern California, that's for sure."

The things Jonah knew how to do... He was just so unbelievably, amazingly hot. The last twenty-four-plus hours had been the equivalent of an upper division course in human sexual practices for David. Graduate level, maybe. That thing with the pressing on the… David shivered just remembering it.

"So, you adjusted okay?"

Craning his neck, David leaned over and tried to look Jonah in the eye. "Sure, I guess. Like, what do you mean?"

"I don't know. I've spent most of my life in one place. What if I get there and I go crazy from lack of sunlight?"

"Sunlight deprivation?" Jonah was smiling down at him and David laughed back. "Is that even a documented condition?"

"Pretty sure it is, yeah." Gaze straying down to David's mouth, Jonah's eyes got that indolent, aroused look in them that David loved. Then Jonah closed them entirely and kissed him, drawing on his mouth with a slow thoroughness that melted David in place. "You'll help me through it, though, won't you? Can I count on you to keep me going when it's raining for the hundred-and-forty-second day in a row and I'm missing home?"

The arm around his back would have held him firmly in place, even if he hadn't been wedged in between Jonah's amazingly long thighs. The kiss was shutting down his higher thought processes and David wanted to promise Jonah anything the man wanted to hear, he really did. But no way was he going to hang around waiting for whatever scraps of attention Jonah felt like tossing his way. Jocks didn't hang with geeks—it was just one of those universal concepts that everyone knew and understood, like Ohm's law or Newton's laws of gravitation.

"Are you kidding? You're going to be too busy to be homesick."

"You think so?" Jonah buried a hand in David's hair, rubbing circles with his thumb over David's cheek. They'd already made love—had sex, whatever—four times, not including the blowjob. Did that make it four point five times, then? Better call it five, then, because four was unlucky. Either way, David wasn't sure he had any more fluids left in him to come with, but Jonah was getting that look in his eyes again and David's body was responding.

"Absolutely. You'll have—" Jonah was kissing his throat and massaging his dick, which was getting harder by the second. "—classes. Papers to write. Research to do."

"That all sounds... God, I love the way you taste." After rolling David onto his back, Jonah was working his shirt up again, kissing his stomach and tonguing his navel. All the while he was pressing the palm of one hand to David's groin, putting the most excruciatingly wonderful pressure on David's cock. "And that all sounds hideous. The only way I'll make it through is if I know I have you to help me."

"You, uh... You're a friendly guy." Jonah's mouth was dangerously close to David's dick, and already he'd memorized the feeling of that first glorious slide into Jonah's mouth. His unruly body was arching and squirming, trying to make the connection that made that unmistakable sensation possible. "You'll make friends."

"Not like you, though. You're different." Jonah tugged aside the waistband of David's shorts and sucked on the exposed pelvic bone, scraping his teeth along the skin there so that David was twisting, trying to evade Jonah's restraining hand, all the better to make real contact.

"Jonah... *Please.*" David was whimpering now, not sure if he could possibly withstand one more orgasm, but hoping like crazy to find out. Maybe it was for the best that he wouldn't see Jonah after they arrived in Portland. He wasn't sure how much more he could take.

It'd be wicked awesome to find out, though.

"I want us to room together after we get there. Who do

we talk to, to make that happen?" Tiny little baby kisses, feathered across David's abdomen, had him moaning, in between long, shuddering breaths. "David? Do you know?"

Jonah's mouth.

He wanted Jonah's mouth on him.

No. He wanted to be fucked—to be ridden, long and slow. With Jonah's hand on his cock, squeezing him.

He wanted—

"David, can you hear me?"

"Huh? Yeah, yeah. Oh, yeah. Can you just do that a little to the left?" Hot breath tickled his balls and then a warm, slick tongue lapped at first one, then the other. For a few brief moments moist heat enveloped them both as—*holy shit*—Jonah mouthed them. Sucked them in and played with them.

He was savoring the feeling, marveling at how something that felt so amazing could be happening to him for the first time, when it suddenly all went away.

A few seconds of perfect heaven… then nothing.

"David, talk to me. I put in for a single room in the on-campus housing. But I should be able to trade that in for a double, don't you think? David?"

"What? Sure, I guess." Prying his eyes open, David's gaze flitted instantly to Jonah's face.

Long strands of streaked auburn hair obscured one eye, but the other was gazing back at David steadily. Jonah's tongue swiped at slightly puffy lips—lips that had just moments ago been caressing David like he'd never been caressed before. That astonishing chest was rising and falling regularly, as Jonah sat and waited. "Do you, really?"

"Sure. Why not? Were you going to… like, um… finish?"

"Eventually, yeah."

"Eventually?" Pushing himself up onto his elbows, David tried for the same steady gaze back, but the ghost of his own high-pitched wail seemed to echo around the room. "What's that mean?"

"It means I want a real answer, not a say-whatever-it-takes-to-get-off answer."

Jonah's expression was serious, no question. He still had that gorgeous, all American, buff athlete look about him, but for the first time David saw through it to the strength of will behind it all. Jonah wasn't going to settle for bullshit and David realized that the ride was over. The Portland station might be two hours away, but the magical world that had existed on this train, where a good-looking guy like Jonah might really be interested in an everyday science nerd like him, was at an end.

David looked down for a moment, trying to find the nerve to say what needed to be said. The hardest part was that he really didn't want to say it. He'd *liked* living in his make-believe world, and he didn't want to do or say anything that would make it end one minute sooner than it absolutely had to.

He looked up at Jonah's face again and knew that the option had been taken away from him. Jonah was waiting and he was going to have to tell the truth, half-naked pathetic spectacle that he'd made of himself or not.

"Yeah, I think you could probably tell them you'd like to trade down to a two-person unit and get about a hundred takers on the spot. You could probably even sell it and make enough to pay for your books for an entire semester. I don't even want to know what you had to do to get one in the first place, but they're in demand, for sure."

"Excellent."

"Yeah."

"So, do we just tell them we want to room together?

How does that part work?" Jonah was beginning to crack a smile again and David knew he'd carry that picture in his head for a long time. His beautiful man, stripped to the waist and smiling at him. His for a little while, anyway.

Crap.

David pinched the bridge of his nose hard and looked away, blinking and willing himself all the while not to cry. He'd known going in that this moment would come. He just hadn't anticipated how fast the time would go, or how much it would hurt when it was all gone.

"David? Do you know? Oh, well, it doesn't matter. We'll figure it out."

"Would you just stop?" David couldn't stand it anymore. If it was over, let it be over. "You don't have to pretend. Can we just admit what it is and let it go?"

"Admit what *what* is?" Jonah was scratching an itch low on his side and the way his arm reached across his body made his pecs bunch up and it was *so* not fair of him. No one should be allowed to be so overwhelmingly attractive in the exact moment that David was having to explain why it would never work between them.

In fact, it was beginning to piss David off that Jonah was making him actually go through the exercise. They both *knew*, didn't they? So why put him through the torture of having to say the words?

"Admit that it was just…" Jonah just stared at him, waiting for who knew what? "That you were just bored; looking for something to pass the time. I don't know!"

"Really? Is this what you do when you're bored? Boy, all I can say is O.C. guys get a bad rap, then."

"Oh, come on, Simpson. You're seriously telling me that you'd have looked twice at me if this had been just another day at school? What? You scoped me out at the station and paid someone off to get the seat next to me? Come on. I've spent my whole life being blown off by guys who look like you. Funnily enough, unless they're looking for help with their science project, vertically challenged science nerds aren't usually the hot guys' first choice."

Instead of backing off like David had expected, Jonah crossed his arms and dug in, as though he was settling in for a protracted battle. "Is that right? Well, maybe I know something they don't, Sato."

"And what would that be?"

"Like maybe that I like a guy with a little something going on upstairs. Like what's between the ears is just as important as what's between the legs." At that, Jonah's gaze dropped to the second area under discussion. "Not that I have anything against that particular bit of geography. I'm especially fond of it, as it turns out. But I've dated enough guys who think having a good outside jumper and knowing how to defend a pick-and-roll are the keys to life."

Relaxing a bit, Jonah reached out and let his hand rest on David's thigh. Resting, his fingers spanned David's thigh, but he drew them together, tantalizing David's nerve endings along the way. "So when I meet a guy who flips my switch in a major way *and* he's got a brain in his head, you'd better believe I'm all over it."

God knew he wanted to believe what Jonah was saying, but a lifetime of experience was telling David that Jonah was only saying what he thought David wanted to hear. Maybe he wanted a regular hook-up, a sure thing, while he got settled in at Mt. Scott. And how much more brutal would it be to get dumped at school, where everyone on the tiny campus would witness his humiliation?

"You don't believe me?"

"Well, let's just say I'd have an easier time explaining string theory than you and me together."

"David." Jonah leaned over and kissed him. Sweet

and… sincere. How a kiss could be sincere, David didn't know, but he knew what he felt. "I know your secret, Sato, and it's just too bad for you."

Instantly suspicious, David eyed Jonah warily. "What?"

"You *want* to believe." Jonah kissed him again, lingeringly this time. "And you will. Just wait and see."

"Jonah?"

"Yeah?"

"What's a pick-and-roll?"

"Move over so I can lie down, and I'll explain it to you."

Kegs and Dorms

Reading Between the Lines
by Jane Davitt

*H*argreaves Hall, the historic center of this modern *college, dates back to 1820. Visitors will note the majestic staircase in the lobby, made in France to Mr. James Hargreaves' specifications and shipped over to be reassembled here by a team of French carpenters. Made of carved oak, it dominates the space and is dramatically lit by the stained glass skylight in the dome above…*

Coming back to college two weeks late sucked, even if he was a senior so it wasn't as if he didn't know his way around the place. Seth hitched his backpack higher on his shoulder and headed for the double doors of Hargreaves Hall, which housed the administrative offices and some formal reception rooms for when the college wanted to get fancy with the fundraising. He'd been looking forward to his final year and the late start had spoiled it; classes had started, roommates had been assigned, and he'd never catch up on what everyone had done over the summer because it was old news by now.

He just hoped that having his appendix unceremoniously yanked out like that wasn't going to stop him making the soccer team. His dad wouldn't mind if it did; he'd made his views plain about the game and how much better it would've been if Seth had been playing football instead. Seth had done what he always did when the subject came up; smiled, said nothing, and then, when his dad had run out of ways to get his message over, he'd taken his soccer ball and gone out to practice. The soccer team at Hargreaves had been set up about five years earlier and was popular enough that, even as good as Seth was, he wasn't guaranteed a place; but compared to football, it was low in status. No cheerleaders, not much funding, and scoring a goal didn't mean you automatically got laid that night by some hero-worshiping jock-groupie with bouncy hair and perky tits.

Seth didn't care about status and he sure as hell didn't care about cheerleaders; well, not the female ones, anyway. Didn't need them to get laid. When he'd scored in extra time and taken the team to the semi-finals (where they'd lost 4-2, but what the hell; it was their best year ever), he'd gotten a blowjob from Joel, one of the defenders, that'd left his legs weak as water and his brains leaking out of his freaking ears. For the rest of the year, he'd only had to walk into the changing room and get a whiff of the smell in there, liniment, sweat, and grass, to get half-hard, his balls tingling pleasantly. Good times...

No Joel this year, though; he'd graduated and Seth didn't even have an address for him. Just a happy memory.

He walked through the open doors, his mood mellowing because he was here now, and it'd only been two weeks, and this was going to be one hell of a year, it really was...

Classes were about to start. The lobby was emptying quickly as students who'd been checking notice boards, or talking to the office staff, headed off to lecture halls and labs, using the doors at the back of the lobby. The buildings that had been added to the original structure over the years had resulted in a hollow square, with the hall itself forming one of the sides and the remaining three tucked behind it, out of sight as you walked or drove up to the building. In bad weather, students exited the lobby to the right or left on the ground floor, or ran up the stairs and took the doors there that led to the first floor rooms, cursing the layout if their destination lay on the far side of the square. In good weather, they went out into the square of grass and flowerbeds and trees that took up the central space and cut across it. A Maine winter turned the square into narrow, icy paths between snow banks.

Seth worked his way through the thinning crowd, his goal the housing office, to get his room assignment. He'd put in a request to share with a buddy from the year before, but Andy had called him over the vacation and said that he'd taken a year off to go backpacking around Europe, which Seth, remembering Andy's piss-poor grades, took to mean he'd given up. Seth's own grades were reasonable. Not good, not bad, just good enough. That was something else his dad hadn't agreed with and Seth, wincing under the icy blast of his father's anger, and for once agreeing that the man had a point, had agreed to improve them.

He was at the foot of the staircase when he heard a thump, followed by a heartfelt, "Shit!" and glanced up to see someone falling down the stairs, arms windmilling wildly, pens and paper flying through the air as the contents of a dropped binder spilled out. The binder slid and bounced and landed at Seth's feet at about the same time as its owner, and the people around him burst out into laughter.

"What the fuck is wrong with you?" Seth demanded, glaring around at them. At six-three, with a deep voice and muscles to spare, he didn't have to do more than glare. The laughter died away as he squatted down and put his hand on a shoulder encased in a battered leather jacket, in a shade of brown that matched the long, curly hair hanging down over the face. Pretty hair, but it was a man who'd fallen; the body was sturdy and the jean-clad ass was most definitely male. "You okay, buddy?"

The head turned, the hair got clawed out of the way, and he stared into furious, green eyes and a snarl. There was a moment when the eyes warmed, a flash of something like recognition passing over the man's face, then it disappeared. "Get your fucking hands off me, you jerk."

"Hey!" Seth protested. "I didn't push you down the stairs, you know."

"He knows," a voice said. "He just doesn't care."

Seth twisted his head and peered up at a girl he vaguely remembered from his time volunteering at the Drama Club as a scenery painter the year before. "Hi, Molly."

She fluttered her hand at him, her mouth set in a sardonic smile, and stepped over the prone body and walked away.

Seth sat back on his heels and watched the man roll to his back, his face tight with pain. He didn't offer to help, but when the man leaned back against the base of the newel post and closed both eyes, he stood and walked up the stairs to where the man had begun his descent. There was a smear of something on the step; fruit, maybe. He took out a tissue and wiped it up. Yeah; peach. Overripe, juicy, and lethal. He walked back down, gathering pens and paper as he went.

"That was evidence," the man snapped. He was standing now and letting the post take his weight. About five-eleven, Seth estimated, and skinny as a bean pole, all sharp features and elbows, his hair the only soft part about him. "I could sue."

"Good luck with that." Seth picked up the binder and dropped what he was carrying into it, trying not to let it all slip from his grasp and hit the floor again. He zipped it closed and held it out.

"You want a fucking thank you?"

Seth gave it some consideration, more because he was enjoying the impatience radiating off the man than any desire for gratitude from him. "I'll pass. You wouldn't do a good job of making me think you meant it, anyway." He tapped his watch. "Got to go. See you."

Really green eyes, he thought as he walked away, the tissue tossed into the first trash can he passed. Had to be a new student; he was the kind of guy who stood out, for all the wrong reasons, and Seth was sure he'd never seen the man before.

Ellie Collins, a motherly looking woman who ran the housing office with a smile in place at all times and a complete lack of sympathy for anyone who upset or challenged her arrangements, greeted Seth with her smile dimmed in deference to his operation. He suffered through five minutes of a harrowing account of her uncle's appendectomy and then cleared his throat.

"I should probably go find my room, Mrs. Collins." He tried to look pathetic. "I drove myself here; set off at four this morning and I've got my first class in an hour…"

She clucked. "Well, of course you want to rest a little. Don't overdo it this first week."

"No, ma'am," he said obediently and mendaciously.

"We had so many new students… and since Mr. Blake left…" Her lips primmed disapprovingly. "*Such* a nuisance; I'd gotten you two a lovely corner room as well…"

"So where am I?" Seth gave her a hopeful smile. "Still in the corner room?"

"Oh, my, no." She passed him a sheaf of paper, a pen, and a key. "Third floor in Latham," she said briskly. "Room 322. You're sharing with a student who transferred here from the West Coast—*also* at the last minute—and I'm sure you'll get along just fine."

"Transferred? Why?" he blurted out.

Her smile became triangular, all points. "Well, you'll have to ask him that, won't you, Mr. Brookes?"

The room was about as far away from the stairs as it was possible to get, but, looking on the bright side, although it wasn't one of the larger, brighter corner rooms, it was near the end of a corridor and flanked by a storage closet on one side, which would cut down on the noise.

Seth dumped his backpack and one suitcase on the floor outside his room and gave his stomach a careful massage. Carrying his case had pulled the incision a little, but he didn't feel any pain. He'd finish emptying his car later; he just had time to move in and get to class. He fit his key to the lock and opened the door.

The room was dark, the curtains pulled and the blinds lowered. Seth blinked until his eyes had adjusted and dragged his luggage in, letting the door close behind him. He flicked on the light and a lump on one of the beds stirred.

"Hey, man…"

The sleepy protest was aggrieved, but not hostile. "Sorry." Seth hesitated, his hand on the light switch. "Look, I've got to see what I'm doing; you want me to draw the curtains?"

"I want you to let me sleep." The man yawned, still mostly buried under the sheets. "What time is it, anyway?"

"Nine-thirty. And I've got a class at ten and I need to—"

"What? Fuck!" The sheets were thrown back and Seth got an eyeful of just about everything there was to see.

Sadly, he'd seen it all before, as the guy had been on the soccer team, playing in goal, and they'd hooked up one night. "Nathan? What the hell are you doing in my room? Ma Collins said I was sharing with some guy who'd transferred in."

"Seth," Nathan said, his eyes focusing with what looked like an effort. He stood and swayed in place. "Head rush. Ow. Hey. Good to see you. Where the fuck are my clothes?"

"How the fuck would I know?"

"Good point, good point…" Nathan nodded vaguely and then glanced down. His face brightened. "Panic over; I'm standing on them."

"Tell me we're not sharing a room?" Seth begged. "I am *not* dragging your ass out of bed every morning."

"No, it's cool." Nathan was dressing with a rapidity Seth would've admired if he hadn't known it was a skill developed because Nathan was always late for everything. "In a way we kind of are, because I got the room you and Andy would've had, but you're here, not there, so maybe it's more like kind of not."

Seth sighed, Nathan's babbling having its usual effect on him, which was to make his head ache. "I've been sick, you know," he said plaintively. "Rushed to the hospital, sirens wailing, lights flashing."

"Awesome." Nathan was looking for his socks now, his forehead furrowed, his short, dark hair sticking up in spikes. Seth could see the socks hanging off a well-filled bookcase in the corner, but he didn't pass the information on.

"No, terminally embarrassing, but never mind that now. For the last time; why my room?"

Nathan leered at him cheerfully. "Not just your room,

buddy, and you weren't here. So me and Gabe took advantage of the fact."

"Gabe? That's who I'm sharing with?"

"Gabriel Rossiter," Nathan said, finally awake. "Wild man in bed, but something tells me last night was a once and only, you know? A man knows these things. And besides, he told me so just before he left. My socks. Where are my socks?" Seth pointed and Nathan beamed. "Cool. I'm not going to be late."

"You've got a ten o'clock class, too? We can walk over together and you can tell me what I've missed."

"Ten? No. Nine. Chem lab." Nathan shrugged philosophically. "Too late for that. No, I mean breakfast; they stop serving it at ten, and man, do I need coffee!"

"Yeah, me, too, but it'll have to wait." Seth gathered up what he'd need for his class and headed for the door. "Nathan? That was Gabe's bed you were sleeping in, right?"

Nathan smiled brightly. "Well, I was in with him, you know, doing the cuddle and grab thing, but around four, he said I was drooling on him and made me move to yours."

Clean sheets. First thing he'd do when he got back to his room. And when this Gabe showed up, he'd give him some pointers on how not to piss off your roomie, because it sounded like the guy needed them.

And he'd slept with Nathan. Shit, how awkward was that? Sharing a room was one thing, but a one-night stand, too?

By the end of the day, Seth was exhausted, his head throbbing from the auditory assault it'd been subjected to. People had been talking at him all day, asking him questions, the same questions, over and over; or, in the case of his professors, not dealing at all well with the fact that he'd missed two weeks of the semester, no matter how good his excuse.

He'd made notes, hit the library, begged and bartered for summaries of what he'd missed, and eaten junk food on the run, which had left him feeling hungry and queasy. He opened the door to his room, juggling a stack of books, intending to do nothing with them but leave them on the nearest flat surface.

This had to be the way zombies felt; mush for brains and wobbly legs. His bed called out to him with a siren song. He needed a shower, too, but that could wait. Bed. Silence. A total absence of thought; mindless, just like a good zombie should be. He'd change the sheets later. Nathan wasn't contagious. At least…

"What the fuck are *you* doing here?"

Seth eyed the stairway surfer with a complete lack of surprise. The way his luck had been going recently, who else *would* he be teamed up with? "I already know you're clumsy, hostile, and ungrateful; you want me to add 'stupid' to the list? Because it's pretty fucking obvious that I'm here because it's my room."

The way that the room was set up made it look as if it was split down the middle, each half containing a bed, night table, built-in closet, bookcase, and desk. By the end of his first week as a freshman, Seth and Andy's gear had mixed and matched until the room was a friendly clutter, and each room they'd shared in the years that followed had looked the same. The men Seth had brought back never complained; the women Andy dated sometimes had. This room was still neat, still tidy. Gabriel's half had books in abundance and there was a laptop on the desk, but there was nothing personal out, no photos, no scummed-over plates of food, no dirty laundry. Not a slob then. Good…

though Seth would take slob over neat-freak any day of the week.

He glanced to the right and saw a door leading to a tiny bathroom; no more than a toilet and a sink, but one of the much-anticipated perks of being a senior. Luxury. His freshman year, taking a leak had involved a five-minute trek; not an issue in the day, but a major pain in the ass in the middle of the night.

Seth dumped his books on his table and took the three steps needed to bring him close enough to his bed that all he had to do was fall forward—except that probably wasn't the best idea. A crash landing would hurt. He settled for crawling onto it with a moan of pleasure that sounded orgasmic even to him and sprawled out, facedown.

"Before you get comfortable…"

"Already know," he said, the pillow muffling his words. "Remind me to kick your ass later. My bed. Mine. You and your dates use your bed. Got it? Hey!"

The sudden, crushing weight on his back was accompanied by a hand around the back of his neck, pushing his face into the pillow, so that his next protest was inaudible. Psycho-roomie leaned down, his curls brushing Seth's cheek. "Don't you even think about bullying me, you jock asshole," Gabe hissed. "I'll cut off your fucking balls."

Okay, enough was enough. Ignoring the stab of pain from his stomach, Seth bucked up and dislodged Gabe, sending the man to the floor. He got to his hands and knees, staring down at his assailant, and then felt nausea rip through him. Luckily, the rooms also came equipped with plastic wastepaper bins, and his was close enough that he managed to grab it before throwing up the burger and fries he'd had for lunch, kneeling on the floor, his body convulsing.

"That is so gross," Gabe muttered under his breath,

but he didn't renew his attack, which was something.

Seth spat to clear his mouth and tried not to breathe in because he had puke in his nose—Gabe was right; it *was* gross—and his stomach was still restless.

"You done?"

"For now," he said, his voice a scratchy husk.

The bin was taken from him and he looked up, startled. Gabe passed him a bottle of water, the top already twisted off, and a handful of tissues. "Clean up."

"Need the bucket to spit in," Seth said.

Gabe sighed and put it down again. "Hurry up. It stinks."

Seth rinsed and spat, longing for a toothbrush, and blew his nose. "Thanks," he said.

"Just getting the mess dealt with," Gabe told him. "I have to sleep in here, too. I'll take care of this; you open a freaking window or something." He snatched the soggy tissues from Seth's hand and disappeared into the bathroom.

Seth staggered to the window, and, once it was open, leaned out, gulping early fall air; warm, but with a cool breeze stirring it, like lukewarm water with ice floating in it. By the time Gabe came back into the room, he felt better. Hollow. Pissed. But better. The mirror on the wall didn't agree; under the thick mop of fair hair that never looked tidy, his face was washed-out and pasty, his gray eyes bloodshot. He'd looked better after a weekend of partying, which didn't seem fair.

"So, what's your deal?" Gabriel set the bin, clean and smelling faintly of disinfectant, down by Seth's desk, and then crossed the invisible line to his own side of the room where he sat on his bed, cat-green eyes narrowed suspiciously. "Flu bug? Food poisoning? Drugs?"

"Or let's go for option four," Seth said. "I just had my appendix out and some asshole used me for a trampoline."

For the first time in their short acquaintance, Gabe looked at him as if he was human, not one step below belly button fluff. "I didn't know that. They told me you were coming back late and I just assumed you were goofing off."

"Do you always assume the worst?" Seth demanded. "Because, no, I wasn't. My appendix burst and there were complications, which I prefer not to talk about, because if you think the puke was gross—"

"Blood isn't gross," Gabe said. "It's beautiful. Keeps you alive, carries oxygen... it's very neat. Puke, well, that just reeks."

"This might be the part where you apologize," Seth said. "Start with the bit where you let Nathan sleep in my bed."

"Sorry, Goldilocks." Gabe looked anything but guilty. "If it helps, I changed it when I got back."

Seth turned his head and realized that the bed Nathan had left in a tangled mess was neatly made, disarranged only slightly by their scuffle. He backtracked to the moment when he'd buried his face in the pillow, and, yeah, it'd smelled of nothing more than laundry detergent.

"Oh." That seemed inadequate, but on the other hand, he wasn't going to fall all over the guy for doing the right thing. "Cancel that part of the groveling, then."

Gabe's expression hardened. "I don't grovel and I don't apologize. If it bothers you that much that a gay slept in your bed, go boil the mattress in bleach."

Seth answered that by going to lie on the bed again, this time keeping an eye on Gabe. Fool me once...

"For your information," he said, choosing his words carefully, "you fucking Nathan *is* a problem, but it's not because you're both guys."

"No?" The scorn in the single, disbelieving word was

echoed in the curl of Gabe's mouth. "So what is it?"

"Clumsy, hostile, ungrateful, violent, and you have terrible taste in men…" Seth grimaced. "If you ever quote me on this, I'll deny it, because I don't want his feelings to get hurt, but he's a selfish prick when it comes to sex. Took me one night to find that out when he came and fell asleep right after, leaving me… not happy."

Gabriel smiled, thin and sharp. "You, too?"

"Yep." Seth closed his eyes as the tension in the room slipped down a notch. "I can point you at some better prospects if you like, and I'll make myself scarce for the night if you do the same for me, as long as it's not too often. I need to study this semester. Didn't do too much of that last year."

"I didn't think jocks bothered with anything as geeky as cracking open a book."

"You're just determined to dig that hole you're in so deep you can't see sunlight, aren't you?" Seth could feel sleep creeping up on him and tapping his shoulder, but he ignored it. If he closed his eyes, he'd crash, and he had too much to do. "I play soccer, sure, but it's what I do for fun; I'm studying math, and one reason I was slacking off was because it was too easy."

There was a short silence. Most people would have offered up some personal information in return, but Seth had already given up on fitting Gabe into the hole labeled 'normal.'

"It's four," Gabe said eventually, and walked over to boot up his laptop.

"What is?" God, he could fall asleep right now, he could just… fall…

"Two plus two." Gabriel turned his head and gave Seth a smile, all teeth. "I like to help struggling jocks and I bet that one was giving you a hard time, huh? It's my mission in life. Or maybe it's just a hobby, who knows?"

"Or maybe it's because you're a jerk," Seth said with a yawn. "I'm going to ask to be reassigned rooms tomorrow by the way. It's nothing personal; I just can't stand you."

"Me?" There was something that sounded like genuine surprise in Gabe's voice. "What the fuck did I do?"

Seth rolled over and let the pillow muffle his despairing moan. There was a waiting pause as if Gabe expected an answer, but he fell asleep before he could frame one that even verged on tactful.

Gabriel didn't look up from his laptop as Seth walked into their room the next day, but his mouth curved in a knowing smile. "No room at the inn, Mary?"

"If you mean, am I about to start packing, then no." Seth took a deep breath. "Okay. We're stuck with each other, but there's no need for this to be a problem. Let's just start over. Hi. I'm Seth Brookes."

"You have got to be fucking kidding me." Gabriel rolled his eyes. "Whatever. I'm Gabriel Rossiter, I'm busy, if you don't bother me I won't kick your ass, and are we done now? Because this paper's due on Friday and today, if it hadn't escaped your notice, is Thursday."

Just ignore him, Seth told himself silently. Control the urge to punch him and pretend he's being reasonably civil. And look up Nathan sometime soon, because how come he at least got the guy to talk to him? What's he got that I haven't?

He made an effort and kept his voice pleasant and casual. "What are you studying?"

"'B' is for 'butt out', 'u' is for 'I warned you', 's' is for—"

"Forget it." Seth said, interrupting Gabriel before he got to the 'y'. He put his can of root beer on his desk—he didn't like it that much, but everyone he knew loathed it, so no one ever tried to steal his stash—and booted up his own laptop.

He was busy, too.

The night before, Seth had crashed, waking once around three to stagger, half-asleep, to the toilet. Gabriel's presence hadn't really registered. Tonight was different. He got back from a late shower with a towel around his hips; risky, as there was always the chance that some bright spark might grab it and run off. That had happened to Seth once the year before, leaving him no other option but a dignified saunter through a gauntlet of cat-calls and whistles, but getting dressed to walk a few yards was just way too much effort.

He closed the door behind him and caught Gabe in the act of pulling a t-shirt off over his head, blindfolded by the fabric for just long enough for Seth to see the scar slashed across pale skin that clearly hadn't see the sun all summer.

Seth held back the sound that rose to his lips, knowing that shock and pity were the last things Gabe would want. The scar was nasty, running across ribs and chest, ending a finger's width away from Gabe's right nipple. The cut—from a knife?—had healed, but the new skin was still pink around it. It wasn't more than a few months old.

Gabe froze, then yanked the t-shirt off and stared at Seth, daring him to comment. There was another t-shirt on the bed, and Seth had to wonder if Gabe would have spent the whole year trying to keep his scar hidden in a series of quick changes. Except… he would have stripped off for Nathan when they had sex, wouldn't he? There it was again; that sense that for some reason Seth was being singled out for special—read worse—treatment, and why? It made no fucking sense at all.

He couldn't stop staring, not at the scar, not now. In nothing but a pair of black boxer briefs, Gabe looked good, the angles and edges of his body, accentuated by his clothes, now revealed as muscle and sleek lines. His chest was smooth, his hipbones jutting out and framing a flat stomach bisected by a thin line of hair. Seth felt his cock respond to the view with an eagerness that left him breathless. Fuck. Too long since—too long.

"What?" Gabe said, his voice stretched taut and singing, like a plucked wire.

"You're hot," Seth said frankly. "That's all."

"Freak," Gabe said after a pause, but there was something in his voice that hadn't been there before; uncertainty, curiosity? "Get off on scars, do you?"

Seth shrugged. "That wasn't what I was looking at." He let his gaze dip down. "Hot night, too," he said with a smile. "I'm sleeping bare. If you want to give me pleasant dreams, you could, too."

"Just because I'm gay, doesn't mean I'll roll over for you. Snap your fingers at me and I'll snap them for real." The snarl was back, as were the threats.

"You went for Nathan, so I'm guessing your standards aren't that high," Seth said, "but mine are, and you don't meet them. Eye candy; sure, you're all of that, but I like to be on speaking terms with my dates."

"We're speaking now."

"Barely." Seth let his towel drop and stood for a second, allowing Gabe to look his fill. If the guy needed to know his scar didn't stop someone finding him hot—and a hard-on was a simple way of getting the message across—then he didn't mind giving him that reassurance. "But it's a start."

He nodded a goodnight and slid into bed, his back to Gabe. The room remained lit by the lamp beside Gabe's bed for a moment longer, and then it was clicked off with a sharp finality.

Seth was half-asleep when Gabe spoke, making him jerk awake again, his heart pounding.

"It was a knife."

"What? Oh… yeah, I figured that myself." He winced. His appendectomy scar was short and neat and he'd been out of it when it happened, and it had *still* fucking hurt like hell when he came around.

"But you didn't ask." Gabe shifted, his bed creaking. "Guess you get points for that."

Enough points to earn the answer to a question he hadn't needed to ask. So how many were left? One point? Two?

"Nathan," Seth said, needing to know that at least. "Did *he* ask?"

Gabe chuckled, sounding dryly amused by something not at all funny, a scrape over raw skin. "Oh, yeah. And he thought it was 'way fucking cool'." The last words were a bitterly accurate mimicry of Nathan's breathless voice.

That explained why Nathan—asshole—hadn't even earned an 'I'll call you,' but not why Gabe had gone for him in the first place. Somehow, Seth didn't think his credit was good enough to make that question safe to ask.

He flipped his pillow over, and put his face against the cool cotton. "Well, good —"

"Shut the fuck up," Gabe said, with less heat to the words than usual but plenty of snap. "I'm trying to sleep here."

Seth rolled his eyes and then closed them. Situation normal…

By the end of the month, they'd achieved a state of partial truce; Gabe still made hedgehogs look cuddly, his face closing down when Seth ventured even an innocuous question, but he'd borrowed Seth's pencil sharpener one night with a grunt of thanks and nodded to Gabe twice in the hallway as they passed each other.

Seth, slipping back into college life and catching up without too much difficulty in class and socially, didn't really care. He was guaranteed a place on the soccer team once Coach Brennan deemed him fit enough, and until then he was training as hard as he could and joining in the practice games as a sub. Gabe eyed him sometimes when he came in, flushed with exertion, but though Seth would've liked to have recounted the penalty he'd scored, or the truly awful refereeing call that had let the opposing team get a free kick, he kept quiet and so did Gabe.

Gabe, new though he was, seemed to have made an impression on the campus. He was studying English, a nugget of information Seth had been grudgingly given after Gabe had decided it was harmless enough, and had joined the Drama Club with credentials that led to him being chosen as Assistant Director for the production of King Lear they were staging. Seth couldn't wrap his head around Gabe assisting anyone, but from all accounts, Gabe was helpful, insightful, and hadn't made anyone cry yet, although Molly had told Seth it'd been close one night with the girl playing Cordelia.

"He told her to lose the gum and learn her lines, right in front of everyone, and she blew this bubble, looking bored and he reached out and popped it with his finger, and it went all over her face, and then *she*—"

"Molly, I *know* what an asshole he is, okay?"

"No, he was right, and she knew it. I've never seen Dian apologize to anyone, but once she got the gum out of her hair, she was sweet as sugar."

"Hmm."

Molly giggled. "I know. I told Gabe to watch his back, but he just grinned. I like him. I wasn't sure at first, but he's really funny once you get to know him, and he knows his stuff."

No, Seth didn't care that Gabe wasn't warming up to him, as long as Gabe was reasonably polite—and he really didn't care that there was no chance of getting to touch the body he saw half-naked most days. Gabe might be hot—and he was, no question about it—but fucking your roommate wasn't really a good idea; too much potential for awkwardness if they split up, and someone on the faculty would probably find out, in that mysterious way they had of tapping into gossip, and the requested transfer might suddenly become possible.

This was safer. Seth was dutifully studying and training, but he knew what all work and no play did and he was taking care of the danger of becoming dull with a helping hand from one of his teammates. Chris, all blue eyes and blond hair, with a wicked gleam in his eyes, didn't fuck, and his public dates were all female, but he was available and willing for a blowjob or two. Chris was about Seth's size, a solid chunk of muscle to rub off on, both of them sweaty and grinning, hands all over the place, mouths meeting and sliding, messy, hungry kisses, stopping only when they needed to breathe, harsh gasps echoing around the empty changing room as they drove each other on.

Chris was fun. Uncomplicated, undemanding fun. Seth didn't have anything in common with him beyond a liking for the same beer and the shared belief that Manchester United was over-rated, but who cared?

Finding Chris on his knees in the showers one night, that smiling mouth busy sucking Gabe's brains out of his cock, was something he *did* care about, though.

Seth had left the changing rooms early, after giving

Chris' bare ass a single, regretful look. He had a paper due and no time to hang around. Discovering that he'd left his iPod in his locker had him groaning. He liked to wear it when he was running laps before the game, and losing it to an opportunistic thief would be a pain. The changing rooms for the soccer field—and the field itself—were far enough away from the main buildings that no one but the soccer team ever used them, but it was still a risk he didn't want to take. He jogged back, resenting each wasted moment. Leaves crunched and swirled around him; fall was coming early this year. When winter arrived, they'd have to move their games inside to the indoor pitch. Hard to kick a ball through six inches of snow.

There was a light on in the showers and the rush of water was loud enough that it took Seth a moment to realize that there was a conversation going on. He retrieved his iPod, glanced around the changing room, and frowned. Chris' clothes were still there, but Chris had already showered once, and the other heap of clothing wasn't a sweaty soccer kit, but a pair of jeans and a scarlet shirt that looked pretty fucking familiar since he'd watched Gabe button it slowly that morning, Gabe's attention on the book he was reading, laid flat on the desk in front of him, his fingers lingering over the task.

Gabe and Chris? What the *fuck*? Seth walked to the archway leading into the showers and paused, mostly hidden in the shadows as the changing room was lit only by the light spilling out from the shower room. Gabe was leaning back against a wall and Chris was on his knees, the spray striking his back and cascading off the tanned, muscular skin.

Gabe's eyes were open, staring ahead, a fixed, unhappy look in them, but his hands were stroking Chris' hair, urging him on, and when Chris paused for breath and took his mouth away, Seth got a flash of Gabe's cock.

Hard. Part of Gabe was getting off on this, anyway. And why not? Chris was good at it. It was strange watching and knowing just what Chris was going to do next… yeah, there was that bob of the head as Chris swirled his tongue around and dived back in; there went Chris' hand, sliding between Gabe's legs to cup and massage those balls.

And there went Gabe, his eyes finally closed, his face contorted with painful pleasure.

Seth could have hung around to watch Chris rock back on his heels and bring himself off with a few strong, forceful jerks, but what was the point? He'd seen it all before.

He left, moving quietly, not looking back, his thoughts circling, not around Chris, but Gabe.

"Seth! Hey, wait up!"

Seth turned and squinted against the sun flooding the quad. Chris' hair blazed brightly in its light, an undeserved halo.

"Hi," he said as Chris caught up to him. He tried not to make it sound accusing. It wasn't as if they were exclusive in any way, and he'd spent the last two days reminding himself of that.

"Can we talk?" Chris said abruptly.

Seth thought about making a witty, snappy comment, but really, it was just too much effort. "Sure," he said with a sigh and walked with Chris to a stone bench set against a wall, out of the sun and therefore empty.

The seat was cold, but there was something fitting about his butt being as numb as the rest of him. He'd been in a weird space the last few days and he couldn't figure out why. Seth wasn't the stereotypical math geek who tried to reduce people to equations; numbers and the complex way they played together fascinated him, but he could still handle the abstract confusion of people and emotions. Usually.

"Before you say anything, I saw you and Gabe the other night." He wanted to confess that up front. Chris stammering through a confession of his own wouldn't be fun for either of them. "I went back for my iPod, and, well…"

"You did?" Chris looked stunned. "You were *there*?"

"I didn't hang around getting off on it," Seth snapped. "I got the hell out."

"No, of course, I mean—I didn't mean—I— Fuck." Chris rubbed his hands through his hair. "He's driving me fucking crazy," he muttered, the words directed at himself.

"Gabe?"

"Yeah." Chris leaned back. "He came onto me. Big time. Wanted to meet me that night. You know what for. And I said yes, because, well, I was curious, you know? He's interesting. Different."

"He's a fucked-up son of a bitch," Seth said and regretted it as soon as he'd said it because Chris looked disappointed and just a little wary. "Chris, I'm not getting possessive on your ass. You and me, we're just, well, it's casual, right? Fun, but that's it."

Chris nodded. "That's how I saw it." He grimaced. "I fucked that up, huh?"

"It's made it kind of complicated," Seth said truthfully.

"Yeah… I guess it's a lot to get over, seeing us like that."

"I'm not traumatized for life, if that's what you mean." Seth grinned. "Anyone else, and I might have joined you."

"Huh?" Chris gave him a bewildered look. "I don't

get it. If it wasn't seeing us that freaked you, what's the problem?"

"Uh... you got off with my *roommate*?" It seemed pretty damn obvious to Seth. "And the next time I blew you, I can guarantee that's what I'd be thinking about."

"Why?" Chris could be blunt at times. "You don't even like him." Enlightenment dawned. "Oh, I get it. That's why you're pissed; because I was with someone you can't stand?"

"Who said I couldn't stand him?" Seth felt lost in a maze and he knew damn well who'd planted it. "Chris, the guy's hated me since we met, but it's not mutual, and I don't have a clue why. If he'd give me a chance—but he doesn't even talk to me. Our room at night makes a cemetery look like party central; you have no idea of how awkward it is. And now... awkward just got worse. I haven't said anything to him, but, shit..."

Chris gave him a helpless look. "Really sorry, Seth. And if I'd known he was just interested in one time, I wouldn't have gone for it. Not if it meant pissing you off." He scrunched up his face. "Guess he's just out to get some notches on his belt, huh?"

"He ditched Nathan after one night, too," Seth said, "so, yeah, maybe... except..."

"Nathan?" Chris rolled his eyes and then winked at Seth. "Well, I don't blame him for that, but me, I'm a keeper, right?"

Seth gave Chris' leg an affectionate pat. "Yeah, you are. Gabe's a jerk. But..."

"What?"

"If he's going for numbers, who else has there been beside you and Nathan? You know word would've gotten out if he'd been doing the rounds."

"True." Chris thought it over and then shrugged. "Beats me." He glanced at his watch. "Shit, I'm late for a tutorial. See you later?"

"Sure." Seth smiled at Chris' back as the man left in a hurry, a book bag bumping against his back. It wasn't Chris he was mad at; never had been. It was Gabe. Gabe had gone after something of Seth's and hadn't cared if he'd ruined it. And even that didn't make Seth as angry as he should have been. More concerned, really, and puzzled.

And wasn't that a scary thought?

"Why did you go after Chris?" Attack first; deal with the fallout later.

Gabe glanced up, frowning. He'd been scribbling notes on a script, three books scattered around him on the bed. It was a shame, really; he'd been in a good mood, for some reason, and Seth had gotten what might have passed for a grin when he came in.

"Chris?"

Oh, now that was too fucking much. "Guy who blew you in the changing rooms on Monday. Or doesn't that narrow it down enough?"

"Bitch," Gabe said pleasantly. "I know who he was—and yes, I remember his name—I just didn't know that you... Oh, he told you, did he?"

"No. He knows when to keep his mouth shut as well as what to do with it." Seth swung around in his chair to face Gabe. "I went back to get something from my locker and saw you. Any more of my exes you want to fuck with? I could give you a list, if it'd help."

"I didn't know Nathan was an ex of yours," Gabe said, carefully enough that Seth saw the ambiguity. "How the fuck could I?"

"But you knew Chris and I were—" Seth couldn't think of a good word to describe his relationship with

Chris. "That we…"

"Did what I did on Monday? Yeah, I knew." Green eyes met his with a studied indifference. "I borrowed him for fifteen minutes; you're always telling me I can help myself to your stuff if I put it back where I found it."

"I meant my *things*," Seth said. "Chris isn't a fucking calculator or a t-shirt."

There was a pause and then Gabe asked, "Did you really tell him he was out of luck now? Just because of one lousy blowjob?"

"Looked like a good one from where I was standing."

"Take pictures, did you?"

Seth shook his head. "This isn't getting us anywhere. I want to know why you did it. You could've gone with any one of a dozen guys if you wanted an itch scratched and you know it. Why Chris?"

For the first time in the conversation, Gabe's gaze wavered, but a moment later he smiled, a thin sneer of a smile, sour as a slice of lemon. "To annoy you. Guess it worked, huh?"

"Yeah, it did," Seth told him. "But not for the reason you think. Chris is a friend and you used him. I don't think it bothers him all that much that you weren't interested in a repeat performance, but now he knows—"

"That he can't have you again, he's regretting it," Gabe put in. "My, my… you must have hidden depths."

"Go to hell," Seth said, through the beat of blood in his ears. "And stay the fuck away from me and my friends, got that?"

"Or what?" Gabe said and arched his eyebrows expectantly. "Go on; tell me. I really want to know how imaginative you can get when it comes to threats."

"Why don't you like me?" It slipped out before he could stop it, and it should have sounded pathetic, a lonely kid on a playground trying to make friends, but even as he braced himself, flinching, Seth realized that it'd come out just as he'd meant it; as a question.

Like most of the ones he'd asked Gabe over the weeks they'd known each other, it didn't get an answer. "Give me one good reason why I should." Gabe curled his lip. "God, get over yourself, okay?"

Seth eyed him. No good reason, then, or he was sure Gabe would have been specific, in scathing, biting detail. Fine. He was just mad enough now that he was prepared to cross the line. There was something going on here, and he wanted to know what.

Wanted it as much as he wanted Gabe. His initial, unthinking attraction to the guy's body had become a baffled, aching frustration. He didn't like Gabe much, but the man was a mystery and a challenge and Seth went for those, always had. It was why he liked math; so many puzzles to solve, with tidy solutions. Gabe wasn't tidy; he was a seething, tangled mess, but that was okay, too.

He wanted to touch Gabe, put his hands on smooth skin and scarred, feel the heat leap off it and into him, watch that sulky, angry mouth soften enough to be kissed—or kiss it anyway and take whatever pain it brought him, because it would be worth it.

A month of silence and he'd learned to read Gabe, a slow, laborious acquiring of knowledge that had taught him patience. He hadn't realized he was doing it until one day when he'd looked over at Gabe, sipping a coffee and listening to music turned up so loud that Seth could hear it faintly through the ear buds pushed into Gabe's ears. He'd looked, identified the band as The Headstones, and thought absently that Gabe was going to jerk off tonight, late, when Gabe thought he was the only one awake. A stealthy, quick session, usually punctuated by a single, muffled grunt that always brought Seth's hand to his mouth to be bitten hard as the best way to stave off a climax he couldn't allow himself, because he knew he couldn't be that quiet. He was getting used to falling asleep with his dick a solid, throbbing weight between his legs. Getting used to it, and, sometimes, getting off on it. The next morning, when Gabe left to piss and brush his teeth, or whatever he did in the bathroom, the climax that came, hours-delayed, left him shaking, his body loose and trembling.

He'd looked at Gabe and known that about the man, and something had changed for him, because if he could be that aware of Gabe, it seemed as if it had to go both ways. Gabe had looked back at him, a long, measuring stare that Seth had met with heat burning his face, his body ready for sex that wasn't going to happen.

"I don't hate you," Gabe said unexpectedly, making Seth realize that he'd been sitting there thinking when Gabe had probably been expecting him to continue the discussion. "I just don't want to get to know you any better."

Seth opened his mouth and closed it again. Why bother asking why? "Fine by me."

Gabe nodded. "Good." He went back to drinking coffee and Seth went back to thinking.

Seth wasn't sure where the idea of snooping came from; it wasn't his style to be sneaky or pushy. But then, he'd never had to be. Gabe was the first person he'd met who'd been metaphorically encased in glass; transparent, sure, but frustratingly hard to touch. Seth felt as if his fingernails were bleeding from scrabbling fruitlessly to get through and he'd had enough.

The answers had to lie in Gabe's past; Seth knew they'd

never met before the encounter in the lobby, and Gabe's antipathy had kicked in as soon as they had, which just wasn't reasonable. Seth waited for Gabe to leave for class and watched him through the window to make sure that he had. From his vantage point, Gabe was a small, lonely figure, but before he'd crossed the grass to the main building, he'd been hailed by two or three people and a girl had joined him, long, red hair hanging down her back in a thick braid, her head close to Gabe's.

Seth turned away. He wasn't going to go through Gabe's private stuff; that was a line he wasn't ready to cross yet, but he just needed a starting point, and that was the name of Gabe's previous college. He squatted down beside Gabe's bookcase—books on a shelf weren't private—and went through the textbooks until he found one with a sales slip in it from a campus bookstore near Sacramento.

Armed with that, he booted up his laptop and went to work. It didn't take long to call up a handful of local newspaper articles from April involving a junior, four seniors, and a knife.

He watched the text waver and blinked it clear and steady again. It had been passed off as hazing or an April Fool joke gone wrong, depending on which paper you read. Only one used the word 'attack,' and when he thought of that vicious slash across Gabe's chest, he couldn't really get behind the idea of it being harmless fun.

The knife had been used to cut up meat for a cookout on the shores of Folsom Lake. Somehow, it had gotten from there to a clearing, where Gabe had been blindfolded and tied to a tree. The knife had been used to cut his clothes off him, with no reason given for why that had seemed like a good idea, but he'd struggled and the knife had slipped. The seniors had been high; Gabe had been drunk... No charges had been pressed. The police had shrugged, the faculty closed ranks, and Gabriel Rossiter had silently slipped away, to surface on the other side of the country.

Which explained part of it, but not all. Seth clicked on one last link and flinched. This article, unlike the others, had photographs; a smiling Gabe in front of a theater poster for a production of—shit—King Lear, his name on it as director, and four headshots of the seniors.

Seth studied the four men. None of them looked like him, so it couldn't be that... and they didn't look like Nathan or Chris, either, which was just as well. The thought of Gabe fucking men who reminded him of the ones who'd hurt him was enough to make Seth feel sick to his stomach.

He closed down his laptop. He knew why Gabe had transferred and where his scar was from, but he still didn't have a fucking clue why Gabe didn't like him.

Maybe Gabe just didn't like him in a Doctor Fell kind of way. Just one of those things. Sometimes two people just didn't click. Seth had met someone like that; hot, funny, perfect ass... and he'd gotten closer and the guy just hadn't smelled right. Not the kind of smell a shower and soap took care of; it was more something missing than something there that shouldn't have been.

Gabe smelled good enough to eat and, God, Seth wanted a taste. He sat on his bed and got hot just thinking of the places on Gabe that he wanted to put his tongue. Sliding it into the waiting warmth of Gabe's mouth would be a good place to start. He had a feeling that once he started kissing Gabe, it'd be a while before he wanted to stop, but his tongue would fit in a lot of other nook and crannies, too. He'd never rimmed anyone; the idea had its appeal, but when it came down to doing it, it seemed on the gross side. He wanted to rim Gabe. Wanted to pin

Gabe down, spread those legs wide, put his hands on that tightly muscled ass and spread it as wide as Gabe's legs and fuck that hole with his tongue and fingers until Gabe was whimpering, howling, open and ready, and *fuck*, he was going to be late for class, because he couldn't go anywhere until he'd taken care of the hard-on doing its best to break his zipper.

He arrived at the lecture out of breath but just in time. It hadn't taken long to come. He'd just licked his lips, his hand busy, and imagined he could taste Gabe. Bam. Cleaning up had taken longer; he'd shot hard enough that the optimistic handful of Kleenex he'd had ready just didn't stand a chance.

It'd been messy, just like everything connected with Gabe was.

"They have stalking laws in this state, you know."

Seth smiled without turning and drew his brush over stretched canvas. "I won't report you, don't worry."

"Seriously." Gabe sounded annoyed, which was normal, but there was some curiosity in there, too, which was gratifying. "What the fuck are you doing here?"

"Painting scenery," Seth told him and caught a drip of black paint before it could roll down onto not quite dry bushes and grass at the bottom of the flat. "I did it last year, too. See that flat over there? The drawing room scene? That was me."

Gabe walked over to it and studied it in silence for a while. Seth continued to paint. Molly wouldn't yell at him if he didn't finish this; she was too aware of how scarce good volunteers were, but he'd said he'd have it done and he liked to keep his word. Around them, the theater hummed with activity; people practicing lines; the thuds and yells of a sword fight… a productive bustle. Backstage was quieter. Seth took a deep breath, inhaled dust and paint fumes and sneezed.

"Bless you," Gabe said absently. "You know, this isn't bad."

"Thank you kindly," Seth said lightly, refusing to let his pleasure at the compliment show in his voice. If he'd known this was all it would take to get Gabe talking, he'd have signed up with Molly earlier.

"For a thumb-fingered four-year-old." The well-timed cruelty of the follow-up was intensified by a scornful snicker.

Seth lost it then. Completely, utterly, lost it. The brush got jammed back into the tin of paint, where it sank deep enough to coat a third of the handle, and he stalked over to Gabe, filled with a frustration so complete that it left no room for indecision or doubt.

Seth put his hands on Gabe and turned him roughly, then jerked him in close, fingers clamped around handfuls of Gabe's shirt, the fabric soft and thin, crumpling without resistance. "You—" Words. He needed words to tell Gabe what a little shit he was, but they wouldn't come out of his mouth. He stared down at Gabe's startled face, where green eyes were dark, lips parted as if Gabe was about to speak—but there was nothing that Gabe could say that he wanted to hear.

He could taste Gabe's breath, apple-spiced because Jan had brought in hot cider for everyone; could feel the air disturbed between them as they exhaled and drew breath back into their lungs in harsh, rough gasps, as if they'd been running.

There was a flush rising to the surface of Gabe's cheeks and he was waiting—waiting—

"You want me." Seth said it aloud, needing to hear it spoken, even if it came out incredulous, bewildered.

"God, you do—"

Gabe's chin had tilted up, just enough to make a kiss easier, an inch of invitation, but Seth wasn't going to take what was on offer, not here. Not after weeks of being ignored. The refusal must have shown, because Gabe's face hardened and he brought his hands up and out, a sharp movement that broke Seth's grip on him.

"Dream on."

Seth shook his head. Gabe hadn't stepped back; that meant more than whatever he said. "No. You do. You always have. I just don't know why you didn't—but you're going to tell me." He leaned in and put his mouth so close to Gabe's that anyone looking at them would have thought they were kissing, shaping his words carefully. "You're going to tell me you're fucking sorry, too."

Gabe stepped back and licked his lips slowly, tasting, before rubbing at them gently with his fingers as if he'd been kissed, as if he'd been touched by more than breath and words.

"I've never lied to you; I don't plan on starting."

"Well, fuck that, too." Seth felt his mouth tighten. "The shit you've pulled and you're not sorry?"

A gleam of amusement glinted in Gabe's eyes. "You're too easy."

"Yeah, I bet it's been fun, but it ends now, okay?" Seth turned his head and sighed. "I'm going to be another hour here, but after that—"

"You can buy me a drink," Gabe said. "The Dog's Dinner over on Grant?"

Seth considered that. It was cheap, it had booths, and mid-week it wasn't likely to be crowded, so they could talk without getting interrupted. "Sure. And you can buy me a plate of wings."

"Their suicide wings are good," Gabe said, with a hint of challenge in his voice

"Bring it on, babe." Who needed taste buds?

He half-expected this to be an elaborate version of most of Gabe's putdowns, his momentary euphoria washed away with the paint as he cleaned the brush and his hands, but after he'd finished, Gabe was waiting for him, slumped back in a seat and studying the stage with a thoughtful frown.

"Goneril keeps standing too far over to the left in one scene so that she can stare at Albany. Less getting into character as his oh-so-loving wife and more wanting to get into his pants after rehearsal. It's driving me fucking crazy."

"Was that the start of a beautiful conversation?"

Gabe stared up at him without moving. "I probably deserve it, but can you stop being an asshole? Please?"

That word, in Gabe's mouth, did things to Seth. It had featured in too many of his fantasies not to trigger a flash of arousal. "Okay. For tonight at least, we'll just start over." He patted his stomach. "Beer and wings? We can walk and build up an appetite."

Gabe snorted. "Are you kidding? I'm hungry enough that I'll be nibbling on you by the time we get off campus." His eyes widened as if he'd spoken without realizing how it would sound, and Seth let him see that it'd registered. Gabe, flustered for the first time since they'd met, kept talking, the words tumbling out. "But sure, we can walk. I wouldn't want you to get pulled over, and this way you won't have to worry—"

"Hey." Seth shook his head. "Not worrying, because I'm not going to have that much to drink—got a lecture at eight in the morning—but it's a nice night to walk."

They left the theater in silence, which was normal, but

a silence that lacked the tension Seth had gotten used to. He didn't miss it. Not that the atmosphere between them could be described as relaxed, because it wasn't, but it wasn't unfriendly.

By the time they reached the road leading to town, they were exchanging glances and sneaking peeks at each other. Seth let Gabe win this round and broke the silence by laughing. "Okay, I can't keep this up. Talk to me."

Gabe's mouth quirked up in a small grin. "Sure. What about?"

Seth's smile faded. "I don't know. I'm so used to *not* talking to you that I don't know where to start."

"Tell me why you play football."

"Soccer."

"Football," Gabe said firmly and flashed him a teasing look. "My grandfather was English and he brought me up properly."

"Do you play?" Seth asked and didn't trouble to hide his eagerness. "The team's full, but we always need people to practice with who know what they're doing."

Gabe shrugged. "Haven't kicked a ball in anger for a while, but, yeah, I know how to play." He walked on a few paces and toed a soda can that had been tossed at a trash can by someone who couldn't aim. It flew up in the air and Gabe kicked it in the direction of the trash, where it struck the side of the can and landed back on the ground. Gabe shrugged again. "Like I said; it's been a while." He bent to pick up the can and deposited it neatly in the trash.

"Wednesday night at six?"

"Maybe," Gabe said with a finality that closed the topic as they continued to walk toward the gate. He cleared his throat, as if regretting his abruptness. "So, do you have a team that you support?"

"Liverpool," Seth said promptly. "You're not the only

one with English ancestors."

"Huh." Gabe nodded and started to say something, but Seth interrupted him.

"Why now? All these weeks... why tonight?"

Gabe stared ahead. "There didn't seem much point to continuing to keep you at arm's length. You'd found out how I feel about you." He turned his head. "And I'm wondering what else you know about me."

"We should be having this discussion at the bar," Seth said, and knew they weren't going to be able to postpone it for the twenty minutes it would take to get there. "Shit, don't get in a fight with me and walk away? Please? I'm *really* hungry."

"You can go and eat wings without me."

"They wouldn't taste the same. I'd chicken out—"

"Was that a pun?"

"Maybe. I'd chicken out and go for mild or something wimpy like that."

Gabe rolled his eyes. "So it's my duty to force you to go for the hot and spicy?"

"Absolutely," Seth said firmly.

They reached the gate, where ivy, turning a rich, dull red, wound around huge stone pillars and the boundary wall. The wall was crumbling in places, but it was deemed historic and picturesque for some reason, and the ivy was allowed to remain.

"Are you going to tell me?"

Seth sighed. "I know how you got that scar," he admitted. "It wasn't hard to look it up online. I'm sorry. Believe me, I wasn't being nosy; I just thought it might help me figure out what was going on."

"And did it?" Gabe's voice was tight with an emotion that Seth hoped wasn't anger. He was so tired of Gabe being angry with him for nothing; this wasn't nothing, but he still didn't want to break the fragile peace between them.

"Not really."

"That's because you don't know what really happened." Gabe shrugged. "I lied. They lied. There was a whole lot of lying going on."

Seth winced away from the desolation he saw in the one glance sideways that he allowed himself. "You don't have to talk about it, you know. I meant it when I said I didn't want to poke and pry."

"But you want to know why I've acted the way I have." It was a flat statement and Seth didn't have time to reply before Gabe continued. "So you're going to need to know, and I'm not sure..." He shook his head, a brisk, impatient movement that made his long hair fly out and then settle again, strands clinging to his face until he brushed them away. "Get me drunk. I don't have to get up early, and it's probably the only way I'll spill my guts."

Seth thought of sharp, bright blades and pale skin split and bleeding, and shivered. "We'll get carded, even at the Dog," he warned.

Gabe patted the pocket of his jacket. "According to my ID, I'm legal."

Easy to guess what *that* meant. Seth's father viewed the laws against underage drinking as pointless, and as long as he left his car keys behind, Seth had been allowed to drink from the age of eighteen; he didn't drink to rebel and he didn't—usually—drink to excess. It didn't go with training. His ID was sincere and convincing and, given that it would get only a cursory look, they'd be safe enough.

"Don't try and use it anywhere else," he told Gabe. "Most of the places in town are really strict."

"I guess if the wings are hot enough, I might start talking just to cool my tongue, even if I'm only drinking Coke, but the ID's not fake; I skipped a year after graduating and went over to the UK to meet up with my family there. I'm twenty-two in January."

Seth watched the traffic pass them, headlights blazing against the twilight. "I don't turn twenty-one for another month. Coke's fine with me, if there's a problem with my ID. Unlike yours, it's not entirely legal."

"Thought you only drank root beer."

It was pathetic how quickly he grabbed onto the evidence that Gabe had been paying attention to what he did. "I'm flexible when it comes to soda. No can is safe."

"How about other things?"

Seth turned his head, puzzled, and then got it. "Oh! No. Just guys. You?"

"The same."

Well, that took care of that. The conversation, stilted and jerky as it was, still felt smooth as silk compared to their usual interactions. He allowed himself to relax into it and somehow, with their talk ranging from the rehearsal to all the gossip Seth could remember from the previous year's productions, they made it to the bar and into a booth without touching on anything controversial.

It was Gabe, not Seth, who got a hard stare from the barman, but his ID stood up to scrutiny and they settled in a quiet corner with a pitcher, two glasses and wings on the way. The pitcher was cold enough that ice was flaking off it, melting and sliding to puddle on the table. Gabe caught a shard of it of his fingertip and Seth watched it turn to water and trickle down Gabe's finger to his cupped palm. He wanted to lick the cool water off Gabe's skin; wanted it with an intensity that felt him feeling open and exposed. He couldn't hide around Gabe; it was as if, from that very first moment, Gabe had slipped, unnoticed, behind Seth's barriers and settled in.

"You want to know why I pushed you away?" Gabe

asked. "Said out loud, it sounds stupid, but I guess it should do, because it was."

"It really, really was," Seth said, which made Gabe's expression lighten from brooding to something resembling amused.

"True. But you're still going to think I'm crazy. I won't blame you if you want to walk away."

"I could leap in and say I won't do that, but I don't know; I might," Seth admitted. "It'd have to be pretty fucking weird to scare me away, though."

Gabe took a long drink of icy beer, set his glass down, and licked his lips, which distracted Seth enough that he missed the first words Gabe said and had to replay them in his head.

"I remind you of Rick?" He thought back to the newspaper articles; the men who'd been involved. None of them had names that shortened to Rick. "Who's Rick?"

"My boyfriend." Gabe's full mouth was a pinched, pained line. "Or he was back then. You're really similar to him in looks. Guess I've got a type."

"Nathan and Chris?" He wasn't sure what made him blurt that out. Way off topic, but his head was whirling. He looked like someone Gabe clearly loathed? Shit. That was just—*shit*. "They don't look anything like me—Chris is blond, but that's about it. Is that why you went for them?"

Gabe wriggled and looked uneasy. "Kind of. I mean, Nathan was just an impulse, you know? I was new and it'd been a *long* time since—God, all fucking summer— months—and he was all over me…"

"That's Nathan," Seth said ruefully. "He's hard to say no to—the first time, anyway."

"The second time; not so much of a problem, right?" Gabe's eyes were lit with a knowing twinkle. "God, he's an opportunistic little shit, but you can't help liking him."

"Yeah." Seth didn't care too much about Nathan. Chris, on the other hand… "Chris didn't come on to you."

Gabe sat back and gave the ceiling—painted a utilitarian beige and not at all interesting—a prolonged inspection. Seth kicked out and got Gabe's ankle and his attention.

"Hey!"

"You—" 'Seduced' just didn't sound right. It conjured up images of Chris as a distressed Victorian virgin or something. Seth settled for something less melodramatic. "You did what Nathan did to you. Pushed him into agreeing to have sex."

Gabe looked uncomfortable. Good. "I didn't—oh, God, I did, didn't I?"

"Yeah. Why?" Seth could be remorseless and stubborn on the track of an answer and this one was important. "Did you know we had a thing?"

"A thing?" Gabe pursed his mouth. "You mean the casual sex thing? *That* thing?"

"Keep your fucking voice down," Seth hissed.

"Why? I thought you were out."

"I am."

"Home as well as here?"

"Shit, yes, but don't change the subject."

Out. Well, yes, he supposed he was. He didn't feel like sharing with Gabe the way that his mother still talked about marriage for him and grandchildren for her. She knew he was gay, but she hadn't accepted it. Seth's father had. He wasn't sure which was worse. Watching his father's love, approval, and support go from willingly given to dutifully extended…

"The subject being my choice of casual fuck? You use him that way; why is it a mystery that I did, too?"

203

"That's fucking cold, even for you." It came out as a snapped rebuke, but he didn't regret it. He'd let Gabe get away with too much already.

"Not cold," Gabe said patiently. "Truth. He doesn't want more than that, neither do you, neither did I. Everyone was happy, or they should have been. If I'd thought he meant more than that, trust me, I'd have gone with someone else."

"No." The wings arrived right then, a platter of them, with two side plates and extra napkins. As conversation stoppers went, they were a good one, the smell curling up to tantalize Seth's nose and taste buds, meaty, spicy, tangy. He took one good sniff and then folded his arms on the table and leaned in, letting his size matter, deliberately going for intimidating. "You didn't know me when you went with Nathan, but you saw how much I didn't like it. You picked Chris just because he was mine and you wanted to fuck with me. Maybe even fuck me secondhand, though that would be on the—"

"Crazy side." Gabe's face was pale in the dim light of the bar, his eyes the only spark of color. "What kind of psycho do you think I am? You remind me of someone I... don't like and so I pushed you away, and yes, I had a bad experience with him, but it doesn't mean I've sworn off sex. Chris and Nathan were both hot, available, no strings attached. That's it."

Seth studied him and couldn't tell if he was lying or not. Maybe he believed it. Maybe it was true.

Maybe the wings were getting cold.

He took one and sat back to eat it, gnawing it to the bone and washing down the explosion of heat in his mouth with gulp after gulp of beer. Gabe sat and watched him, still tense, still pissed.

Seth nodded at the platter. "Eat," he said after swallowing a mouthful of chicken. "If you're waiting for an apology, you're not going to get one. It was a valid hypothesis."

"You always throw me when you say stuff like that," Gabe said. "Jock body, geek brain. You're confusing."

"No, you're just stereotyping me." Gabe took a chicken wing and Seth waited for him to take a bite before adding, "Was Rick brainy, too?"

Gabe wasn't pale now. He choked, his eyes watering, and slugged back most of his beer. "God, these are hot... No, not really. He wasn't at college to study; his father and grandfather were both alumni and..." His voice faltered and then he took a deep breath. "He more or less bought a place there, and his father would've done the same to get him a degree if it looked like Rick was flunking. It's part of life; you come from a family that can donate Olympic-sized pools or new science labs, and you tend to reap the benefits, you know?"

"Yeah." Seth shrugged. "My family's not hurting, but we don't have that kind of money; I have to work. And, to be honest, I wouldn't have it any other way."

"That's very admirable of you," Gabe said solemnly.

Seth grinned and flicked some beer at him. "Asshole."

"Rick's family... that ties in to what happened."

"You don't have to tell me, you know."

"Yeah, I kind of do. It's probably good for me to talk about it and I owe you an explanation." Gabe looked less than enthused, but determined. "You know how I got the scar on my chest."

"Hazing gone wrong, most of the articles said. Though you were a junior, so it didn't make a lot of sense."

"Warning gone right," Gabe corrected him flatly. "You're out, and I've never been anything else." Off Seth's look, he explained, "My dad's gay. A discovery he made about the same time Mom told him I was on the way. They were both cool about it, though, and he stuck around. Then Mom died in a car crash—no, it's okay; I was six. I don't remember enough to be upset. Dad raised me, and that's how I got interested in the theater."

Seth had a mouthful of chicken, but he made a fairly polite attempt at a questioning grunt.

"My dad's Simon Rossiter." Seth must have looked as blank as he felt, because Gabe burst out laughing. "Oh, man... That's going to crush his ego. He's an actor. Stage actor. Not mega-famous, no, but ..."

"I'm sorry," Seth said abjectly. "I don't have a clue about stuff like that. But it must've been cool. My parents didn't disown me, but they freaked when I told them I was gay."

"Not always," Gabe said. "He went off with my one of my boyfriends once, and I've lost count of how many of his have made passes at me."

"Ouch."

"Tell me about it. God, I keep wandering off-topic, don't I? Kind of a no-brainer to work out why... Rick wasn't out. Not at all. Not even at college, where most of us were relaxing for the first time in our lives and having some fun. Rick was a leading light at the same fraternity his dad and grandfather were pledged to, and believe me, he didn't want them to know about us."

"So how did you meet?"

"Drama club; where else? He was in this play I was directing and he needed work on one scene; I stayed behind to coach him, and bam. Halfway through the scene, we were all over each other. Literally. Messy."

Seth didn't like the hint of fondness in Gabe's voice, but it disappeared a moment later.

"That night at the lake, it was Rick who spiked my drinks so I was drunk as a fucking skunk. Rick who took me into the woods for his buddies to find me. Rick who—

" Gabe broke off. "Shit. I thought I'd processed all of this, but I haven't."

"I'm not surprised," Seth said, aghast at the betrayal. "That's just unbelievable. Why did he do that?"

"Because I'd told him I was in love with him and it scared him. He had to admit that he was in love with me—he *was*—and that meant that what we had wasn't experimentation or buddy fucking but the way he was made. So he turned to his friends and they said they'd take care of it. Of me. And that was how they did it. Tied me up and used that knife to make me promise I'd back off and stop trying to—oh, how did they put it?—turn a good guy gay."

"Sick, sadistic little fucks." Seth couldn't speak past the hard knot of loathing in his throat. He could picture it; Gabe drunk, laughing, thinking that Rick and he would soon be kissing, hands urgent and eager—then the betrayal, the fear—the pain.

He shook his head. "Why did you let them get away with it? You could have got them in so much goddamned trouble."

"You weren't listening." Gabe's smile was pained. "I told you. I loved Rick. I wasn't going to say anything that would out him. When they took my statement I didn't know how involved he was, and I was protecting him. When I found out the truth, it was too late." He drew a pattern on the table in the puddle of water, staring at the random squiggle with a frown. "They didn't mean to cut me, you know; that was an accident. They'd gotten drunk or high to give them the guts to do it. They were just… they were trying to help a buddy. In their own eyes, they were the good guys."

"You have got to be fucking kidding me," Seth muttered. "Jesus."

"Yeah. Well, I stayed the year; I wasn't going to run

away, but I couldn't go back after summer vacation. It wasn't because I was scared of them; I held all the aces and they knew it. I just—I need this degree. I need to be able to concentrate on work and so I transferred. Easy enough; you might not have heard of him, but other people have, especially on this coast, and they all wanted to get Simon Rossiter's son for their drama department."

"Your dad... how come he didn't go after those fuckers? My dad would've sued their asses off." Even after he'd found out that Seth was gay.

"He was on tour at the time and I'm a legal adult, remember? I told him an edited version; had to, I couldn't hide the scar, but he bought the whole drunken fun gone wrong thing. He wanted to; it made life easier for him."

Seth opened his mouth to protest and then subsided when Gabe gave him a warning glare. He cleared his throat. "So you came here for a fresh start and then..."

Gabe met his gaze with a level look. "And then I met you. You look so much like Rick, and I wanted you and hated you and didn't want to be anywhere near you from the moment I saw you—oh God, finding out you were sharing a room with me was hell."

"Perfect word for it," Seth agreed fervently.

Gabe winced. "I'm so sorry. Really. Really, really sorry. It was a shitty thing to do to you. I guess I wasn't as over it as I thought. So much for all the therapy sessions over the summer."

"But are you over it now?" Seth asked, because that was really what mattered. He could forgive the past if the future looked brighter.

To his dismay, Gabe didn't reply with an instant assurance that yes, he was. "I—I think so. I'm talking to you, right?"

"I want to do more than talk," Seth said. "A hell of a lot more."

Gabe picked up a napkin and began to shred it methodically, tiny pieces fluttering to the table. "I know. You haven't exactly been subtle about it."

"Geek and jock; I'm lacking the subtle gene on both sides," Seth said acidly. For God's sake... it wasn't as if he'd been throwing himself at the guy, or wandering around, dick out and waving in the breeze.

"I'm not saying I'm not interested, just that I'm not sure—"

"Gabe, unless he's my long-lost twin, which, no, is not likely, we look similar, not identical. You're not looking at me." Gabe's gaze met his, startled and uncertain. Seth leaned in. "*Look* at me," he said softly. "Really look. And you'll see I'm not him."

"I know."

"Yeah? Prove it. My eyes. Same color?"

Gabe leaned in, too, so that they were separated by inches not feet. "Yours are gray and his were... I guess they were more of a blue. It's dark in here."

"Hair?" Seth demanded.

"Same style—"

"I'll cut it."

"But yours has more blond in it. He—his curled, too, over the ears, and yours sticks up more."

Seth grinned. "Yeah. Straight up. The untamable mop, my mom used to call it. Okay. Nose, mouth, freckles?"

Gabe sat back and slashed his hand through the air. "Enough. I get it. You're the same height and build and you both have light hair and grayish eyes. The rest is my imagination—but I can't *help* it."

Seth took out some bills and dropped them on the table. "I'm heading back. This is just getting us nowhere. And, no, I'm not storming off; we tried and it didn't work. As long as you don't go back to treating me like shit—"

"We didn't try everything."

"What?"

Gabe added his share of the bill and beckoned a waitress over. She compared the money on the table with what they'd ordered and gave them a sunny smile before scooping it up. She didn't offer them any change, but she threw in a wiggle of her ass as she walked away.

"We didn't try everything," Gabe repeated. He stood. "Come on. Let's get out of here."

They walked through the town in a silence that was less comfortable now. Seth was replaying the conversation in his head and trying to find a place where he could have said something differently and gotten a better result. Gabe was tense, his hands jammed into the pockets of his jeans.

They passed an alley and Gabe paused, grabbed Seth's arm and nudged him toward it. "In there."

"Why?"

"Because I want to kiss you, stupid." Gabe ran his tongue over his lips, not nervously, but in preparation, as if he was checking for residue from the wing sauce.

"Oh." Seth walked into the alley, but glanced back to arch his eyebrows at Gabe. "You know, for a man who reads poetry and stuff, your seduction routine needs work."

"Got you in here, didn't it?"

Seth stopped, far enough into the shadows to be discreet, not so far down the alley that they were in sight of anyone emerging from the back of the stores and restaurants that formed it. It seemed quiet enough for them to get away with a kiss.

"If you think insulting me is what got me here, you—"

Gabe's kiss stopped whatever he was going to say next. It wasn't forceful or bruisingly hard; more of a brush of Gabe's mouth over Seth's, but it was enough. Seth let the wall behind him hold him up and Gabe moved closer, those hands sliding up Seth's arms to his shoulders, and then higher still to cradle Seth's face and draw it down.

Kissing Gabe was bone-meltingly good. Seth was lost after that first touch, his hands finding the shape of Gabe's head through the lavish mass of hair, cool as water against his fingers. Seth thought of Gabe trailing that long hair over him as Gabe kissed his way down, and moaned, a needy, desperate sound that Gabe met by thrusting his tongue deep into Seth's mouth, a rapid flicker of an invasion, over too soon. But Seth didn't care because Gabe's mouth was locked onto his now, sliding like liquid a moment later, the contact shifting, but never broken.

He found he could breathe through his nose, which was good because he didn't want this to stop for something as mundane as that. Gabe was different now; not the hostile man Seth knew best, nor the apologetic, unsure man in the bar. This was Gabe as he'd probably been before the betrayal that had been carved into his body and heart; passionate, open, playful.

Hot.

Seth took his mouth away, voicing his loss with a disappointed whimper, even if he'd been the one to break the kiss. He'd thought of something he wanted—needed—to do more. He fastened his teeth into Gabe's neck in a rough kiss and sucked, hard enough to draw a moan from Gabe, who arched up against him, not struggling at all; hard enough to leave a mark. It would fade, as the scar across Gabe's ribs wouldn't, but it was going to be there for the rest of the night, and it was fresh and new and wanted.

He licked at the skin where it was hot and felt Gabe's hand press against his cock where it pushed eagerly against his zipper. The zipper that Gabe was easing down with a care that felt more like a tease than concern for vulnerable flesh and sharp, metal teeth.

"God, not here," he whispered. "Gabe... we can go back to our room."

A hand, cool against warmer skin, slid past Seth's stomach and down. "I can't wait that long to touch you."

"*Gabe—*"

The tips of Gabe's fingers grazed the side of Seth's cock, sending a shock of arousal through him that was repeated when Gabe dug that hand deeper and curled those fingers awkwardly but firmly around the shaft.

"God, you're so hard. I got you like this with a kiss?" Gabe wasn't laughing at him; just staring at Seth with a fierce longing. "Want to see what you did to me, biting me like that?" He drew Seth's hand to where his cock, as rock-solid as Seth's, thrust and pushed against his jeans.

Seth heard himself groan from a distance, through the seashell roar in his ears, and let his hand curve to the shape needed, his palm filled with a promise. Gabe hummed approvingly and rubbed against Seth's hand like a cat, insistent and demanding.

"We really can't," Seth said. Weak... so weak. He wanted to shove Gabe's jeans down, just far enough to bare that cock and ass. Wanted to stroke and touch, explore and discover... Wanted to get to his knees in this dark, dank alley and do things to Gabe's cock with his mouth that would make the man tremble and cry out, his hands digging into Seth's shoulders.

Wanted to stand, spin Gabe around, put him against the wall and fuck him, hard and fast, watching Gabe's hands flex against the brick, fingers spread as wide as his legs, fuck him until Gabe came with a shudder and a cry, his come pale splatters against the wall, his body writhing in Seth's grip.

Reality banished the fantasies as a car drove by, the wash of light from its headlights illuminating the entrance to the alley. Seth grabbed Gabe's wrist and tugged up, the loss of the warm touch making him ache with regret. "Not here," he repeated and this time made it sound firm. "We get back and I'm up for anything, whatever you want, but I'm not letting you jerk me off in public."

"Fuck." Gabe tore free of Seth's slackening grip and stepped back. "What is *wrong* with you? I thought you wanted me?"

"I do, just not here, not like this." Seth couldn't understand Gabe's problem. He could hear voices as a group of people got closer to the entrance, walking along the sidewalk and laughing. "Hear that? We're going to have an audience in about thirty seconds."

Gabe bit his lip and then shrugged, his face closed down and sullen. "Whatever."

Seth reached out and Gabe flinched away. "Hey… don't," he said. "Don't do this. Just… just come here, will you?" Gabe shook his head, but Seth wasn't going to let the spark between them fizzle out like this. He waited until the group of people had passed by, none of them even glancing into the alley, and then put his arms around a stiff, unresponsive Gabe and hugged him, nuzzling into cool, silky hair until he found an ear to kiss. "I want you. I do, okay? Now can we get back to where there's a bed?"

Gabe sighed and relaxed, returning Seth's hug briefly, but there was still something bothering him; he wouldn't meet Seth's questioning looks as they walked back to the college, and conversation was limited to Seth making comments that Gabe replied to in monosyllables.

Seth edged closer and bumped his arm against Gabe's shoulder, which at least got Gabe to glance at him. "Sorry."

"You did it on purpose."

Was that a faint smile? Seth slid his arm around Gabe's shoulders. "Oops?"

"You are such a clown." Gabe leaned into Seth's side for a moment and then pulled free. "Okay, you can walk faster than this when there's sex waiting at journey's end, can't you?"

"'Journeys end in lovers' meetings'," Seth said, surprising himself. Where the hell had that come from? "God, did I just quote Shakespeare? Are you infecting me with culture?"

Gabe grinned. "You most certainly did, and I'm impressed. Or I would be if you could tell me the play."

"Has to be one I studied at school, so... uh, Midsummer Night's Dream?"

The snort from Gabe was enough to tell him that he'd blown that one. "Twelfth Night," Gabe corrected. "Your gold star just got taken off you."

"Damn," Seth said, and walked just a little quicker.

Their room looked different somehow now that Gabe and he had walked into it both smiling, together. Which had gotten them some curious stares from the guys they'd passed in the hallway; people were used to them not getting along. Seth flicked on the light, closed and locked the door, and looked around. The chaos of his side of the room was still offset by the orderly neatness of Gabe's side, but it looked less of a battle for control than a difference in style. And was that his t-shirt on the floor by Gabe's bed? The line dividing them was blurring, vanishing; had disappeared even more in that moment of revelation in the theater.

And Gabe was moving into his space, one hand stroking the side of Seth's face even as the other hand was deftly unfastening the button and zipper of Seth's jeans.

"Bed," Seth said. "Don't care whose." He began to head that way, his hand on Gabe's arm, drawing him along, but Gabe dug his heels in for just long enough to reach back and flip the light switch.

"Don't do that," Seth protested. "It's pitch-black in here. At least let me put on one of the lamps…"

"No." Gabe wrenched free, his voice shaking. "No lights."

Oh. That explained the dark alley, at least. Seth rubbed his fingers over his forehead. "Gabe, I've seen it. It doesn't bother me."

"I wanted you to see it before." Gabe was there, in front of him; enough light was seeping in from the corridor for Seth's rapidly adjusting eyes to know that much, but he couldn't see Gabe's face. "I—it was like I wanted you to see what you'd done to me, and no, don't bother telling me how totally fucked up and weird that sounds, because I know, okay?"

It did, but that didn't mean that Seth didn't get it, because he did.

"And now, well, now I *don't* want you to see it." Gabe moved, turning away. "It's ugly. It looks ugly, it feels awful when I touch it, and people see it and I don't know which is worse; when they look away or when they stare. Chris stared. He didn't mean to, but he did. That was why it was a one-time only with him, if you really want to know."

Seth took a deep breath and wished, intensely, for five minutes alone with Rick and the other assholes who'd done this to Gabe. Dwelling on what he'd do to them was soothing, but not all that helpful when it came to helping Gabe. In the end, there were two choices; he could give in and leave the lights off, hoping that Gabe would get past this hang-up, or he could turn them back on and risk losing Gabe.

He couldn't go for the easy option. Not when he guessed, deep down, it'd just confirm Gabe's belief that the scar mattered. He turned on a lamp, the golden glow subdued, but enough for there to be nowhere to hide for either of them, and began to undress, letting his clothes fall to the ground.

"You've seen me half-naked," he said. Top, shoes, socks... "Let me give you the tour." Jeans, shorts... naked. Gabe's gaze was like heat on Seth's bare skin, but the man wasn't moving closer. Seth sighed and pointed to his stomach. "I'll start with the most recent. Appendix operation; see? They did a good job, but it's left a scar and I'll die with that still on me."

"That's different."

"No. It's a scar. I'm not perfect." Seth turned slightly and tapped his right calf. "See that? It's a present from a barbed wire fence I got friendly with when I was ten. Tore me up and ruined my birthday because I spent most of it at the hospital getting a tetanus shot and God knows how many stitches. I forget it's there, mostly, but you can see it, can't you?"

Gabe drifted closer and peered down. "Yeah. I can see it."

"Knees. Covered with nicks and dents. I had this tendency to ride my bike places a bike wasn't meant to go at speeds that guaranteed I'd limp home bleeding."

"That big brain of yours only works when it comes to math, huh?"

"Something like that." Seth raised his eyebrows. "Is this getting through to you, or do you want to see more?"

Gabe smiled. "Yes and yes. The whole deal, though, not just the scars."

"You can look, but you don't get to touch until you give me something to look at," Seth said and hoped that he hadn't pushed too hard, too fast.

Gabe worried at his lower lip with his teeth and then

nodded. "Guess that's fair."

When Gabe had finished undressing, Seth took his first open look at a body he'd been sneaking peeks at for weeks now, building a picture in snatched scraps. The scar was paler now, healing well, and it just didn't hold Seth's attention. Not when there was so much else to look at. Gabe wasn't muscled the way Seth was, but there was a sturdy strength to him coupled with a vibrant energy that made Seth want to touch him and soak it up. "God, I wish we hadn't taken so long getting here."

"Flattering," Gabe said. He eyed Seth's cock and the gleam in his eyes deepened. "So is that."

"Back at you," Seth retorted. Gabe was hard, too, his chest rising and falling as he took quick, shallow breaths. "Turn around?"

"Why?"

"I want to see the back view."

"My ass is hot, too," Gabe said, turning and then glancing back. He prodded it. "See? Firm and bitable."

"Mmm," Seth said, coming up behind Gabe and wrapping both arms around him, needing to bridge every gap between them, physical and emotional. "I'll take you up on that when you least expect it."

Gabe leaned back against Seth, all pliant acceptance for the moment, at least, and tilted his head to rest on Seth's shoulder. Seth sighed and bent his head to bite and lick gently at Gabe's neck, letting the way Gabe rolled his head to give him access guide him when it came to choosing his next target.

"Vampire," Gabe murmured, the word lost in a moan as Seth began to suck up a mark. "Oh, God, that feels good…"

"Don't want your blood," Seth said and dropped one hand to pump Gabe's cock in a slow, leisurely counterpoint to what his mouth was doing between words. "Other bodily fluids, now…"

"That sounds gross considering the full list, but I guess if we stick to spit and spunk, I can go along with it."

Seth chuckled, smothering the sound in the crook of Gabe's neck. "Yeah, they were what I had in mind."

Gabe arched into Seth's grip, his hands reaching back to cup Seth's ass and bring them even closer. Seth's cock was riding the cleft of Gabe's ass now, trapped in the shallow groove. Gabe continued to talk, his body moving smoothly, his voice ragged around the edges. "We need to have the talk?"

"I'm clean and I've got enough condoms and lube in the drawer over there for an orgy. You?"

"The same. Well, maybe not as well-supplied as you… but enough for tonight."

"You feel well-supplied to me, babe," Seth said with a smirk and knew Gabe well enough that the elbow jabbed at his ribs hit air, because he'd twisted out of the way.

"You have any kinks, preferences, weird habits I need to know about?"

"Nope," Seth said. "I save the cuffs and chains for the second date, and if I'm going to be honest—"

"About sex? Isn't that, like, illegal?"

"Shut up." Seth cupped Gabe's balls and gave them a squeeze that wouldn't have popped a soap bubble. "I'm baring my soul here. I haven't—shit, I've never fucked anyone. Been fucked, yes, but not often. Uh, three times, if we're counting, and the first—not a good memory. Hurt like hell because he rushed it."

"Hey, I'm not Mr. Experience myself, " Gabe assured him. "I've done both, and liked it on both ends, but, yeah, not a lot. Usually ended up with a blowjob or jerking each other off. Which is cool."

"Mmm." Seth dragged his fingernails across Gabe's belly, low down, not hard, but, judging from Gabe's groan of pleasure, just hard enough. "Want to be my first?"

Gabe twisted his head and stared at him. "God, you don't fuck around, do you? Yeah, sure." He turned in Seth's embrace and planted a kiss on Seth's mouth, slow and sweet. "Want to work up to that, though? Or don't you think you've got the energy for a repeat performance?"

"With you, I could maybe manage an encore or two," Seth said.

"Listen to you being optimistic…" Gabe pursed his lips. "Your bed. It's messy anyway."

"Fine, but we sleep in yours to avoid the wet spot."

"You want to sleep with me?" There was genuine surprise in Gabe's voice.

"The beds are doubles; there's room." Seth frowned. "You don't want to?"

"I just—I never have. Not all night." Gabe shrugged. "If I kick you out, don't take it personally."

"I'm going to wear you out," Seth told him to cover the unexpected pang of hurt. "You won't have the energy to kick anything."

"Talk, all talk…" Gabe ducked his head and bit Seth's nipple, a sharp, hot sting that made Seth's stomach muscles clench as his body jerked reflexively in a mixture of protest and yearning. "Show me what you've got."

They landed on Seth's bed in a tangle of arms and legs, mouths locked together, hands exploring. Seth filled a palm with the solid jut of Gabe's ass and squeezed it, surprised at the flash of possessiveness he felt. Too soon to be thinking like that, and given Gabe's addiction to one-night stands…

He took his mouth away from Gabe's and said bluntly, "Is this the only chance I'm going to get with you? Just tonight?"

Gabe blinked. "Not necessarily. *You* don't stare. Not in a way that pisses me off, anyway. Why?"

"Seems to be the way you do things."

"Not with you," Gabe said and ran a fingertip down Seth's nose. "Unless that's the way you want it."

"I don't."

Gabe closed his eyes and rolled to his back. "Good to know. Want to suck me?"

"Jesus, you're romantic."

Green eyes stared at him through lowered lashes. "Not answering my question."

Seth straddled him and dropped a brief kiss on Gabe's smiling mouth. "Yeah, I want to."

He took his time getting there, though, getting to know every inch of Gabe's chest and stomach as he moved down the bed, ignoring Gabe's protests and the not-at-all subtle prods his stomach was getting from Gabe's cock. Gabe's nipples, cinnamon brown, the skin around them pebbled against the tip of Seth's tongue, were worth lingering over, and the hollow at Gabe's throat, where the skin was smooth as cream, was worth returning to, over and over. He kept his hands on Gabe because he liked to feel the tremors running through the body beneath him, but did no more than stroke a hip or Gabe's arm from time to time.

When he reached the scar, he didn't hesitate, but, anticipating Gabe's response as Gabe had gone tense and still, he held Gabe down, one hand locked around Gabe's upper arm, the other pushing down on the opposite thigh.

"Don't." Gabe sounded panicky.

"It's just skin. It's part of you," Seth told him. "Unless it hurts?"

"What? No, it—it doesn't hurt."

"Good." He dragged his tongue along the mark the knife had left and then kissed his way back to where he'd started. The texture of the new skin was different;

smoother in places, ridged where it met older skin. "Just skin," he repeated.

Gabe was peering down at him, eyes wide and shocked, face twisted. "I don't know how you can do that."

"It's not a big deal." Seth quirked his mouth in a half-smile. "And no, I don't have a weird fetish for scars. You see it and remember how you got it, all the pain. I see it and it's just a line. And it's fading."

"No, it's not."

"Yes, it is." Seth tapped the scar. "When I first saw it, it was redder than this. It's faded, shrinking. It won't go away, but in a year or so, it'll just be this white line."

"How the fuck do you know that?"

Seth let his forehead rest against Gabe's ribs to hide his face. "My dad's a plastic surgeon, okay? I've picked up some stuff over the years listening to him talk. Spare me the boob job jokes; heard them all before."

"I went to see one of them," Gabe said hesitantly. "He said pretty much what you did and told me to come back if it didn't fade."

"You didn't believe him?"

"I didn't want to risk believing him and then getting disappointed. My dad did, though, and he wouldn't pay for any surgery after that. Said we should wait."

"Good call." Point made, Seth moved down the bed a few inches. "Belly button. Now, those I *do* have a thing for."

"You have got to be kidding me—hey! Tickles!"

Seth gave his best evil chuckle and dipped his tongue into the shallow depression again, swirling it around.

"I can tickle, too," Gabe said ominously. "Except I leave bruises."

"Kinky." Seth took pity on him and the next lick was across the glossed-wet head of Gabe's cock. The salt-musk taste filled his mouth and made it water. God, he loved doing this... Loved the rush of reducing someone to a needy, gasping quiver, sounds spilling from their mouth as their come shot into his mouth, unexpected, always, a sudden rush of it, so much to swallow, though his memories of jerking off told him differently.

And when he had swallowed the taste lingered, reminding him, so that he could walk into class, that acrid, thick liquid still flavoring every breath, and answer questions or chat, looking relaxed, laid back... *swallow*. He could brush his teeth, but where was the fun in that?

Gabe was fun to play with, fun to tease, but Seth's cock was throbbing eagerly and not at all interested in waiting. He dipped his head and let the shape of Gabe's cock reshape his parted lips, loving the familiar act and the pleasure of discovering what Gabe tasted like, felt like against his tongue, silk-thin skin over hardness, the weight of those balls warm in Seth's palm as he rolled them and squeezed gently.

Gabe bucked up, fucking his mouth, and Seth threw in an extra flick of his tongue across the smooth head to reward the enthusiasm. Most people just lay there and let him do whatever he wanted to them; this was new and, he had to admit, he kind of liked it. An image from a porn movie flashed through his head; a man on his back, another guy straddling his chest, his cock nudging its way into an open mouth and then sliding in and out. In the movie, the man on top had come all over the other guy's face, the camera just a little too close in for it to really be sexy, but even so, Seth decided he'd like to try it that way some time.

For now, though, maybe he didn't want Gabe to have this all his own way... He wrapped his hand around the base of Gabe's cock and jerked him off, his mouth positioned so that the rounded, wet head bumped into his lips or his darting tongue every second or third stroke.

Gabe tried to thrust up and go deeper into Seth's mouth, but Seth held him down easily enough.

"Fuck you," Gabe panted out without hostility, but with a good deal of intensity. "I'm sorry, okay? All of it, I'm sorry, just do it, do it—*God* —"

Seth felt a stab of satisfaction he knew was petty, but as he really thought that he was owed an apology, the guilt was minimal. He didn't bother with reassurances; just opened his mouth wide and slid his hands away so that Gabe could do what the hell he wanted. With a sob of relief, Gabe arched up in one powerful surge of his body and came a few strokes later, his hands running roughly through Seth's hair and then clamping down on Seth's shoulders for the final thrust into a space Seth was making as welcoming as possible.

Hearing Gabe gasp out his name as he climaxed was almost enough to send Seth over the edge, but he hung on. He didn't want to miss any of this, not the sounds Gabe was making, raw, incoherent attempts at words, or the silence that followed, broken by Gabe's ragged breathing. He watched the flush on Gabe's face deepen and noted the sheen of sweat across his forehead.

Gabe was wiped out. Totally. Just from one blowjob. Sweet. Seth felt a click he associated with working out a complex equation and knowing that the answer was right on some level that didn't need proof. This, this thing between them, was right, too. It was only just beginning and it'd gotten off to one hell of a rocky start, but it was solid now.

Gabe lifted one hand and clamped it around Seth's arm with more strength than Seth would have expected him to have, given that he looked as if his muscles had been turned to cooked spaghetti. "Get your ass down here and kiss me."

Seth lay down beside Gabe and wiped his hand across

his mouth, feeling self-conscious. He could still taste Gabe's come and he liked it, but it didn't mean that Gabe would.

"Oh, please," Gabe said and pushed Seth's hand down. "Like I've never tasted it."

"Freak," Seth told him and leaned in to kiss and be kissed, his cock jerking eagerly as it was pressed against Gabe's stomach and hot, damp skin.

Gabe's tongue licked and lapped at Seth's mouth, which sent Seth's arousal up a notch higher. He moaned and broke the kiss. "Gabe... you keep this up and I'm going to come."

Gabe chuckled, a drowsy, wicked ripple of amusement, and shimmied just enough to make Seth drive his teeth into his lip to distract himself from the urgent need to fuck something, anything; skin, hand, fresh air.

"Thought you wanted to fuck me?"

"Are you still up for that?"

"Give me ten minutes and I might be, but ooh, you're not going to last that long, are you?"

A finger teased the tip of Seth's cock, sliding in the pooled wetness there, and he bit down again, this time on Gabe's shoulder; his lip stung. "Fuck. *Fuck*—"

"That's what I was suggesting, yes."

"Okay." With an effort, Seth rolled away from Gabe and groped around in the nightstand for what he needed. "I don't know how you want to do this..."

Gabe didn't answer in words; he just went to his stomach and folded his arms under his chin. Figured that he'd choose a position where he couldn't see who was fucking him, and his scar was hidden, Seth supposed, wishing that Gabe had stayed on his back. Or maybe it was easier to do it this way and he was reading too much into it?

He rolled the condom on and gritted his teeth when

Gabe spread his legs and raised his ass up. "You're killing me here, you know that?"

Gabe wiggled his ass and glanced back through the hair falling down over his face. "I want to. I want you so hot for me that you don't think about what you're doing and freak."

"Oh, because telling me not to freak is useful," Seth complained. He tilted the bottle of lube and let some drip down onto his fingers. "And I don't want to hurt you, so feeling like I want to get balls deep in you right now, without waiting longer than it takes to line up and shove, maybe isn't that good."

"You won't hurt me." Gabe sounded serene and a lot more confident than Seth was.

Seth took a steadying breath. One finger. He'd done that before, anyway, and knew how to ease in, how much pressure to apply and when to take it slow. So intimate, this; his finger sinking deep into hidden, secret places; more so than it would be when it was his cock pushing in with a care that would be excruciating. His finger was bare; his cock wouldn't be. The drag and cling of the hot flesh surrounded his finger, muscles squeezing it tight. He worked the lube in as deeply as he could and then, remembering that two fingers had hurt him, the irregular bumpy shape they made difficult to accommodate, he slicked up his cock until it was shiny and wet.

'Tell me if this doesn't feel good," Seth murmured, finger back inside Gabe's ass again, working its way in and out slowly as Gabe sighed and spread his legs wider, then tilted his hips to meet it. Seth kissed the back of Gabe's neck through the silky hair that lay in a tangle over it, and nuzzled through it until his lips met smooth skin. "I'll stop, I swear I will."

"Just do it," Gabe said, his voice soft, relaxed, as if they were both locked in a dream and nothing really mattered. "Fuck me. Please." The final word, added as an afterthought, Gabe's tone too meek for Seth not to feel suspicious, was still enough of a turn-on for his remaining doubts to dissolve to nothing.

He put the head of his cock against the yielding flesh and pushed his way inside, inch by inch, the lube and Gabe's complete cooperation making it easy. Short strokes, each one leaving him a little deeper inside, until he was in as far as he could go. He glanced down and felt a dizzying disorientation; a sense of loss because his cock wasn't there for him to see; Gabe had it, held it, fucking owned it. It didn't last long. His body, driven by instinct, was already moving, withdrawing just enough to make the next slide forward the perfect length. Friction brought heat, encompassing, consuming. Wildfire. He was aware of every part of his body and concentrating only on Gabe until he was sure Gabe was with him.

Gabe's hands were fisted in the sheets, kneading the crumpled cotton, and his head hung down. The bow of his back, with the ridges of his spine showing, pale dents against his skin, was a curve Seth wanted to draw, tracing it onto paper with a smooth, unbroken line. He could map it, analyze it, reduce it to an equation, that curve— or, when this was over and they were lying together, exhausted, satiated, he could run his fingers down it, lick the salt of sweat from it, kiss each bump...

"Seth—"

He reached around, losing the momentum of his thrusts for a moment, and felt the renewed hardness hanging heavy and full between Gabe's legs. Gabe moaned gratefully and Seth left his hand there, his fingers closing around a shape that he was beginning to know. He could have drawn that, too, with an accuracy Gabe might not have appreciated; if the camera added ten pounds, most men added an inch. He braced himself on one hand

and went back to what he'd been doing, matching and meeting Gabe's movements as he fucked Gabe's ass and Gabe worked his cock into the circle of Seth's hand.

Next time, they were going to do this face to face. He wanted to see Gabe's expression and be sure that Gabe saw him, just him, with no memories to cloud his vision.

He wanted—wanted— He cried out, three years of listening to his classmates through thin walls enough incentive to make it quiet enough to be lost in the background noise, though he knew that Gabe could hear him. Cried out and felt his balls tighten and his world stop spinning, leaving him stranded in an endless moment of stillness, poised on the edge, before gravity remembered him and he came crashing down, hips hammering in a relentless beat, cock spilling, spurting.

Seth's hand fell away from Gabe's cock for a moment, but before Gabe could replace it with his own, Seth put an arm around Gabe's waist and lowered them to the bed, spooning up beside Gabe, cock still inside him.

This was better. He wriggled his arm free and put his hand back where it had been, neither of them speaking, because this wasn't over yet and words would have broken the charm. He used his mouth to kiss, finding places on Gabe's neck and shoulder that made Gabe shudder and press back, internal muscles flexing around Seth's cock. He wouldn't be able to keep it there much longer, but he wanted to be inside Gabe when Gabe came.

His caresses became more demanding and his kisses harder. Gabe grunted and ground that ass back against Seth, spurring him on. His hand blurred on Gabe's cock, feeling the slip-slide of skin, and he knew when Gabe was about to climax as surely as he would have known if it'd been his own cock he was jacking.

Warm and wet, Gabe's come coated his belly and Seth's hand, and Seth sighed and pushed inside Gabe one last time before regretfully easing out.

They were going to have to clean up. Big time. They were most definitely going to need to switch beds.

Right now, though, he just wanted to close his eyes and go back to kissing the back of Gabe's neck from time to time, his arm around Gabe, holding Gabe close, his fingers stroking the scar as if he could smooth it away.

This early in spring the ground was cold and newly thawed, but it was firm enough to be playable. Seth could see bright splashes of color under trees dotted with leaves the green of apples. He loved this time of the year. He took a deep sniff of fresh spring air.

"It's just a game," Gabe said with a roll of his eyes, eyes that matched the leaves.

Seth gave the love of his life, the man he adored beyond reason or sense—most of the time—a solid punch on the arm. "It's the fucking semi-finals."

"And if you win, you'll expect me to get excited all over again for the final. I can't do it. It's just too emotionally exhausting. I'm going over to the theater to see if Molly put the fear of God into that shit-for-brains electrician who fucked up the lighting."

Seth stopped Gabe from leaving by taking the folder containing Gabe's notes on the play that went with him everywhere—if he'd been told Gabe showered with it, it wouldn't have surprised him—and sitting on it.

"Hey!"

"You're staying. You're watching. And did I mention cheering? Oh, and providing a shoulder to cry on later if needed."

Gabe smiled, his words cloaked by the noise of the spectators gathered around the pitch. "I was thinking more of how to reward you when you win; that's much more appealing."

"Soccer—"

"Football."

"*Soccer* is a team game," Seth said absently, his attention drifting. "I won't be winning; the whole team will. If we do." He squinted over at the opposition bench where the blue and white of Pemberley College was a pale blot on the landscape, which was dominated by the red of the Hargreaves supporters. "They're going to be tough to beat…"

"I don't do orgies," Gabe said flatly. "So you'd better make sure you do something heroic out there. I don't get creative for games with no goals, either, and if you *dare* let this go to extra time and a fucking penalty shoot-out…"

Unmoved by Gabe's threats or the insistent tugs as he tried to free his binder, Seth smiled at him. "So you're staying to watch?"

Gabe sighed. "You know I am. I'll stay up here, though. Chris said he'd save me a seat next to him, but he'll be with Julia, and you know what she's like around me."

"Jumpy," Seth said. "Yeah…" He tugged at Seth's hair. "I've got to go. Coach wanted us all in the dressing room before the match to go over some stuff."

"Off you go," Gabe said amiably.

"I'm taking this with me," Seth said and held the binder up high, where Gabe couldn't reach it, even if he jumped; not that Gabe would do anything so doomed to fail. Gabe would probably knee Seth in the balls and tweak the folder from his hand as he collapsed, groaning, to the ground.

"If you do, I'll find Chris and watch the game sitting on his knee."

"Julia would rip your head off and tell us to use it as a ball," Seth countered.

"Funny you should say that," Gabe began, a spark of interest appearing in his eyes. "In the past, football was played using—"

"Tell me later," Seth said hastily. He dropped the folder onto the bench by Gabe and began to walk away, pushing past the people climbing up to this top row of seating as the bleachers filled.

He glanced back once. The folder was open on Gabe's knee and he was poring over it, which Seth had expected, but Gabe lifted his head and smiled at Seth, and mouthed something that looked like "good luck."

Seth raised his hand in acknowledgment and went to find Coach.

He didn't need good luck. He had Gabriel on his side and by his side.

And one hell of an incentive to win.

What It's All About
by Tory Temple

He *knew* he should have worn boxers instead of briefs tonight. Maxwell Tisdale crouched in the brambles and winced as yet another thorn scratched his bare thigh.

Not that boxers would have offered much more protection than his briefs, but Max wished for them anyway. There was something so much more vulnerable about hiding in the woods in tighty-whities.

Max knew he was going to look like he'd been in a fight with his mother's prize Persian cat. The stings of the thorns and branches were all over his chest and legs, but he didn't dare come out of his hiding place. Hell Week was almost over, and so far this was the most humiliating thing he'd been asked to do as a pledge. Considering what fraternities used to do to their pledges, Max was getting off easy.

"Still feels like hazing," he muttered out loud into the cool autumn air. Thank God it was still warm enough this late in the season that he didn't freeze his balls off.

"It is," came the unexpected response.

Max jerked his head up and scanned the wooded area where he was hiding. There was no one immediately visible. "Hazing's illegal."

"Dude, you're in your fucking skivvies in the woods at night, supposedly playing 'hide and seek,' and you have to try and make it back to the house without a brother seeing you. Of course it's hazing." The disembodied voice seemed to be coming from the wide oak to Max's left.

He peered through the fast-encroaching twilight and tried to ignore the calls and whistles of his frat brothers in the distance. "The rules of hazing are mostly just about physical brutality. Oh, and drinking."

That was answered with a snort. "What about exposure to the elements? I thought I read that somewhere in the stupid rules."

Max considered that. "It's not like it's cold," he said lamely, although as it grew darker, the air grew cooler. "And Greg said none of us could stay out here longer than an hour." The senior frat brother had looked stern while saying it, but Max heard the snickers behind him, and how the hell were they supposed to tell when an hour was up, anyway? They'd all been stripped of everything but their underwear.

"Whatever, man. It sucks that we're both out here, and you know what? I bet they're not looking for us. I bet you a hundred bucks that they're sitting on the porch laughing their asses off." The voice sounded bitter.

"So why are we both hiding out here instead of heading back to the house?" Max squinted his eyes and tried harder to see who he was talking to. There were twenty-two new pledges to the Kappa Delta house, and Max had only known three of them before Hell Week started. Supposedly, he would know all of the pledges by the time the week was over, but they'd really been kept too busy to socialize.

He gave up trying to determine which of his fellow pledges was talking to him and concentrated on the right corner of the roof of the frat house. Max could barely see it through a break in the trees, but he knew that if he kept his eye on it, he wouldn't feel lost out here in the woods.

"Fuck this shit," Max's pledge brother finally said. "I'm going for it. What are they going to do to me? Lock me in the basement?"

Max shrugged even though the other man couldn't see him. "Dunno, dude. No hazing." He figured if he said it enough, it would be true. But Max had to admit that, so far, the Kappa Delta brothers had been kinder than he'd anticipated.

"Whatever. I'm going."

There was a flash of movement and a rustle of leaves, and Max peeked out of the bramble bush in time to see a medium-sized body dashing for the house. He had short, dark hair that Max could see was cropped closely in the back, a trim waist, and a nice ass. The outline of the nice ass was visible through tight gray boxer-briefs.

He wondered if he'd be kicked out of the frat if they knew he was gay. It was something Max had thought about a lot before deciding to rush, and he specifically picked Kappa Delta because of the nondiscrimination clause in their by-laws. But there was always the chance of some homophobe giving him shit.

At the moment, though, the only thing Max cared about was getting back to the house when his hour was up. He and Erik, his roommate, were two of the four pledges on the kitchen schedule to cook. Max knew he'd catch serious shit if they didn't have dinner on the table by the time the other members sat down to eat.

Max and Erik didn't live in the frat house; their university had a rule that no freshmen or sophomores could live there. They still cooked, though, and other pledges did the dishes, and then they all usually trooped home through the streets to their dorm.

The last bit of twilight faded into night and stars winked on above Max's head. He didn't like feeling so alone in the woods, even though the house was easy to see if he looked hard enough. Screw this shit, he was going in.

He darted out of the brush, receiving another long scratch down his stomach as he bolted up and out. Leaves and twigs crackled under his feet as Max headed for the house. He wasn't sure what he feared more at this point: breaking the stupid rules of the game, or not having enough time to cook dinner.

Max burst out of the wooded area behind the house and stopped short in the clearing. Nine of the senior members of Kappa Delta were sitting on the benches on the back porch, grinning at him.

"Congratulations, Tisdale!" Greg called. "You and Page are among the first idiots to figure it out. Nicely done!"

Max blinked at the laughing men on the porch. Page? Devin Page? Is that who'd been in the woods with him? He shook his head and started for the porch steps, painfully aware of his near-nakedness. "So where're the rest?" he asked, glancing back over his shoulder toward the woods. "It's getting cold."

"We're keeping track," Greg said cheerfully, holding up a roster. "If they haven't figured out that no one's looking for them and they're dumb enough to stay in the woods, we'll send you and Page out looking for them."

"I have to cook." It was a feeble protest, and he didn't really mean it, anyway. Max knew he'd rather go looking for his stray brothers than cook.

"So we'll haul you out of the kitchen if we need you." Greg clinked beer bottles with Adam Zane and both men grinned at Max.

Max stifled a sigh and headed up the porch steps. "Sure."

A strong arm shot out to block his path. "You mean 'yes'."

Shit, he had the hardest time remembering that. Max straightened and looked Greg in the eye. "Yes, sir."

"Thanks, Tisdale. Looking forward to dinner." Greg dropped his arm and let Max pass.

The back door led straight into the kitchen. Max went in to find Erik already pouring spaghetti noodles into a huge pot of boiling water. "Hey. Let me get my jeans on and I'll be right there."

"Hurry up, man. It's almost seven." Erik looked worried, but Erik always looked worried. Max was used to it.

"Is it my fucking fault they made us play that idiotic game just so they could laugh? And how the hell did you get back here so fast?" Erik was a rabid rule follower and slightly obsessive-compulsive. Max wouldn't have been surprised if Erik had spent the night in the woods just because the senior brothers had told him to.

Erik sprinkled salt into the bubbling water and then snatched a pepper grinder from the counter. He started grinding pepper with a vengeance into the pot and shot Max an incredulous look. "We have to *cook*. I had to weigh the options of getting in trouble for coming out of the woods or getting in trouble for not cooking. Have you seen those guys when their dinner isn't on the table?" Erik shook his head and continued wrenching on the top of the grinder. "Good thing I guessed right. …Dude, go put your fucking pants on already. I bet you Meeks and Weintraub aren't gonna make it in here to help us."

Max rolled his eyes. Erik was probably right. Meeks and Weintraub were okay guys, but not the brightest.

"Yeah, gimme five."

He headed out of the warm kitchen into the cooler, dimly-lit hallway. He'd left his clothes in the upstairs bathroom, like he'd been instructed to do, so Max climbed the stairs to the second floor and pushed open the third door in the hallway.

"You could knock."

Startled, Max stepped back. The overhead light in the hallway was bright enough that he hadn't realized the bathroom light was also on and the room wasn't empty. Devin Page tugged his shirt down over a well-toned chest and arched a brow at Max.

"Uh." Max fumbled for words. "Sorry? The door wasn't all the way closed." He became even more painfully aware of the fact that Devin was fully dressed and he was still in his underwear.

Devin's brow shot up even higher. "Yeah, it was."

"Okay. Um, sorry, man. Can I get my clothes?" Max prayed to anyone listening that his cock wouldn't start to react to the flash of bare skin he'd seen before Devin had pulled his shirt down.

Devin stepped to one side and motioned at the bathroom, so Max slipped by him and shut the door. As an afterthought, he clicked the lock on the knob and wondered if he actually heard a chuckle on the other side or if it was just his imagination.

The only thing Max knew about Devin Page was that he was a freshman like Max, lived in a different dorm, and they were pledging the same fraternity. Other than that, the man was a total mystery.

He has a nice ass, his subconscious whispered.

Max glowered at himself in the mirror. He was pretty sure the frat by-laws forbade perving on the other pledges, but the strip of Devin's bare stomach, combined with the memory of Devin's ass as he made his earlier dash through the woods, was enough to get Max's cock stirring.

"All right, all right," he muttered, well aware that he'd left Erik downstairs fretting over the spaghetti. There was no way Max would be able to cook with a hard-on anyway, so he might as well take care of it before going back downstairs.

A handy jar of Vaseline was just inside the medicine cabinet. This was a fraternity house, after all. Max was sure they all went through lube, lotion, and petroleum jelly like crazy.

The thought of all the men in the house jacking off was enough to get Max even harder. There were some pretty cute guys in his frat, although he felt a little shallow and guilty when he wondered if that was one of the reasons he'd pledged here. Max contented himself by remembering that his father had encouraged Kappa Delta.

The Vaseline was cool and slick on his palm and cock. It turned warm within moments and Max shuddered at the conflicting sensations. He enjoyed different extremes during sex and wasn't averse to a little pain now and then, or even being restrained. And there had been that time with his old boyfriend Wayne and the ice cubes...

Another shudder wracked Max's body and his cock grew even stiffer. He couldn't help looking up at himself in the mirror. Brown eyes looked back, nearly obscured by a lock of sandy-brown hair that usually got lighter in the summertime. Max fixed his gaze on himself and stroked his prick with deliberate slowness.

His cock felt great in his hand. Max hadn't used quite enough petroleum jelly, so there was a slight sting and burn from the friction of his palm. It added that familiar zing that he usually needed to get him off more quickly, so he tugged harder at himself and felt the tightness in his spine and balls.

Max wanted to ease off for a minute, to go a little

slower and not come so quickly, but his timing was shitty and he knew he'd catch hell from Erik if he didn't get his ass back downstairs and into the kitchen. There'd be time later to take it slow and think about Devin Page—whoa, wait a second.

He would have stopped altogether, but Max's mind flashed back to Devin's ass and the line of that strong, muscular back as Devin had made that earlier dash through the woods. Max's hand moved even faster on his dick as he recalled the firm cheeks that had been outlined so beautifully through Devin's briefs.

With the hand not on his cock, Max reached down and squeezed his balls as hard as he could. The unexpected nudge of pain was enough to send him over, and his prick spasmed in his palm and shot three ropy ribbons of fluid onto the sink in front of him.

Max had to grip the edge of the counter again to keep himself from wobbling. It had been a hard climax, harder than he'd thought it would be. He wondered if thoughts of Devin Page had anything to do with that. Max guessed it didn't matter, really. There were plenty of guys who graced the pages of his mind's fantasy novel.

A quick wipe-up, wash-up, and zip-up, and then Max hopped downstairs and back into the kitchen. "Did you start the sauce?" he started to ask Erik, but stopped short.

Devin was stirring a vat of spaghetti sauce and looking very serious about the spices he was adding. "I got it," he said unnecessarily, never even looking in Max's direction.

Erik shrugged at Max. "He's got it. You could do the bread, though." He nodded at the two long loaves on the counter, waiting to be cut.

Max cast one more look in Devin's direction. When the guy still didn't bother turning around to look back,

Max made a face and went to dig out the bread knife. "You're not on the roster to cook this week," he said to Devin, although Max was pretty sure Devin knew that.

"You left your wingman alone," Devin answered. "I had to step in and assist. Never leave your wingman."

Erik smothered a laugh and Max saw Devin glance over and smile, still stirring. Max rolled his eyes and began to carefully slice the long loaves of French bread. He thought that might be a Top Gun reference, but even though Tom Cruise was hot, Max thought the guy was a weirdo and therefore made it a point not to watch his movies.

The three of them worked together in the kitchen until Andy Merrill bolted in the back door, breathing hard, clad only in red satin boxers. "Gimme five minutes," he gasped. "Be right back."

"Nice drawers," Max smirked. "Can I feel them?"

Andy's expression turned stony. "It was laundry day. My girlfriend gave them to me for Valentine's Day and they were the only clean ones I had. How the hell did I know they'd make us strip down and go play in the woods?" He took himself upstairs, and Max could hear him grumbling in the hallway.

"So where's Capshaw?" Erik turned down the heat under the noodles and went to look out the kitchen window. "Still in the damn trees?"

"I don't know. But we're almost done, so that means he's doing dishes by himself." Max spread butter on the four long halves of bread and sprinkled them with garlic salt before sliding the trays into a warm oven.

The back door slammed open again and Benji Capshaw flew in. "Not doing dishes!" he barked. "You fuckers. I'll be right back." He disappeared through the hallway door just as Andy came back in, fully dressed. "I'm not doing dishes by myself," he informed Andy. "You're helping me. Fucker."

They managed to complete their meal and have it all on the table by the time the senior members trooped in and sat down. Max was relieved to note that all twenty-two of the pledges were accounted for. Just another Tuesday afternoon at the Kappa Delta house. Max took his seat next to Erik and waited to see if Devin would occupy the vacant one on his left.

When Devin chose to sit on Erik's other side and the two of them murmured jokes to each other throughout the meal, Max thought it might be time to get new jerk-off material. Devin was clearly into Max's roommate.

It wasn't until the pledges were trooping home later that evening that it occurred to Max that he hadn't even known Erik was into guys. Almost three months as roommates and it had never occurred to Max to ask.

There were probably a lot of things it hadn't occurred to Max to ask Erik. They were as opposite as they could get, but Max didn't necessarily see it as a bad thing. Erik was anxious, high-strung, and excitable. But, fortunately for Max, Erik was also organized, timely, and reliable. Max had some trouble with the "organized" part, himself. Good thing he had Erik to tell him when the hell they were actually supposed to be places.

Obviously, Devin had found something he liked in Erik. Max could hear the two of them laughing and whispering behind him. So much for his vague plans of making a play for Devin. Oh well, it wasn't as if college wasn't full of guys.

Max wondered if any of those other guys had an ass that looked as good as Devin's in boxer briefs.

The party was in full swing by the time Max got there, but since he had yet to attend any college party that wasn't in full swing from start to finish, Max knew by now it was the norm.

A red plastic cup was shoved in his hand as soon as he crossed the threshold, and a guy who looked like he was thirty-five held out a jar. The jar was stuffed full of bills and coins. "Five bucks," the dude yawned. His eyes were red and he smelled like weed.

Max dug out some crumpled bills and quickly counted how many days were left in the month. His parents were good about depositing his monthly allowance on time, but some months seemed to stretch on forever. He stuck the bills in the overflowing cup and headed for the keg in the corner.

As usual, he had to wait for some over-excited partygoer to finish their keg stand before Max could get himself a cup of beer. He was pleased to note, however, that it wasn't the usual cheap swill from the corner liquor store, but a nice microbrew that had a richer flavor.

He cruised the small apartment, looking for familiar faces. He found one in the kitchen.

"Tisdale!" Benji Capshaw grinned at him and hopped down off the counter. "We need a fourth for beer pong. You're just in time."

"Whose team? Yours? You stink at beer pong." Max looked doubtfully at Benji and remembered the last time Benji had suckered Max into playing with him. Max had had a terrible hangover that lasted two days.

"I know." Benji gave him a mournful look. "But you don't want to disappoint the ladies, do you?" He leered and gestured at two girls Max recognized from their floor in the residence hall.

In truth, he didn't give a shit about the ladies. They were nice girls and Max guessed they were pretty enough.

One of them had on some kind of shimmery crap that made her skin sparkle. Maybe it was hypnotizing Benji.

"Oh, fine," Max sighed, draining his cup to fortify himself. "Buy me pizza later."

"Only if we win!" Benji toddled drunkenly over to the card table where the cups had already been set up and poured.

Thirty minutes later, Max knew there was no way they were going to win. He didn't care so much about that, but he mourned the loss of pizza. Midnight was when his hunger pains always struck.

The girls they were playing with were giggling and whispering to each other. Benji frowned at them. "S'op it," he slurred. "Jus' stop. No more laughin'. Distracts me from playin' good. 'Cause you're real pretty."

That only made them laugh more, of course, and Max couldn't restrain an eye roll. He was drunk, but not as drunk as Benji. When one of the girls landed the ping pong ball in another cup, however, Max knew he'd be quickly on his way to catching up unless he walked away now.

"Done," he announced, waving away the cup that the girl held out to him. "Nope. No more. Gotta exam in the morning. No more beer."

"Max!" Benji whined, reaching for the girl's cup. "You said!"

"Nah, you just heard wrong." Max nodded sagely. "Think about it."

He didn't feel bad for taking advantage of his drunk friend, not when Max had been serious about the test he had to take at ten the next day. He especially didn't feel bad when both of the girls made pouty faces and attached themselves to Benji, one on either side. Benji would get over Max's bail-out soon enough.

Max drained his cup and tossed it toward the trash.

The clock over the kitchen stove caught his eye and he winced. Past one already. He made a mental note next time to get started earlier at night. College parties were like Las Vegas: they went on until sunrise, and hardly anyone ever knew what time it was.

He pushed through the crush of bodies near the door and stumbled out into the fresh fall air. Max waved to a couple of guys he knew from his pre-law program and they raised their cups in salute. He wondered how long it would be until they discovered the time and remembered they were taking the same exam Max was tomorrow morning.

The walk back to his dorm was short. Max let himself in with his passkey and hoped the elevator wasn't out of order again. Living on the seventh floor had seemed like a great idea until he'd been forced to climb the steps more than once. There had been a rumor that a kid had committed suicide by prying open the elevator doors and jumping onto the top of the car, but Max sort of thought that might be one of the college's urban legends.

The elevator was working, thankfully. His hallway was dimly lit, but Max managed to weave his way down to his own room. Key, key, where the hell did he put his key... there! In his left front pocket, like always. Max congratulated himself on his prowess and fumbled with the lock. There was a bandana in the way, for some reason, so he yanked it off and tossed it to the floor before managing to get the door open.

Erik gave a startled squeak and sat up in bed. "What the hell?" he asked Max, pulling the bed covers around him.

Maybe Max had had more beer than he'd thought. He stared at Erik and couldn't figure out why Erik was so surprised to see him. "Why is there music?" he asked, wandering toward the radio with his iPod docked on top.

"Because I like music while I'm having sex," came the smooth response that definitely wasn't Erik.

Max whirled around and stared at the bed. "Devin?"

Devin Page sat up and arched a brow. "You said he'd know what it meant if you hung something on the doorknob," he said to Erik.

"Well… I thought he would," Erik said lamely. "But we've never tried it before, so maybe he didn't know."

Devin chuckled and lay back down, pulling Erik to him. "Clearly." He looked over at Max. "Now you know. Want to come back in an hour or so?"

"Uh. I. Well. Um. What?" Max blinked at him.

"We're busy. Can you come back in an hour? I don't care if you stay, but I think Fischer here might have some trouble performing." Devin gave Max a lazy grin that spoke volumes.

Erik didn't say anything, but when he gave Max a pleading look, it was apparent that he agreed with Devin.

"Uh. Sure?" Max backed hastily out of the room. "Right. An hour. I'll come back in an hour." He shut the door and stood in the hallway, staring at it.

After a moment, he turned and went back down the hallway to the central common room. The couches there were comfortable, so Max lay down on the one in the corner and stared up at the ceiling.

Devin was fucking his roommate. Didn't that just figure?

Max found out after a couple of weeks that Devin was doing more than just fucking Erik. The guy was actually *dating* him. At least, that's what it seemed like to Max.

They went to the movies a lot, and Devin came over to get Erik for coffee a few times. Max figured they were dating.

So when Max caught Devin feeling up one of the endless blonde girls that were forever hanging around the Kappa Delta house, he nearly swallowed his tongue in surprise. "Hey!" he said, unsure of what was actually going on.

"Hey yourself." She smiled. Her name might have been Amanda, but Max wasn't sure. "There's room for three."

Devin grinned that same lazy grin and kept one eye on Max, even while nuzzling into Amanda's neck. "Sure," he drawled. "Room for three."

"Got stuff to do," Max mumbled, and hurried to the kitchen. It was their week to cook again.

Amanda's and Devin's laughter followed Max down the hall.

"He's into girls too," Max said to Erik later that week.

"Duh, no shit." Erik dumped his laundry basket full of clean socks on the floor and sat down to sort them. "Damn it." He held up a red shirt that had gotten mixed in with his whites and stared mournfully at the resulting pink socks. "I should just save my laundry for my mom to do at the holidays."

"You know he's into girls, too? Is he seeing any of them?" Max didn't care about Erik's pink socks.

"How the hell should I know? He's not my boyfriend or anything. Hey, if I wash these again, will the pink come out?"

"I don't think it works like that." Max had accidentally

dumped black jeans in his own wash and everything with white on it came out gray. "And I sort of thought he was. Your boyfriend, I mean."

"Nah. We just messed around a few times and went for chili fries. He doesn't date. Fuck, my mom's going to be mad that I ruined more socks." Erik sighed and continued matching up pairs.

Max watched him for a few moments before speaking up again. "So, are you still seeing each other?" He wanted to kick himself as soon as the question was out. It wasn't like Devin was showing any interest in Max, after all.

Erik shrugged. "Kind of. Sometimes. We're supposed to go to a party on Friday." He stopped and looked up at Max. "Why? Are you interested in him?"

"What? Oh, heh. No. Um." Max bent his head and started fiddling with his laptop screen. His cheeks flamed with heat and he could feel Erik watching him.

Erik snorted and turned back to his wash. "The guy fucks anything that walks. Let him know you're into him and he'll nail you faster than lightning."

His cock gave an involuntary twitch. God, he would love for Devin to nail him. But, on the other hand... did he? Max had more than his fair share of sexual experience. He'd discovered his high school's chapter of GLBT youth group when he was in his sophomore year, and it had been a real eye-opener for him in terms of his own sexuality.

But he'd never wanted to be the guy who someone else fucked and then left.

"Whatever." Max laughed, trying to play it off. "I'm not into him."

"Me either." Erik shrugged. "But he's good in bed."

Max pretended not to hear.

In truth, Erik's innocent statement fueled Max's fantasies for the next few weeks. It was all he could do to keep himself from getting hard every time he was in Devin's presence, which turned out to be a lot. They were thrown together constantly because of fraternity functions.

The latest function was one that Max hoped wasn't a regular thing. Kappa Delta was giving a dance for their pledges, complete with the Zeta Pi sorority girls as dates. The rest of the pledges were thrilled; Max couldn't care less. Sororities were definitely not high on his interest list.

He wandered the edges of the university's event hall and stuck a finger in his collar, trying to pull it away from his neck. Not only was it a stupid dance, but it was a stupid *formal* dance. His mom had gladly given him the extra hundred dollars for the tux rental.

"Pictures!" she'd squealed into the phone. "You must send pictures, Maxie."

Max had no intention of capturing this for posterity, but he hadn't told her that.

He leaned on the wall with a sigh and tried to calculate how long it would be until one of the giggling sorority pledges zeroed in on him. There was a gaggle of them across the way. Max tried not to make eye contact.

"Don't make eye contact," someone murmured in his ear, echoing his thoughts.

Max looked over to see Devin slouching against the wall next to him. His tux fit him well, and Max tried not to glance down to see how snug it was in the crotch region. "I'm trying not to. But I don't think they care."

Sure enough, two of them had detached from their pack and were slinking their way across the dance floor. Devin chuckled. "Play it cool."

There was no time to reply before the two girls stood

before them. They both had long hair and wore dresses that hugged their slim figures. They were pretty enough, Max guessed. Any of the other pledges would have been thrilled to have been approached. Well, except maybe for Erik.

"Ladies." Devin grinned. "You smell good."

They tittered and nudged each other with tanned arms. "I'm Jackie," said one, giving Max the eye.

"Cool." Max extended his hand, which Jackie shook. She waited for a moment before saying, "And you're…?"

"Paul," Devin piped up, ignoring the other girl that was trying to get his attention. "He's Paul and I'm Todd." Devin inched closer to Max, letting their sleeves brush.

Max smiled weakly at Jackie and shrugged one shoulder. "What he said."

The girls exchanged glances and then Jackie looked back at Max. She made a small fanning motion with her hand and looked pained. "Sort of hot in here, isn't it? Don't they have the air on? Boy, it's sure making me thirsty."

Max thought that might be his cue to go and fetch her a drink, although, since they were on campus, all the drinks at the dance were non-alcoholic. "Uh," he started to say, but Devin interrupted him.

"And for me, too," he purred, leaning in close to Max and nuzzling along Max's jawline.

Max's body responded instantly despite his initial shock. He knew Devin was playing a part for the girls, but Max's cock had no idea. Max shifted a little as his dick started to firm up and the hairs on the back of his neck prickled with anticipation.

Jackie blinked at Devin and then turned to give the other girl a raised eyebrow. Her friend raised her eyebrow back and the two of them turned on their expensive heels and left. Max watched as they returned to their group and immediately began whispering.

"Come on," Devin hissed, grabbing Max's sleeve and tugging him toward the door. "Before they can point us out to someone who knows our real names."

Max followed Devin automatically, but his mind was racing. It wouldn't be long until the girls talked to one of the senior frat members about the two guys who were into each other, and then where would he and Devin be? Max still had no clue if being gay would cause a problem.

Devin was laughing as they burst outside into the chilly night. "Over here!" He pulled Max around the side of the building and into a small alcove in the brick. Devin leaned against the wall and laughed hard enough to bring tears to his eyes. "Fucking hilarious. Did you see them? God, that was funny."

"We could get in trouble." Max looked around uncertainly, but leaned next to Devin anyway, stealing the opportunity to be close to him.

"Nah, we're clear. There isn't even anyone in the damn frat with the names Paul and Todd." Devin chuckled a bit more and rubbed at his eyes with the heel of his hand.

"But when we go back in…" Max trailed off when he realized he was sounding like Erik, all worried about something that was probably not a big deal.

Devin snorted and nudged Max with a shoulder. "We're not going back in. That'd be social suicide for sure. They won't miss us, man. All of them were halfway to loaded. Didn't you see Greg and those guys hiding their flasks in their jackets? It was only the pledges that weren't allowed to have any fun."

Max considered that and decided Devin was right. "Okay. So what are we doing instead?"

Devin looked over at him and the sliver of moonlight through the campus trees caught the blue of his eyes.

"Shoot," he drawled, edging closer to Max, "could think of plenty to do."

The undercurrent of sex that oozed out of Devin's voice went straight to Max's semi-hard prick. Max went from halfway erect to at attention in moments. Damn Devin anyway, how was he doing that? The guy wasn't anything special.

Except he was, for some reason. He was hot and young and his body was pressing up against Max's in just the right way. "Come on, Max," Devin whispered with a grin. "I know you've got an idea or two." Devin snuck his hand out and rested it over the bulge in Max's rented slacks.

"I'm not getting come in these pants," Max squeaked. "They're not mine."

It was a stupid thing to say, but Devin laughed anyway. The shaft of moonlight had moved and was no longer highlighting the blue of his eyes, but Max knew they were twinkling. He'd watched Devin enough to know.

"I won't let you get come in your pants. In my mouth is better." Devin winked and dropped to his knees on the pavement. Max had a moment of concern for the knees of Devin's slacks, but then realized he was way too worried about their respective trousers. He was about to get—oh, holy fuck.

Max's pants were unzipped and his cock was in Devin's mouth before he'd even registered any of it. And it wasn't just any mouth, as Max quickly came to realize. It was one of the softest, tightest mouths he'd ever had around his dick. He couldn't help thrusting up in response, then realized he'd better try and slow down to enjoy it.

The brick was rough against the back of Max's head, but every other sensation paled in comparison to the gentle, sucking pulls his prick was receiving. He'd had blowjobs before and thought that they were good.

Apparently he had been wrong.

Devin looked up and smiled a little before going back to what he was doing. A long, sweeping stroke up the side of Max's cock with his tongue, then an easy swirl around the head with a little dip into the slit before going back down the other side. Max's hands automatically went to Devin's hair, and he wove his fingers into the longish strands.

"You're good at this," Max gasped, his hips once more jutting forward of their own accord.

"I know," came the answer, and it didn't really sound smug as much as matter-of-fact, but by then Max didn't care. He just wanted more of it.

Devin complied by going down farther, his lips closing around Max's shaft and everything inside his mouth going soft and relaxed and wet. Max could feel Devin's throat open for him. Devin swallowed and then the tight suction was back, making Max thunk his head against the brick wall behind him.

Max could feel his toes curling inside his good dress shoes. The tension in his body was building and something had to give, despite the fact that he could have stood there all night long with Devin sucking his cock. Max's balls gave the familiar warning sign of going high and tight all at once, so Max shut his eyes and tried to pull away. Not everyone liked come in their mouths.

Devin must have sensed what Max was about to do and immediately reached up to slide his hands around Max's ass. It effectively trapped Max in place, and Max had no other choice. "Oh fuck, right now," was all he could whisper before he jerked forward and started to come.

His orgasm was pulled out of him by Devin's mouth. Devin milked and sucked Max until he was shaking and lightheaded. Max let go of Devin's head and grabbed the wall for support when he felt himself slide sideways. "Whoa. Uh."

"Max, for Christ's sake," Devin whispered harshly. "A little help?"

Max blinked and looked down to see Devin still kneeling on the cement, his slacks unzipped and his leaking cock in his fist. "Damn, sorry." He dropped down next to Devin and slid his hand over the slick tip.

"Fast. I like it fast." Devin let his hand fall away and he closed his eyes, chest heaving.

Max gave it to him fast. He always liked learning someone new and Devin was no exception. The man had a smooth, uncut cock that was nicely thick around. His foreskin was insanely soft to the touch and Max stared at it, fascinated. Most of the guys he'd been with had been circumcised.

Devin made a soft sound and arched forward into Max's hand, so Max got down to business and started jacking Devin quickly. He could have wished for a little bit of lube, but Devin didn't seem to mind the lack of it. In fact, the tighter Max's hand got, the more noise Devin made.

The possibility of discovery became more real as Devin got closer to climaxing. He panted and moaned and generally made a bunch of noise that Max thought someone was sure to overhear. Clearly, it was up to Max to make it good but make it fast.

He leaned forward and slammed his mouth down over Devin's while tugging hard on that cock. Devin gasped into Max's mouth and began to shudder. "Yes, there," he moaned, trying to get closer to Max and shoving through the tunnel of Max's fingers. "God!"

One more tight stroke and then finally Devin was coming with trembling little jerks against Max's hand. His come was warm and sticky in Max's fingers and the smell of sex rose up between them, making Max's own cock give a renewed twitch. Shit, he wished they were somewhere with four walls and a bed.

Devin leaned against Max heavily and tried to catch his breath. "Thanks," he grinned, planting a kiss on Max and looking much more relaxed than a few minutes ago. "That was just how I like it."

Max fought off the ridiculous urge to blush and was about to respond when a flash of light caught his eye. "Oh, fuck," he murmured, pushing away from Devin and scrambling to his feet. He yanked the handkerchief out of his vest pocket and hastily wiped his hand off before reaching down and pulling Devin up with him. "Put your dick away!"

Devin blinked the hazy look out of his eyes and turned his head to see what Max was staring at. The shine of the flashlight on the pavement around the corner of the building was obvious, and he started to chuckle. "Campus security," he whispered. "Classic."

"God, come on," Max pleaded, when Devin seemed in no apparent hurry to pull up his slacks. "This is the last thing I need."

Another soft laugh was Devin's answer, but he tucked himself away and did up his zipper. "Calm down. They can't do anything to us."

Max fumbled with his fly and didn't respond. He couldn't get the button through the hole and settled for yanking his white dress shirt down over the zipper just as the security guard rounded the corner and spotted them.

"Hello," the guard said suspiciously. "What are the likes of you two doing out here?" He lifted his flashlight to illuminate their faces, making Max and Devin both squint and shade their eyes.

"Just getting air." Devin sounded nonchalant and he leaned back against the brick. "Really hot in there."

The guard's gaze lit on the pledge pins on their jackets. "Frat dance, huh?"

"Yeah, man. The chicks were all over us, so we just needed time to come out here and plan our method of attack." Devin winked and Max could hear the fake friendliness he infused in his words. The guard couldn't have been more than five years their senior.

"Heh. Yeah, I hear what you're saying." The guard grinned and lowered his flashlight.

"We're headed back in right now." Devin nodded. "Hey, wanna come with us? I'll introduce you." He gestured with his head toward the door of the building.

Max held back a snort. Devin was playing with the guard like he was a toy, but somehow Max didn't think the guy was smart enough to figure it out.

"Nah, I'm on the clock." The guard sounded regretful. "But maybe I'll stop in afterwards? I'm off in two hours."

Devin pushed off from the wall and tugged at Max's jacket to indicate he should do the same. "Hey, great! I'm Paul and this is Todd. Come on in later and find us. We'll introduce you to some really lovely ladies." He leered slightly and the guard looked pleased.

"Sure, okay. You two go on inside, now, so I don't get in trouble." He smiled and then seemed to remember something. "Uh... you weren't drinking out here, right?" He shone his flashlight at their feet, looking for contraband.

"Come on, man. You see any empties?" Devin spread his arms and shook his head, then took a step or two toward the side of the building. Max followed him.

The guard laughed. "Okay, just checking. See you guys later, maybe."

"Definitely!" Devin gave a little wave and took off in the opposite direction, Max at his heels.

When they were clear of the guard, Max breathed again. "You told the girls that I was Paul and *you* were Todd."

Devin laughed. "Did I? Does it matter?"

"I don't like the name Todd. I have a cousin named Todd who's a real asshole."

For some reason, Devin found that uproarious. He began laughing hard enough to bring tears to his eyes, and Max had no choice but to laugh with him.

"Oh, man," Devin said a while later, wiping his eyes with the back of his hand. "You're funny, Tisdale." There was warmth in Devin's voice and Max knew he wasn't being insulted.

"So now where are we going?" Max looked around to see where they'd wandered to under the guise of getting away from the security guard.

Devin turned onto a small bike path that cut through the center of campus. "Woodstock's."

Woodstock's had excellent pizza and stayed open until three a.m. Max approved of this plan, so he walked in silence with Devin until they reached the small, walk-up pizza place that was just on the west edge of the school grounds.

They each ordered two slices from the window and sat down at one of the rickety tables. Devin shrugged off his jacket and inhaled his first slice. Max picked off his pepperoni pieces one by one and ate them.

Devin watched him. "So, you're kind of a rule follower, aren't you." There was no question mark in his voice.

Max looked up, startled. "Um. Maybe? I guess so. My dad's an attorney, it's kind of ingrained in me."

"No wonder. My dad's a cop, which makes that even funnier." Devin laughed a little and dropped his pizza crust before starting on his other piece. "But that's cool. Just gives me something to work with." He winked and took an enormous bite.

The implications of that statement were numerous, but Max decided it meant that he and Devin would be spending more time together.

Cool.

They finished their pizza slices and decided to split one more. When the final piece was demolished, Devin raised his arms over his head and stretched. "You got class tomorrow?"

Tomorrow was Friday, a typical day off for most students. Max had made the error of registering for a Friday class back in the summer when he didn't know better, but quickly realized his mistake when school started. He'd been able to withdraw and take the debate class on Tuesdays and Thursdays instead.

"No class. I have to work at ten, though." The campus bookstore didn't offer much money, but it was something. Jobs on campus were hard to come by, especially for freshmen.

"Yeah? Meet me for coffee at nine. Over at The Grinder; you know it?"

"I know it." Max did; he and Erik had studied there before.

"See you tomorrow, Tisdale." Devin got up from the table and winked at Max before sauntering off into the darkness of campus.

He was awake at 6:45, even though by the time Max had finally fallen asleep the night before it had been two a.m. Bits and pieces of what he and Devin had done together had kept sneaking in around the edges of sleep, preventing it from overtaking Max and instead just making him hard. He finally ended up jerking off in the middle of the night, glad for the freedom of Erik being gone.

Max got up when the sun peeked through the blinds. He showered and ignored the gritty feeling of too little sleep from his eyes. It was a common occurrence in college anyway, resulting from either studying or partying. Max had quickly grown used to it his first month here.

He purposely gave no thought to his clothing, because to do otherwise would imply that this was some kind of date or something. It wasn't a date, it was just coffee, and then Max had to work so there wouldn't be time for anything else.

But, Christ, Max wanted there to be time.

Erik had come home sometime during one of Max's rare periods of sleep, so Max was quiet about dressing and running a comb through his hair. He closed the door gently behind him and didn't bother waiting for the hall elevator, preferring instead to take the steps two at a time down to the ground floor.

The Grinder was just off campus and Max set out in that direction, glad that he'd remembered a hoodie to fend off the chill of the fall morning. It was a short walk to the coffee shop and he arrived at two minutes after nine, snagging a small table in the front window so he could see Devin arrive.

By 9:29, Max knew he was being stood up.

The clock on the wall ticked over to 9:30 just as Max realized that Devin was probably not going to show. He was absurdly grateful that the table where he sat held magazines and the daily paper. Max grabbed one of them and started leafing through it as if he'd meant to be there alone the whole time.

At five minutes before ten o'clock, Max dropped the magazine back on the table and walked out the door. He retraced his steps across campus to the bookstore and arrived at 10:01, still pinning on his nametag even as he took his place behind the register.

"New shipment of textbooks," Jenny informed him. "You look tired."

"Thanks," Max snapped, unaware until that moment that he'd moved past 'annoyed' and into 'pissed off.' "Tell Cheryl to do the fucking books. I did the last three orders."

Jenny leaned on the register counter and raised a brow. "Bad morning?" she asked, not ruffled by Max's mood. "Or bad night?" The last comment was accompanied by a slight leer. Jenny loved to hear about Max's exploits with the 'homosexual agenda,' as she put it.

"Nothing. No. Neither." Max grabbed a fresh roll of register tape and began putting it in, just for something to do.

"Oh, Max. Don't you know by now that you're going to tell me everything, even if you think you can keep it to yourself? You wait and see. I'll owe you a beer by the end of the day if you haven't told me." Jenny smiled at him and flipped a streak of her turquoise hair over her shoulder before she walked away.

She was right, of course, and on his lunch break Max sat on the bench outside the bookstore's back door and watched Jenny smoke.

"I got stood up this morning."

"Heh, welcome to a woman's world. You date guys; you've never been stood up before?" She turned her head to blow out a puff of smoke and then looked at Max curiously.

"I don't really date." Max scuffed the heel of his tennis shoe along the pavement. "I mess around a lot, though. And you know what sucks? I have to see this guy all the time. He's a pledge, too."

Jenny frowned and stubbed out her cigarette. "That

was stupid of him. He knows he'll be seeing you at that stupid fraternity and he still stood you up?" Jenny wasn't fond of college organizations and didn't mind saying so.

"It's not stupid." That was his patented response each time. "And yeah. Dunno, we were both kind of drunk when we made the date, but." Max shrugged. "It would have been cool."

"So what are you going to say when you see him?"

Max hadn't really thought that far ahead. "Uh. No idea. Nothing, I guess. It was just coffee." Coffee with Devin Page.

"Oh, whatever." Jenny rolled her eyes and stood up. "Guys are so weird. Girls have a whole plan of attack when things like this happen to them. Let me know if you want help strategizing." She shook her head and went back inside.

Max stared out at the small back alley. It was just coffee.

As it turned out, Max was kept busy enough with notes and classes and research papers and exams that he didn't have a lot of time to think about being stood up. For a few days, at least, because three nights later there was a pledge meeting at the house.

The topics of their pledge meetings were usually something banal. The last one had been called "The University Social Scene" and was all about how to avoid getting roofies in your drink or why it was generally frowned upon to do it to others. Max had stopped listening after ten minutes and spent the next hour kicking Erik's shin.

Tonight's meeting was about their upcoming final exams and how pulling all-nighters was not actually conducive to doing well. Max could almost hear the collective eye rolls from his pledge brothers.

Devin was late. Max told himself he only noticed because, when the front door opened, Devin brought in a rush of cold night air with him. Otherwise, Max hadn't even realized that Devin had been missing from the group that sat in the front room of the house.

That was total bullshit, of course. Max had known from the moment he walked in that Devin wasn't there. Pretending otherwise was making him feel better, though, so Max continued to feign indifference when Devin sat down right next to him on the couch.

It was hard as fucking hell to concentrate on whatever the speaker was babbling about, but Max tried. He tried as hard as he could to ignore Devin's thigh pressed up against his own and the heat radiating off Devin's body. He thought he was doing a pretty good job of it, but his dick had other ideas.

Thank Christ he hadn't hung up his jacket when he'd walked in. Max draped it over his lap to hide his developing erection and stared as hard as he could at the woman who was still talking.

"Bathroom," Devin whispered, and then he was off the couch and crossing the room. Max watched him disappear down the hallway and heard the downstairs bathroom door close.

Oh, no. No way was Max jumping because Devin told him to. There was just no damn way, not after feeling like an idiot all week. He wasn't going to do it. Max would let the guy wait for him in the bathroom all fucking night.

Except Max found himself getting up and skirting the edges of the room, heading out the opposite doorway that Devin had gone through, and then going the long way through the kitchen and dining room. He entered the empty hallway from the back and slipped into the bathroom, closing the door behind him.

Devin was perched on the edge of the sink, grinning at him. "Hi, Tisdale."

"You're a dick." The words were out before Max even knew he was thinking them.

The grin vanished from Devin's face. "What?"

Max scowled. "A dick. I said you're a dick. You heard me."

Devin pushed off the sink and took a step toward Max. "What the hell is wrong with you?"

"The fact that you're a dick. That's what's wrong with me." Okay, so maybe now he was getting a little repetitive, but it felt good to keep saying the words.

Blue eyes narrowed. Devin stepped in even closer and appeared to study Max's face. "I liked you. We had fun. So what's with the attitude?"

Christ, did the guy really not know? Max forced himself to stand his ground and not let Devin back him up against the bathroom door. "Friday morning," he explained. "You and me, coffee? The Grinder? You left me sitting there alone like an asshole for an hour. You could have at least called and made a lame excuse if you didn't want to go. I would have pretended to fall for it."

Devin blinked and stared at Max blankly. "Friday morning? What?"

Oh. Oh, shit. Devin didn't remember. Max closed his eyes and sagged. "Thursday night after you and I—after we—um, you know."

"Had pizza?" Devin tilted his head and Max thought he detected a glimmer of a smile.

"Right, sure. After we had pizza." Which was after they'd messed around up against the side of a building. "You asked me to meet you for coffee at The Grinder the next morning." Max had a sinking feeling that this was not going to turn out well.

"I asked you to meet me... aw, damn." Guilt crossed Devin's features and he sighed. "Max. I was really, really drunk that night."

Max frowned. They'd both been drinking, but Devin had seemed pretty with it. Especially when his mouth had been wrapped around Max's cock. "How drunk?"

"Drunk enough that I don't remember asking you out." Devin dropped his gaze and bit his bottom lip endearingly.

"But you remember us having pizza." Max could hear the doubt in his own voice.

Devin nodded. "Uh huh. And I remember sucking you off against the wall." He glanced up from under his lashes and Max's prick gave a traitorous twitch.

Sternly telling his dick to calm down, Max gave Devin a long look. It was true that they'd both been drinking, although Max hadn't realized Devin had been that drunk. But he didn't know the guy that well, did he?

Ignoring the fact that he'd known Devin well enough to stick his cock in Devin's mouth, Max sighed and nodded. "Okay. It's cool."

Devin moved in closer and curved his mouth into a half-smile. "You should have called me," he murmured. "Woken my ass up and yelled at me to get down to The Grinder."

"You should have been there in the first place," Max countered, not moving away even though he knew he should. Devin just smelled so good, like some combination of clean clothes and light aftershave.

"You're right." Devin grinned and tilted his head to nuzzle behind Max's ear. "I suck. Let me make it up to you."

"How?" Max shivered, goosebumps rising on his skin from Devin's warm breath.

Devin smiled against Max's neck. "You could fuck

me up against the sink." He dug in his back pocket and produced a condom. "See? Always prepared."

He was about to say no, because, God, they were in the bathroom for Christ's sake, and there was a fucking meeting going on down the hall, and oh holy shit they'd be in so much trouble if they were caught. Just, no.

That was before Devin pressed his erection up against Max's hip, however, and it was definitely before Devin reached down and cupped Max's cock over his jeans. "Come on," Devin murmured. "I want to feel this in my ass. Do it."

It was too much temptation. Max pulled out of Devin's grasp and shoved at Devin's shoulder to turn him around. Devin grabbed the edge of the sink; Max could see Devin's eyes glinting at him in the mirror. "Unzip," Max told him.

Devin nodded and undid his fly. He let his jeans drop to his ankles and stepped one foot out of them. "There," he said softly, pointing to the cabinet under the sink. "There's hand lotion under there. I checked."

Well, that was presumptuous of him. Max thought for a moment that he should be annoyed, but Devin's ass was round and smooth and right there in front of him, so all thoughts of irritation fled. He dropped his own jeans to his hips, snatched the condom from the edge of the sink, and rolled it on. A quick look under the sink revealed the bottle of lotion.

Max coated his fingers with too much of the slippery stuff, but when he carefully slid one finger into Devin's hole, Devin didn't seem to care that Max was getting lotion everywhere.

"Oh, yeah," Devin whispered into the stillness of the bathroom. "Yeah. Another one. Don't be shy."

"Tight." Max swallowed hard and gave Devin another finger, stretching and easing the way. "Jesus. You're so tight."

Devin moaned by way of response and spread his legs. It made his back arch and his ass rise. "Come on. Come on, come on, come on."

"Okay, easy," Max whispered. He withdrew his hand and lined up, smearing a little more lotion on the already-lubed condom. "I don't want to hurt you."

Devin wiggled. "I'll tell you if you do." He dropped his head and Max could see his fingers tighten on the edge of the sink. "Max, for fuck's sake. Do it."

Max eased forward little by little, feeling the tight ring of muscle give way for him until he was totally buried and his balls rested at the curve of Devin's ass cheek. His cock throbbed and he stayed perfectly still, afraid of coming right then. "Wait," he panted. "Oh, shit. Don't move."

"Fuck that." Devin clenched hard around Max and circled his own cock with a hand. He began to stroke himself, clenching and unclenching as he did. "I said do it!"

There was no way for Max to resist, and he didn't really want to. He gripped Devin's hip with one hand and moved. Out just a little, then back in. Again, then again, until a fine sheen of sweat broke out on his forehead and Max was trembling with the effort to hold back his orgasm.

Devin was making soft gasps and little moans that Max could just hear over the sound of his own breathing. His hand moved faster on his prick and his hips jerked forward and back in time with Max's strokes. "Yes," he groaned, head falling back. "Max. Right now."

Max forced his eyes open and craned his neck to see in the mirror. He was just in time to see Devin tug hard on his cock and spray warm ribbons of come over his hand and the sink. His ass tightened even more around Max's prick, and that was enough to make Max shudder and start to come, too.

He slammed in one more time and froze where he was, filling the condom and feeling the tingles spread out through his limbs. Devin helped by pushing back against Max, keeping him buried deep while Max's cock throbbed and twitched.

The only sound in the small bathroom was their mingled panting breaths, until Devin groaned a little and shifted. Max slipped out of him and did a quick condom clean-up. "You okay?" he asked Devin while tying off the rubber and hiding it in the trash. "God, it stinks like sex in here."

"I'm great." Devin grinned at Max in the mirror and then bent to tug his jeans up. "And this is a frat house. They'll never notice. Either that, or they'll secretly congratulate whoever got laid in the bathroom."

Thankfully, the hand soap dispenser wasn't empty like it usually was. Max washed his hands and face and caught a glimpse of himself in the mirror. Oh, there was no way anyone would think anything but that he'd just gotten lucky. His eyes were bright, his cheeks were pink, and his chest was slightly puffed out. One glance at Devin revealed the same 'I just got off' signs.

They were screwed.

"You worry a lot," Devin laughed, edging Max aside so he could wash his hands and face too.

"I do not." Max frowned. "Erik worries a lot. I just worry about everyday stuff."

Devin smirked. "Erik does worry a lot. But you're a close second. Ready?"

Max opened the door and peeked out. The meeting in the living room was still going. "You go first," he whispered.

"Okay," Devin mock-whispered back, really loudly. "Me first."

Max scowled and shoved him out the door into the hallway. "Smartass."

"Yeah," Devin chuckled. He shoved his hands in his front jean pockets and wandered back in the direction of the living room, tossing Max a wink over his shoulder before disappearing through the doorway.

It wasn't until Max had counted to two hundred and slipped out of the bathroom that he realized Devin hadn't asked him for another date.

"So you should have asked *him*," Jenny said, exasperation plain in her voice. "He just let you... you know. Fuck him. You could have just said 'meet me for pizza and more fucking tomorrow.' But maybe without the 'more fucking' part." She continued shelving new textbooks on the row under the one Max was working on.

He sighed and scanned ISBN numbers. The scanner made an irritating beep noise with each one and that was giving him a headache. "I wanted him to ask me."

Jenny snorted. "Now you sound like a girl. Get over it. Clearly the boy doesn't ask people out unless he's drunk. Why you'd want to go out with someone like that is a mystery anyway, but you're a guy and I don't pretend to understand you. God, Max. Snap out of it!"

Max looked down at the top of her turquoise head. "You're right."

"I know. Hurry up, you're falling behind. I'm almost done with this row."

Max frowned and kept scanning. The rest of the day was spent doing much the same thing as he and Jenny worked side by side with the new stock. Max refrained from mentioning Devin again, but in his head the wheels were turning.

Six hours passed quickly and when Max got back to his room, Erik was getting dressed to go out. Or rather, he was getting undressed. Max studied him.

"Is that a sheet?"

"Yeah." Erik sighed and studied himself in the full-length mirror on the back of their door. "I can't figure out how to tie it so my ass isn't showing."

"Why the hell are you wearing a sheet?"

The sheet in question dropped to the floor in a puddle of fabric and Erik kicked it. It billowed up and then down again in pretty much the same place. "Because that toga run is tonight, remember? You said you were going to go. Better get your sheet." He snorted and picked up his own sheet again, trying to find a way to tie it on that didn't allow for glimpses of naked flesh.

Damn, Max had forgotten about the toga run. It was an unofficial university tradition the week before finals. A vast number of students dressed up in white sheets and not much else and ran through town at ten minutes to midnight. They ended up at various bars, of course, and the students under legal drinking age without a decent fake I.D. card dispersed to other places to get drunk for no reason. Other than to celebrate the toga run, naturally.

"Here, let me tie the fucking thing," Max sighed, yanking the corners of the sheet over Erik's shoulder and knotting it.

"Cool." Erik studied himself in the mirror. "I got kicked out of Boy Scouts because I couldn't tie knots. Where's your sheet, man?"

"I, um. Think I'm gonna skip it." Max shoved some books off his bed and flopped down.

"What!" Erik was dangerously close to a screech and Max winced. "You have to go with me, Max. No way I'm running through the goddamn streets by myself."

Max laughed. "By yourself? There'll be five hundred other people with you." At least.

Erik propped his hands on his hips and scowled. "Don't be an asshole. Come with me so I don't have to hate you."

"You won't hate me when you have the hangover of death and I'm bringing you water and aspirin." Max craned his neck to look for his mp3 player amid the mess on his nightstand.

"I'll hate you a lot for not having a hangover with me. Max, you're a fucking pussy, get the hell up and go with me!"

What the fuck else was there to do, really? Sit around and mourn the date he and Devin never went on? Max rolled his eyes and sat up. "I don't have a white sheet."

Erik went to his bottom drawer and pulled out a light blue one. "Here. Good enough. No one cares what color the sheet is. Cool, we're gonna have fun." He was grinning in his exuberance as he shoved the sheet in Max's direction.

Max constructed a decent toga out of his sheet and found himself nearly shoved out the door by a buoyant Erik. "Awesome, come on, we have to meet the KD guys in front of The Spotted Elk at eight. Here!" Erik shoved a flask into Max's hand. "Drink a little of that, you'll feel better." Clearly, Erik had already been drinking some of whatever was in there.

He let Erik propel him toward The Spotted Elk, an extremely raucous and popular bar in the center of town. There were already dozens of toga-clad students milling about the area. Max had to grin when he saw some of the get-ups they'd concocted for themselves. He winced inwardly at the idiots wearing sandals, though. They were bound to get their feet crushed in the melee.

Greg and Andy were among the dozen or so frat brothers

in front of The Spotted Elk and they grinned madly when they saw Erik and Max. "Toga!" they shouted, raising their arms above their heads and revealing that they wore very little under their sheets. Max glanced around for Devin before berating himself for looking in the first place.

There was more disorganized milling about as the crowd grew and things got noisier. Max continued to share Erik's flask until it was sadly empty, but the Jack Daniels that had been in there had been enough to start a nice buzz for Max. He assumed they'd meet for beers at someone's place after the run, and he was grateful to Erik for making him come out after all.

It seemed as if everyone was content to just stand around in bed sheets and not actually run anywhere, but just as Max was thinking that he'd need more liquor soon before his buzz totally died, a pretty blonde coed was boosted up to the top of a trash can under the street light.

"Hi, togas!" she screamed. The crowd hooted and hollered back at her, which she seemed to like because she planted her hands on her hips and batted her eyelashes at them. "Listen up! The run starts here and goes through town to the other side of campus! Your ending point is at Jolly Roger's on Cherry Avenue!"

"My Jolly Roger wants your Cherry Avenue!" yelled one of the too-drunk crowd members. It made no sense, but it got a huge laugh anyway and the girl giggled and rolled her eyes.

"Ready, togas?" The blonde held up three fingers. "Three... two... RUN!"

Max got yanked by the arm along with the surging crowd. Erik was laughing and running with the throng, so Max did his best to keep up. There were people everywhere, all around him, and Max wondered fleetingly how the girls and some of the shorter guys weren't being totally dragged under.

The students swarmed down the road, filling the street and sidewalks. Max wondered, if he lifted his feet from the ground, whether he'd still be carried along by the crowd, and decided not to try it. It was taking all his concentration just to stay near Erik and some of their brothers.

When the enormous swarm of people reached the dead end at Peach and Hickory, there were two ways to turn. The street came to a T and Max assumed they'd go right, since that was the shortest and straightest way to the other side of campus. Erik and the others obviously had the same thought and headed in that direction, but as Max tried to follow them, he was met head-on by a giant group of runners that had the opposite idea.

He grabbed for the back of Erik's sheet, but missed. Erik was swallowed up by the oncoming crowd and Max found himself shoved into the corner of the bank building that loomed to his left. There was a vague sensation of pain as his bare arm scraped along the brick.

"Wrong way!" one of the runners shouted gleefully. Max gave him the finger and tried pushing against them. It got him nowhere except rammed straight back against the wall, scraping his arm even further.

Max was about to give up and let himself be swept along in the other direction when he felt tight fingers around his wrist. Someone yanked him, stumbling, out of the dangerous spot and into the crowd that was running in the direction he'd first wanted to go.

It was dark and the streetlights weren't sufficient light for Max to see who his rescuer was. He was dragged along for another few yards before Max was wrenched out of the main throng of people and hauled into a side street.

Devin bent over, hands on his knees, chest heaving. "That was a goddamned madhouse."

Max swallowed and stared at him. "One, how the hell did you find me in there? And two, thanks, but I would have been fine on my own." He knew it sounded snotty, but there was still lingering resentment there, apparently.

"I was behind you the whole time. I got there just as that blonde chick started us off. And you might have been fine, but you're bleeding." Devin lifted his chin at Max's arm.

Max looked down, expecting to see scrapes and a bit of blood. What he actually saw were long gashes that leaked thin crimson trails down his arm that dripped from his elbow. "Uh." His head reeled. Looking at other people's blood was not an issue, but his own was another story.

"Whoa. Come here." Devin pulled gently at Max's other arm and led him farther away from the noise and clamor. They retreated a few more feet and stopped in the doorway of a closed hardware store. "Sit for a second," Devin advised, pushing Max down to the step.

Max didn't argue. He sat gingerly, doing his best to avoid looking at his arm. Max held it out to his side at rather an awkward angle and leaned his head back against the door. "Thanks," he relented, knowing that Devin had done him a favor by pulling him out of the crowd. It was sort of embarrassing, but Max's mom had raised him to show some manners.

"No problem." Devin sat next to him and untied Max's sheet. "You'll have to get yourself another one," he apologized, using the fabric to wipe at Max's bleeding arm. "Tell your mom you ruined it in the wash. That's what I do. Then she sends me new stuff."

"It's Erik's. He'll make a huge issue out of it." Max watched as Devin used gentle patting motions to clean up most of the blood.

Devin chuckled and continued swiping at Max's scrapes. "Nah, you gotta be really dramatic and overboard when you tell him what happened. That's the way to handle Erik; make whatever happened to you way worse than anything that's happened to him. He'll be in awe and forget to be pissed."

Max blinked. Devin was right. That was exactly the way to handle Erik, only Max hadn't realized it until Devin said it. "That's pretty observant," Max said thoughtfully. "I didn't know you had spent that much time with Erik." Max was *not* jealous.

"I didn't, really. I just like to watch people. But even so, Erik's easy." Devin laughed and then bent his head to study Max's arm. "This is still bleeding, and it's got dirt and junk in it. You need to wash it off and then bandage it, at least for tonight."

He chanced a look downward at his injured arm, ready to jerk his eyes away if the blood was still dripping. Devin had done a great job, however, of mopping up and cleaning what he could, and though the wounds still oozed beads of blood, Max was able to look at it without feeling nauseated.

"I guess I'll go back and clean up," Max said. "Not really how I planned to finish the run, but whatever."

"Come on." Devin grinned and nodded his head in the direction of the street that was emptying itself of toga-clad students. "Come back to my room and I'll help. I don't want to hear about you fainting while trying to wash off your own blood."

Max was glad for the cover of nighttime when he felt his cheeks heat. "My mom always wanted me to take over her practice, but my dad knew I wasn't cut out for it the first time I fell off my bike. I split my lip open and didn't stop screaming at the blood for hours." He heaved himself off the step and followed Devin back down the alley.

"Your mom's a doctor and you can't handle blood? Hilarious." Devin laughed and winked at him.

"Your dad's a cop and you committed lewd acts in public with me." Max said it before he thought better of the statement, but Devin just laughed some more and shook his head.

"True enough. Not to mention doing numerous other things that would send my old man to an early grave. Good thing I'm in college and can use stupidity as an excuse, huh?" Devin didn't sound concerned as he pushed through a small cluster of people that still lingered in the street.

The walk back to Devin's dorm was quick. He lived in the closest residence hall to the edge of campus. Max glanced up at the two-story building before Devin swiped his key card and opened the front door. "Greentree's supposed to be the quiet dorm, right?"

Devin snorted. "Yeah, whatever the hell that means. My parents saw in the information package that Greentree was for the students who wanted 'a studious, quiet environment.' What that should actually say is that it's for the parents who want the studious environment. This dorm parties like all the rest of them."

Indeed, Max could hear the low thump-thump of a stereo as they climbed the stairs and headed down the hall to Devin's room. He concentrated on the noise rather than the fact that they were going to Devin's room, and Max probably knew what would happen when they got there. Or his dick did, anyway, since it was starting to wake up. Damn it.

The last room on the right side of the hallway had a dry-erase message board stuck to it. There was a very detailed Jolly Roger flag drawn on the board and a ferocious looking skull and crossbones leering at them. "Roommate," Devin explained. "Art student. He leaves me love notes like that all the time. When he's here, anyway. Usually he's at his girlfriend's place."

Max had no idea if Devin was just offering information or if he wanted Max to know they'd be alone. Then he cursed himself for reading too much into a totally innocent situation. Devin was just being cool about Max's arm and there was nothing else to it.

The room was divided into two obvious categories: clean and disastrous. One side of the room looked as if a bomb had hit it. Laundry, art supplies, empty mineral water bottles, and CDs littered the bed, the desk, and the floor. There were half-sketched drawings taped to the walls.

"Wow," Max said in awe, impressed by the mess.

"I know, right?" Devin pushed some books aside and gestured at the bed. "You can sit there. I told Brett if he didn't keep his shit on his side that I'd hang up a fucking curtain down the middle of the room. So far he's done pretty good." Devin bent and rummaged through his bottom drawer, coming up with a small first aid kit. "And I told my mom I'd never need this."

"Remind me to thank her."

Devin examined his palms and wrinkled his nose. "Lemme go wash my hands." He zipped out the door and was gone for a few moments before returning. "Okay, clean. You sure you're not going to pass out on me?"

Max took a quick glance at his arm. "Nah, I'm okay. It's mostly stopped bleeding." The crusted blood on his arm was still making him queasy, but there was no way he was going to tell Devin that.

The bed dipped when Devin sat next to Max. "I need to scrub some of that junk off. It'll probably hurt." He sounded apologetic, and Max's cock reminded him that it was still interested, especially when Devin used that concerned-sounding voice.

"Yeah, whatever. No problem." Max concentrated on disinterest and was grateful his voice wasn't squeaking.

Devin ripped open an anti-bacterial wipe and began dabbing at Max's arm. It didn't hurt, no more than his arm did already, so Max sat quietly and watched Devin's bent head.

When the wipe was rust colored from the dried blood, Devin tossed it in the trash and used another one to finish cleaning up. "Oooh," Devin said, studying the scrapes. "Those have crap in them. Let me rinse your arm with this, okay?" He held up a small bottle of hydrogen peroxide. "Shouldn't sting."

Max shrugged and pretended indifference. "Whatever. If it needs to be cleaned."

"It does." Devin reached behind his head and tugged his white t-shirt up and off. He placed it under Max's arm like a towel and began to gently squirt the liquid over the cuts.

The sting of his scrapes was eclipsed immediately by Max's total awareness of Devin's bare chest. His prick sprang to full attention, not that it had far to go, but Max was grateful for the sheet that he'd carried back with him to Devin's room. He shoved it down over his lap and tried not to move while Devin tended to him.

When Max's arm was clean and dry, Devin dressed it lightly with gauze. "Sleep with that on for tonight," he mused, looking at the bandage critically. "Take it off tomorrow and keep it clean."

"You sure you're not pre-med?" Max asked. He was pleased that his voice sounded normal.

To Max's delight, Devin blushed. "Oh yeah, I'm sure." He busied himself with cleaning up and then came back to sprawl out next to Max on the bed. "Wanna go out?

There are a hundred toga run parties happening right now."

"I guess," Max said, pretending indifference. He didn't want to go out at all; he wanted to stay right here on Devin's bed with Devin lying warm and cuddly right next to him.

"Okay." Devin stayed where he was. He made no move to get up, instead just propping his head on his hand and smiling at Max. "Or we could just order pizza. I've got a six pack under the bed."

"I guess," Max said again, knowing now he sounded anything but indifferent.

Devin chuckled. "I like my men agreeable," he murmured, just before snaking a hand up around Max's neck and tugging Max down to him. Devin darted out the very tip of his tongue to lick at the indentation on Max's top lip. "That means they're open to the power of suggestion."

Max shamelessly opened his mouth when he felt Devin's tongue. He slid down into the space between Devin and the wall and stretched out against the lean body. His arm brushed up against Devin's chest and awakened the stinging again, but Max didn't care when Devin grinned at him and slid a thigh in between Max's legs.

"Are we staying in?" Max whispered.

"For now." Devin's eyes fluttered closed and he fit himself more snugly against Max. "Oh, there's the spot." He nudged his hips forward, and Max could feel Devin's thick length press up alongside his own rigid cock.

Max spread his legs just a little and then they were lined up perfectly, only two pairs of thin denim separating them. Max's cock rubbed along the inside of his jeans as Devin pushed against him.

"I can take my jeans off." Max groaned and pushed back.

"You will," Devin smiled. "The next time. This time, I want… this." He rocked up again and brought a hand around to clutch and squeeze Max's ass. "Like this, okay?"

There really wasn't any need for Devin to ask permission, but Max pretended to give it and nodded anyway. He would have nodded to anything Devin asked him to do. "God, yes. Like this." He arched his neck and closed his eyes, grinding hard.

There was a soft suckling at his exposed neck and Max gasped. Devin had taken advantage of the skin Max presented and was licking and nibbling just under Max's jaw. The added sensation went right down Max's spine to his balls, and he groaned out loud.

Devin clutched at Max's ass, pulling him closer as they both searched for friction, and Devin continued sucking and biting at Max's neck. Max could feel the inside of his jeans grow damp and knew he was close to coming. It would have been embarrassing, coming in his pants like he was still in high school, but Devin was obviously about to do the same thing. Max went with it.

"Devin, fuck," Max grunted, rubbing hard and sinking into the feeling of impending orgasm. There was heat and hardness and a thigh between his legs, and it was all adding up to the perfect combination. Max whimpered and thrust forward. His dick dragged along the rigidness of Devin's and then he was coming, jerking in Devin's arms and gasping out loud to the ceiling.

A tight mouth and sharp teeth fastened onto Max's neck as Devin came almost immediately afterward. Devin was silent as he spilled, his fingers digging in hard to the soft part of Max's ass and his hips making small pumping motions. He finally lifted his mouth from Max's neck and relaxed his hold.

"That's what I wanted," Devin grinned.

Max smiled and settled himself into the curve of Devin's arms. His eyes were heavy and he longed to put his head down and sleep, but his jeans were going to be sticky and uncomfortable in an hour. Max glanced down and made an effort to squeeze his hand between them to fiddle with his fly.

"Yeah, perfect idea," Devin whispered, eyes twinkling. "That'll make it easier later."

His prick gave a renewed twitch and Max shoved down his damp jeans. Devin did the same and Max tossed his shirt over the side of the bed. They curled around each other again, warm skin against smooth flesh, and Max was asleep within moments.

Max woke in the morning to a quiet room and empty bed.

"He just left you there in his dorm room? The fuck?" Jenny looked incredulous while trying to appear bored. It wasn't working.

"He left a note," Max shrugged. "Said he had an early class and he'd text me or something."

"And did he?"

"He'd have to have my cell phone number for that." Max thought that came out sounding bitter, then realized he *was* bitter, so who cared?

Jenny wrinkled her nose at him and twirled a piece of her hair, newly dyed pink over the previous turquoise, around her finger. "He said he'd text but doesn't have your cell number? Either this dude is really forgetful or he's blowing you off, Max. And for God's sake, would you stop making your dick available to him at every opportunity? He's not going to buy the cow if blah blah blah, you know."

"Jen, Christ. I don't want to marry him. I don't even want a relationship with him." Max shook his head. The box of textbooks in his arms was growing heavy, so he put it on the floor and sat on it.

"So then, what's the problem? You're getting laid and you don't have to deal with the relationship shit." She cracked her gum and examined the ends of her hair.

"The problem is… um. Okay, well. Maybe I do want a relationship. Or something. A date would be good. Hell, I don't know, Jen. I like him."

Jenny stared at him. "Tell him that, dumbass."

Max snorted. "That I want a date or that I like him?" He shook his head. "Doesn't matter, I'm not doing either one. I'll look like a gir—" Max cut himself off, but not in time.

"You know," Jenny mused, arching a pierced brow, "my mom told me it was okay if I went away to school and tried being a lesbian. I told her to get bent, but you know what? I should have listened to her. Men are stupid, and I don't care if you do like cock. You're still stupid." She snatched the price scanner from a shelf and flounced away.

Max sighed and watched her disappear around the end of the aisle. It was kind of a dickish thing to say, but he hadn't meant to insult her. Jen was cool.

He made a note to buy her some flowers or a pack of cigarettes or something. Max only realized he was still sitting morosely on the box of books when the shop's shift manager came down the aisle and gave him a curious look.

The remaining four days before Finals Week passed for Max in a blur of studying, coffee, and all-nighters.

Somehow he'd thought that all-nighters were just a college urban myth and that people didn't really stay up till six a.m., but when he found some of the residence hall members camped out in the library at two o'clock in the morning, Max realized that, yes, all-nighters were more than just legend.

There was no time to think about Devin, or so he told himself. Max's head was too full of information from his pre-law classes. And if Max had one or two wet dreams during the week, well, it was only because he wasn't thinking about sex during the day, so his subconscious was taking over for him at night, right?

That's what he told himself. It seemed to make sense.

Max's exams were simultaneously easier and harder than he'd expected. When he finished on the Thursday before winter break, he had no clue how he'd done. He couldn't find it in himself to care, though, because he was exhausted and it was nearly vacation time and the Kappa Delta house was throwing a Christmas/holiday/winter-themed thing that promised lots of beer and loud music. It sounded pretty good to Max.

He and Erik went together. Erik whined and moaned during the short walk to the house about how terribly he'd done on his finals. Max knew that meant the guy had done exceptionally well, but he was in a good enough mood that he let Erik complain instead of telling Erik to shut the fuck up. When the music was audible from down the block, Erik cut himself off mid-sentence and grinned.

"Party! I'm gonna get wasted." Erik paused for a moment. "Not out of control, though."

"Of course not." Max chuckled and nudged Erik with an elbow. "That'd be dangerous, right?"

Erik regarded him seriously. "I can show you statistics on how many university students die from alcohol poisoning every year."

Max held up a hand. "I believe you. Let's just go drink a beer or ten, huh?"

Erik whooped and dashed down the street toward the sound of the music.

Max followed Erik with a smile, feelings of fondness for Erik combining with the relief at having lived through his first semester of college and anticipation for a full month of vacation. Feelings for or about Devin Page didn't fit anywhere into that equation.

Or so Max thought, until he walked through the front door of the frat house and was handed a brimming cup of beer by Devin.

"Happy No More Fucking Finals Day, Tisdale," Devin grinned, licking foam from his upper lip. "Drink up."

"Uh. Hi," Max stuttered. He couldn't help raking a quick glance down Devin's body and back up. Standard college frat boy attire—jeans, nondescript t-shirt, dark blue hoodie—but Max could only remember what Devin's bare skin had looked and felt like the night they'd spent together in Devin's bed.

He didn't realize he was standing there staring until Devin moved in a little closer. "Max?" Devin murmured, his voice barely audible above the music.

Max froze, hyper-aware of Devin's nearness. "Yeah?" Oh God, oh God, please let Devin say he wanted to get the hell out of there and he wanted Max to go with him.

Devin put his mouth close enough to Max's ear that Max could feel the heat of his breath. "Do me a favor."

Thank Christ Max was wearing long sleeves and Devin couldn't see the goosebumps on his arms. "Sure," he said, his voice cracking. "Let's go."

Devin pulled back and blinked. "Go? I don't want to go, man." The corner of Devin's mouth curved. "I just want you to drink your beer. You look like you need it."

Oh. Oh, right. Max gave himself a mental shake and

forced his hand to bring the cup to his lips. He took a fortifying drink and made himself grin at Devin. "Cheers, dude."

"There you go!" Devin slammed his own cup against Max's and sloshed beer over the edge. He drained what was left of his drink and then looked mournfully into the cup. "Refill time. You're two behind me. Come find me when you catch up!" He wandered off in the direction of the kitchen and Max assumed the keg was that way.

Vodka gelatin shooter cups lined the edge of the pool table in the living room. Max made his way toward the edge of the room and watched Erik swallow three shooters in a row. He wondered what Erik's definition of 'not out of control' was, and realized Erik was not usually a heavy drinker. Looked like tonight was going to be an exception.

Billy Ashton, one of the other pledges that Max hadn't known well at the beginning of the year but now liked a lot, approached with two gelatin shooters. "Maxie!" he shouted, his mouth already stained orange from too much gelatin. "Shoot 'em up, buddy!" He pressed the small paper cup into Max's hand and lifted his own in salute.

Max laughed and downed the shooter with one quick swallow. He and Billy crushed their cups together and yelled "Woof!" at the tops of their lungs. Billy grinned in delight and dragged Max by the arm to the group of men around the coffee table. "Max wants to play speed quarters with us!" Billy informed them.

He didn't, really, but the chorus of "Maaaaax!" from his frat brothers was hard to resist. Max squeezed into a space on the couch and made himself comfortable, perfectly happy to ignore wherever Devin might be.

Speed quarters degenerated into some form of throwing the coins instead of bouncing them, but no one cared.

Max alternated between accepting more vodka shooters and drinking more beer than he'd intended. It was fun, though, and he just about managed to forget that Devin was somewhere else in the house.

When Billy knocked over a full cup of beer and soaked three guys' jeans, the game broke up. Max realized he was hungry and wove unsteadily to the kitchen to see if there was any food other than orange-flavored gelatin.

He'd just managed to wedge his way into a group of guys who were hovering over the chips and salsa when someone spoke his name in a low, worried tone. Max looked over his shoulder to see Devin nibbling on his lower lip. "Oh, hey."

"Hey. C'mere." Devin jerked his head toward the back porch and then turned in that direction.

The last time Devin had asked Max to meet him somewhere in the house, they'd ended up fucking in the bathroom. Max almost considered not following the guy, but even through his own buzz, Max had caught a certain tenseness to Devin's words. Better just go and see what was wrong.

He went out the back door and elbowed past a cluster of men. Devin was sitting on the bottom step, one hand rubbing the neck of the person sitting next to him. Max got halfway down the porch stairs before he realized that it was Erik.

"What's up?" Max made his way down to the bottom and sat next to Erik. "Whoa. Erik, man. You okay?"

Erik sat with his elbows propped on his knees and his head hung low. He grunted at Max. "Okay. Yup. Uh huh."

Devin looked at Max over Erik's head. "Not okay," he sighed. "He's pretty smashed. Not like I've ever seen him, anyway. Hey Erik, you got a little carried away, huh, buddy?"

"Nah. M'good. Jus' a few shooters. Then some beer. And more shooters after that." Erik spoke directly to the ground and kept himself very still, as drunk people often did when things were spinning around them. Max winced in sympathy.

"Yeah, he's loaded." Max sighed and felt his buzz fade. "I'll keep an eye on him. He'll probably start hurling soon."

"Let's at least get him out into the yard," Devin suggested. "Have him sit on one of those lawn chairs by the edge of the woods."

They half-carried, half-dragged a protesting Erik to the chairs and pushed him down into one. He slumped over and tried to sleep. "Lemme 'lone."

"Can't." Devin laughed a little and sat down next to him. "Someone's gotta make sure you don't choke when you throw up."

"That's gross," Erik mumbled, echoing Max's thoughts. "Don't feel good."

Devin rolled his eyes and Max snorted. "You shouldn't have downed all those vodka shooters."

Erik moaned. "Don't say vodka."

They didn't have long to wait before Erik launched himself out of the chair and stumbled to the nearest tree. He threw up what looked to be like a gallon's worth of orange gelatin and Max made a face and turned away. "You need to handle that," he said to Devin.

"He's handling it himself," Devin laughed, unconcerned. "I'm just monitoring. I don't do the whole 'rub your back' routine when you're drunk. You get yourself fucked up, you can deal with the pain. I'm just here to make sure he doesn't die."

It seemed fair enough to Max. He sat down in Erik's abandoned chair and turned it to face away from his puking roommate. The party continued around them, and Max amused himself by watching three of his stupid fraternity brothers try and do handstands on top of the porch railing.

"I think he's done," Devin said after about half an hour.

Max looked around and saw Erik leaning heavily against the tree, head hung low. "You sure?" he asked doubtfully.

"No. But he hasn't hurled in fifteen minutes, so he's done for now. Want to help me get him back to your room?" Devin stood up and stretched.

"You don't want to just toss him in one of the upstairs bedrooms?" Max had no idea how they were going to drag Erik three blocks and then halfway through campus to their dorm.

"Can't. House rule, remember?" Devin made an annoyed face.

He was right, Max realized. It was a rule that anyone who got too drunk to walk either stayed on the couch or floor of the house. No brother wanted to stumble his way to bed only to find another frat member passed out in it.

"Shit." Max wasn't enough of a dick to just let Erik tough it out on his own, and apparently Devin wasn't either. The party was still in full swing, so there was nowhere for Erik to lie down unless they managed to get him back to his own bed. "How are we getting him back to campus?"

"I've got ten bucks. We'll squeeze into a cab." Devin shrugged and checked his wallet.

Max knew that spending ten dollars on cab fare was a lot for him, but then realized he had no idea what Devin's monthly budget was. Maybe his parents didn't keep him on as tight a financial leash as Max's did. It didn't matter; Devin was offering to get a taxi and that solved the bulk of their problem with Erik, so Max nodded.

"I'll call." Max used his shoulder to hold his phone to his ear as he and Devin each got under one of Erik's arms. Max quickly gave the address of the house as they steered Erik toward the front yard.

A taxi pulled up within minutes and they shoved Erik into the back seat. Devin crawled back there with him and Max got in the front, praying Erik would wait until they were outside again if he had to throw up.

Thankfully, the ride was uneventful. Max and Devin got Erik out of the cab and nearly all the way to the residence building before pausing to let Erik puke once more.

"This is your one free pass, Young," Devin sighed as he waited for Erik. "Next time you do this, don't expect sympathy or a free cab ride."

"Fuck off," Erik mumbled, reaching for the stair railing. "Fuck your sympathy. And your cab ride. Fuck."

Max raised an eyebrow, but Devin just chuckled. "Sure. I'll remind you again in the morning. Come on, up you go." He propelled Erik into the elevator with Max in tow until they reached Max and Erik's floor. Max brushed past both of them and went to unlock their room, praying that Erik wouldn't wake up their bastard of an R.A. A canned lecture on underage drinking was the last thing Max needed to hear.

Erik groaned and made a lunge for his bed as soon as they got through the door. Max caught his arm and Devin yanked on his shirt just in time to keep Erik from taking a faceplant. They mostly dragged him the rest of the way across the floor and deposited Erik on top of the covers.

"And my work is done," Devin announced as Erik began to snore almost immediately. "Put the trash can by the bed and leave him alone."

Max did as he was told. "Should we... I don't know, take off his shoes or something?"

"Hell, no, we ain't his momma." Devin laughed softly and winked at Max. "He'll live to drink another day. Come on, let's go sit in the common room."

Okay, the common room. A public place right in the middle of the dorm floor, the room that separated the men's side from the women's. There wasn't any harm in going down the hall to sit there with Devin, Max thought. They were just going to talk. Like friends or something.

"Sure." Max nodded and took one last glance at his sleeping roommate. Erik would be fine until morning, most likely. Max didn't envy the hangover. He reached into the mini-fridge under his own bed and grabbed two sodas, tossing one to Devin. Devin nodded his thanks and they made their way quietly back down the long hallway to the common room.

Someone had left the lights off and the TV on. An old western was playing with the sound down low, so Max just left it. They sprawled on the couch in the corner and popped open their soda cans.

"Got plans for vacation?" Max asked. He wondered what kind of holiday Devin's family had. His own family gatherings were small but cozy, and there was always Christmas dinner.

"Sleep a lot. Eat my little sister's cooking. She goes crazy for those cooking shows and makes me try her new recipes." Devin paused to take a drink and Max couldn't help watching his throat work as Devin swallowed. "Sometimes the food sucks, but most of the time she does a good job."

There was no mention of a family holiday, so Max didn't press. He nodded and made a noise of agreement. "Sleeping sounds good. Maybe give my liver a rest."

Devin grinned. "Yeah, remember in the welcome packet we got before school started? There were the pamphlets and stuff about underage drinking and all the stats they tried to scare us with. My mom tried to sit me down with them and talk about it."

"Mine, too." Max laughed and took a drink of his soda. "When she got to the sex stats, she choked."

"Mine wanted to talk about the one where female college freshmen were at a high risk for sexual assault. She wanted to make sure I wasn't one of the ones assaulting them, I guess." Devin gave Max a sideways glance. "She didn't say anything about guys, though. My mom likes to pretend she doesn't know."

Max watched Devin's leg slide closer to his own and swallowed hard. "Would she be mad?"

"I don't know. My dad might flip, but he wouldn't kick me out or anything." Devin leaned even closer. "But they're not here. What I do at school and who I choose to do it with isn't any of their business, right?"

The flickering light of the television was mirrored in Devin's eyes. Max found himself reacting, as always, to Devin's nearness. "Right," he whispered.

There was only a fraction of space between them, but Devin stayed very still. His mouth was curved in a smile, and it took Max a moment to realize that Devin was waiting for him to bridge the distance. It wasn't smart, and somehow Max knew that this was going to end up like all the other times, but there was still enough alcohol in him from the party to use as an excuse for impaired judgment.

Max kissed him.

Devin tasted a little like the bitterness of beer and a lot like the sweetness of soda. His mouth opened for Max immediately and their tongues swept together with familiarity. Max liked that he knew Devin's taste.

There was a lingering awareness that they were in a terrible place for a make out session, but a lot of students on Max's floor had already gone home for the holiday and the ones who were left were probably out partying. The floor was still and silent except for the sound of the television and the soft sounds Devin was making as Max kissed him.

They kissed for a long time in the muted silence. Slowly, Max felt Devin easing him back on the couch. Devin stretched out lengthwise on top of him and nudged against Max's hip. "I want to fuck you," Devin murmured.

"Here?" Max squeaked, even though "yes" was his first reaction.

"No. Well, yeah. Anywhere. But right here's not a good idea." Devin smiled down at him and nuzzled Max's cheek. "I do want to touch you, though." He lifted his hips slightly and put a hand between them, searching for Max's cock over his jeans.

Seeing as how Max's dick was threatening to rip through his fly, it wasn't hard for Devin to find and squeeze. Max hissed and bit down hard on his lower lip. "That's probably not a good idea either," he managed, but thrust up into Devin's hand anyway.

"I'll make it fast." Devin winked and nuzzled Max again. "Max, come on. Touch me, please?" He rocked into Max's thigh and then quickly flipped open his top button.

Max looked down to see the tip of Devin's cock poking out from his jeans. He wore no underwear, and the tip of the man's dick was already glistening. There was no way in fucking hell that Max could stop his hand from reaching out to feel, so he didn't. One finger grazed across the top of Devin's prick.

Devin's eyes fluttered closed and he fumbled with Max's fly. "Uh huh, come on." His fingers found Max's zipper and then Devin closed a warm hand around Max's dick, drawing it out of his jeans and holding it firmly. "Stroke with me," Devin whispered. "Do what I do." He rubbed with his thumb at the underside of the shaft.

Max's body responded immediately. His cock leaped in Devin's hand, but he tried to imitate what Devin was doing to him. He found the ridge of Devin's prick and rubbed there with his thumb, squeezing out more fluid and making Devin moan softly.

They dragged their erections through each other's fists for a minute or two, until both of them were writhing against the other and Max knew he was going to blow. "Devin," he pleaded, unsure of what he was asking for except more of something.

"Yeah. Want. Max, please." The words were low and gravelly. Devin cupped and squeezed and stroked and Max tried to copy his movements, but his own hips were jerking forward helplessly with each rub and tug of Devin's hand.

Devin ground against Max, his hand never stopping its squeezing and rubbing, until he sucked in a hard breath and his eyes went wide. Max looked down in time to see Devin come in a little arc of white, ribbony spunk over Max's fingers. His cock jumped and pulsed in Max's hand, though the rest of him remained frozen.

Max wanted to raise his hand to his mouth and taste Devin's come, but Devin's momentary pause was over and he began stroking Max again in earnest. "Come on. Now you. Now you." Devin smiled at him and leaned forward to lick at the corner of Max's mouth.

The warm tongue on his lips was the final push. Max rolled his bottom lip under his teeth and arched his neck on the couch. His orgasm rushed up in a trembling wave and the heat poured out of him into Devin's hand. Max jerked and writhed under the weight of Devin's body, all his muscles flexing and contracting as he came.

Their short, panting breaths mingled with the low noise from the TV, but there was no other sound in the room. Max closed his eyes and let the drowsiness steal over him. Devin lay there, too, seemingly in no hurry to move.

The sound of people coming up the stairwell finally made them jerk apart. Devin slid off the couch and tucked his cock back into his jeans just before two girls arrived on the landing and eyed them suspiciously. Max had gotten his t-shirt pulled down over his open fly in time, so he just smiled weakly at them and waited for them to go down the hall.

When the girls were gone, Devin grinned and winked. "Could've given them a show. They might have liked it."

"Want to have breakfast tomorrow?" Max blurted, which sounded very different from whatever else he'd planned to say. He couldn't remember what it was, though.

Devin leaned against the wall and studied Max. "Thought you were leaving tomorrow."

"I am. Not till the afternoon, though. Late flight." Max held his breath.

There was another long silence. Finally, Devin pushed off the wall and approached the sofa. He leaned down and brushed his lips lightly over Max's, then pulled back and stood up straight. "Freshman year of college isn't about dating. *I'm* not about dating." There was a faint air of apology in his words. It pissed Max off.

"You're about fucking, though."

Devin smiled a little. "Yeah. I am. Have a good break, Max." He left quietly, and Max could hear his footsteps echoing in the stairwell.

Max looked at the television in time to see the cowboy tip his hat at the farmer's wife before he rode away.

The end of December merged into the beginning of January, and by the time Max started packing up all the clean laundry his mother had washed for him, he was definitely ready to return to school. Living under his parents' roof had seemed constricting in high school, but trying to do it after living on his own for the first semester of college was more hellish than he'd thought it would be.

A sealed container of peanut butter cookies from his mom was under his clean shirts and a hundred dollar bill from his dad was in Max's wallet. He got a kiss, a hug, and a handshake at the airport, and then, just like that, Max was climbing out of a taxi in front of his residence hall.

Maybe second semester wouldn't be as confusing as the first had been.

Devin had crossed Max's mind much less frequently than he'd anticipated. Being at home for the holidays was distracting. There were friends to catch up with and family to visit, not to mention Christmas and New Year's coming right on top of each other and taking up a lot of Max's energy. There just wasn't time to dwell on Devin Page and the way he'd brushed Max off before vacation.

But being here, back at school and with the very real possibility of seeing Devin sometime in the next few days, Max was finding it difficult to pretend he wasn't thinking about it.

He was distracted from his thoughts momentarily by the cheerful arrival of Erik. "Maxie!" Erik greeted him happily, no worse for the wear from his night of debauchery before they'd left. "Good to see you, man! What'd you get for Christmas?"

They spent some time sharing holiday stories while they unpacked, interrupted only by the relentless knocking on their door by other returning friends. Erik finally just propped the door open with a trash can so they could wave at people who stuck their heads in the room.

When they'd finished putting clothes away and their duffel bags had been shoved back under their beds, Max and Erik sprawled on the floor and shared the last soda left in their mini-fridge. "Meeting tonight," Erik reminded Max. "Welcome back dinner or something, isn't it?"

Max nodded. He'd gotten the fraternity's second-semester calendar at his home address. Tonight's meeting wasn't mandatory because not all students would be back on campus yet, but if Erik was going, then Max would go. He had no idea if Devin would be there, but it didn't matter. It was probably time to forget about Devin.

Devin wasn't there when they got to the house, he didn't make an appearance at dinnertime, and he still hadn't shown up by the time Max finished the strawberry shortcake for dessert. Max decided that Devin wasn't back from vacation, because he wasn't usually one to pass up free dinner or beer, both of which were in abundance.

Besides, it hurt to think that Devin might be back at school and had just blown the whole thing off.

Second semester of classes started three days later and Max still hadn't seen Devin, but that wasn't unusual. They weren't in the same program or dormitory. The only time they were really together was at fraternity functions, but other than the welcome back dinner, there hadn't been any meetings.

So when Max walked into the first official frat meeting of the spring semester and found out that Devin had depledged from the Kappa Delta house, it hit him like a ton of bricks.

"He did what?" Max looked at Greg incredulously. The meeting had just been called to order and the announcement made. A couple of the other pledges were looking around in amazement too.

"Page didn't feel that Kappa Delta was the right fit for him." Greg spoke in a serious tone, no humor present. Depledging from a fraternity or sorority was never a joke.

"Isn't he supposed to... I don't know, make a formal announcement or something?" Max was still unsure that this wasn't some sort of practical joke on the pledges.

Greg sighed. "He did. He came to me and requested a meeting with all brothers who were back from vacation. He explained his reasoning and turned in his pledge pin. He did everything right and went about it in a respectful way."

"Oh." Max blinked and looked at Erik, who shrugged.

"Dunno. He never seemed like the frat type to me, but what do I know?"

"Don't worry about it, Tisdale," Greg said. "All frats have guys who depledge. It's rare for a pledge class to be the same size at the end of the year as it is at the beginning. Okay, moving on. Dues need to be in by the end of the month..."

The meeting continued, but Max didn't listen to the rest of it.

"What does 'depledged' mean?" Jenny took a bite of her tuna wrap and chewed while she looked at Max. "I'm not hip on all your frat speak."

He ignored her vague tone of disdain. Jenny had always made it clear what she thought of organized... well, anything. "It means he turned in his pin and quit."

"Okay. And this is a big deal, because? I'm not trying to be a bitch; I seriously don't know." She took a sip of soda and munched thoughtfully.

Max picked up a small pebble and began using it to draw little designs in the dirt at his feet. "Well, because fraternities are supposed to be for life. These guys are supposed to become like my flesh and blood brothers. When a frat offers you a bid during rush week, they're telling you that they like you and they think you'll fit in well. Depledging could be seen as a huge insult, especially after a whole semester."

"Oh." Jenny rattled ice around in her cup. "So, does he get ostracized or something? Run out of town on a rail? Tarred and feathered?"

"Nah. If he wants to rush another frat, he has to wait until next year is all. And Greg seemed cool with it when he told me, but I don't know. It's like he never existed; no one talks about him or anything." Max understood why they wouldn't, but it still seemed weird to totally wipe out any traces of a former member.

She stood and tossed her trash into the can. "But, like, you can still talk to him if you want to, right? No one's going to tell on you?"

Max snorted. "No, Jen. No one's going to tell on me. It's just that it's been three weeks now and I haven't seen him anywhere."

"Did you go to his dorm?"

"No."

"Did you call him?"

"No."

"Oh, well then." Jenny raised a brow and gave Max her best sarcastic smile. "You're right, it's really weird that on a college campus of seventeen thousand students, you haven't seen one guy that isn't even in the same program as you. Someone alert the media to this freaky happenstance."

"Okay, Jen." Max rolled his eyes. Her sarcasm tended to run away from her. "So it's not that weird. I guess

Kappa Delta was one more thing he didn't think freshman year was about."

"That makes no sense to me and I don't want you to explain it, because our break's over. But jeez, Max. Just go see him if you want to, okay?" Jenny shook her head and disappeared inside the building.

It sounded easy, but really wasn't.

Except it turned out to be a thousand times easier than Max thought.

"You and Page hang out, right?" Greg dumped a plastic bag on the counter next to where Max was trying to chop fresh basil for a quick pesto sauce. He'd wanted plain old spaghetti again, but Erik's mom had watched a lot of cooking shows while Erik had been home for Christmas. Erik came back to school with a file box full of new recipes.

"Uh." It was on the tip of his tongue to say no, but Max looked curiously at the bag instead and forgot.

Greg pulled out two hoodies and a t-shirt, all emblazoned with Kappa Delta's Greek letters. "So yeah, his parents ordered this shit for him before the holidays. Can you pass it over for me? I don't care if he doesn't want it. You can keep it or something."

Max frowned. "I don't really see him." The sweatshirts were nice colors. The light blue one would look good with Devin's eyes, but why did Max care about that? He shoved the clothes back into the bag and nodded. "Yeah, whatever. I'll get it to him."

"Excellent. Hey, not too much garlic in that sauce, right?" Greg winked and pointed his thumb and forefinger at Max like a gun before sauntering out of the room.

Erik came over and scooped up Max's basil leaves. "You

ever think that guy's a tool sometimes?" he muttered.

Max laughed, because he did.

The bag with Devin's clothes ended up staying in Max's closet for another week before he stopped being a pussy and shook off his case of nerves.

"Just go over there," Jenny had said when Max had told her about the bag. "Leave it at his door with a note, if you don't want to see him."

But as Max stood in front of Devin's door, the last thing he wanted to do was just leave the bag and walk away. There was something about Devin that had always compelled Max; something that Max had never even thought about when screwing around with other guys. Max didn't know what to call it or why it was so gripping, but it wouldn't let him leave Devin's doorway without at least knocking to see if the guy was there.

Max took a deep breath, dropped the bag of clothes on the floor, and knocked.

It was anti-climactic. Nothing happened.

He considered knocking again, but it wasn't like it was a giant house and Devin was lost somewhere on the second floor. It was a seven and a half by fourteen foot dorm room. Clearly, Devin wasn't there.

Max left the plastic bag where it was and turned away, defeated. Maybe he'd see if Erik wanted to go out and drown some sorrows with him, or—

"Max, hey."

Max looked back over his shoulder at Devin. Devin was blinking blearily and rubbing his eyes with the heel of one hand. Max couldn't help but notice the bare chest and sticking-up bed head. "Oh, shit, I woke you. Sorry, man." Except he wasn't really that sorry, since it had been a really long time since Max had seen Devin and he was looking just as good as ever. Even with the bed head.

"Nah, it's cool. It's probably close to ten, I should get

up." Devin yawned and held the door open a little wider. "Want to come in?"

"Um, it's noon. And sure." *No!* Max's inner Jiminy Cricket warned, but Max shushed it. Jiminy Cricket was stupid.

"Noon? Damn." Devin laughed a little and went back to the disheveled bed. He crawled between the pale green sheets and yawned again. "Don't mind me. I'll wake up in a few minutes. What brings you all the way out to Greentree, Maxie?" He grinned adorably, stretching his arms way over his head.

I wanted to see you, was the first thing that sprang to mind, but Max choked that response back and remembered the clothes. "Uh, these." He handed over the bag and then felt vulnerable without anything in his hands. "Greg wanted me to bring them to you."

Devin frowned and took the bag. He pawed through the clothes for a moment before dropping it on the floor with a sigh. "That looks like shit my mom would order. You want 'em?"

Max nodded. "Yeah, I guess. We're about the same size. So how come you quit and didn't tell me?"

The last part of the sentence was out of his mouth before Max realized he'd said it aloud. Where the hell was his Jiminy Cricket now? Probably off having a cigarette, since he realized Max didn't listen to him.

Devin sat up slowly, leaning back against his headboard and letting the sheet pool in his lap. "Well now," he mused. "There wasn't any real reason for me to tell you, right?" He looked up at Max with a cocked brow.

"We were friends," Max said, knowing it sounded accusatory.

"And because I let you fuck me," Devin finished. Max blushed.

"That's got nothing to do with it."

"No? It sounds like that's what you meant." Devin sighed and scrubbed a hand through his hair, making it stick up even more. "Look, Tisdale. I like you. You're funny, you're smart, you're totally easy on the eyes, and even the way you worry about unnecessary shit is kind of cute. But I told you, right? I don't want a relationship. That isn't what college is about."

Max wasn't sure how they'd gone from talking about why Devin had depledged the frat to their non-existent relationship, but he tried steering things back in the other direction. "Yeah, I got it. You told me. But why'd you quit, huh? Why'd you leave Kappa Delta?"

Devin gave him a hard stare. "Because I was in that fucking fraternity for my old man. All I heard about when I was growing up was how Kappa Delta made him who he is today, and how it would do the same for me. College is about brotherhood." He stopped and shook his head and picked at a small hole in the bed sheet. "Fuck that noise. I knew three days after Rush Week that brotherhood wasn't for me. I go my own way, not the way of the Greek, whatever that means." Devin rolled his eyes and gave a half-hearted shrug. "So I depledged. He still doesn't know."

Something occurred to Max while he stood there watching Devin pick at the sheet. "Yeah. I'm guessing he was probably the one who gave you a detailed list of what college is 'supposed' to be about. It's about brotherhood, but not about relationships. It's about fun, but not dating. It's about fucking whoever whenever you can, but leaving right after." Max laughed humorlessly. "Whatever, dude. You were brave enough to depledge, but not brave enough to go on a fucking coffee date with me. You're full of shit."

He turned to go, slamming the door open against the wall and not bothering to shut it again. Max strode down the hallway, eyes straight ahead, chest heaving with anger that he didn't even know had been there.

It was only when he reached the sidewalk that he realized he was still holding the bag with Devin's clothes. Max ditched it in the bushes.

Jenny's eyes were huge behind her pink-tinted sunglasses. "Shut the fuck up," she whispered, awed. "You did not."

Max shrugged and tossed a piece of his pizza crust to the begging sparrows. "I did, yeah. I was kind of a dick. But Jen, I was really pissed, you know? What a fucking coward."

"Wow. I'm impressed, Max. I would never have said you had the balls." She picked delicately at her pizza and ate a piece of pepperoni.

"Oh, thank you. You're really a bitch sometimes."

She seemed pleased with that and smiled prettily. "Buy me another piece of pizza and I'll tell you what else I think."

He didn't really want to know, but Max bought her another piece of pizza anyway. "You eat a lot. For a girl."

"What the hell do you know about girls?" She snorted at him and took a big bite of pizza.

"Nothing." Max paused thoughtfully. "Except they smell pretty good a lot of the time." He took the slice of pizza from her and took a bite of it, then handed it back. "So what else do you think?"

Jenny peered at him over the tops of her sunglasses. "I think you're very cute and much too nice for the likes of Darren Page."

"Devin."

"Whatever. That's how little I care about him. I can't even remember his name. But you're way too cute and could get laid a lot from guys and girls both, so it's too bad you're not bisexual. You'd get a lot of action. How long are you going to pine for him and can I set you up with my friend John who's gay?"

Max furrowed his brow. He'd known Jenny for a few months now and was still taken aback by her frankness. "Uh. No? I don't want to be set up. But thank you. And I don't know, Jen." He sighed and watched her polish off the piece of pizza. "Stupid to pine over something I didn't have."

She smiled and wiped her mouth. "Maybe. But it's still disappointing, right?"

"Yeah. It was."

"So, pine for a week. I'll tell you when your time's up." Jenny stood and tossed her plate in the trash. "Come on, that new manager gave us the evil eye when we clocked back in three minutes late the other day."

Max followed her back inside, wondering what she would do if he ended up pining for Devin for longer than a week. Then he got disgusted with himself for thinking he was going to pine at all. He was too irritated with Devin to pine.

The new manager was lurking by the time clock when Jenny and Max retrieved their cards from the rack and went to punch them. Max slid his in first, but much to Max's amusement, Jenny watched the digital clock tick down to the very last possible second before punching her card and slipping it back into the metal holder. "Not late," she said airily to the manager, and wandered off toward the front register.

Max gave the manager an uneasy smile and made to follow her, but was stopped by a hand on his arm. "Hey," Pete said in an undertone. "I think there's a shoplifter out there. Keep an eye on him." He nodded toward the front of the store.

The bookstore was virtually empty except for one or two students milling around the comic book aisle. "Which one?" Max asked. None of them looked suspicious.

"That one with the green t-shirt. He keeps cruising around without looking at anything and checking his watch."

At the moment, Max couldn't see who Pete meant, but he nodded anyway. "Oh, yeah. Sure, I'll watch him." God forbid a broke student should lift an eighty-cent pack of gum. It wasn't like they carried expensive shit in the store.

Pete nodded and indicated Max should get back to work, so Max headed out toward the book cart he'd abandoned before his break. Green t-shirt was nowhere in sight.

"Your manager thinks I'm going to steal something."

The book Max was holding fell to the floor, though he made a valiant attempt to at least grab for it before it hit. The effort was unsuccessful. Max blinked at Devin and replied, "You could if you tried hard enough. There aren't any cameras in here."

"Good to know. Maybe I'll try to lift my textbooks for next semester. Then I can pocket the cash my dad sends." The green t-shirt was making Devin's eyes look brighter.

"How did you know I worked here?" He honestly couldn't remember ever telling Devin where he worked.

Devin crossed his arms and then leaned them on the book cart. "I know more about you than you think."

"Like what?"

"Like where you work," Devin laughed. He grew serious again after a moment. "And that you're smarter than I am."

"Oh, yeah? How do you figure?" Max bent and picked

up the dropped book just to have a moment to gather his thoughts. Devin appearing in the bookstore had been the last thing Max had expected, especially after just talking about him outside with Jenny.

Devin bent down with Max and faced him. "Because you were right. Because I was a coward. Because I was listening to shit that my father was spouting without really thinking about whether it did or didn't apply to my life."

There was nothing that Devin said that Max disagreed with, so he simply nodded and waited to see if Devin had anything else to say. The green t-shirt was really distracting in the way that Max's dick seemed to like how it was bringing out the little gold flecks inside the blue of Devin's eyes.

When it appeared that Devin was done talking, Max furrowed his brow and studied the book he was holding. "So, you came by my work just to tell me that?" He glanced up at Devin, then back down again. "Uh, thanks, I guess."

"No."

"No?"

Devin sighed and shook his head. "I'm fucking it all up, I'm sorry." He reached out and took the book from Max, then knelt down on the floor. "I mean no, I didn't come by just to tell you that. I came by to see if… you know, um. If you wanted to… get coffee." He stared hard at the floor.

Max could feel the corner of his mouth lifting. He knelt down next to Devin and leaned in, brushing his lips over Devin's. Devin responded at once, kissing Max back eagerly.

"Sure," Max murmured into the kiss. "Dating is what college is all about."

Kegs and Dorms

Printed in the United States
140427LV00004BA/3/P

9 781603 705264